Royal Seductions: Secrets

MICHELLE CELMER

Bestselling author **Michelle Celmer** lives in southeastern Michigan with her husband, their three children, two dogs and two cats. When she's not writing or busy being a mum, you can find her in the garden or curled up with a romance novel. And if you twist her arm really hard you can usually persuade her into a day of power shopping.

Michelle loves to hear from readers. Visit her website at www.michellecelmer.com or write to her at PO Box 300, Clawson, MI 48017, USA.

THE DUKE'S
BOARDROOM AFFAIR

BY
MICHELLE CELMER

To my Aunt Janet, who,
besides being totally cool and tons of fun,
told me my first dirty joke when I was a kid.
Why does a honeymoon only last six days?
I think you remember the rest…

One

Victoria Houghton had never been so humiliated.

Watching her father lose in a hostile takeover the hotel that had been in their family for generations had been almost more than she could bear—and now she was expected to be a personal assistant to the man who was instrumental in sealing the deal?

The Duke of Morgan Isle, Charles Frederick Mead, lounged casually behind his desk, smug and arrogant beneath the facade of a charming smile, the crisp blue of the Irish Sea a backdrop through a wall of floor-to-ceiling office windows behind him. Dressed in a suit that was no doubt custom-made, his casual stance was at odds with the undeniable air of authority he oozed from every pore.

"I was told I would be taking on a managerial

position," she told him. And along with it a generous salary and profit sharing. Or had they changed their minds about that part, too?

He leaned back and folded one leg casually atop the other. "Until the second phase of the hotel opens, there's nothing for you to manage. And since my personal assistant recently left, you will temporarily replace her."

He must have thought her daft if he believed she would buy that flimsy excuse. She would work in housekeeping, changing linens and scrubbing commodes, if it meant not seeing this man every day. He may have looked pleasant and easygoing, but underneath he was cold and heartless.

"So put me in the part of the hotel that's already completed," she said. "I'll do anything."

"There aren't any openings."

"None?"

He shook his head.

Of course there weren't. Or so he said. To men like him, lying was as natural as breathing. And what of their financial agreement? Surely he didn't expect to pay an assistant the exorbitant salary they had quoted in her contract? "What about my salary and profit sharing?"

He shrugged. "Nothing in the terms of your contract will change."

Her brow perked up in surprise. What was he trying to pull?

"If you consult your attorney, he'll confirm that we're honoring our end of the deal," he assured her.

According to her father, their own attorney had sold them out to get in good with the royal family, so unfortunately he wouldn't be much help. She doubted there was a single attorney on the island who would take on the monarchy, so basically, she was screwed.

"And if I refuse?" she asked, though she already knew the answer.

"You violate the terms of your contract."

He had no idea how tempted she was to do just that. She'd never wanted this job. But refusing it would devastate her father. The sale of his hotel—her legacy—to the royal family for their expansion project had been contingent on her being hired as a permanent manager, and at nearly twice the salary she had been making before. Not to mention incredible benefits. He wanted assurances that she would be well taken care of. And she was helpless to object.

Losing the hotel had put unneeded strain on his already weakening heart. Despite sitting on the prime resort land of the island, since the opening of the newly renovated Royal Inn hotel, occupancy in their much smaller facility had begun to drop. The way the lawyers for the royal family had begun buying up ocean-side property, both she and her father feared it would only be a matter of time before their number was up.

And they had been right.

In his fragile state, more bad news might be all it took to do him in. Since the day her mother and older brother were killed in an automobile accident, when Victoria was only five, he had been her entire life. He had sacrificed so much for her. She couldn't let him down.

With renewed resolve, she squared her shoulders and asked, "When do you expect the second phase of the hotel to open?"

"The additions and renovations are scheduled for completion by the beginning of the next tourist season."

The next tourist season? But that was nearly six months away! Six *days* would be too long to work for this man, as far as she was concerned. But what choice did she have?

Something that looked like amusement sparked in his deep, chocolate-brown eyes. Did he think this was funny?

"Is that a problem?" he asked.

She realized the duke was baiting her. He *wanted* her to violate the terms of her contract so he could get rid of her. He didn't want her services any more than she wanted his charity.

Well, she wouldn't give him the satisfaction of seeing her buckle. He may have broken her father, but there was no way he was going to break her.

She raised her chin a notch and looked him directly in the eye, so he would see that she wasn't intimidated. "No problem."

"Excellent." A satisfied and, though she hated to admit it, *sexy* grin curled the corners of his mouth. Which she didn't doubt was exactly what he wanted her to think.

He opened the top drawer of his desk, extracted a form of some sort, and slid it toward her. "You'll need to sign this."

She narrowed her eyes at him. "What is it?"

"Our standard nondisclosure agreement. Every employee of the royal family is obligated to sign one."

Another trick? But after a quick scan of the document, she realized it was a very simple, basic agreement. And though she wouldn't be working directly for the royal family but instead for the hotel chain they now owned, she didn't feel it was worth arguing. Their secrets would be safe with her.

Yet, as she took the gold-plated pen he offered and signed her name, she couldn't escape the feeling that she had just sold her soul to the devil.

She handed it back to him and he tucked it inside his desk, then he rose from his chair. Short as she was, she was used to looking up to meet people in the eye, but he towered over her. At least a foot and a half taller than her measly five foot one. And he looked so...perfect. His suit an exact fit, his nails neatly trimmed and buffed, not a strand of his closely cropped, jet-black hair out of place.

But men like him were never as perfect as they appeared. God knows she'd met her share of imperfect men. Despite his looks and money and power, he was just as flawed as the next guy. Probably more so. And being that he was an attorney, she wouldn't trust him as far as she could throw him—which, considering their size difference, wouldn't be very far.

"Welcome to the company, Victoria." He extended a hand for her to shake and, determined to be professional, she accepted it.

His hand enfolded her own, gobbling it up, big and warm and firm. And she felt a strange stirring in the pit of her belly. A kind of fluttering tickle.

His hand still gripping hers, he said, "Why don't we discuss your duties over lunch?" But his eyes said he had more than just lunch in mind. Was he *hitting* on her?

You have got to be kidding me.

She came this close to rolling her eyes. The tabloids

were forever painting him as a shameless, ruthless womanizer, but she had always assumed that was just gossip. No man could possibly be that shallow. Perhaps, though, they weren't so far off the mark.

If he believed for an instant that he would be adding her to his list of female conquests, he was delusional.

As graciously as possible she pried her hand loose. "No. Thank you."

He regarded her curiously. Maybe he wasn't used to women telling him no. "My treat," he said, dangling the word in front of her like bait.

Did he really think she was that hard up?

"We're going to be working somewhat closely," he added, and she could swear she heard a hint of emphasis on *closely*. "We should take the time to get to know one another."

They wouldn't be working *that* closely. "I prefer not to mix business with pleasure."

She wondered if he would insist, citing it as part of their contract, but he only shrugged and stepped around his desk. "Well, then, I'll show you to your office."

Instead of taking her back through the outer office, past the grim-faced, aged secretary she'd met on the way in, he led her through a different door to a smaller, sparsely decorated, windowless office with little more than an empty bookcase, a comfortable-looking leather office chair, and an adequately sized desk. On it's surface sat a phone, a laptop computer and a large manila envelope.

"Everything you need is on your computer," he explained. "You'll find a list of all your duties, along with any phone numbers you may need as well as a copy of my personal schedule. If you're unsure of how to use the program you can ask Penelope, my secretary, for help."

"I'm sure I can figure it out."

He picked up the envelope and handed it to her. "Inside is a badge for this building, and another that will give you access to the business offices at the palace—"

"The *palace?*" She never imagined that going to the palace would be a part of the job description.

"I keep an office there and often attend meetings with King Phillip. Have you ever been there?"

She shook her head. She'd only seen photographs. Not that she hadn't imagined what it would be like.

"Well, then, I'll have to give you a tour."

Okay, maybe there would be *some* perks to this job. The idea of being in the palace, and possibly meeting members of the royal family, filled her with nervous excitement. Then she reined in her wayward emotions by reminding herself that this was not going to be a fun job. And given the choice, she would rather be anywhere but here.

"You'll also find a set of card keys," he continued, "for both your office and mine. They're marked accordingly. And in a separate envelope is your personal security code for my house."

Why on earth would he give her access to his house?

"My driver will be at your disposal twenty-four hours a day. Unless, of course, I'm using him, in which case you will be reimbursed for your petrol use."

A driver? She couldn't imagine what she would need that for. This job just kept getting stranger and stranger.

He gestured to a second door, adjacent to the one connecting their offices.

"That door leads to Penelope's office and will be the entrance that you use. She'll take you on a tour of the building, show you the break room and facilities. If you need to speak to me specifically, call first. The line to my office is marked on the phone. If I don't answer that means I'm busy and not to be disturbed."

"All right."

"My business calls go through Penelope, but any personal calls will be routed through your office or to the cell phone I'll supply you."

Answering phones and taking messages? Not the most challenging job in the world. But the duke was obviously a man who liked things done a certain way, and if nothing else she respected that. More than once her employees at the Houghton had suggested she was a little too rigid when it came to her business practices, but she had never felt an ounce of regret for running a tight ship.

She had been working since the age of twelve, when her father let her help out in the Houghton Hotel office after school. But only after earning her master's degree in business at university was she promoted to manager. Her father had insisted she earn her education, should she ever need something to fall back on.

And, boy, had she fallen back.

"Take some time to look over your duties, then we can discuss any questions you have," he said.

"Fine."

"I have to warn you, I've been without an assistant for a week now, and I'm afraid things are in a bit of a mess."

Honestly, how hard could it be, being a glorified secretary? "I'm sure I can manage."

"Well," the Duke said, with one of those dazzling smiles, "I'll leave you to it, then."

He turned and was halfway through the door before she realized she had no idea how she was supposed to address him. Did she call him Sir, or Sire? Did she have to bow or curtsy?

"Excuse me," she said.

He turned back to her. "Yes?"

"What should I call you?" He looked puzzled, so she added, "Mr. or Sir? Your Highness?"

That grin was back, and, like his handshake, she felt it all the way to the pit of her belly.

Stop that, she warned herself. He only smiled that way because he *wanted* her to feel it in her belly.

"Let's go with Charles," he said.

She wasn't sure if that was proper. Calling him by his first name just felt too...casual. But he was calling the shots, and she wasn't going to give him any reason to accuse her of violating the contract. "All right."

He flashed her one last smile before he closed the door behind him, and she had the distinct feeling he knew something she didn't. Or maybe that was just part of the game. Either way, she refused to let him intimidate her. If they thought they were going to force her out, they had no idea who they were dealing with. She hadn't earned her reputation as a savvy businesswoman by letting people walk all over her.

She took a seat at her new desk, finding the chair to be as comfortable as it looked. But the office itself was cold and impersonal. Since she would be spending at least six months here, it wouldn't hurt to bring a few photos and personal items into work.

She opened the laptop and booted it up. On the desktop were the documents he had mentioned. Convinced this job couldn't get any worse, she opened the one titled *Duties*. Starting at the top, she read her job description, working her way down the two-page, single-spaced list, her stomach sinking lower with each line, until she could swear it slipped all the way down near the balls of her feet. *Personal assistant, my foot.*

She had just agreed to be Charles Frederick Mead's indentured slave.

TWO

Charles sat at his desk, watching the time tick by on his Rolex. He gave Victoria five minutes before she stormed into his office in a snit about her employment duties. And he'd bet his ample net worth that she'd forget to call first.

For a woman with her education and experience, the backward step from managing a five-hundred-room hotel to the duties of a personal assistant would be tough to navigate. If it were up to him, he'd have found her a position in the hotel. But it wasn't his call. His cousins, King Phillip and Prince Ethan, were calling the shots.

The Houghton Hotel hadn't been acquired under the best of circumstances—at least, not for the Houghton family—and the royal family needed to know if Victoria was trustworthy before they allowed her into the fold. The logical way to do that was to keep her close.

He could see that she was still distraught over the loss of their hotel and property, but, sadly, the buyout had been inevitable. If not the Royal Inn, some other establishment would have swooped in for the kill. At least with the royal family they were given a fair deal. Other prospective buyers, with less interest in the country's economy, might have been far less accommodating. But it was possible that Victoria and her father, Reginald Houghton, didn't see it that way. But at the very least, she could show a little bit of gratitude. The royal family had saved them the embarrassment of both professional and personal financial devastation.

He'd barely completed the thought when his phone rang. Three short chirps, indicating the call originated from Victoria's office. She remembered.

He glanced at his watch. She was early. Only three and a half minutes.

He answered with a patient, "Yes, Victoria."

"I'm ready to discuss my duties," she said, and there was a distinct undertone of tension in her voice that made him grin.

"That was quick," he said. "Come on in."

The door opened a second later, and she emerged, a look on her face that could only be described as *determined*. For a woman her size, barely more than a nymph, she had a presence that overwhelmed a room. A firestorm of attitude and spunk packed neatly into a petite and, dare he say, *sexy* package. He usually preferred women with long, silky hair—and typically blond—but her shorter, warm brown, sassy style seemed to fit her just right.

He wasn't typically drawn to strong-willed women, but Victoria fascinated him. And he wouldn't mind at all getting to know her better. Which he would, despite what she seemed to believe. It was a simple fact: women found him irresistible. It was exhausting at times, really, the way women threw themselves at him. He didn't help matters by encouraging them. But he just couldn't help himself. He loved everything about women: Their soft curves and the silky warmth of their skin. The way they smelled and tasted. In fact, when it came to the female form, there wasn't a single thing he didn't adore.

This time, he had his sights set on Victoria. And he had yet to meet a woman he couldn't seduce.

"You have questions?" he asked her.

"A few."

He leaned back in his chair and folded his arms. "Let's hear it."

She seemed to choose her words very carefully. "I assumed my duties would be limited to more of a…secretarial nature."

"I have a secretary. What you'll be doing is handling every aspect of my private affairs. From fetching my dry cleaning to screening my e-mail and calls. Making dinner reservations and booking events. If I need a gift for a friend or flowers for a date, it will be your responsibility to make it happen. You'll also accompany me to any business meetings where I might require you to take notes."

She nodded slowly, and he could see that she was struggling to keep her cool. "I understand that you need to fill the position, but don't you think I'm a little *over*-qualified?"

He flashed her a patient and sympathetic smile. "I realize this is quite a step down from what you're used to. But as I said before, until the second phase opens…" He shrugged, lifting his hands in a gesture of helplessness. "If it's any consolation, since my last assistant left, my life has been in shambles. There will be plenty to keep you busy."

For a second she looked as though she might press the issue, then thought better of it. It wasn't often anyone outside of the family contradicted him. It was just a part of the title.

She spared him a stiff, strained smile. "Well, then, I guess I should get started."

He was sure that once she got going, she would find managing his life something of a challenge. He wished he could say the same for seducing her, but he had the sneaking suspicion it would be all too easy.

Charles hadn't been kidding when he said his life was in shambles.

After a quick tour of the building with Penelope, who had the personality and warmth of an iceberg, Victoria started at the top of his to do list. Sorting his e-mail. She had to go through his personal account and first weed out the spam that had slipped through the filter, then compare the sender addresses on legitimate mail to a list of people whose e-mails were to be sorted into several separate categories. Which didn't sound like much of an undertaking, until she opened the account and discovered over *four hundred* e-mails awaiting her attention.

There were dozens from charities requesting his donation or endorsement, and notes from family and friends, including at least three or four a day from his mother. A lot of e-mails from women. And others from random people who admired him or in some cases didn't speak too fondly of him. Cross-referencing them all with the list of addresses he'd supplied her would be a tedious, time-consuming task. And it seemed as though for every e-mail she erased or filed, a new one would appear in his inbox.

When eyestrain and fatigue had her vision blurring, she took a break and moved down to number two on the list. His voice mail. Following his instructions, she dialed the number and punched in the PIN, and was nearly knocked out of her chair when the voice announced that he had two hundred and twenty-six new messages! She didn't get that many personal calls in a month, much less a week. And she couldn't help wondering how many of those calls were from women.

It didn't take long to find out.

There was Amber from the hotel bar, Jennifer from the club, Alexis from the ski lodge, and half a dozen more. Most rang more than once, sounding a bit more desperate and needy with each message. The lead offender for repeated calls, however, was Charles's mother. She seemed to follow up every e-mail she sent with a phone call, or maybe it was the other way around. No less than *three* times a day. Sometimes more. And she began every call the exact same way. *It's your mum. I know you're busy, but I wanted to tell you...*

Nothing pressing as far as Victoria could tell. Just

random tidbits about family or friends, or reminders of events he had promised to attend. A very attractive woman from a good family she would like him to meet. And she seemed to have an endless variety of pet names for him. Pumpkin and Sweetie. Love and Precious. Although Victoria's favorite by far was Lamb Chop.

His mother never requested, or seemed to expect, a return call, and her messages dripped with a syrupy sweetness that made Victoria's skin crawl. How could Charles stand it?

Easily. By having someone else check his messages.

She spent the next couple of hours listening to the first hundred or so calls, transcribing the messages for Charles, including a return phone number should he need to answer the call. Any incoming calls she let go directly to voice until she had time to catch up. Between the e-mail and voice mail, it could take days.

"Working late?"

Startled by the unexpected intrusion, she nearly dropped the phone. She looked up to find Charles standing in the doorway between their two offices. She couldn't help but wonder how long he'd been standing there watching her.

"I'm sorry, what?" she said, setting the phone back in the cradle.

Her reaction seemed to amuse him. "I asked if you're working late."

She looked at her watch and realized that it was nearly eight p.m. She'd worked clear through lunch and dinner. "I guess I lost track of the hour."

"You're not required to work overtime."

"I have a lot of work to catch up on." Besides, she would much rather have been busy working than sitting home alone in the flat she had been forced to rent when her father could no longer afford to keep the family estate. Since she was born, that house had been the only place she had ever called home. But there was a new family living there now. Strangers occupying the rooms that were meant to belong to her own children some day.

Every time she set foot in her new residence, it was a grim, stark reminder of everything they had lost. And Charles, she reminded herself, was the catalyst.

He held up what she assumed was to be her new phone. The most expensive, state-of-the-art gadget on the market. "Before Penelope left she brought this in."

She felt a sudden wave of alarm. His secretary was gone? Meaning they were alone?

She wondered who else was in the building, and if working alone with him was wise. She barely knew him.

"Is everyone gone?" she asked in a voice that she hoped sounded nonchalant.

"This is a law firm. There's always someone working late on a case or an intern pulling an overnighter. If it's safety you're concerned about, the parking structure is monitored by cameras around the clock, and we employ a security detail in the lobby twenty-four seven."

"Oh, that's good to know." Still, as he walked toward her desk to hand her the mobile phone, she tensed the tiniest bit. He was just so tall and assuming. So...*there*.

"It's a PDA as well as a phone. And you can check e-mail and browse the Internet. If you take it to Nigel in tech support on the fourth floor tomorrow morning, he'll set everything up for you."

"Okay." As she took it from him their fingers touched and she had to force herself not to jerk away. It was barely a brush; still, she felt warmth and electricity shoot across the surface of her skin. Which made no sense considering how much she disliked him.

"I've been going through your phone messages," she told him. "Your mother called. Many times."

"Well, there's a surprise," he said, a definite note of exasperation in his voice. "I should probably warn you that when it comes to dealing with my mother, you have to be firm or she'll walk all over you."

"I can do that." Being *firm* had never been a problem for her. In fact, there had been instances when she'd been accused of being *too* firm. A necessity for any woman in a position of power. She had learned very early in her career how not to let people walk all over her.

"Good." He glanced at his watch. "I'm on my way out, and since it would seem that neither of us has eaten yet, why don't you let me take you out to dinner?"

First a lunch invitation, now dinner? Couldn't he take no for an answer? "No, thank you."

Her rejection seemed to amuse him. He shrugged and said, "Have it your way."

What was that supposed to mean? Whose *way* did he expect her to have it? His?

"I'm going to the dry cleaners tomorrow to pick up your laundry," she said. "Do you have anything dirty at home that I should take with me?"

"I do, actually. My housekeeper is off tomorrow

morning but I'll try to remember to set it by the door before I leave for work. Would you like my car to pick you up?"

"I can drive myself." Her father had always had a driver—until recently, anyway—but she never had felt comfortable having someone chauffer her around. She was too independent. She liked to be in control of her environment and her destiny. Which had been much easier when her father owned the company. When she was in charge. Answering to the whims of someone else was going to be…a *challenge*.

He shrugged again. "If that's what you prefer. I guess I'll see you in the morning."

Unfortunately, yes, he would. And nearly every morning for the following six months. "Good night."

For several very long seconds he just looked at her, then he flashed her one of those devastating, sexy smiles before he walked out of her office, shutting the door behind him.

And despite her less-than-sparkling opinion of him, she couldn't help feeling just a tiny bit breathless.

Victoria checked her caller ID when she got home and saw that her father had called several times. No doubt wondering how her first day had gone. All she wanted to do was fall into bed and sleep, but if she didn't call him back he would worry. She dialed his number, knowing she would have to tread lightly, choose her words carefully, so as not to upset him.

He answered sounding wounded and upset. "I thought you wouldn't call."

It struck her how old he sounded. Too frail for a man of sixty-five. He used to be so strong and gregarious. Lately he seemed to be fading away. "Why wouldn't I call?"

"I thought you might be cross with me for making you take that job. I know it couldn't have been easy, working for those people."

That was the way he'd referred to the royal family lately. *Those people*. "I've told you a million times, Daddy, that I am not upset. It's a good job. Where else would I make such a generous salary? If it does well, the profit sharing will make me a very wealthy woman." She found it only slightly ironic that she was regurgitating the same words he had used to convince her to take the position in the first place.

"I know," he conceded. "But no salary, no matter how great, could make up for what was stolen from us."

And she knew that he would live with that regret for the rest of his life. All she could do was continually assure him that it wasn't his fault. Yet, regardless of whose mistake it was, she couldn't help feeling that she would spend the rest of her life paying for it.

"Is it a nice hotel?" he asked grudgingly.

"Well, I didn't actually see the hotel yet."

"Why not?"

Oh, boy, this was going to be tough to explain. "There isn't a manager's position open in the hotel right now," she said, and told him about the job with the duke, stressing that her contract wouldn't change.

"That is completely unacceptable," he said, and she could practically feel his blood pressure rising, could just imagine the veins at his temples pulsing. He'd already had two heart attacks. One more could be fatal.

"It's fine, Daddy. Honestly."

"Would you like me to contact my attorney?"

For all the good that would do her. "No."

"Are you sure? There must be something he can do."

Was he forgetting that it was his attorney who was partially to blame for getting them into this mess?

"There's no need, Daddy. It's not so bad, really. In fact, I think it might be something of a challenge. A nice change of pace."

He accepted her lie, and some of the tension seemed to slip from his voice. He changed the subject and they went on to talk about an upcoming party for a family friend, and she tried to remain upbeat and cheerful. By the time she hung up she felt exhausted from the effort.

Performing her duties would be taxing enough, but she could see that creating a ruse to keep her father placated would be a long and arduous task. But what choice did she have? She was all her father had left in the world. He had sacrificed so much for her. Made her the center of his universe.

No matter what, she *couldn't* let him down.

Three

Charles lived in an exclusive, heavily gated and guarded community fifteen miles up the coast in the city of Pine Bluff. His house, a towering structure of glass and stone, sat in the arc of a cul-de-sac on the bluff overlooking the ocean. It was a lot of house for a single man, but that hardly surprised her. She was sure he had money to burn.

Victoria pulled her car up the circular drive and parked by the front door. She climbed out and took in the picturesque scenery, filled her lungs with clean, salty autumn air. If nothing else, the duke had impeccable taste in real estate. As well as interior design, she admitted to herself, after she used her code to open the door and stepped inside the foyer. Warm beiges and deep hues of green and blue welcomed her inside. The foyer opened up into a spacious living room with a rustic stone fireplace that climbed to the peak of a steep cathedral ceiling. It should have looked out of place with the modern design, but instead it gave the room warmth and character.

She had planned to grab the laundry and be on her way, but the bag he had said he would leave by the door was conspicuously not there. Either he hadn't left yet or he'd forgotten. She was guessing the latter.

"Hello!" she called, straining to hear for any signs of life, but the house was silent. She would have to find the clothes herself, and the logical place to look would be his bedroom.

She followed the plushly carpeted staircase up to the second floor and down an open hallway that overlooked the family room below. The home she had grown up in was more traditional in design, but she liked the open floor plan of Charles's house.

"Hello!" she called again, and got no answer. With the option of going either left or right, she chose right and peered into each of the half-dozen open doors. Spare rooms, mostly. But at the end of the hall she hit the jackpot. The master suite.

It was decorated just as warmly as the living room, but definitely more masculine. An enormous sleigh bed—unmade, she noted—carved from deep, rich cherry dominated the center of the room. And the air teemed with the undeniable scent of the woodsy cologne he had been wearing the day before.

She tried one more firm "Hello! Anyone here?" and was met with silence.

Looked like the coast was clear.

Feeling like an interloper, she stepped inside, wondering where the closet might be hiding. She found it off the bathroom, an enormous space in which row upon row of suits in the finest and most beautiful fabrics she had ever seen hung neatly in order by color. Beside them hung his work shirts, and beside them stood a rack that must have had three hundred different ties hanging from its bars. She wondered if he had worn them all. The opposite side of the closet seemed casual in nature, and in the back she discovered a mountain of dirty clothes overflowing from a hamper conveniently marked Dry Cleaning.

It was shirts mostly. White, beige, and a few pale blue. She also noted that his scent was much stronger here. And strangely familiar. Not the scent of a man she had known only a day. Perhaps she knew someone who wore the same brand.

Purely out of curiosity she picked up one of the shirts and held it to her face, inhaling deeply.

"I see you found my laundry."

She was so startled by the unexpected voice that she squealed with surprise and spun around, but the heel of her pump caught in the carpet and she toppled over into a row of neatly hung trousers, taking several pairs with her as she landed with a thump on the floor.

Cheeks flaming with embarrassment, she looked up to find Charles standing over her, wearing nothing but a damp towel around his slim hips and an amused smile.

She quickly averted her gaze, but not before she registered a set of ridiculously defined abs, perfectly formed pecs, wide, sturdy shoulders, and biceps to die for. Damn her pesky photographic memory.

"I didn't mean to startle you," he said. He reached out a hand to help her up and she was so tangled she had no choice but to accept it.

"What are you doing here?" she snapped when she was back on her feet.

He shrugged. "I live here."

She averted her eyes, pretending to smooth the creases from her skirt, so she wouldn't have to look at all that sculpted perfection. "I'd assumed you'd left for work."

"It's only seven-forty-five."

"I called out but no one answered."

"The granite in the master bath was sealed yesterday, so I was using the spare room down the hall."

"Sorry," she mumbled, running out of places to look, without him realizing she was deliberately not looking at him.

"Something wrong with that shirt?" he asked.

She was still clutching the shirt she had picked up from the hamper, and she realized he must have seen her sniffing it. What could possibly be more embarrassing?

"I was checking to see if it was dirty," she said, cringing inwardly at that ridiculously flimsy excuse.

Charles grinned. "Well then, for future reference, I don't make a habit of keeping clean clothes in the hamper."

"I'll remember that." And she would make a mental note to never come into his house until she was entirely sure he wasn't there, or at the very least fully clothed. "Well, I'll get out of your way."

She turned and grabbed the rest of the clothes from the hamper, stacking them in her arms. He stepped out of her way and she rushed past him and through the doorway.

"Might as well stick around," he said.

She stopped and turned to him, saw that he was leaning casually in the closet doorway. She struggled to keep her eyes from wandering below his neck. "Why?"

"I was going to call my driver, but since you're here, I'll just catch a ride into work with you."

He wanted to ride with *her?* "I would, but, um, I have to stop at the dry cleaners first. I don't want to get you to work late."

"I don't mind." He ran his fingers through the damp, shiny waves of his hair, his biceps flexing under sun-bronzed skin. She stood there transfixed by the fluidity of his movements. His pecs looked hard and defined, and were sprinkled with fine, dark hair.

He may have been an arrogant ass, but God, he was a beautiful one.

"Give me five minutes," he said, and she nodded numbly, hoping her mouth wasn't hanging open, drool dripping from the corner.

"There's coffee in the kitchen," he added, then he turned back into the closet, already loosening the knot at his waist.

The last thing she saw, as he disappeared inside, was the towel drop to the floor, and the tantalizing curve of one perfectly formed butt cheek.

Charles sat in the passenger side of Victoria's convertible two-seater, watching her through the window of the dry cleaner's. He would have expected her to drive a more practical car. A sedan, or even a mini SUV. Not a sporty, candy-apple-red little number that she zipped around in at speeds matched only on the autobahn. And it had a manual transmission, which he found to be a rarity among females. Sizewise, however, it was a perfect fit. Petite and compact, just like her. So petite that his head might brush the top had he not bent down.

She was full of surprises today—the least of which was her reaction when he greeted her wearing nothing but a towel. To put it mildly, she'd been flustered. After her chilly reception last night in the office, he was beginning to wonder if she might be a bit tougher to seduce than he had first anticipated. Now he was sure that she was as good as his. Even if that meant playing dirty. Like deliberately dropping his towel before he cleared the closet door.

Victoria emerged from the building with an armload of clean clothes, wrapped in plastic and folded over one arm. She tucked them into the trunk, then slipped into the driver's seat. Her skirt rode several inches up her thighs, giving him a delicious view of her stocking-clad legs.

If she noticed him looking, she didn't let on.

"They got the stain out of your jacket sleeve," she told him, as she turned the key and the engine roared to life. She checked the rearview mirror for oncoming traffic, then jammed her foot down on the accelerator and whipped out onto the road, shifting so smoothly he barely felt the switch of the gears.

She swung around a corner and he gripped the armrest to keep from falling over. "You in a hurry?"

She shot him a bland look. "No."

She downshifted and whipped around another corner so fast he could swear the tires on one side actually lifted off the pavement.

"You know, the building isn't going anywhere," he said.

"This is the way I drive. If you don't like it, don't ask to ride with me." She took another corner at high speed, and he was pretty sure she was doing it just to annoy him.

If she drove this way all the time, it was a wonder she was still alive. "Out of curiosity, how many accidents have you been in?"

"I've never been in an accident." She whipped into the next lane, cutting off the car directly behind them, whose driver blared its horn in retaliation.

"Have you caused many?"

She shot him another one of those looks. "No."

"Next you'll try to tell me you haven't gotten a speeding ticket."

This time she stayed silent. That's what he figured.

She took a sharp left into the underground parking at his building, used her card key to open the gate, zipped into her assigned spot, and cut the engine.

"Well, that was an adventure," he said, unbuckling his seat belt.

She dropped her keys in her purse and opened her door. "I got you here alive, didn't I?"

Only by the grace of God, he was sure.

They got out and walked to the elevator, taking it up to the tenth floor. She stood silently beside him the entire time. She could never be accused of being too chatty. Since they left his house she hadn't said a word that wasn't initiated by a question. Maybe she was in a snit about the towel. She had enjoyed the free show, but didn't want to admit it.

The elevator doors opened at their floor, and as they stepped off he rested a hand on the small of her back. A natural reaction, but she didn't seem to appreciate his attempt to be a gentleman.

She jerked away and shot lasers at him with her eyes. "What are you doing?"

He held his hands up in a defensive gesture. "Sorry. Just being polite."

"Do you touch all of your female employees inappropriately?"

What was her problem? Here he thought she'd begun to warm to him, but he couldn't seem to get an accurate read on her.

"I didn't mean to offend you."

"Well, you did."

A pair standing in the hallway outside his office cut their conversation short to look at him and Victoria.

"Why don't we step into my office and talk about this," he said quietly. She nodded, then he almost made the monumental error of touching her again, drawing his hand away a second before it grazed her shoulder.

He couldn't help it; he was a physical person. And until today, no one had ever seemed to have a problem with that.

Penelope was already sitting at her desk, tapping away at her keyboard. The only hint of a reaction as he ushered Victoria to his office door was a slight lift of her left brow. He liked that about his secretary. She was always discreet. He also knew exactly what she was thinking. He'd lost another assistant already. Not all that unusual, until he factored in that he hadn't even slept with this one yet.

"Penelope, hold my calls, please." He opened the door and gestured Victoria inside, then closed it behind them. "Have a seat."

Her chin jutted out stubbornly. "I'd rather stand, thank you."

"Fine." He could see that she wasn't going to make this easy. He rounded his desk and sat down. "Now, would you like to tell me what the problem is?"

"The *problem* is that your behavior today has been completely inappropriate."

"All I did was touch your back."

"Employers are not supposed to walk around naked in front of their employees."

He leaned forward and propped his elbows on the desk. "I wasn't naked."

"Not the entire time."

So, she had been looking. "Need I point out that you were in *my* house? When I walked into *my* closet I had no reason to expect you would be there. Sniffing my shirts."

Her cheeks blushed pink, but she didn't back down. "And I suppose the towel accidentally fell off."

"Again, if you hadn't been ogling me, you wouldn't have seen anything."

Her eyes went wide with indignation. "I was not ogling you!"

"Face it, sweetheart, you couldn't keep your eyes off me." He leaned back in his chair. "In fact, I felt a little violated."

"*You* felt violated?" She clamped her jaw so tight he

worried she might crack her teeth. She wasn't easy to rile, but once he got her going…damn.

"But I'm willing to forgive and forget," he said.

"I've read your e-mails and listened to your phone messages. I know the kind of man that you are, and I'm telling you to back off. I don't want to be here any more than you want me to, but you have done such a thorough job of ruining my family that I need this position. The way I see it, we're stuck with each other. If you're trying to get me to quit, it isn't going to work. And if you continue to prance around naked in front of me and touch me inappropriately I'll slap a sexual harassment suit on you so fast you won't know what hit you."

He couldn't repress the smile that was itching to curl the corner of his mouth. "I was *prancing?*"

Her mouth fell open, as though she couldn't believe he was making a joke out of this. "You really are a piece of work."

"Thank you."

"That wasn't a compliment! You have got to be the most arrogant, self-centered—" she struggled for the right word, but all she could come up with was "—*jerk* I have ever met!"

He shrugged. "Arrogant, yes. Self-centered, occasionally. But anyone will tell you I'm a nice guy."

"Nice?"

"And fair."

"Fair? You orchestrated the deal that ruined my father. That stole from us the land that has been in our family for five generations, and you call that fair? We

lost our business and our home. We lost *everything* because of you."

He wasn't sure where she was getting her information, but she was way off. "We didn't *steal* anything. The deal we offered your father was a gift."

Her face twisted with outrage. "A *gift?*"

"He wouldn't have gotten a better deal from anyone else."

"Ruining good men in the name of the royal family doesn't make it any less sleazy or wrong."

This was all beginning to make sense now. Her lack of gratitude toward the royal family and her very generous employment contract. And there was only one explanation. "You have no idea the financial shape that the Houghton was in, do you?"

She instantly went on the defensive. "What is that supposed to mean? Yes, my father handled the financial end of the business, but he kept me informed. Business was slow, no thanks to the Royal Inn, but we were by no means sinking."

Suddenly he felt very sorry for her. And he didn't like what he was going to have to do next, but it was necessary. She deserved to know the truth, before she did something ill-advised and made a fool of both herself and her father.

He pressed the intercom on his desk. "Penelope, would you please bring in the file for the buyout on the Houghton Hotel."

"What are you doing?" Victoria demanded.

Probably making a huge mistake. "Something against my better judgment."

Victoria stood there, stiff and tight-lipped until Penelope appeared a moment later with a brown accordion file stuffed to capacity. She handed it to Charles, but not before she flashed him a swift, stern glance. Penelope knew what he was doing and the risk he was taking. And it was clear that she didn't approve. But she didn't say a word. She just walked out and shut the door behind her.

"The contents in this file are confidential," he told Victoria. "I could be putting my career in jeopardy by showing it to you. But I think it's something you need to see. In fact, I know it is."

At first he thought she might refuse to read it. For several long moments she just stared at him. But curiosity must have gotten the best of her, because finally she reached out and took the file.

"Take that into your office and look it over," he said.

Without a word she turned and walked through the door separating their offices.

"Come see me if you have questions," he called after her, just before she shut the door firmly behind her. And he was sure she would have questions. Because as far as he could tell, everything her father had told her was a lie.

Four

Victoria felt sick.

Sick in her mind and in her heart. Sick all the way down to the center of her soul. And the more she read, the worse she felt.

She was barely a quarter of the way through the file and it was already undeniably clear that not only had the royal family not stolen anything from her and her father, they had rescued them from inevitable and total ruin.

Had they not stepped in, the bank would have foreclosed on mortgages she hadn't even been aware that her father had levied against the hotel. And he was so far behind in their property taxes, the property had been just days from being seized.

The worst part was that the trouble began when Victoria was a baby, after her grandfather passed away and her father inherited control of the hotel. All that time he'd been riding a precarious, financial roller coaster, living far above their means. Until it had finally caught up to him. And he had managed to keep it a secret by blatantly lying to her.

She had trusted him. Sacrificed so much because she thought she owed him.

Because of the royal family's generous offer, she and her father had a roof over their heads. And she had the opportunity for a career that would launch her further than she might have ever dreamed possible. Yet she still felt as though the rug had been yanked violently from under her. Everything she knew about her father and their business, *about her life,* was a lie.

And she had seen enough.

She gathered the papers and tucked them neatly back into the file. Though she dreaded facing Charles, admitting her father's deception, what choice did she have? Besides, he probably had a pretty good idea already that something in her family dynamic was amiss. If nothing else, she owed him an apology for her unfounded accusations. And a heartfelt thank-you for… well…*everything*. His family's generosity and especially their discretion.

And there was only one thing left to do. Only one thing she *could* do.

She picked up the phone and dialed Charles's extension. He answered on the first ring. "Is now a good time to speak with you?"

"Of course," he said. "Come right in."

She hung up the phone, but for several long seconds

just sat there, working up the courage to face him. And she thought yesterday had been humiliating. Getting her butt out of the chair and walking to his office, tail between her legs, was one of the hardest things she'd ever done.

Charles sat at his desk. He had every right to look smug, but he wore a sympathetic smile instead. And honestly she couldn't decide which was worse. She didn't deserve his sympathy.

She handed him the file. "Thank you for showing me this. For being honest with me."

"I thought you deserved the truth."

She took a deep breath. "First, I want to thank you and the royal family for your generosity. Please let them know how much we appreciate their intervention."

"'We'?" he asked, knowing full well that her father didn't appreciate anything the royal family had done for them.

Although for the life of her, she couldn't imagine why. Pride, she supposed. Or stubbornness. Whatever the reason, she was in no position to make excuses for him. Nor would she want to. He had gotten them into this mess, and any consequences he suffered were his own doing.

"And while I appreciate the opportunity to work for the Royal Inn," she said, removing her ID badge and setting it on his desk, "I'm afraid I won't be accepting the position."

His brow furrowed. "I don't understand."

She had taken this job only to appease her father, and now everything was different. She didn't owe him anything. For the first tine in her life she was going to make a decision based entirely on what *she* wanted.

"I'm not a charity case," she told Charles. "I owe you too much already. And unlike my father, I don't care to be indebted to anyone."

"You've seen the file, Victoria. We were under no obligation to your father. Do you honestly believe we would have hired you if we didn't feel you were qualified for the position?"

She didn't know what to believe anymore. "I'm sorry, but I just can't."

"What will you do?"

She shrugged. She was in hotel management, and the Royal Inn was the biggest game on the island. She would never find a position with comparable pay anywhere else. Not on Morgan Isle, anyway. That could mean a move off the island. Maybe it was time for a change, time to stop leaning on her father and be truly independent for the first time in her life. Or maybe it was he who had been leaning on her.

"I'll find another job," she said.

"What will you do until then?"

She honestly didn't know. Since the buyout, what savings she'd had were quickly vanishing. If she went much longer without a paycheck, she would be living on the streets.

"I have an idea," Charles said. "A mutually beneficial arrangement."

She wasn't sure she liked the sound of that, but the least she could do was hear him out. She folded her arms and said, "I'm listening."

"You've seen the shambles my life is in. Stay, just long enough to get things back in order and to hire and train a new assistant, and when you go, you'll leave with a letter of recommendation so impressive that anyone would be a fool not to hire you."

It was tempting, but she already owed him too much. This was something she needed to do on her own.

She shook her head. "You've done too much already."

He leaned forward in his seat. "*You* would be the one doing *me* the favor. I honestly don't have the time to train someone else."

"I've been here *two* days. Technically someone should be training me."

"You're a fast learner." When she didn't answer he leaned forward and said, "Victoria, I'm desperate."

He did look a little desperate, but she couldn't escape the feeling that he was doing it just to be nice. Which shouldn't have been a bad thing. And she should have been jumping at his offer, but she couldn't escape the feeling that she didn't deserve his sympathy.

"Do this one thing for me," he coaxed, "and we'll call it even. You won't owe me and I won't owe you."

She would have loved nothing more than to put this entire awful experience behind her and start fresh.

"I would have to insist you pay me only an assistant's wage," she said.

He looked surprised. "That's not much."

"Maybe, but it's fair."

"Fine," he agreed. "If that's what you want."

"How long would I have to stay?" she asked.

"How about two months."

Yeah, right. "How about one *week?*"

He narrowed his eyes at her. "Six weeks."

"Two weeks," she countered.

"Four."

"*Three.*"

"Deal," he said with a grin.

She took a deep breath and blew it out. Three weeks working with the duke. It was longer than she was comfortable with, but at the very least it would give her time to look for another job. She had interviewed hundreds of people in her years at the Houghton, yet she had never so much as put together a résumé for herself. Much less had to look for employment. She barely knew where to begin.

"I'll have Penelope post an ad for the assistant's position. I'll leave it to you to interview the applicants. Then, of course, they'll have to meet my approval."

"Of course."

"Why don't we catch an early lunch today and discuss exactly what it is I'm looking for?" His smile said business was the last thing on his mind.

Were they back to that again?

If she was going to survive the next three weeks working for him, she was going to have to set some boundaries. Establish parameters.

"I'm not going to sleep with you," she said.

If her direct approach surprised him, he didn't let it show. He just raised one brow slightly higher than the other. "I don't know how you did things at the Houghton, but here, *lunch* isn't code for sex."

On the contrary, that's exactly what it was. Practically everything he said was a double entendre. "I'm not a member of your harem."

One corner of his mouth tipped up. "I have a harem?"

Was he forgetting that she'd listened to his phone messages? "I just thought I should make it clear up front. Because you seem to believe you're God's gift to the female race."

He shot her a very contrived stunned look. "You mean I'm *not?*"

"I'm sorry to say, I don't find you the least bit attractive." It was kind of a lie. Physically she found him incredibly attractive. His personality, on the other hand, needed serious work.

He shrugged. "If you say so."

He was baiting her, but she wouldn't give him the satisfaction of a response. "Have a list of employment requirements to me by end of day and I'll see that the ad is placed." She already had a pretty good idea of the sort of employee he was looking for. More emphasis on looks than intelligence or capability. But she was going to find him an assistant who could actually do the job. And she would hopefully be doing it sooner than three weeks. The faster she got out of here, the better.

"You'll have it by five," he said.

"Thank you. I should get back to work." She still had a backload of e-mail and phone messages to sort through.

She was almost to her office when he called her name, and something in his voice said he was up to no good. She sighed quietly to herself, and with her hand on the doorknob, turned back to him. Ready for a fight. "Yes?"

"Thank you."

"For what?" she asked, expecting some sort of snappy, sarcastic comeback or a sexually charged innuendo.

Instead, he just said, "For sticking around."

She was so surprised, all she could do was nod as she opened the door and slipped into her office. The really weird thing was, she was pretty sure he genuinely meant it. And it touched her somewhere deep down.

If she wasn't careful, she just might forget how much she didn't like him.

It was almost four-thirty when Charles popped his head into her office and handed Victoria the list of employment requirements. And early, no less.

"Are you busy?" he asked.

What now? Wasn't it a bit early for a dinner invitation? "Why?"

"You up for a field trip?"

She set the list in her urgent to-do pile. "I guess that all depends on where you want to go." If it was a field trip to his bedroom, then no, she would pass.

"I have a meeting at the palace in half an hour. I thought you might want to tag along. It would be a chance for you to learn the ropes."

A tickle of excitement worked its way up from her belly. Anyone who lived on Morgan Isle dreamed of going to the palace and meeting the royal family.

But honestly, what was the point? "Why bother? I'll only be working for you for three weeks."

"Yes, but how will you train your replacement if you don't learn the job first?"

He had a point. Although his logic was a little

backward. But the truth was, she really *wanted* to go. After all, when would she ever get an opportunity like this one again?

"When you put it that way," she said, pushing away from her desk, "I suppose I should."

"A car is waiting for us downstairs."

She grabbed her purse from the bottom desk drawer and her sweater from the hook on the back of the door, then followed him through the outer office past Penelope—who didn't even raise her head to acknowledge them—to the elevator. He was uncharacteristically quiet as they rode down and he led her through the lobby to the shiny, black, official-looking Bentley parked out front. Not that she knew him all that well, but he always seemed to have something to say. Too much, usually.

They settled in the leather-clad backseat, and the driver pulled out into traffic. She wasn't typically the chatty type, but she felt this irrational, uncontrollable urge to fill the silence. Maybe because as long as they were talking, she didn't have to think about the overpowering sense of his presence beside her. He was so large, filled his side of the seat so thoroughly, she felt almost crowded against the door. It would take only the slightest movement to cause their knees to bump. And the idea of any sort of contact in the privacy of the car, even accidental, made her pulse jump.

When she couldn't stand the silence another second, she heard herself ask, "Not looking forward to this meeting?"

The sound of her voice startled him, as though he'd forgotten he wasn't alone. "Why do you ask?"

"You seem…preoccupied."

"Do I?"

"You haven't made a single suggestive or inappropriate comment since we left your office."

He laughed and said, "No, I'm not looking forward to it. Delivering bad news is never pleasant."

He didn't elaborate, and though she was dying of curiosity, she didn't ask. It was none of her business. And honestly, the less she knew about the royal family's business, the better.

The drive to the palace was a short one. As the gates came into view, Victoria's heart did a quick shimmy in her chest. She was really going to visit the royal palace. Where kings and queens had lived for generations, and heads of state regularly visited. Though she had lived on Morgan Isle her entire life, not ten miles from the palace, she never imagined she would ever step foot within its walls. Or come face-to-face with the royal family.

Charles leaned forward and told the driver. "Take us to the front doors." He turned to Victoria. "Normally you would use the business entrance in the back, but I thought for your first visit you should get the royal treatment."

The car rolled to a stop, and royally clothed footmen posted on either side of the enormous double doors descended the stairs. One opened the car door and offered a hand encased in pristine white cotton to help her out. It was oddly surreal. She'd never put much stock in fairy tales, but standing at the foot of the palace steps, she felt a little like Cinderella. Only she wasn't there for a ball. And even if she were, there were no single princes in residence to fall in love with her. Just an arrogant, womanizing duke.

Which sounded more like a nightmare than any fairy tale she'd ever read.

She and Charles climbed the stairs, and as they approached the top the gilded doors swung open, welcoming them inside.

Walking into the palace, through the cavernous foyer, was like stepping into a different world. An alternate reality where everything was rich and elegant and larger than life. She had never seen so much marble, gold, and velvet, yet it was tastefully proportioned so as not to appear gaudy. She turned in a circle, her heels clicking against marble buffed to a gleaming shine, taking in the antique furnishings, the vaulted and ornately painted ceilings.

Though she had seen it many times in photos and on television documentaries, and on television documentaries, those were substitute for the real thing.

"What do you think?" Charles asked.

"It's amazing," she breathed. "Does everyone who visits get this kind of welcome?"

"Not exactly. But I feel as though everyone should experience the entire royal treatment at least one time. Don't you think?"

She nodded, although she couldn't help wondering if he had done this out of the kindness of his heart or if instead he had ulterior motives. She knew from experience that men like him often did. How many other women had he brought here, hoping to impress them with his royalty? Not that she considered herself one of his *women*. But he very well might. In fact, she was pretty sure he did. Men like him objectified women, saw them as nothing more than playthings.

And she was buying into it. Playing right into his hand. Shame on her for letting down her guard.

She put a chokehold on her excitement and flashed him a passive smile. "Well, thank you. It was a nice surprise."

"Would you like to meet the family?" he asked.

Her heart leapt up into her throat. "The f-family?"

"We have a meeting scheduled, so they should all be together in the king's suite."

The *entire* family? All at once? And he said it so casually, as if meeting royalty was a daily occurrence for her.

But what was she going to tell him? *No?*

"If it's not a problem," she said, although she didn't have the first clue what she would say to them.

"They're expecting us."

Expecting them?

She went from being marginally nervous to shaking in her pumps.

He stepped forward, toward the stairs, but she didn't budge. She couldn't. She felt frozen in place, as though her shoes had melted into the marble.

He stopped and looked back at her. "You coming?"

She nodded, but she couldn't seem to get her feet to move. She just stood there like an idiot.

Charles brow furrowed a little. "You okay?"

"Of course." If she ignored the fact that her legs wouldn't work and that a nest of nerves the size of a boulder weighed heavy in her gut.

A grin curled one corner of his mouth. "A little nervous, maybe?"

"Maybe," she conceded. "A little."

"You have nothing to worry about. They don't bite." He paused then added, "Much."

She shot him a look.

He grinned and said, "I'm kidding. They're looking forward to meeting you." He jerked his head in the direction of the stairs. "Come on."

She didn't pitch a fit this time when Charles touched a hand to the small of her back to give her a gentle shove in the right direction. But he kept his hands to himself as he led her up the marble staircase to the second floor, gesturing to points of interest along the way. Family portraits dating back centuries, priceless heirlooms and gifts from foreign visitors and dignitaries.

It all sounded a bit rehearsed to her, but the truth was, as the family lawyer, he'd probably taken lots of people on a similar tour. Not just women he was hoping to impress. And it did take her mind off of her nerves.

"The family residence is this way," he said, leading her toward a set of doors guarded by two very large, frightening-looking security officers. He gestured to the wing across the hall. "The guest suites are down that way."

Feeling like an interloper, she followed him toward the residence. The guards stepped forward as they approached, and Victoria half-expected them to tackle her before she could make it through the doors. But instead they opened the doors and stepped aside so she and Charles could pass. Inside was a long, wide, quiet hallway and at least a dozen sets of double doors.

Behind one of those doors, she thought, waited the entire royal family. And what she hadn't even considered until just now was that each and every one of them knew the dire financial situation she and her father had been in. For all she knew, they might believe she was responsible. She could only hope that Charles had told them the truth.

"Ready?" he asked.

Ready? How did one prepare herself for a moment like this? But she took a deep breath and blew it out, then looked up at Charles and said, "Let's do it."

Five

Victoria was tough, Charles would give her that.

Typically when people were introduced to members of the royal family, it was one or two at a time. Victoria was meeting King Phillip and Queen Hannah; Prince Ethan and his wife, Lizzy; and Princess Sophie and her fiancé, Alex, all at the same time.

Everyone was gathered in the sitting room of Hannah and Phillip's suite, and they all rose from their seats when he and Victoria entered.

If she was nervous, it didn't show. Her curtsy was flawless, and when she spoke her voice was clear and steady. It never failed to intrigue him how a woman so seemingly small and unassuming could dominate a room with sheer confidence. He could see that everyone was impressed. And though it was totally irrational, he felt proud of her. Hiring her had in no way been his idea. He had merely been following orders.

After the introductions and several minutes of polite small talk, an aide was called in to give Victoria a tour of the business offices and familiarize her with palace procedure.

"I like her," Sophic said, the instant they were gone. It had been at her insistence that they had hired Victoria in the first place.

Charles nodded. "She's very capable."

"And attractive," Ethan noted, which got him a playful elbow jab in the side from his very pregnant wife, Lizzy.

"Stunning," Hannah added.

"Quite," Charles agreed. "And she would have been an asset to the Royal Inn."

"Would have been?" Phillip asked.

Sophie narrowed her eyes at Charles. "What did you do?"

"Nothing!" He held both hands up defensively. "I swear."

He explained Victoria's outburst and admitted to showing her the file on the Houghton sale. "She seems to think we see her as some sort of charity case. She has no idea her expertise. Nor does she have the slightest clue how valuable she is. Had it not been for her, I think the Houghton would have collapsed years ago."

"Then it will be up to you to see that she learns her value," Phillip said.

Easier said than done when she was suspicious of his every move. "She's stubborn as hell. But I'm sure I can convince her."

"Stubborn as hell," Alex said, glancing over at Princess Sophie. "She'll fit right in, won't she?"

Now she narrowed her eyes at him. "Is it so wrong that I don't want my wedding to be a spectacle? That I prefer small and intimate?"

"You have other news for us?" Phillip asked Charles, forestalling another potential wedding argument.

Yes, it was time they got to it. Charles took a seat on the couch beside Sophie, rubbing his palms together.

"I gather the news isn't good," Ethan said.

"The DNA test confirmed it. She's the real deal," Charles told them. "Melissa Thornsby is your illegitimate sister and heir to the throne."

"We have a sister," Sophie said, as though trying out the sound of it. Phillip and Hannah remained quietly concerned.

"And here I believed I had the distinction of being the only illegitimate heir to the throne," Ethan quipped, even though he was the one who had taken the time to investigate their father's notorious reputation with women, and the possibility of more illegitimate children. But who could have imagined that King Frederick would have been so bold as to not only have an affair with the former prime minister's wife but to father a child with her? And he never told a soul. Had Ethan not stumbled across a file of newspaper clippings King Frederick had left hidden after his death, they might never have learned the truth.

"She's older than Phillip?" Lizzy asked.

"Twenty-three days," Charles said.

Everyone exchanged worried glances, but Hannah

broached the subject no one else seemed willing to speak aloud. "Could she take the crown?"

This was the part Charles hadn't been looking forward to. "Technically? Yes, she could. Half Royal or not, she's the oldest."

Hannah frowned. "But she wasn't even raised here."

"She was born here, though. She's still considered a citizen."

In an uncustomary show of emotion, Phillip cursed under his breath. Losing the crown for him wouldn't be an issue of status or power. Phillip truly loved his country and had devoted his entire life in the preparation to become its leader. To lose that would devastate him. "We'll fight it," he said.

"I don't think it will come to that," Charles said. "She doesn't seem the type to take on the role as the leader of a country. Despite a first-rate education, other than heading up a host of charities, she's never had a career."

"As a proper princess wouldn't," Phillip said, sounding cautiously optimistic. "Meaning she could very well fit right in."

"Would she be the type to go after our money?" Sophie asked.

Charles shook his head. "I seriously doubt it."

"Why?"

"Because she has almost as much money as you do. She inherited a considerable trust from her parents on her twenty-first birthday, and her aunt and uncle left her a fortune. She's at the top of the food chain in New Orleans high society."

"How did she take the news?" Hannah asked.

"According to the attorney, it was definitely a shock, but she's eager to meet everyone. So much so that she's dropping everything so that she can move here. Temporarily at first. Then she'll decide if she wants to stay."

"Her place is here with her family," Sophie said.

"We can't force her to stay," Lizzy pointed out.

"True," Hannah said, looking pointedly at Phillip. "But if we make her feel welcome she'll be more inclined to."

It was no secret that when Ethan joined the family, Phillip had been less than welcoming to his half brother. But in Phillip's defense, Ethan had gone out of his way to be difficult. Since then, they had put their differences aside and now behaved like brothers. Not that they didn't occasionally butt heads.

"When will she come?" Phillip asked.

"Saturday."

"We'll need to see that a suite is prepared," Sophie said. "I suggest housing her in the guest suite at first, with restricted privileges to the residence."

"I agree," Phillip said. "Lizzy, can you please handle the details?"

Lizzy nodded eagerly. Going from full-time employment to royal status had been rough for her. And despite a somewhat trying pregnancy, she was always looking for tasks to keep her busy until the baby arrived. "I'll take care of it immediately."

Phillip turned to Sophie, who handled media relations. "We'll have to issue a press release immediately. I don't want to see a story in the tabloids before we make a formal announcement."

Sophie nodded. "I'll see that it's done today."

"Speaking of the tabloids," Alex said, "you know they're going to be all over this. And all over her." Having recently been a target of the media himself when his ex-wife fed them false information about his relationship with the princess, he knew how vicious they could be.

"She'll be instructed on exactly what she should and shouldn't say," Charles assured him. "Although given her position in society, I don't think handling the press will be an issue."

"I'd like to keep this low-key," Phillip said, then he rose from his seat, signaling the end of the meeting. "Keep us posted."

Hannah tugged on his sleeve. "Are you forgetting something, Your Highness?"

He looked down at his wife and smiled. "You're sure you want to do this now?"

She nodded.

He touched her cheek affectionately, then announced, with distinct happiness and pride, "Hannah is pregnant."

Everyone seemed as stunned as they were excited.

Sophie laughed and said, "My gosh! You two certainly didn't waste any time. Frederick is barely three months old!"

Hannah blushed. "It wasn't planned, and I only just found out this morning. We'd like to keep it quiet until closer to the end of my first trimester. But I was too excited not to tell the family."

"I think it's wonderful," Lizzy said, a hand on her

own rounded belly. She shot Sophie a meaningful glance. "At this rate we'll have the palace filled with children in no time."

Sophie emphatically shook her head. "Not from me you won't. Alex and I have already discussed it and decided to wait until he's not traveling back and forth to the States so much."

"You say that now," Lizzy teased. "Things have a way of not working out as you plan."

She would know. Her pregnancy had been an unplanned surprise. She'd gone from palace employee to royal family member with one hasty but genuinely happy *I do*.

"What about Charles?" Sophie said, flashing him a wry grin. "He's not even married yet. Why not pick on him?"

"When it comes to marriage," Phillip said, sounding only slightly exasperated, "*yet* is not a word in Charles's vocabulary."

Phillip was absolutely right. And this was not a conversation Charles cared to have any part of. The last thing he needed was the entire family meddling in his love life.

"Wow," he said, glancing down at his watch. "Would you look at the time. I should be going."

"What's the matter, Charles?" Sophie asked. "Have you got a hot date?"

In fact he did. Even though the "date" in question didn't know it yet.

Phillip just grinned. "If you hear anything else from Melissa or her attorney, you'll let us know?"

"Of course." He said the obligatory goodbyes, then

made a hasty retreat out into the hall. Before he could escape the residence, Ethan called after him.

"Charles, hold up a minute." He wore a concerned expression, which was enough to cause Charles concern himself. Ethan was one of the most easygoing people he knew.

"Is there a problem?" he asked.

Ethan paused for a moment, then sighed and shook his head. "I guess there's really no tactful way to say this, so I'm just going to say it. The family is asking, as a personal favor, that you not have an affair with Victoria."

For an instant, Charles was too stunned to speak. Then all he could manage was "I beg your pardon?"

"You heard me."

Yes, he had. But he must have been mistaken. He'd devoted his life to his family, true, but that didn't give them the right to dictate who he could or couldn't sleep with. "What are you suggesting, Ethan?"

Ethan lowered his voice. "I don't have to *suggest* anything. It's common knowledge that the employees you sleep with don't last. Normally that isn't a problem because they're *your* personal employees, and how you run your firm is your own business. But Victoria is an employee of the royal family, as are you, and as such, policy states there can be no personal relationship. If we can convince her to stay, her expertise will be a great asset to the Royal Inn. That isn't likely to happen if you and she become...*intimately* involved."

"That's a little hypocritical coming from you," Charles said. "Seeing as how you knocked up a palace employee."

It was a cheap shot, but the arrow hit its mark.

Ethan's expression darkened. "Make no mistake Charles, this is something the *entire* family is asking. Not just me."

And what if Charles said no? What if he slept with her and she refused to stay? Would he be ousted as the family attorney? "This sounds a bit like a threat to me."

"It's nothing more than a request."

Though only a cousin, Charles had always been an integral part of the royal family. For the first time in his life he felt like an outsider.

And he didn't like it.

"Do whatever it takes to make her stay," Ethan said, and there was a finality to his words that set Charles even deeper on edge.

"I need to go fetch my assistant," Charles told him, then he turned and left before he said something he might later regret.

He found Victoria in the main business office with one of the secretaries. For the life of him he couldn't remember her name. She was explaining the phone and security system to Victoria. As he approached they both looked up at him.

"Finished already?" Victoria asked.

Charles nodded. "Ready to go?"

"Sure." She thanked the secretary, whose name still escaped him, grabbed her purse, and followed Charles out. She practically had to jog to keep up with his brisk, longer stride. He led her out the back way this time, where she would come and go should the position ever call for her coming back to the palace.

"Meeting not go well?" she asked from behind him, as they passed the kitchen.

"What makes you think that?"

"You're awfully quiet. And you seem to be in a terrible rush to leave," she said, sounding a touch winded.

He made an effort to slow his pace. It wasn't the meeting itself that was troubling him. That had gone rather well, all things considered. "It was fine," he said.

The car was waiting for them when they stepped out of the back entrance. They got in, and he almost directed the driver to take them back to the office, but then he remembered that he was treating Victoria to dinner.

Instead he told him, "The Royal Inn."

"Why are we going to the Royal Inn?" she asked.

"I'm taking you to Les Régal De Rois for dinner," he said. He expected an argument or an immediate refusal. Instead she just looked amused, which rubbed his already frayed nerves.

"Is that an invitation?" she asked.

"No. Just a fact."

"Really?"

He nodded. "Yep."

"What about my car?"

"It'll be fine in the parking garage overnight. I'll arrange for my car to pick you up in the morning."

She mulled that over, looking skeptical. He steeled himself for the inevitable argument. In fact, he was looking forward to it. He needed a target to vent a little steam. Even though he was supposed to be convincing her to stay, not using her for target practice.

Instead she said, "Okay."

"Okay?"

"I'll go to dinner with you, but only if I get to choose the restaurant."

He shrugged. "All right."

"And you have to let me pay."

Absolutely not. He never let women pay. It had been hammered into him from birth that it was a man's duty—his *responsibility*—to pick up the check. As far as his mother was concerned, chivalry was alive and kicking.

"Considering your current employment status, it might be wise to let me cover it," he said.

She folded her arms across her chest. "Let me worry about that."

Would it hurt to let her *think* she was paying? But when it came time to get the bill, he would take it. It's not as if she would wrestle it out of his hand. At least, he didn't think she would. She may have been independent, but he knew from experience that deep down, all women loved to be pampered. They liked when men held doors and paid the check. Expected it, even.

"Fine," he agreed.

She leaned forward and instructed the driver to take them to an unfamiliar address in the bay area. For all he knew she could be taking him to a fast-food establishment.

The driver looked to Charles for confirmation, and he nodded.

What the heck. He was always up for an adventure.

Six

It wasn't a fast food restaurant.

It was a cozy, moderately priced bistro tucked between two upscale women's clothing stores in the shopping district. The maître d' greeted Victoria warmly and Charles with the proper fuss afforded royalty, then seated them at a table in a secluded corner. It was quiet and intimate and soaked in the flickering glow of warm candlelight. Their waiter appeared instantly to take their drink orders—a white wine for Victoria and a double scotch for him—then he listed the specials for the evening.

"I recommend the prime rib," Victoria said, once he was gone.

Charles drew the line at letting his date order for him, and he used the term *date* very loosely. Besides, his encounter with Ethan had pretty much killed his appetite.

"I take it you come here often," he said.

"I love this place," Victoria said with a smile. An honest to goodness, genuine smile. And the force of it was so devastating it nearly knocked him backward out of his chair. She might not have smiled often, but it was certainly worth the wait.

The waiter reappeared only seconds later with their drinks. Charles took a deep slug of scotch, relishing the smooth burn as it slid down his throat and spread heat through his stomach. Three or four more of these and he would be right as rain, but he'd never been one to find solace in a bottle.

Victoria took a sip of her wine, watching him curiously. "Would you like to talk about it?"

"Talk about what?"

"Whatever it is that's bothering you." She propped her elbow on the table, dropped her chin in her hand, and gazed across the candlelight at him, her eyes warm, her features soft in the low light.

She really was stunning. And not at all the sort of woman he was typically attracted to. But maybe that was the appeal. Maybe he was tired of the same old thing. Maybe he needed to spice things up a bit.

The family had put the kibosh on that, though, hadn't they? And since when did he ever let anyone tell him whom he could or couldn't pursue?

"What makes you think something is bothering me?"

"That's why I agreed to dinner," she said. "You looked as though you needed a sympathetic ear."

She certainly looked sympathetic, which for some reason surprised him. He never imagined her having a soft side. But he wasn't one to air his troubles, Although, would it hurt to play the pity card this one time? And maybe, in the process, do his job and convince Victoria to stay with the hotel?

He pulled in a deep, contemplative breath, then blew it out. "Family issues," he said, keeping it cryptic. Baiting her. But if he expected her to try to drag it out of him, boy, had he been wrong.

She just sat there sipping her wine, waiting for him to continue.

He dropped another crumb. "Suffice it to say that the family wasn't happy to hear that you're not staying with the Royal Inn."

"I'm sorry to hear that."

"I've been instructed to do whatever it takes to convince you to stay."

If she was flattered, it didn't show on her face. "But that isn't what's bothering you," she said.

Who was baiting whom here?

Though he'd had no intention of telling her what was really said, he supposed that if anyone could understand a backstabbing, meddling family, it was her.

"I've been asked by the family not to pursue you socially."

A grin tipped up the corners of her mouth. "In other words, don't sleep with me."

Her candor surprised him a little, but then, what did she have to lose? This was only a temporary position for her. "That was the gist of it, yes."

"And that upsets you?"

"Wouldn't it upset you?"

"I suppose. But then, I don't have a notorious reputation for sleeping with my employees."

He couldn't help but wonder where she'd heard that. "According to whom?"

"The girls in the palace office talk."

He couldn't exactly deny it, but still he felt… offended. Whom he dated was no one's concern. Especially the girls in the office. "What else did the *girls* have to say about me?"

"Are you sure you want to know?"

Did he? Did it even matter? When had he ever cared what people thought of him?

But curiosity got the best of him. "I'm a big boy. I think I can handle it."

"They told me that your assistants never last more than a few weeks."

Again, he couldn't deny it. But that was just the nature of business. Assistants' positions notoriously had a high turnover rate. Most were overworked and underpaid.

Were the girls in the office taking that into account?

Not to say that he was an unfair employer. But he didn't owe anyone an explanation.

"And I'm not your usual type."

"I have a type?"

"Tall, leggy, impressed by your power and position."

Could he help that people were impressed by his title?

"Oh, and they told me that you objectify women," she added. "But I already knew that."

Wait, what? He *objectified* women? "No, I don't."

She looked a little surprised by his denial. "Yes, you do."

"I have nothing but respect for women. I *love* women."

"Maybe that's part of the problem."

"What the hell is that supposed to mean?" And why did he even care what she thought of him?

"This is upsetting you," she said. "Maybe we should just drop it."

"No. I want to know how it is that I objectify women."

She studied him for a minute, then asked, "How many different women have you dated in the last month?"

"What does that have to do with anything?"

"Humor me."

"Eight or ten, maybe." Maybe more. In fact, if he counted the casual encounters in bars or clubs that led back to his bedroom, that number was probably closer to fifteen. But that didn't mean anything. Wanting to play the field, not wanting to settle down yet, did not equate into disrespect for the opposite sex.

"What were their names?" she asked.

That one stopped him. "What do you mean?"

"Their names. The women you dated. They had names, right?"

"Of course."

"So, what were they?"

He frowned. That was a lot of names. Faces he could remember, or body types. Hair color, even eye color. Names he wasn't so good with.

"I'll make it easy for you. Of the last twenty girls you dated, give me *three* names," she said.

Three names? What about the blonde from the bar last week. The bank teller with the large and plunging… portfolio. It was something simple. A *J* name. Jenny, Julie, Jeri. Or maybe it was Sara.

He was usually pretty good under pressure, but now he was drawing a blank.

"You can't do it, can you?" Victoria said, looking pleased with herself. "Here's an easy one. How about your last assistant? What was her name?"

Now this one he knew. Tall, brunette. Low, sultry voice...

It was right there, on the tip of his tongue.

"Oh, come on," she said. "Even I know this."

He took a guess, which he knew was probably a bad idea. "Diane."

"Her name was Rebecca."

"Well, she looked like a Diane to me." Mostly he'd just called her honey, or sweetheart, so he wouldn't *have* to remember her name. Because after a while they all just sort of bled together. But that didn't mean anything.

She shook her head. "That's really sad."

"So I'm not great with names. So what?"

"Name the last five male clients you met with."

They popped into his head in quick succession. One after the other, clear as if he'd read them on a list. And though he said nothing, she could read it in his expression.

The smile that followed was a smug one. "Easier, isn't it?"

He folded his arms across his chest, not liking the direction this was taking. "What's your point?"

"You remember the men because you respect them. You see them as equals. Women on the other hand exist only for your own personal amusement. They're playthings."

Though his first reaction was to deny the accusation, it *was* an interesting…hypothesis. And one he had no desire to contemplate at that particular moment, or with her.

He downed the last of his drink and signaled the waiter for the check. "We should go."

"We haven't eaten yet."

"I have to get an early start in the morning."

Her smug smile grew, as though she was feeding off his discomfort. To make matters worse, before he could take the bill from the waiter, she snatched it up. "My treat, remember?"

There didn't seem much point in arguing. And since it was only drinks, he would let her have her way this once.

She paid in cash, leaving a generous tip considering they hadn't even eaten, then they rose from their chairs and walked in silence to the door. The car was already waiting for them out front.

"I'll see you tomorrow," she said.

"You don't want a ride?"

She shook her head. "No, thanks."

"It's quite chilly."

"I'm just a few blocks from here. I could use the fresh air."

"I'll walk you," he said, because God forbid she would also accuse him of not being a gentleman.

"No, I'm fine," she said, with a smile. "But I appreciate the offer."

There was something very different about her tonight. He'd never seen her so relaxed. So pleasant and…happy.

At his expense, no doubt.

"See you tomorrow at the office." She turned to

walk away, but made it only a step or two before she stopped and turned back. "By the way, have you decided what to do?"

"What do you mean?"

"Your family? Not pursuing me. Will you listen to them?"

Good question. And despite all the hemming and hawing and claims that no one could tell him who he could or couldn't see, he had an obligation to the family. Ultimately, there was really only one clear-cut answer.

He shrugged. "I don't really have much choice."

"Well, in that case…"

Another one of those grins curled her mouth. Playful, bordering on devious, and he had the distinct impression that she was up to no good.

She stepped closer, closing the gap between them, then reached up with one hand and gripped his tie. She gave it a firm tug, and he had no choice but to lean over—it was that or asphyxiation. And when he did, she rose up on her toes and kissed him. A tender, teasing brush of her lips against his own.

Before he could react, before he could cup the back of her head and draw her in for more, it was over. She had already let go of his tie and backed away. His lips burned with the need to kiss her again. His hands ached to touch her.

He wanted her.

"What was that for?" he asked.

She shrugged, as though she accosted men on the street on a regular basis. "Just thought you should know what you're missing."

* * *

Victoria knew that kissing Charles was a really bad idea, but he had looked so adorably bewildered by their conversation in the restaurant, so hopelessly confused, she hadn't been able to resist. She thought it would be fun to mess with his head, knock him a little further off base. But what she hadn't counted on, what she hadn't anticipated, was the way it would make *her* feel.

She'd kissed her share of men before, but she felt as though, for the first time in her life, she had *really* kissed a man. It was as if a switch in her brain had been flipped and everything in her being was saying, *He's the one*.

Which was as ridiculous as it was disturbing.

Yet her legs were so wobbly and her head so dizzy that once she'd rounded the corner and was out of sight, she collapsed on a bench to collect herself.

What was wrong with her? It was just a kiss. And barely even that. So why the weak knees? The frantically beating heart and breathless feeling? Why the tingling burn in her breasts and between her thighs?

Maybe that was just the effect he had on females, something chemical, or physiological. Maybe that was why he dated so many women. They genuinely couldn't resist him.

That was probably it, she assured herself. Pheromones or hormones or something. And the effect was bound to wear off. Eventually she would even grow immune to it altogether.

She just hoped to God that he hadn't noticed. That before she let go he hadn't felt her hands shaking, that he hadn't seen her pulse throbbing at the base of her throat or the heat burning her cheeks. That he hadn't heard the waver in her voice before she turned and walked away. If he knew what he did to her, he could potentially make her life—the next few weeks, any-way—a living hell.

When she felt steady enough, she walked the two blocks to her flat. She unlocked the outer door and headed up the stairs to the third floor. The building was clean and well tended, but the flat itself was only a fraction the size of her suite at the family estate.

She stepped inside and tossed her keys and purse on the table by the door. It would be roomier once she emptied all of the boxes still sitting packed in every room. But her heart just wasn't in it. It didn't feel like home.

The light on her answering machine was flashing furiously. She checked the caller ID and saw that every one that day was from her father. He was probably eager to talk to her about the royal family, tell her more lies to cover his own mistakes.

Well, she wasn't ready to talk to him. The sting of his betrayal was too fresh. She would end up saying something she would later regret.

She erased the messages without listening to them and turned off the ringer on her phone. At times like this she wished she had a best girlfriend to confide in. Even a casual friend. Only now, with her career in the toilet, was she beginning to realize what she'd missed out on when she made the decision to devote herself entirely to her career. For the first time in her life she truly felt alone. And when she thought of her father's betrayal, the feeling intensified, sitting like a stone in her belly.

All those years of dedication and hard work, and what had it gotten her? Thanks to her father, she had lost nearly everything.

But was it fair to blame it all on him? Didn't she shoulder at least a little bit of the blame? Had she allowed it to happen by not questioning his handling of the finances? By not checking the books for herself?

By trusting him?

But what reason had he given her not to?

She shook her head and rubbed at the ache starting in her temples. Self-pity would get her nowhere. She needed to get over it, pick up the pieces, and get on with her life. And the first thing on her agenda: finding Charles a new assistant and finding herself a new job. Despite their desire to keep her in their employment, she would never feel comfortable working for the royal family. She couldn't shake the idea that their job offer had nothing to do with skill, that they had hired her out of pity.

She would never feel as though she truly fit in.

First thing in the morning she would place an ad for the assistant's position and phone her contacts at the various employment agencies in the bay area. In no time she would have Phillip a new assistant. A *capable* assistant.

And until then, she would stay as far from Charles as humanly possible.

Seven

So much for keeping her distance from Charles.

As promised, he sent his car to fetch Victoria before work the next morning. When she heard the knock at her flat door, she just assumed it was the driver coming up to get her. But when she opened the door, Charles stood there.

He leaned casually against the doorjamb, looking attractive and fit in a charcoal pinstripe suit, a grin on his face. And not a trace of the ill ease he'd worn like a shroud the night before.

"Good morning," he said, then added, "*Victoria.*"

Okay. "Good morning…Charles."

"I thought you would be impressed. I remembered your name."

He'd apparently taken what she said to heart. She

was genuinely and pleasantly surprised. It didn't last long, though.

"I'd say that I deserve a reward," he said, with an exaggerated wiggle of his brows.

The man was a shameless flirt, and though she hated to admit it, his teasing and innuendo wasn't nearly as offensive as it used to be.

And to be fair, he had remembered her name right from the start. Which meant nothing when she considered that she and her father were the topic of many a conversation prior to her employment with him. Of course he would remember her.

You're rationalizing, Vic.

The best response was no response at all.

"I just need to grab my jacket," she said. "Wait right here."

She dashed off to her bedroom, grabbed her suit jacket, and slipped it on. She was gone less than a minute, but when she returned to the door, it was closed and he wasn't there.

Had he gone back to the car?

"Nice view," she heard him say, and turned to find him standing in her cluttered living room gazing out the window.

He was *in* her flat.

The fact that it was in total disarray notwithstanding, he was just so *there*. Such a distinct and overpowering presence in a room that until that very moment had always felt open and spacious. Now they might as well have been locked in a closet together for the lack of breathing room.

Just relax. This is not as bad as it seems. You're completely overreacting.

She folded her arms across her chest, doing her best to sound more annoyed than nervous. "You don't take direction well, do you?"

He turned to her and smiled, and she felt it like a sucker punch to her belly. The worst part was that she was pretty sure he knew exactly what that smile was doing to her. And he had intended exactly that.

You just had to kiss him, didn't you?

He gestured out the window. "You have an ocean view."

Barely. Only a few snippets of blue through the buildings across the road. Nothing like the view from his home. Although it was looking decidedly more pleasing with him standing there.

Ugh. She really had to stop these random, destructive thoughts.

"I don't recall inviting you inside," she said.

"Yeah, you might want to work on those manners."

She shook her head. "God, you're arrogant."

He just grinned and gestured to the city street below. "How do you like living in the heart of the city?"

It was different. Her father's estate, *their* estate, had been in a rural setting, but she'd spent the majority of her time working in the city. A home in the bay area seemed the logical choice. "It's…convenient. Besides, I needed a change of pace. A place that didn't remind me of everything I've lost."

She cringed inwardly. Why had she told him that? It was too personal. Too private. She didn't want him getting the idea that she liked him. She didn't want to *like* him.

He nodded thoughtfully. "And how is that working out for you?"

Lousy, but he probably already figured that out.

"I'm ready to go." She walked to the door, grabbing her keys and purse from the table.

He didn't follow her. He just stood there, grinning, as though he knew something she didn't. "What's the rush?" he asked.

She looked at her watch. "It's eight-twenty."

He shrugged. "So?"

"Isn't the car waiting?"

"It's not going anywhere without us."

She didn't like the way he was looking at her. Or maybe the real problem was she liked it too much. Yesterday she would have considered his probing gaze and bone-melting grin offensive, but this morning it made her feel all warm and mushy inside.

Kissing him had definitely been bad idea.

"I've been doing some thinking," he said, taking a few casual steps toward her.

Her heart climbed up in her throat, but she refused to let him see how nervous he was making her. "About?"

"Last night."

She was tempted to ask, *Which part?* but she had the sinking feeling she already knew. So instead she asked, in what she hoped was a bored and disinterested tone, "And?"

He continued in her direction, drawing closer with every step. "I think I've had a change of heart."

Uh-oh.

She hoped he meant that he'd had a change of heart

about the way he objectified the opposite sex, but somehow she didn't think so.

"Now that I know what I'll be *missing,* maybe I won't be cooperating with the family after all."

Oh, yeah, kissing him had been a *really* bad idea.

He was coming closer, that look in his eyes, like any second he planned to ravish her. And the part that really stunk was that she wanted him to. Desperately. She had assumed that playing the role of the aggressor last night, socking it to him when he was all confused and vulnerable—and a little bit adorable—would somehow put her in a position of control.

Boy, had she been wrong.

He'd managed to turn the tables on her. At that moment, she'd never felt more *out* of control in her life. And the really frightening thing was, she kind of liked it.

"I mean, what's the worst that will happen?" he said.

Hopefully something really bad. "Hanging?"

He was standing so close now that he could reach out and touch her. And though every instinct she possessed was screaming for her to back away, she wouldn't give him the satisfaction of so much as a flinch.

"And then I got to thinking." He leaned in, his face so close to hers she could smell the toothpaste on his breath. "Who says they even have to know?"

Bloody hell, was *she* in trouble. If he decided to kiss her right now, she would have no choice but to kiss him back. And then he would know the truth. That she wasn't nearly as rigid as she'd led him to believe.

His eyes locked on hers. Deep brown irises with flecks of black that seemed to bleed out from his pupils.

Full of something wicked and dangerous. And exciting. And God knew she could have used a little excitement in her life.

No, no, no! Excitement was bad. She liked things even-paced and predictable. This was just chemical.

It took everything in her, but she managed to say, with a tone as bland as her expression, "Are you finished?"

"Finished?"

"Can we go to work now?"

The grin not slipping, he finally backed away and said, "You're tough, Victoria Houghton."

Didn't she wish that were true. Didn't she wish that her heart wasn't pounding so hard it felt as though it might beat right through her rib cage. That her limbs didn't feel heavy with arousal. That her skin would stop burning to feel his touch.

Don't let him know.

"Yes, I am," she lied.

A playful, taunting grin lifted the corners of his lips, and he reached past her to open the door. "But I'm tougher."

By three o'clock that afternoon Victoria managed to catch up on the backlog of calls and e-mails. No thanks to Charles, who, in a fraction of that time, proved himself to be a complete pain in the neck.

He popped into her office a minute after three, for what must have been the fifth time that day. "I heard the phone ring. Any answer to the employment ad?"

He knew damned well that she had just placed the ad with the employment agency that morning and they weren't likely to hear anything until at least tomorrow.

He parked himself behind her chair, hands propped on the back, his fingers brushing the shoulders of her jacket. The hair on her arms shivered to attention and she got that tingly feeling in the pit of her belly. But telling him to back off would only give him the satisfaction of knowing that he was getting to her.

"It was your mother," she told him, leaving off the *again* that could have followed. The woman was ruthless. The kind of mother who drove her children away with affection. It probably didn't help matters that Charles was an only child and the sole focus of her adoration.

No wonder he didn't want to settle down. He was already smothered with all the female attention he could handle.

"What are you working on?" he asked, leaning casually down to peer at her computer monitor, his face so close she could feel his breath shift the hair by her ear.

"A template for an updated, more efficient call and e-mail log."

He leaned in closer to see, his cheek nearly touching hers, and, did he smell delicious. She wanted to bury her face in the crook of his neck and take a long, deep breath. Nuzzle his skin. Maybe take a nibble.

"How does it work?" he asked.

"Work?"

"The spreadsheet."

Oh, right. "When I input the number or e-mail address, it automatically lists all the other pertinent information, so you don't have to waste any time looking it up yourself. It's color-coded by urgency."

"That's brilliant," he said.

She couldn't tell if he meant it or was just being sarcastic. "Oh, yes, I'm sure they'll award me the Pulitzer. Or maybe even the Nobel Peace Prize."

The rumble of his laugh vibrated all the way through her. "You said my mother called again. What did she want this time?"

She swiveled in her chair and stuck a pile of phone messages in his face, so he had no choice but to back off or get a mouthful of fuchsia paper. "To remind you about your father's birthday party. She wanted to confirm that you're spending the *entire* weekend with them."

He took the messages and sat on the edge of her desk instead, riffling through them. "What did you tell her?"

"That you would be there. *All* weekend. And you're really looking forward to it."

He shot her a curious look. "Seriously?"

She flashed him a bright and, yes, slightly wicked smile. "Seriously."

He narrowed his eyes at her. "You didn't really."

"Oh, I did."

She could have sworn that some of the color drained from his face. "That's odd, because I seem to recall telling you to tell her that I wouldn't be able to stay the whole weekend."

"Did you?" she asked innocently. "I guess I forgot."

He knew damned well that she hadn't forgotten anything.

"That's evil," he said.

She just smiled. That was what he got for messing with her—although, in all fairness, she had been the one to kiss him. But she had the feeling that there would be nothing fair about this unspoken competition they had gotten themselves into.

"Just for that, I should drag you along with me," he told her.

A duke bringing his personal assistant home for a weekend visit with the folks. Like that would ever happen. She had the sneaking suspicion that being royals, they clung to slightly higher standards. Or maybe they would make her stay in the staff quarters and take her meals in the kitchen.

Was that what she had been reduced to? Servant's status?

She and her father may not have been megarich, but they had lived a very comfortable lifestyle. The outer edges of upper crust. And to what end? Had he only been honest, lived within their means, she wouldn't be in this mess.

But now was not the time or the place to rehash her father's betrayal.

"I could ring her and tell her you don't want to stay," she told Charles. "That you have better things to do than spend time with your parents. Although, you know, they're not getting any younger."

"Wow," he said, shaking his head. "You and my mother would get along great."

She doubted that. His mother didn't strike her as the type to socialize with the hired help.

"Was there anything else you needed?" she asked, wanting him off her desk. He was too close, smelled too good. "I'd like to get back to work."

"Pressing business?" he asked.

"Keeping up on all the calls and e-mails from your female admirers is a full-time job."

"Maybe, but right now," he said, locking his chocolate eyes on hers and leaning closer, so she was crowded against the back of her chair. "I only have one special woman in my life."

Uh-oh.

Please, please, Victoria silently pleaded, *let it be anyone but me.*

He held up the message slips. "And I'd better go call her and tell her just how much I'm looking forward to the party."

She let out a quiet, relieved breath.

He rose from the corner of her desk, but his scent lingered as he walked to the door. "Buzz me if you hear about the ad."

"The second I hear anything," she promised. Hoping this would be the last time she saw him until it was time to leave for the evening.

Even that would be too soon. Maybe she could just sneak out unnoticed.

It was a dangerous game they had begun playing, but she wasn't about to surrender. She wouldn't let him win. He needed to be knocked down a peg or two. Put in his place. And she was just the woman to do it.

Eight

Charles's mother rang back not fifteen minutes later. The woman was ruthless.

Victoria struggled to sound anything but exasperated by her repeated calls. "I'm afraid he's in a meeting," she said, just as he had instructed her. In a meeting, on another line. He never took personal calls at work. "But I would be happy to take a message."

"I don't mean to bother," she said, which is how she began all of her phone conversations, whether it was the first or tenth call of the day. "I'm just calling about the party, to extend a formal invitation."

Again? Hadn't Victoria already sent an RSVP for him? How many times did she have to invite her own son? "I'll let Charles know," she said automatically.

"Oh, no, not for Charles," she said. "For *you*."

For *her?* But…

Oh, no, he didn't. He *wouldn't.* "For *me,* ma'am?"

"He told us you'll be joining him for the weekend," she gushed excitedly. And the weird thing was, she actually sounded *happy.* "I just wanted you to know how eager we are to meet you. Charles rarely brings his lady friends home."

Lady friends? Did she think…? "Ma'am, I *work* for Charles."

"Oh, I know. But he values your friendship. And any friend of Charles is a friend of ours. His father and I just wanted you to know that you're welcome."

Friendship? Since when were she and Charles friends?

"So, we'll see you then?" his mother asked.

Did Victoria really have the heart to tell her the truth? She sounded so genuinely eager to meet her. How could she tell her it was nothing more than a cruel trick?

So she said the only thing she could. "Yes, of course. I'll see you then."

Victoria was out of her chair before she hung up the phone. Not bothering to knock, she barged into Charles's office. And got the distinct feeling he'd been waiting for her to do just that. He was sitting back in his chair, elbows on the armrests, hands folded across his chest. But it was too late to turn around now.

"You call *me* evil?" she said.

He smiled. "I take it my mother phoned you."

"That was low, even for you."

He looked pleased with himself. "An eye for an eye. Isn't that what they say?"

"I do not what to spend a weekend at your parents's estate."

"Neither do I. But I guess neither of us has a choice now."

"They're not *my* parents. I have no obligation to be there."

He shrugged. "So, ring her back and tell her you don't want to come. I'm sure they won't be too offended."

She glared at him.

"Or, you could come with me and you might actually have fun."

"I seriously doubt that."

"Why?"

"Why? *You* don't even want to go!"

"My parents are good people. They mean well. But when it's just the three of us it can get...stifling. I get there Friday night, and by Saturday afternoon we've run out of things to talk about. With you there it might take a little bit of the pressure off."

"I wouldn't have a clue what to say to your parents. They're completely out of my league."

His brow edged into a frown. "How do you figure?"

"I'm an *employee* of the royal family."

"So what? You're still a person. We're all just people."

Was he really so naive? Did he truly not understand the way the world worked? They were royalty, and she was, and always would be, a nobody in their eyes. Or was this just part of the game he was playing? Lure her to his parent's estate so he could humiliate her in front of his entire family?

His intentions weren't even the issue. The real problem was that she simply didn't trust him.

"You know, you don't give yourself nearly enough credit." He rose from his chair and she tensed, thinking he might come toward her, but he walked around to sit on the edge of his desk instead. Since he'd last been in her office he'd taken off his jacket, loosened his tie, and rolled the sleeves of his dress shirt to his elbows. He seemed to do that every day, after his last meeting.

Casual as he looked, though, he still radiated an air of authority. He was always in control.

Well, almost always.

"Tell me," he said. "How could a woman so accomplished have such a low self-esteem?"

"It has nothing to do with self-esteem. Which I have my fair share of, thank you very much. It's just the way the world works."

"When you met my cousins, did they look down their noses at you?"

"Of course not."

"I think my parents might surprise you. It can't hurt to come with me and find out. Besides, the party should be a blast. Good food and company. And if at any time you feel uncomfortable, I'll take you home."

If she went at all, she would be driving herself. *If* she went?

She couldn't believe she was actually contemplating this. If nothing else, out of curiosity. At least, that's what she preferred to tell herself. There were other possible motivations that were far too disturbing to consider. Like wanting to see the kind of man Charles was around his family. What he was *really* like.

"Fine. I'll go." she said. Then added, "It's not as though I have much choice."

"Smashing," he said, looking truly pleased, which had her seriously doubting her decision.

What was he up to?

"We leave in the afternoon, two weeks from this Friday and return Sunday afternoon."

"I'll meet you there," she said. She wanted her car, in case she needed a quick getaway. And surprisingly, he didn't argue.

"Pack casual," he said. "But the party Saturday night is formal."

Formal? She was expecting an intimate family gathering. Not a social event. "How many people will be there?"

He shrugged. "No more than a hundred or so."

One *hundred?* Her heart seized in her chest. All more wealthy and influential than her.

Smashing.

"You have a dress?" he asked.

From a charity event four years ago. It would be completely out of fashion by now. She didn't exactly have the money to spend on expensive gowns. And for a party like this, nothing less than the best would do.

"I'm sure I can scrounge something up," she said, hoping she sounded more confident than she was feeling.

"You're sure?" he asked. "If it's a strain on the budget right now—"

"It's fine," she snapped. That was the second time

he'd made a reference to her diminishing funds. "It isn't as though I'm destitute."

He held his hands up defensively. "Relax. I wasn't suggesting that."

My God, listen to yourself. Maybe Charles was right. Maybe her self-esteem had taken a hit lately. Maybe her confidence was shot. Why else would she be so touchy?

Maybe she needed to get out with people. Reestablish her sense of self. Or something like that.

She softened her tone. "I'm sorry. I didn't mean to snap."

"If you really don't want to go to the party—"

"I'll go," she said firmly. "For the whole weekend."

Who knows, maybe a short vacation would be good for her. A chance to forget about the shambles her life was currently in and just relax.

And who knew? She might even have fun.

Victoria unlocked her flat door at exactly seven-thirty the following evening. Early by her standards, yet it had felt like the longest day of her life.

Since she'd kissed Charles the other night, then accepted his offer to join him at his parents, the teasing and sexual innuendo hadn't ceased. When they were alone, anyway. When anyone else was around he was nothing but professional. He treated her more like a peer than a subordinate. It was his way of showing that he did indeed respect her.

And maybe the teasing wasn't as bad as it had been at first. Not so immoral. Not that she would allow it to progress to anything more than that.

She dropped her purse and keys on the hall table and headed straight for the wine rack, draping her suit jacket on the back of the couch along the way. She opened a bottle of cabernet, her favorite wine, poured herself a generous glass, kicked off her pumps, and collapsed on the couch.

Charles left work at the same time, making sure to let her know, in the elevator on the way down to the parking structure, that he had a dinner date. As if she cared one way or the other how or with whom he chose to spend his free time. Although she couldn't help wondering who the unlucky girl could be. Amber from the club, perhaps? Or maybe Zoey from the fund-raiser last Friday? Or a dozen others who had called him in the past few days. Or maybe someone new.

Whoever she was, Victoria was just glad it wasn't her.

Are you really? an impish little voice in her head asked. *Aren't you even a little curious to know what the big deal is? Why so many women fall at his feet? They can't all be after his money and title.*

It had to be the wine. It was going straight to her head. Probably because she'd skipped lunch. Again.

You'll waste away to nothing, her father used to warn her, in regard to her spotty eating habits. And it would certainly explain her peculiar lack of energy. Not to mention the noisy rumble in her stomach. She sipped her wine and made a mental list of what was in her refrigerator.

Leftover Thai from three days ago that was probably spoiled by now. A few cups of fat-free yogurt, sour skim milk and a slightly shriveled, partial head of romaine lettuce. The contents of the freezer weren't much more promising. A few frozen dinners long past their expiration date and a bag of desiccated, ice-encrusted peas.

She was weeks past due for a trip to the market, but lately there never seemed to be time. Besides, she'd never been much of a cook. There had never been time to learn. On late nights at the Houghton she ate dinner in her office, or their housekeeper doubled as a cook when the need arose. In fact, in her entire life Victoria had never cooked an entire meal by herself. She wasn't even sure if she knew how.

Nor did she have the inclination to learn.

She sat up and grabbed the pile of carryout menus on the coffee table. The sushi place around the corner was right on top.

That would work.

She grabbed the cordless phone and was preparing to dial when the bell chimed for the door. Who could that be? She hoped it wasn't her father. She hadn't returned any of his calls, and he was probably getting impatient.

Maybe if she didn't answer, whoever it was would go away.

She waited a moment, holding her breath, then the bell chimed again.

With a groan she set the phone and her nearly empty glass on the coffee table and dragged herself up from the couch, a touch dizzy from the wine, and picked her way to the door. She peered through the peephole, surprised to find not her father but Charles standing there.

What in heaven's name did *he* want?

She considered not opening the door, but he'd probably

seen her car parked out front and knew she was home. She just couldn't force herself to be rude.

She unlatched the chain, pulled the door open and asked, "What do you want?"

Despite her sharp tone, he smiled. He was still wearing his work clothes. Well put together, but with just a hint of the end-of-the-day rumples. And he looked absolutely delicious.

Bite your tongue, Vic.

"I realized I still owe you dinner," he said. In his hand he held a carryout bag from the very restaurant she had just been about to phone. As though he had somehow read her mind.

That was just too weird.

"I hope you like sushi," he said, shouldering his way past her into her flat. Uninvited yet again.

So why wasn't she doing anything to stop him?

"And if I don't like sushi?" she asked, following him to the kitchen.

"Then you wouldn't have a menu for a sushi restaurant conveniently by the phone." He set the bag on the counter. "Would you?"

How did he…?

He must have seen it there that morning. The first time he barged in uninvited. "I thought you had a date."

The idea that someone stood him up was satisfying somehow, although, what it really meant was she was his second choice. The veritable booby prize.

"I do." He set the bag on the countertop and grinned. "With you."

What was it she just felt? Relieved? Flattered?

Highly doubtful.

She folded her arms across her chest. "I don't think it can be considered a date when the other party knows nothing about it."

He pasted an innocent look on his face. "Did I forget to tell you?"

He took off his jacket and handed it to her. Like an idiot, she took it. And came this close to lifting it to her nose to breathe in his scent, rubbing her cheek against the fabric. She caught herself at the last second and folded it over her arm instead.

Stop it, Vic.

He wasn't paying attention, anyway. He was busy emptying the bag, opening the carryout containers.

The aroma of the sushi wafted her way, making her mouth water. And if she didn't eat something soon, the wine was going to give her a doozy of a headache.

"I'll have dinner with you," she said, then added, "just this once."

He shrugged, as though her refusing his company had never even crossed his mind. Could he be more arrogant? Or more cute?

No, no, no! He is not cute.

It took only a few disastrous office romances to make her vow never to get involved with a coworker again. Not to mention the other laundry list of reasons she would never get involved with a man like him.

This was just dinner.

"I wasn't sure what you liked, so I got a variety," he said.

"I guess." There was enough there to feed half a dozen people. She would have some left over for lunch and dinner tomorrow. And since he went through all this trouble, the least she could do is offer him a drink. "I just opened a bottle of cabernet."

"I thought you would never ask," he said with a grin, then gestured to the cupboards. "You have plates?"

"To the left of the sink." She draped his jacket neatly over the back of the couch over her own and poured him a glass of wine, then refilled her own glass. She really should slow down, wait to drink until she'd eaten something, but the warm glow of inebriation felt good just then. And it wasn't as if she was completely sloshed or anything. Just pleasantly buzzed.

The dining table was topped with half-unpacked boxes, so she carried their glasses to the coffee table instead. It was that or eat standing up in the kitchen, and she honestly didn't think her legs would hold her up for long. She considered going back into the kitchen to help him, but the couch looked so inviting, she flopped down and made herself comfortable. Some hostess she was, making him serve her dinner. But he didn't seem to mind.

Besides, that's what he got for showing up out of the blue.

"Do you have a serving platter?" Charles called from the kitchen.

"Somewhere in this mess," she said. The truth was she usually just ate straight from the carryout containers. "I haven't gotten that far in my unpacking." She paused, guilt getting the best of her, and called, "Do you want help?"

"No, I've got it."

Good. She rested her head back on the cushions, sipped her wine, and closed her eyes. When she opened them again, he was setting everything down on the coffee table.

"Wake up. Time to eat."

"Just resting my eyes," she said. She sat up and he sat down beside her, so close their thighs were touching. His was solid and warm. She didn't normally let her size bother her, but he just seemed so large in comparison. Intimidating, although not in a threatening way, if that made any sense at all. And, God help her, he was sexy as hell with his collar open and his sleeves rolled up.

She took a tuna roll, dipped it in soy sauce, and popped it into her mouth. He did the same. The delicious flavors were completely lost on her as she watched him eat. He even managed to chew sexy, if that was possible.

She peeled her eyes away, before he noticed her staring, just as the doorbell chimed again.

"Expecting someone?" he asked, like maybe she had a date with some other man that had slipped her mind.

"Not that I recall." She sighed irritably and dragged herself up and walked to the door.

If she weren't so relaxed from the wine, she would have remembered to check the peephole. And if she had, she would have seen it was her father standing there.

Nine

Victoria stepped into the hall and edged the door shut behind her so her father wouldn't see who was sitting on her couch. "Daddy, what are you doing here?"

"You haven't returned my calls. I was concerned."

I'll bet you were, she thought. *Concerned that all of those lies have started catching up to you.* The idea made her heart hurt, but she was too angry to cut him any slack right now.

Besides, now was not the time for that unpleasant discussion. "I'm a little busy right now."

"Too busy for your own father?" He looked old and tired, but she couldn't feel sympathy for him.

She needed another day to think about exactly what she wanted to say to him. Not that she'd thought of much else lately. Maybe she just needed time to be less angry. "I'll call you tomorrow."

His mouth fell open and he stared at her, aghast, as though he couldn't believe she would deny him entrance into her home. "Victoria, I demand to know what's going on."

The door pulled open and Charles appeared behind her wearing a concerned expression. "Everything okay, Victoria?"

She knew he meant well, he was being protective, and in many instances she might have appreciated his intervention.

Now was not one of them.

He'd just done more harm than good.

"What is he doing here?" her father said, spitting out the question.

As if she owed him any explanation at all. Or cared that he was displeased. "Having dinner."

"Dinner?" he said, not bothering to hide his disdain. "You're having dinner with *him?*"

"Yes, I am."

He looked from her to Charles, and she knew exactly what he was thinking. "Are you—?"

"It's just dinner," she said, not that it was any of his business. "And right now you should leave. We'll talk about this another time."

But her father wasn't listening. He was too angry. He knew better than to let himself get upset. It wasn't good for his heart. Or maybe his heart was just fine now, and that was a lie, too.

"How could you do this to me?" he asked. "How could you betray me this way?"

How could *she* do this? Who was he to accuse her of deception? "There's been some betrayal going on, but it certainly isn't coming from my end."

"What do you mean?" He shot Charles a venomous glare. "What has he been telling you?"

"What you should have told me a long time ago."

The angry facade slipped a fraction. "I don't know what you're talking about."

"I saw the files from the sale of the hotel, Daddy. I know about all of your debt. All the lies you told me."

"He's trying to turn you against me."

He was still going to deny it? Lie to her face? At the very least she had expected a humbled apology, maybe a plea for forgiveness. Instead he continued to try to deceive her?

She wanted to grab him and shake some sense into him.

She was stunned and angry and hurt. And even worse, she was disappointed. All of her life she had looked up to him. Idolized him even. But he had changed that forever.

"The only one doing that is you, Daddy," she said sadly, knowing that she would never look at her father the same way again.

"I should go," Charles said, taking a step backward from the door. This was a little too intense for his taste. Had he known it was her father at the door, he never would have interfered. He had enough of his own family issues to deal with without taking on someone else's.

Victoria held up a hand to stop him. "No. You stay. *You* were invited. My father is the one who needs to go."

Technically, Charles had shown up unannounced and muscled his way inside. But he didn't think now was the time to argue with her.

"I can't believe you're choosing him over me," her father said.

"And I can't believe you're still lying to me," she shot back, although she sounded more resigned than angry. "Until you can be honest with me, we have nothing left to say to each other."

Before her father could utter another word, she shut the door and flipped the deadbolt, and for several seconds she just stood there. Maybe waiting for him to have a change of heart.

After a moment of silence, she rose up on her toes and peered out the peephole. She sighed quietly, then turned to face Charles and leaned against the door. "He's gone."

"Victoria, I'm really sorry. I didn't mean to—"

"It's not your fault. He's the one who lied to me. He's *still* lying to me."

"I'm sure he'll come around."

She shook her head. "I'm not so sure. You have no idea how stubborn he can be."

If he was anything like Victoria, Charles had a pretty good idea. "What are you going to do?"

"I'm not sure. But I do know what I'm not going to do."

"What's that?"

"All my life I've been doing what my father asked of me. What was *expected* of me. Not anymore."

She surprised him by taking his hand, lacing her fingers through his. She gave it a tug. "Come on."

"Where?"

"Where do you think, genius? To my bedroom."

Wait…what? How had they jumped from dinner to her bedroom? "I beg your pardon?"

He'd been out to get in her knickers since the day he met her. And it certainly wouldn't be the first time he'd taken advantage of a situation to seduce a woman—although she seemed to be doing most of the seducing now. Not to mention that he had a strong suspicion she was slightly intoxicated. Again, that had never stopped him before. Yet, something about this just didn't feel right.

He actually felt…guilty.

She tugged again and he felt his feet moving.

"Hey, don't get me wrong," he said, as he let her lead him down the hall. "I'm not one to pass up revenge sex, but are you sure this is a good idea?"

"I think it's an excellent idea." She dragged him into the bedroom and switched on the lamp beside her bed. Only then did she let go of his hand.

Like the rest of the flat, there were boxes everywhere, but in the dim light the bed looked especially inviting. And oh, so tempting.

But he knew he really shouldn't.

She turned to him and started unbuttoning her blouse.

Christ, she was making it really hard to do the right thing. "Maybe we should step back a second, so you can think about what you're doing."

She gazed up at him though thick, dark lashes. "I

know exactly what I'm doing." The blouse slipped from her shoulders and fluttered silently to the carpet.

Ah, hell.

Underneath she wore a lacy black bra. Sexier than he would have imagined for her. But he'd always suspected, or maybe fantasized, there was more to Victoria. That deep down there was a temptress just waiting to break free.

It looked like he was right.

She reached behind her to unzip her skirt, and desire curled low and deep in his gut. "Are you just going to stand there?" she asked.

"I just don't want you to do something you'll regret." Where was he getting this crap? When did he ever care if a woman had regrets? Was he, God forbid, growing a conscience?

"I'm a big girl. I can handle it." She eased the skirt down her legs, hips swaying seductively, and let it fall in a puddle at her feet. She wore a matching black lace thong and thigh-high stockings. And her body? It was damn near perfect. In fact, he was pretty sure it *was* perfect. And he was so mesmerized that for a minute, he forgot to breathe.

"You've been after me for days," she said. "Don't chicken out now."

Calling him a chicken was a little harsh, considering two days ago she'd accused him of disrespect toward the opposite sex. The woman was a walking contradiction. But an extremely sexy and desirable one.

His favorite kind.

She walked toward him—stalked him was more like

it—and reached up to unfasten the buttons of his shirt. She did look as though she knew what she was doing.

One button, two buttons. He really should stop her. It wouldn't take much. Although he suspected that if he turned her down now, he wouldn't get another chance.

Damn it. It shouldn't be this complicated. Maybe that was what was really bothering him. This had complex and messy written all over it.

One more button, then another. Then she pushed his shirt off his shoulders and down his arms. She gazed up at him, sighing with satisfaction, her eyes sleepy and soft. She flattened her hands on his chest, dragging her nails lightly across his skin all the way to his waistband. She toyed with the clasp on his slacks…

Oh, what the hell.

He circled an arm around her waist and dragged her against him. Her surprised gasp was the last thing he heard before he crushed his mouth down on hers. Hard.

She groaned and looped her arms around his neck, fingers sinking through his hair. Feeding off his mouth.

He scooped her up off her feet and they tumbled onto the mattress together. She was so small he worried he might crush her, but she managed to wriggle out from under him, push him onto his back so she could get at the zipper of his slacks. Then she shoved them, along with his boxers, down his hips, and he kicked them away.

"My goodness," she said, gazing down at him with a marginally stunned expression. "We've certainly been blessed, haven't we?"

Though he hadn't considered it until just then, she was awfully petite. What if she was that small everywhere?

"Too much for you?" he asked.

"Let's hope not." She took a deep breath and blew it out. "Condom?"

"In my wallet, in my jacket." Which was in the other room.

"Right back," she said, hopping up from the bed and darting from the room. A bundle of sexual energy. She was back in seconds, long before he had time to talk any sense into himself.

Who was he kidding? They were already well past the point of no return. Besides, she didn't appear to be having any second thoughts.

He sat up and she tossed him his wallet. He fished a condom out, then, realizing one probably wasn't going to cut it—he hoped—he grabbed one more.

"You're sure those will fit?" she asked, but he could see that she was teasing.

"They're extra large," he assured her, setting his wallet and both condoms on the bedside table.

Victoria stood beside the bed, gazing at him with hungry eyes. She unhooked the front clasp on her bra and peeled it off, revealing breasts that couldn't have been more amazing. Not very big, but in perfect proportion to the rest of her. High and firm. The perfect mouthful. And he couldn't wait to get a taste.

She walked to the bed, easing her thong down and kicking it into the pile with the rest of her clothes. He decided, now that he'd seen the whole package, she really was perfect.

And just for tonight, she was all his.

Though he usually liked to be the one in charge, he

didn't protest when she pushed him down onto his back and climbed on him, straddling his thighs, her stockings soft and slippery against his skin. What he really wanted was to feel them wrapped around his shoulders, but she had something entirely different in mind. She grabbed one of the condoms and had it out of the package and rolled into place in the span of one raspy breath.

It was a surreal feeling, lying there beneath her, and the fact that *she* had seduced him and not the other way around. She was unlike any woman he had been with before. Most tried too hard to impress him, to be what they thought he wanted. For Victoria, it just seemed to come naturally. She leaned down and kissed him, teasing at first. Just a brush of her lips, and a brief sweep of her tongue. She tasted like wine and desire. And when she touched him, raked her nails lightly down his chest, he shivered. She seemed to know instinctively what to do to drive him nuts.

They kissed and touched, teased each other until he did not think he could take much more. Victoria must have been thinking the same thing.

She locked her eyes on his, lowered herself over him and took him inside her. Tentatively at first. She was so slick and hot, so small and tight, he almost lost it on that first slow, downward slide. Then she stopped, and for an instant he was afraid he really might be too much for her, too big. But her expression said he was anything but. It said that she could handle anything he could dish out, and then some. It said that she wanted this just as much as he did.

She rose up, slowly, until only the very tip remained

inside of her. She hovered there for several seconds, tor-
turing him, then, with her eyes still trained on his, sank
back down, her body closing like a fist around him. He
groaned, teetering on the edge of an explosion. In his
life he'd never seen or felt anything more erotic. And if
she did that one more time, he *was* going to lose it.

He rolled her over onto her back and plunged into
her. She arched up against him, gasping, her eyes
widening with shock because he was so deep.

He nearly stopped, to ask her if she was okay, but she
was clawing at his back, hooking her legs around his
hips, urging him closer, and that said everything he
needed to know. He may have been bigger than her, but
they fit together just fine. He stopped worrying about
hurting her. All he could think about was the way it felt.
The way *she* felt. And every thrust brought him that
much closer to the edge.

The last coherent thought he had was that this was
too good, too perfect, then Victoria shuddered and cried
out, her body tensing around him, and he couldn't think
at all as she coaxed him into oblivion with her.

Ten

Victoria lay in bed beside Charles, watching him sleep. Typical man. Have sex three or four times then go out like a light.

He looked so peaceful. So…satisfied. A feeling she definitely shared.

In her experience, first times always tended to be a little awkward or uncomfortable. But there was nothing awkward about the way Charles had touched her. She'd once believed that just because a man looked like he would be good in the sack didn't necessarily mean he would be, but Charles had completely blown that theory to smithereens as well.

In fact, he was so ridiculously wonderful, so skilled with his hands and his mouth and every other part of his body, it should have given her pause. He'd obviously had a lot of practice. Yet when he looked at her and touched her, it was as though there had never been anyone else.

It was almost enough to make her go mushy-brained. And she probably would have if she weren't so firmly rooted in reality.

At least now she knew what all the fuss was about.

For a minute there, when he'd first taken off his pants, she honestly thought the size difference might be an issue, but in the end the tight fit and the wonderful friction it created had been the best part. Remarkable size wasn't worth much if a man didn't know how to use it.

And, oh, he did.

The second best part was the knowledge that she was doing something totally wrong for her. Wrong on so many levels. She'd always been the obedient daughter, doing as she was told. She never imagined that a simple thing like being bad could feel *so* good.

But it's just sex, she reminded herself, lest she get carried away and start having actual feelings for him.

She was sure that things would be clearer in the morning, at which point she would realize what she'd really done and feel overwhelming regret. Especially when she got to the office. Wouldn't *that* be awkward? But until then she was going to enjoy it.

She curled up against him under the covers, soaking up his warmth. He sighed in his sleep and wrapped an arm around her.

Nice. Very nice.

She closed her eyes, felt herself drifting off. When she

opened her eyes again, the morning sunlight was peeking through the blinds, and Charles was already gone.

Sleeping with Charles had been a *really* bad idea.

Victoria stood in the elevator at work as it climbed, dreading the moment it reached her floor. The hollow *ting* as the doors slid open plucked every one of her frayed nerves.

He hadn't even had the decency to wake her before he left. He'd just skulked away in the middle of the night. Probably the way he did with all the women he slept with.

Did you really think you were any different?

She had gone from feeling sexy and desirable, feeling *bad,* to feeling…cheap.

He could have at least said goodbye before he left. Maybe given her one last kiss.

You are not going to let this bother you, she told herself as she exited the elevator and walked to her office. Penelope, who typically ignored her, lifted her head as she passed and actually looked at her. Not a nasty look. Just sort of…blank.

She knows. She knows what Charles and I did.

That was ridiculous. It was just a coincidence that she chose today to acknowledge Victoria. After all, she doubted Charles confided in his secretary about his sex life. And how else would she possibly know?

So this was what it felt like to be the office slut.

Fantastic.

Victoria nodded at the old prune, then opened her office door. Feeling edgy and unsettled, she hung her jacket, sat in her chair, and stowed her purse in the bottom desk drawer. Work as usual. This day was no different than any other. Not to mention, this situation was temporary. With any luck, she would hear from the employment agency about a suitable replacement.

She was just about boot to up her computer when the intercom buzzed, startling her half to death, and Charles's voice, in a very professional tone, said, "Would you please come in here, Victoria?"

Her heart jumped up into her throat.

Here we go, the part where he tells you it was fun but it isn't going to happen again. He certainly wasn't wasting any time. Not that she hadn't expected that.

She pressed the call button. "One minute."

The sooner it's over the better. And only once, for a millisecond, would she allow herself to admit that she was the tiniest bit disappointed it had to end. It may have only been sex, but it was damned good sex.

She remembered the invitation to spend the weekend with his family and cringed. That would just be too awkward. She would have to come up with some reason to decline. She doubted he would be anything but relieved.

What had she been thinking? One night of fantastic sex was not worth all of this complication.

She took a deep breath. No point in putting this off any longer. She rose from her chair, walked to the door and pulled it open, stepping inside his office. But he wasn't sitting at his desk.

The door closed behind her, and the next thing she knew, she was in Charles's arms.

"Morning," he said, a wicked grin on his face, and

before she could utter a sound, he was kissing her. Deep and sweet and wonderful. And though everything in her was screaming that this was wrong, she wrapped her arms around his neck and kissed him back.

She didn't care that he was kissing away her lipstick, or rumpling her hair. She just wanted to feel him. To be close to him.

Oh, this was bad.

When he broke the kiss she felt dizzy and breathless. He grinned down at her and said, "Good morning."

She couldn't resist returning the smile. Despite feeling as though her entire world had been flopped upside down, she actually felt…happy.

"If it weren't for the conference call I had this morning," he said, caressing her cheek with the tips of his fingers, "we might still be in bed."

"Conference call?" He left because he had to be at work?

"At six-thirty. You didn't get my note?"

"Note?" He left a note?

"On the pillow."

The rush of pure relief made her weak in the knees. And she didn't even care how wrong it was. "I guess I didn't see it."

A grin curled his mouth. "You didn't think I'd just up and leave without a word, did you?"

She shrugged, feeling ashamed of herself for thinking that. For judging him that way. And automatically assuming the worst. "It doesn't matter."

"Have time to take a break?" he asked with a devilish smile.

"I just got here."

He dipped his head to nibble on her neck. "I don't think your boss will mind."

Office romance. Very bad idea. But neither the affair nor the job were going to last long, so, honestly, why the hell not? Besides, it was really tough to think logically when his hands were sneaking under her clothing, searching for bare skin.

"What about Penelope?" she asked.

He shuddered and shook his head. "Definitely not my type."

She laughed. "That's not what I meant."

"I already told her that I'm not to be disturbed." He kissed her throat, her chin, nibbled the corner of her lips. "It's just you and me."

The old woman would have to be a fool not to realize what was going on, but she already disliked Victoria, so what difference did it make? Besides, Victoria had never been one to care what other people thought of her.

"I'm sure I can spare a minute or two," she said.

He smiled. "It's going to be a lot longer than a minute or two."

He lifted her up in his arms and carried her to the couch. He seemed to like doing that. Taking over, seizing control. And for some reason she didn't mind. Probably because he made her feel so damned good. He was one of those rare lovers who took pleasure for himself only after she had been satisfied first. She had always heard that men like that existed, but she'd never actually met one.

He sat on the couch and set her in his lap. But before he could kiss her, she asked, "Have you done this before?"

"What do you mean?"

"In here, with another assistant." She didn't know where the question came from, or if she even wanted to know the answer. And he looked surprised that she'd asked.

"You know what, never mind. Forget I asked."

She tried to kiss him, before she completely killed the mood, but he caught her face in his hands.

"Hold on, I want to answer that." His eyes locked on hers and he said, "No, Victoria, I haven't."

The way he said it, the way he looked her in the eye, made her believe it was the truth. She had no reason, no *right* to be relieved, but she was. And the tiny part of her that was still doubtful melted into a puddle at their feet.

She wanted this, right here, right now, and she wasn't going to be afraid to take it.

It was almost noon when Victoria finally made it back to her office. And she'd barely been there fifteen minutes, checking phone messages—there were already three from his mother—when Charles quietly opened the door and slipped inside.

She pretended not to hear him skulking around behind her, but when she felt his hands on her shoulders, his lips teasing the back of her neck, he became really hard to ignore.

"Neither of us is going to get anything done if you keep this up," she scolded, but she wasn't doing anything to stop him. Although, she thought, maybe she should. Unlike his office, hers didn't have a sturdy lock. In fact, she wasn't sure if it locked at all.

"Just thought I would pop in and say hello," he said, his breath warm on her skin. She couldn't deny that another hour or so in his office was tempting.

No, you have work to do.

"Your smother called," she said. "Several times."

He stopped kissing her. "My what?"

She turned to look at him. He had a quirky grin on his face. "Your mother," she repeated.

"That's not what you said."

What was he talking about? "Yes I did."

He shook his head. "No. You said *smother*. 'My smother called.'"

She slapped a hand over her mouth. Oh my gosh, had she? Had she really said it out loud? "I'm so sorry. That was completely inappropriate."

Rather than look offended, he laughed. "No. That's perfect. 'My smother.' I'll have to tell my father that one."

"No!" What would his father think of Victoria? Insulting his wife like that.

Charles just shrugged. "He knows what she's like. She drives everyone crazy. He'll think it's hilarious."

She swiveled in her chair to face him. "Please don't, Charles. It's going to be awkward enough. I would be mortified."

He didn't look like he got it, but he nodded. "All right. I won't say anything."

"Thank you."

He backed away from her. She couldn't help wondering if she'd offended him somehow, and she realized the idea truly disturbed her. How quickly she'd gone from disliking him to valuing his friendship.

Too fast.

And when he smiled at her, she realized he wasn't the least bit offended. "Can I take you out to dinner tonight?" he asked.

Two nights in a row? Then again, sitting in bed naked feeding each other sushi couldn't really be counted as having dinner out. And her first impulse was to say yes, she would love to. But did she want to make a habit of being seen with him in public? To be crowned his latest conquest? Just another fling? Even though that was exactly what she was.

"I don't think that would be a good idea," she said.

"Why?"

"We're sleeping together, not dating."

He shrugged. "What's the difference?"

"There's a *huge* difference. Sex is temporary. Superficial."

"And dating isn't? According to whom?"

He had a point. "I suppose it can be, but…it's just *different*."

"I don't date women with the intention of a lasting relationship. So by definition, dating for me is very temporary." He paused, then his brow tucked with concern. "You're not looking for a relationship, are you?"

"With *you?* Of course not!"

He looked relieved, and she knew enough not to take it personally. He was just establishing parameters. It was what men like him did. And it was the truth. He was the last man on earth that she would ever consider for a serious relationship.

"Well, then, what's the problem?" he asked.

"Maybe another time."

He folded his arms over his chest. "You're going to make me chase you, is that it?"

"Chase me? Are you forgetting that I was the one who had to drag you to my bedroom last night?"

"Oh yeah." That devilish, sexy grin was back, and it warmed her from the inside out. He leaned in closer, resting his hands on the arms of her chair. She couldn't help but think, *Oh, boy, here we go again.* "Did I forget to tell you how much I enjoyed it?"

He'd told her several times, but what she'd found even more endearing, most appealing, was that he had been worried about her state of mind, that she might have been acting rashly and making a mistake. She hadn't expected that from a man like him.

Every time she thought she had him pegged, he surprised her.

"Don't you have work to do?" she asked.

He dipped in close and kissed her neck, just below her ear. He'd discovered last night that it was the second most sensitive spot on her body. And he used it to his advantage. "Have dinner with me, Victoria."

She closed her eyes and her head just sort of fell back on its own. "I can't."

"It doesn't have to be a restaurant." He nibbled her earlobe and she shivered. "I'll make us dinner at my place."

Dinner at his house wouldn't be so bad. *But two nights in a row? Won't that be pushing it a little?* Although what he was doing felt awfully good. Could she honestly work up the will to deny herself another night of unconditional pleasure? "I shouldn't," she said, but not with much conviction.

"I'm an excellent cook," he coaxed, pulling her blouse aside to nibble on her shoulder. "My specialty is dessert."

He kissed his way down to her cleavage and a whimper of pleasure purled in her throat. "Well, I do have dry cleaning to drop off. I suppose I could hang around for a little while. And if you happen to have dinner ready…"

He eased himself down on the floor in front of her chair, then pulled her blouse aside, exposing one lace cup of her bra. He took her in his mouth, lace and all, and bit down lightly. Though she tried to hold it in, a moan slipped from her lips.

God, he was good.

He looked up at her with that devilish gleam. "So you'll be stopping by when? Around seven?"

"Seven sounds about right," she said, aware that her door wasn't locked and anyone could walk in. Not that anyone but him ever did. But it was the sense of danger, the possibility that someone *could,* that made her so bloody hot for him. "We really shouldn't do this in here."

"Do what?" He switched to the opposite side and took that one into his mouth.

She grabbed his head, sinking her nails though his hair. "Have sex."

"Who says we're going to have sex?"

"I guess I just assumed."

"Nah." He eased her skirt up around her hips, hooked

his fingers on her thong and dragged it down her legs. He nipped at the flesh on the inside of her upper thigh, the number-one most sensitive area on her body, and she melted into a puddle in her chair.

"Well, then, what would you call it?" she asked, her voice thick with arousal.

He grinned up at her. "Afternoon snack?"

Well, whatever he called it, as he kissed his way upward, she had the sneaking suspicion that neither of them was going to get much work done today.

Eleven

Victoria woke slowly the next morning aware, even before she opened her eyes, something was different. Then it dawned on her.

She wasn't at home.

She was curled up in Charles's bed, warm and cozy between his soft silk sheets.

Too warm and cozy.

She hadn't meant to fall asleep here and risk having someone see her car parked out front. Not to mention that spending the night was just a bad idea. She had planned to go back to her own place, sleep in her own bed. Charles hadn't made it easy, though.

Last night, every time she'd made noises like she was going to leave, he would start kissing her and touching her, and she would forget what she'd been saying. And *thinking.* And when they weren't devouring each other, they lay side by side and talked. About her childhood and his. Which couldn't have been more different.

After a while it got so late, and she'd felt so sleepy. She remembered thinking that she would close her eyes for just five or ten minutes, then she would crawl back into her clothes and drive home.

So much for that plan.

He knew it, too. Charles knew she wanted to leave, and he let her sleep anyway. She wasn't sure how to take that. Most men considered letting a woman spend the night in their house too personal. Did he genuinely want her there, or was it some sort of power play? To see if he could bend her to his will. Did he do that with all of the women he *dated?*

Speaking of Charles…

She reached over and patted the mattress beside her, but encountered only cool, slippery silk.

He had one of those enormous king-size deals that a person could lie spread-eagled in and still not encounter the person lying beside them.

She reached even farther, with the very tips of her fingers, till she hit the opposite edge of the bed.

No one there.

She rose up on her elbow, pried one eye open and peered around. The curtains were drawn and Charles was nowhere to be seen.

Here we go again, she thought. Waking up alone. But how far could he have run this time, seeing as how they were in his house?

Not that he had *run* yesterday morning. He'd gone to work. And he'd left a note.

She sat up and rubbed her eyes. A robe hung over the side of the bed that she was guessing he'd put there for her to use. Thoughtful, yet she couldn't help wondering if all of the women who slept over wore it. Would it smell of someone else's perfume? Would she find strands of another woman's hair caught in the collar? Or did he have the decency to wash it between uses?

His shirt from the night before was draped over the chair across the room, so she padded across the cold wood floor and slipped that on instead. It hung to her knees, and she had to roll the sleeves about ten times, but it was soft and it smelled like him. And she could say with certainty that no other woman had worn it recently.

She stopped in the bathroom and saw that she had a serious case of bed head. An inconvenience of short hair. She rubbed it briskly and picked it into shape as best she could. Next to the sink was a toothbrush still in the package. For her, she assumed.

The man thought of everything. Convenient, if not a little disturbing. He probably had a whole closet full of them. For every woman he brought home.

She brushed her teeth and considered showering, but the stall was dry, and she recalled him saying something about the granite just being sealed the other day. She ventured out into the hallway instead, wondering where he could be.

She poked her head in a few of the rooms, called, "Hello!" But he didn't seem to be anywhere upstairs. Then she caught the scent of freshly brewed coffee wafting up from the lower level, and let her nose lead her to the source.

She found Charles in the kitchen, standing by the sink, the financial section of the newspaper in one hand, a cup of coffee in the other. He was dressed in a pair of threadbare jeans and nothing else, and his hair was even a little rumpled. Very *normal* looking. He looked up and smiled when she stepped in the room. "Good morning."

"Morning."

He eyed her up and down appreciatively. "I left a robe out for you, but honestly, I think I prefer the shirt." He put down the paper and cup, and walked toward her, a hungry, devilish look in his eye, and her stomach did a backflip with a triple twist.

They'd slept together on two separate occasions, so shouldn't that intense little thrill have disappeared by now? Before she could form another thought he wrapped her up in his arms and kissed her senseless, which made her thankful she'd taken the time to brush her teeth.

It should have been awkward or uncomfortable, but it wasn't. It was as though she had spent the night dozens of times before. Maybe he'd had so many women sleep over that it had become second nature waking with a virtual stranger in his house.

Okay, she wasn't a stranger, but still…

She sighed and rested her head on his chest. This was nice. It was…comfortable. Still, she couldn't shake the feeling she was just one insignificant piece to a much larger puzzle that was Charles's romantic life.

"You do this often?" she asked.

"Do what?"

"Sleepovers."

"I'm assuming you mean with women." He eased back to look at her. "Why do you ask?"

She shrugged. "You just seem to have a routine."

His brow perked with curiosity. "I do?"

"The robe, the toothbrush. It was just very…convenient."

"And here I thought I was being polite." He didn't look offended exactly. Maybe a little hurt.

She realized she was being ridiculous. Besides, she didn't want him to get the wrong idea, to think she was being possessive. Because she wasn't.

"I'm sorry," she said. "Forget I said anything. I'm obviously not very good at this."

He grinned down at her. "Oh, no, you were very good. And to answer your question about sleepovers— If I like a woman, and want to spend time with her, I invite her to stay over. Simple as that."

And why shouldn't he? Who was she to judge him? Who he did or didn't spend the night with was none of her business, anyway. She did appreciate his honesty, though.

"Now that we have that out of the way," he said. "Can I interest you in a nonroutine cup of coffee?"

She smiled up at him. "I'd love one."

"Cream or sugar?"

"A little of both."

He grabbed the cup that was already sitting beside his state-of-the-art coffeemaker.

"What will you be up to today?" he asked, as he poured her a cup.

"I should probably work on unpacking. Although, considering my current employment situation, I might have to look into renting a cheaper place. Just until things are settled."

He handed her a steaming cup and she took a sip. The coffee was rich and full-bodied and tasted expensive.

He leaned back against the edge of the counter. "The offer for the job at the Royal Inn is still good. I can even work on getting you out of my office and into a management position sooner if that would sweeten the deal."

She wished she could, but that was no longer an option. The only reason she had even considered it in the first place was for her father's sake.

"You know I can't do that. But thank you. I do appreciate the offer." She leaned against the opposite counter. "What are you doing today?"

"Most likely damage control."

Well, that was awfully direct. Although she wasn't sure how she felt about him referring to their night together as *damage*.

Then he held up the front section of the newspaper and she realized he wasn't talking about them. The headline read in bold type:

Royal Family Reveals Illegitimate Heir

Beside the article was a photo of an attractive woman in her early to mid-thirties who bore a striking resemblance to the king. "Another illegitimate heir?"

"She's their half sister," Charles said. "The result of King Frederick's affair with the wife of the former prime minister."

As if his family hadn't had enough scandal the past couple of years. "Oh, boy."

"Yeah. It's not going to be pretty."

She took the page from him and skimmed the article. Not only was this princess illegitimate, but she was the oldest living heir. Which, the article stated, could mean that she was the rightful heir to the crown itself.

Did this mean King Phillip would lose the crown? A move like that could potentially turn the country upside down.

She was dying of curiosity. But as the family attorney, Charles probably wouldn't be able to tell her more than was divulged in the press release.

"This is what that meeting was about the other day, wasn't it?" she asked.

He nodded. "We wanted to get the press release out as soon as possible, before the tabloids caught wind of it."

From the other room she heard her cell phone ring. It was still in her purse on the couch. "I should get that," she said.

By the time she reached the living room, opened her purse, and wrestled her cell phone out, she'd missed the call. There was no name listed and the number was unfamiliar. Then the phone chirped to indicate that a message had been left. She would listen to it later.

There were also two calls from her father from the night before. Had he called to argue, or was he ready to apologize? She didn't even want to think about that right now.

She needed to get dressed and get back to her own place, before this got too cozy. Besides, she didn't want to wear out her welcome. It would be awkward if he had to ask her to leave.

"Everything okay?"

She turned to find Charles standing in the arch between the living room and the foyer, watching her. She snapped her phone shut and stuffed it back in her purse. "Probably just a wrong number."

"I was about to jump into the shower," he said, walking toward her. "I thought you might like to join me."

Oh, that was so tempting. He was obviously in no hurry to get rid of her. Would it hurt to stay just a little bit longer…?

"I really need to go," she told him.

He didn't push the issue, although if he had, she just might have caved.

"I have family obligations this evening," he said, "but I'm free Sunday night. How about dinner?"

She wondered if he really had family obligations or just some other woman he'd already made plans to see. Although, as far as she could tell, he'd never been anything but honest with her.

She just wasn't ready to trust him yet. "Call me."

He folded his arms across his chest. "Why do I get the feeling that means no?"

She shrugged. "It means call me."

But, in all honesty, it probably did mean no. Even so, she couldn't help wondering, as she headed upstairs to get dressed, if she didn't say yes, would it just be someone else?

The possibility that it might be disturbed her far more than it should have.

* * *

It was amazing that despite being only half Mead, Melissa Thornsby looked so much like her siblings. She had the same dark hair and eyes, and the same olive complexion. She was tall and slim, and she carried herself with that undeniable royal confidence. She even shared similar expressions and gestures. Charles couldn't help wondering: if she had stayed on Morgan Isle after her parents' death, would someone have made the connection years ago?

He stood off to the side of the palace library, where this first meeting was taking place, as introductions were being made. At times like this he couldn't help feeling like an outsider. And, yes, maybe a little envious. But he had his mother, who drowned him in so much attention he couldn't imagine when he would find time for anyone else. And people wondered why he insisted on staying single. He didn't think he could handle his mother *and* a wife demanding his time.

The only catch, he thought, as he watched Phillip cradle his son, was that someday he would like to have children of his own. Not that he needed to be married for that. But he'd seen firsthand what a mess an illegitimate child could cause in a royal family.

Melissa spotted him and walked over.

"You must be Charles." She spoke with an accent mottled with varying intonation. A touch of the New Orleans South combined with a twinge of East Coast dialect, and something else he couldn't quite put his finger on. Very unusual. Especially for a princess.

He nodded. "Welcome home, Your Highness."

She took his hand and clasped it warmly. She carried herself with a style and grace that reeked of old money and privilege. "I wanted to thank you for all you've done. For making all the arrangements."

He was just doing his job. But he smiled and said, "You're welcome."

"It's not every day one is informed they may have an entire family they know nothing about. It could have been messy. I was impressed by how diplomatically the situation was handled, and I'm told that was in most part due to you."

"I really can't take the credit."

"Modest," she said, with a smile. "A good quality." She glanced around the room, as though searching for something. "Is your spouse not here with you?"

"I'm not married."

"Significant other?"

Oddly enough, the first person who came to mind was Victoria. Odd because she was no more significant than any other woman he had dated. "No one special."

"A handsome thing like you," she teased in a deep Southern drawl. "Why, in New Orleans you'd have been snapped up by some lovely young debutante ages ago."

"I could say the same for you," he said. "How could a woman so lovely still be single?"

"Oh," she said, with a spark of humor lighting her eyes, "we won't even go there."

Despite the trepidation of the rest of the family, Charles knew without a doubt that he was going to like his cousin. She had spunk and a pretty damned good sense of humor. He appreciated a woman, especially one in her social position, who didn't take herself too seriously.

Sophie stepped up beside them. "Sorry to interrupt, but I thought I might show Melissa to her suite and get her settled in."

"I certainly could use a breather," Melissa said. "It's been something of a crazy week, to say the least." She turned to Charles. "It was a pleasure meeting you. I hope we see quite a bit more of each other."

"As do I," he said, and honestly meant it. He suspected that Melissa would make a very interesting, and entertaining, addition to their family.

When they were gone, he heard Ethan ask from behind him, "So, what do you think of her?"

Charles turned to him. "I like her."

"She's quite outspoken."

"I think that's the thing about her that I like. Maybe she'll stir things up a bit."

Ethan nodded thoughtfully, and Charles had the distinct impression he felt wary of his new sibling. Which surprised him, since Ethan himself was illegitimate. If anyone were to welcome her with open arms, he would expect Ethan to. Knowing of Melissa's vast wealth, surely they didn't suspect she might be after their fortune. She had also made assurances to her attorney that she had no interest whatsoever in taking her rightful place as ruler of the country. But before Charles could question his wariness, Ethan changed the subject.

"Have you made any progress convincing Victoria to stay?"

He shook his head. "I'm working on her, though. I

think I'll have her mind changed by my father's birthday party."

Ethan's brow perked with curiosity. "She'll be there?"

Charles knew exactly what Ethan was thinking. He would never come right out and ask if Charles had slept with her, but he obviously had his suspicions.

"My mother has taken a liking to her," Charles said. "When she suggested inviting her, I figured it would be the perfect opportunity for her to get to know the family. Maybe then she would be more willing to accept our offer."

It wasn't a complete lie, more a vast stretching of the truth, but Ethan seemed to buy it.

"Good thinking. I'll make sure the others know to expect her there."

So, in other words, they would tag-team her. Try to wear her down. It couldn't hurt.

"We should see that Melissa knows she's welcome, too," Ethan said.

"I'll have my mother ring her," Charles said. Or as Victoria said, his "smother." The endearment brought a smile to his face.

He'd dated a lot of women in his life, but Victoria was different. Maybe part of the fascination was that women usually chased him, and for the first time he found himself the pursuer. And the truth was he sort of liked it. He was enjoying the challenge for a change.

All his life, things had come very easily to him. He would be the first to admit that he'd been spoiled as a child. There had never been a single thing he'd asked for that he hadn't gotten. Even if his father had said no, his mother would go behind his back.

Being told no was a refreshing change. He saw Victoria as more of an equal than just another temporary distraction. Not that he expected it to last. But why not enjoy it while he could?

Twelve

It was almost three in the afternoon when Victoria remembered the message on her cell phone and finally dialed her voice mail. As she listened to the somber voice on the other end, her heart plummeted and a cold chill sank deep into her skin, all the way through to her bones.

Her father had been admitted to the hospital with chest pains and was undergoing tests. The fact that the doctor had called, and not her father himself, filled her with dread. She called the hospital back but they refused to give her any information over the phone, other than to say that he was stable.

Was he unconscious? Dying? His cardiologist had warned that another attack, even a minor one, could do irreparable damage.

Hands trembling, heart thudding almost painfully hard in her chest, she threw on her jacket, grabbed her purse, and raced to Bay View Memorial Hospital as fast as the congested city streets would allow—damned tourists. She swore to herself that if he would just come out of this okay, she would never raise her voice to him, never be angry with him for as long as she lived.

And what if he wasn't okay? What if she got there and he was already gone? How would she ever forgive herself for those terrible things she'd said to him?

She'd lost her mum and her brother. She wasn't ready to lose him too. She couldn't bear it.

At the hospital information desk she was given a pass and directed to the cardiology wing on the fourth floor. When she reached the room, she was afraid to step inside, terrified of what she might see. Would it be like the last time? Her father hooked to tubes and machines?

With a trembling hand she rapped lightly on the door and heard her father's voice, strong and clear, call, "Come in."

She stepped inside, saw him sitting up in bed, his eyes bright and his color good, and went weak with relief. The machines and monitors she'd expected were nowhere to be seen. He didn't even have an IV line.

He was okay.

For now, at least, a little voice in her head said.

"Sweetheart," he said, looking relieved to see her. "I thought you were so angry with me you wouldn't come."

She thought she would be mad at him forever, but her anger just seemed to melt away. He held his arms out and she threw herself into them. She buried her face in the crook of his neck, squeezed him like she never wanted to let go, and he squeezed her right back.

"I'm sorry," they said at the exact same time.

"No," he said. "You had every right to be angry with me. I shouldn't have lied to you."

"It's okay."

"No, sweetheart, it isn't." He cupped her face in his hands. "I should have been honest with you from the start. I thought I was protecting you. And I was ashamed of the mess I'd made out of things."

"We all make mistakes."

He stroked her cheek with his thumb. "But I want you to know how deeply sorry I am. It's been just the two of us for a long time now. I would never do anything to intentionally hurt you."

"I know. It's all in the past now," she said. Hadn't losing the hotel been penalty enough? Was it fair to keep punishing him for his sins? And if she were the one who had made the mistake, wouldn't she want to be forgiven?

He was all she had left. They were a team. They had to stick together.

"What happened to you?" She sat on the edge of the bed and took one of his hands. It felt warm and strong. "Was it another attack?"

He shook his head, wearing a wry smile. "Acid reflux, the doctor said. Brought on by extreme stress. My cardiologist did a full workup just to be safe, and as far as they can tell I'm fit as a fiddle. They should be releasing me any time now."

She doubted *fit as a fiddle* was the term the doctor used. Probably more like *out of the woods*. "I'll wait around and take you home."

"Victoria, I also wanted to say I'm sorry that I was so rude to the duke. I guess I was just a little…surprised. He doesn't seem your type."

No kidding. It had been so long since she'd been in a relationship, she wasn't sure what her type was, anymore. And considering all her past disastrous relationships, maybe it was time to rethink exactly what her type should be.

"I wasn't sure about him at first," she told her father, "since he does have something of a reputation with women. But the truth is, he's not a bad guy. In fact, he's actually quite sweet. When he's not being arrogant and overbearing, that is."

"Is it…serious?"

She emphatically shook her head. "God, no. It's… *nothing*."

He gave her that fatherly *you can't fool me* look. "It didn't look like nothing to me. The way he came to the door to see if you were okay. He has feelings for you."

Not in the way her father suspected. "It isn't like that. We're keeping it casual. *Very* casual."

He raised a brow at her. "Let's face it, Vicki, you don't do casual very well. When you fall, you fall hard."

That used to be true, but she'd changed. The past few years, she hadn't fallen at all. She hadn't given herself the opportunity. She had pretty much sworn off men after her last catastrophic split.

It had been inevitable she would eventually take a

tumble off the celibacy wagon. She just never suspected that it would be with a man like Charles.

"This is different," she told him. "*I'm* different."

"I hope so. I know you think you're tough, but I've seen your heart broken too many times before."

She had no intention of putting herself back in that kind of situation. "Would you mind if we don't have a discussion about my love life? Besides, *your* heart is the one we should be worrying about."

He gave her hand a squeeze. "I'm going to make this up to you, Vicki. All the trouble I caused. I'm not sure how yet, but I will."

"I can take care of myself, Daddy." And if not, it was time she learned how. She'd been relying on him for too long.

All that mattered now was that he was alive and well, and they were back to being happy.

Victoria didn't see Charles again until Sunday night, when he showed up unannounced at her door. He looked delicious in dark slacks, a warm, brown cashmere sweater and a black leather jacket.

Any thoughts she had of turning him away evaporated the instant he smiled. She did love that smile.

"Inviting yourself over again?" she asked, just to give him a hard time.

"I tried calling today, but you didn't answer," he said, as if that were a perfectly logical reason.

"My phone died. I just plugged it in a few minutes ago when I got home."

"Are you going to let me in?"

Like she had a choice. She stepped aside and gestured him in. "Just for a few minutes."

He stepped inside, bringing with him the scent of the brisk autumn air. He took his jacket off and hung it over the back of the couch, then sat down. She sat beside him. Something about him being there was very...comfortable.

Or it could all be an illusion.

"You look tired," he said.

"It's been an exhausting weekend. My father was admitted to the hospital with chest pains Friday night."

He sat forward slightly, and the depth of concern on his face surprised her. "Is he all right?"

"He's fine. It wound up being his stomach, not his heart, but I stayed with him last night and all day today, just to be safe." And while it was nice spending time with him, it made her realize just how comfortable she'd become living alone. It had been something of a relief to get back to her flat. To her home and her things.

"I guess this means things are okay with you two."

She nodded. "It's amazing how a scare like that can alter your perception. When I imagined losing him forever, the rest of it all seemed petty and insignificant."

"You should have called me," he said.

"What for?"

He shrugged. "Support. Someone to talk to."

"Come on, Charles. You and I both know that isn't the way this works. We don't have that kind of relationship. We have sex."

He grinned. "Really great sex."

"Yes," she agreed. "And in the end, that's all it will ever be."

She could swear he looked almost…hurt. "Would it be such a stretch to think of me as a friend?"

If he were anyone else, no. "Until tomorrow, or the day after, when the next woman catches your eye and I get tossed aside? That isn't friendship."

He frowned. "That's a little unfair, don't you think?"

"Not at all. It's quite realistic, in fact. I mean, can you blame me? It's not as if you don't have a reputation for that sort of thing."

"What if I said, for now, I only want to see you."

At first she thought he was joking. Then she realized he was actually serious. "I guess I would say that you're delusional. You're totally incapable of a monogamous relationship."

"Hey, I've had relationships."

"Name the longest one."

He paused, his brow furrowing.

"That's what I thought."

"Maybe I want to try."

In a monogamous relationship, she gave him a week, tops. And that was being generous. "I don't want to get involved. I don't want a commitment." Especially with a man like him.

"Neither do I," he said. "We'll keep it casual."

"Casually exclusive? That doesn't even make sense."

"Sure it does. You've never dated someone just to date them, with no expectations."

Not really. Like her father said, when she fell, she fell hard. That was the way it was supposed to happen, as it did with her parents. They met, they fell in love, they settled down and started a family. But it had never quite seemed to work that way for her. Perhaps she'd been expecting too much?

Maybe this time it would be different. In the past she had entered relationships with the understanding, the expectation, that it would be long-lasting. And when it didn't work out she'd felt like a failure. But this was different. She was entering this relationship with no expectations at all.

"We're attracted to each other," Charles said. "And you can't deny that we're hot in bed."

She wouldn't even try.

"So," he asked. "Why not?"

He made it sound so simple. "How long?"

He shrugged. "Until it's not fun anymore, I suppose."

"Who says I'm having fun now?"

He flashed her that sexy grin. "Oh, I know you are."

Yeah, she was. The sex alone was worth her while.

But what if the only thing keeping Charles interested was the challenge, the thrill of the chase? If she gave in too easily, would he lose interest?

"I'll think about it," she said, and enjoyed the look of surprise on his face when she didn't bend to his will.

He opened his mouth to say something—God only knew what—but the bell for the door chimed.

Before she could move, he rose to his feet. "That's for me."

For him? Who would he invite to her flat?

"Back in a sec." He walked to the door. She heard him open it and thank whoever it was, then he reappeared with a large white box in his arms. The name of an exclusive downtown boutique was emblazoned on the top. Exclusively women's clothing.

What had he done this time?

"What is that?" she asked.

"A gift," he said, setting the box in her lap. It was surprisingly heavy. "I saw it in the shop window and knew I had to see you in it."

What had he done?

"Open it," he said eagerly, grinning like a kid at Christmas.

She pulled off the top and dug through layers of gold tissue paper until she encountered something royal blue and shimmering. She pulled it from the box and found herself holding a strapless, floor-length, sequined evening gown. It was so beautiful it took her breath away.

"Do you like it?" he asked.

"Charles, it's amazing, but—"

"I know, I know. You can afford your own dress and all that." He sat down beside her. "When I saw it in the shop window, I knew it would be perfect for you. And I can see already that it is."

He was right. If she'd had every gown in the world to choose from, she probably would have picked this very one. He'd even gotten the size right.

The price tag was missing, but she was sure that from this particular boutique, it must have cost a bundle. More than she could afford to spend.

"It's too much," she said.

"Not for me, it isn't."

Maybe this was one of the perks of dating a multimillionaire. Even though they weren't technically dating.

Normally she wouldn't accept a gift like this. But it was just so beautiful. So elegant. The designer was one she had always admired and dreamed of wearing, but never could quite fit into her budget.

She considered offering to pay him back, but God only knew when she would have the money. As it was, she was barely making the rent.

Maybe she could say yes, just this once.

"I love it," she said. "Thank you."

"The manager said if it needs altering, bring it around Monday and they'll put a rush on it. I wasn't sure about jewelry or shoes."

"That part I have covered," she said.

She could tell just from looking at it that at least three inches would have to go from the hem. She folded it carefully and lay it back in the box.

"Aren't you going to model it for me?" he asked.

She shook her head and eased the top back in place. "It will just have to be a surprise."

Something told her that if she wore it for him before the party, the novelty might wear off.

See, she told herself, *this is what you would have to look forward to if you let yourself get involved with him.* She would always be fretting about how to keep him interested, worrying that any minute he would get tired of her.

"Could I at least get a thank-you kiss?" he asked, tapping an index finger to his lips. "Right here."

"Just a quick one," she said. Then she would kick him out so she could get to bed early for a change. She had a lot of sleep to catch up on.

She leaned in and pressed her lips to his, but before

she could back away, he cupped a hand behind her head and held her there. And it felt so good, she only put up the tiniest bit of resistance before she gave in and melted into his arms.

One kiss turned into two kisses, which then led to some touching. Then their clothes were getting in the way, so naturally they had to take them off.

When he picked her up and carried her to the bedroom, she had resigned herself to another sleepless but sinfully satisfying night.

Thirteen

Victoria sat with Charles in the back of the Bentley, her luggage for the weekend tucked beside his in the trunk. She had planned to drive herself to his parents's estate. But after a long week of Charles giving her every reason to make the hour-long drive with him—outrageous petrol prices, complicated directions, and who knew, maybe even highway robbery—she had finally relented and agreed to ride with him.

It wasn't as though she was concerned she wouldn't be welcomed. She and Charles's mother had practically become buddies over the past couple of weeks. Mrs. Mead had called every day as usual, but there were times when she called specifically to speak with Victoria, not Charles.

She wanted to know Victoria's preference for dinner

Friday night. Beef or fish? And which room would she prefer to stay in? One facing the ocean or the gardens? Did she prefer cotton sheets or silk, and were there any food allergies the cook should be aware of? Was there a special wine she would like ordered, or would she prefer cocktails? And the list went on. Victoria wondered if she was this attentive with all the guests who stayed with them.

With each call Mrs. Mead expressed how thrilled she and her husband were to be meeting Victoria. And even though Mrs. Mead never came right out and said it, Victoria couldn't escape the feeling that she was reading way more into Victoria and Charles's relationship than was really there. And Victoria was feeling as though she was being sucked into the family against her will. Which might not have been horrible if the man in question were anyone but Charles.

Yes, she and Charles had fun together—and not just the physical kind. He made her laugh, and she never failed to get that shimmy of excitement in her belly when he popped his head in her office or appeared unannounced at her door. But she still hadn't given him a definitive answer about the nature of their relationship.

And call her evil, but keeping him guessing gave her a perverse feeling of power. If she could just ignore the fact that she was coming dangerously close to falling for him. But she would never be that foolish. The instant she gave in, surrendered her will to him, the thrill of the chase would be gone, and Charles would lose interest.

Hopefully she would be long gone before then.

"By the way," she told him, "the employment agency

called just before we left. They have four more possible candidates for the assistant position."

"Splendid," he said. "Make interview appointments first thing next week."

"Why bother?" she asked wryly. "You haven't liked a single applicant yet."

They had all been perfectly capable. And not a gorgeous face or sexy figure in the lot of them. Which she suspected was the reason he'd dismissed them all without consideration.

"I'm sure the right one will come along," he said.

He or she would have to. Victoria's time was nearly up. At this rate she would have to stay longer to train whomever he hired, and she had other irons in the fire. In fact, she was expecting a very important phone call any day now that just might determine her immediate future plans. The opportunity of a lifetime, her father had said.

But she refused to let herself think about that and add even more nervous knots to the ones already twisting her stomach.

The hour-long drive seemed to fly by, and before she knew it they were pulling up to the gates of the estate. She noted it was not at all hard to find—one turn off the coastal highway and they were there.

And only then did she become truly nervous. What if they hated her? Made her feel like she was imposing? Would his parents smother Charles with affection and leave her feeling like the fourth wheel?

Things she maybe should have considered *before* she climbed into the damned car.

As they approached, the gates swung open. The car

followed the long, twisting drive, and she got her first view of his parents' estate. The home that she supposed would one day belong to Charles.

It was utterly breathtaking, and so enormous it made her father's estate look like a country cottage. Built sometime in the nineteenth century, the impressive structure sat on endless acres of rolling green lawns that tapered down to a stretch of private beach. The grounds were crawling with staff, all bustling with activity. To prepare for the party tomorrow night, she assumed.

"What do you think?" Charles asked.

"It's really something," she said, peering out her window. "Has it always been in the royal family?"

"Actually, this house comes from my mother's side. Her family originated on Thomas Isle, the sister island to Morgan Isle. They immigrated here in the late nineteenth century."

"I didn't realize you had ties to Thomas Isle," she said. Up until recently, their respective monarchies had ruled in bitter discord with the other. As few as ten years ago they weren't even on speaking terms.

"Have you ever been there?" he asked, and she shook her head. "It's very different from Morgan Isle. Farming community, mostly, and a little archaic by our standards. Although, in the last few years the entire island has gone with the recent green trend, and all the crops they export now are certified organic. We should go sometime, tour the island and the castle."

She wasn't sure how she felt about taking another trip with him, or the fact that he'd even suggested it. Here they were, going on four weeks of seeing each other, and he still wasn't making noise like he wanted out. The longer they dragged this out, the more attached they would become. Not to mention that if things worked out as she'd planned, she might not be on the island much longer.

The car slowed to a stop by the front entrance, and the driver got out to open the door for them.

As they stepped out into the brisk, salty ocean air, the front door opened and Charles's parents emerged. Victoria was struck instantly by what an attractive couple they made.

Mrs. Mead looked much younger than her husband, and that surprised Victoria. She'd imagined her older and more matronly. In reality Mrs. Mead looked youthful, chic, and stunningly beautiful. And though Mr. Mead was showing his age, he was brutally handsome and as physically fit as his wife. Nothing like the stodgy old man she's been picturing all this time. It was clear where Charles had gotten his good looks.

Talk about hitting the gene-pool jackpot! She could just imagine the gorgeous children she and Charles—

Whoa. Where had that errant and totally unrealistic thought come from? Talk about a cold-day-in-hell scenario. She didn't even know if Charles wanted children.

She didn't *want* to know. Because if the answer was yes, it would make him that much more appealing.

"Your parents are so handsome," she whispered to Charles. "I never imagined your mother would be so young."

"Don't let her face fool you," he whispered back. "She just has an exceptional plastic surgeon."

Victoria hung back a few steps as Mrs. Mead approached them, arms open, and folded her son into a crushing embrace. "It's so wonderful to see you, dear! Did you have a good trip?"

"Uneventful," he said, untangling himself from her arms so he could shake his father's hand. "Happy Birthday, Dad."

"Welcome home, son," his father said with a smile that lit his entire face. There was no doubt, they adored their child. Not that Victoria could blame them.

Charles gestured her closer. "Mum, Dad, this is my colleague, Victoria Houghton."

Victoria curtsied. "I'm so pleased to finally meet you both," she said, accepting Mr. Mead's outstretched hand, then his wife's.

"The pleasure is all ours, Victoria," his mother said, "And please, you must call us Grant and Pip."

Her name was *Pip?* Victoria bit her lip to hold back a nervous giggle.

"I know what you're thinking," Mrs. Mead, *Pip,* said. She looped an arm through Victoria's and led her toward the house. "What kind of a name is Pip?"

"It is unusual," she admitted.

"Well, my parent's weren't that eccentric. My given name is Persephone."

That wasn't exactly a name you heard every day, either.

"I don't know if Charles told you, but I used to be a runway model."

"No, he didn't." But that wasn't hard to believe. At least she hadn't put those looks and figure to waste.

"This was back in the sixties." She shot Victoria a wry smile. "I'm aging myself, I know. But anyway, those were the days of Twiggy. They liked them tall and ghostly thin. I was thin enough, but at five feet seven inches I wasn't exactly towering over the other models. So, because I was the shortest, everyone started calling me Pipsqueak. Then it was shortened to Pip. And that's what people have been calling me ever since. Isn't that right, Grant?"

"As long as I've known you," he agreed.

She didn't seem small, but then, with the exception of young children, everybody was taller than Victoria.

"My parents abhorred it, of course," Pip said, as they stepped through the door into the foyer, Charles and his father following silently behind. "But being something of a rebellious youngster, that only made the name more appealing."

The inside of their home was just as magnificent and breathtaking as the outside. Vaulted ceilings, antique furnishings, and oodles of rich, polished wood. So different from the modern furnishings in Charles's home. It was difficult to imagine him growing up here.

"I'll show you to your room so you can settle in," Pip said. "Then we can meet in the study for a drink before dinner. Grant, would you be a dear and check that Geoffery brought the correct wine up from the cellar?"

"Of course." He flashed Victoria a smile, then walked off in the opposite direction. If it bothered him being sent on errands, it didn't show.

"He's the wine connoisseur," Pip explained. "I'm more of a gin-and-tonic girl."

They climbed the stairs, Charles in tow, and Pip showed her to a room decorated in Victorian-era floral with what she assumed was authentic period furniture. A bit frilly for Victoria's taste, but beautiful.

A servant followed them in with Victoria's luggage.

"Would you like a maid to help you unpack?" Pip asked.

"No, thank you." She'd never been fond of total strangers rifling through her things—or even the maid who had been with her and her father for years.

"Well, then, is there anything you need? Anything I can get you?"

"I'm fine, thanks."

"Mum," Charles said, "why don't we leave Victoria to unpack? You can walk me to my room."

"If there's anything you need, anything at all, just buzz the staff." She gestured to the intercom panel by the door. "Twenty-four hours a day."

Jeez, talk about being smothered with kindness. "Thank you."

"Shall we meet in the study in an hour?"

"An hour is fine, Mum." Charles had to all but drag her from the room. And before he closed the door behind him, he told Victoria, "I'll be by to show you to the study, and later I'll take you on a tour."

The devilish look in his eyes said he had more than just a tour in mind.

"Charles, she's lovely!" his mother gushed the instant they were in his room. "So pretty and petite. Like a pixie."

"Don't let her size fool you. She can hold her own."

"Just the kind of woman you need," she said.

Could she be any *less* subtle?

He should have seen this coming. "Don't start, mother."

She shrugged innocently. She knew he meant business when he called her mother instead of Mum. "Start what, dear?"

"*Pushing* me."

She frowned. "Is it wrong to want to see my only son settle down? To hope for maybe a grandchild or two? I'm not getting any younger."

It was times like this he hated being an only child. "You're only fifty-eight."

She shot him a stern look. "Bite your tongue, young man."

So he added, "But you don't look a day over thirty-five."

She smiled and patted his cheek. "That's my sweet boy."

Ugh. He hated when she called him that. And she wondered why he didn't come around very often. He hoisted his suitcase up on the bed and unzipped it.

"Let a maid do that," she scolded.

"You know I prefer to do it myself."

She sighed dramatically, as though he was a lost cause, and sat on the bed to watch him. "You brought your tux?"

"Of course."

"And Victoria?"

"She would look terrible in a tux."

She gave him a playful shove. "You know what I mean."

"She's all set."

"I thought of offering her the use of one of my gowns, but she's at least two sizes smaller."

"I bought her a gown."

She raised a curious brow. "Oh, did you?"

"Don't go reading anything into it. I just wanted her to feel comfortable."

"It's been ages since you brought a date home."

"We're not dating," he said. Victoria's rules, not his. Although, if this wasn't dating, he wasn't sure what to call it. It was the longest exclusive relationship he'd ever had with a woman.

He'd kept waiting for it to lose its luster, to get bored with her. Instead, with every passing day, he seemed to care more for her. In a temporary way, that is.

"So what *are* you doing," she asked, and the instant the words were out, she held up a hand and shook her head. "On second thought, I don't want to know."

"She's a friend," he said, and realized it was true. A friend with benefits. The two roles had always been mutually exclusive in the past. He'd never even met a woman he would want to sleep with *and* call a friend. She was definitely unique.

And when the inevitable end came, he had the feeling he would miss Victoria.

After drinks in the study, Victoria, Charles, and his parents had a surprisingly pleasant dinner together. Victoria found Pip to be much less overbearing in person, and Grant was quiet but friendly. It was rare he got a word in edgewise, though.

Pip must have asked Victoria a hundred questions about her family and her career, despite the warning looks she kept getting from her husband and son.

"What?" she would ask them. "I'm just curious."

Victoria didn't mind too much, although around the time dessert was served, it was beginning to feel a little like the Spanish Inquisition. When the questions turned a little too personal, to the tune of "So, Victoria, do you think you'll want children someday?" Charles put the kabash on it by taking her on that tour he'd promised. Which ended—*surprise*—right back in her room between the covers. Which is where they stayed for the rest of the night.

They were up bright and early for breakfast at eight, then spent hours with his parents chatting and looking through family photos, taking a long walk through the gardens and along the shore. And Victoria couldn't have felt more welcome or accepted.

She had expected Pip to grow bored with her almost immediately and cast her aside in favor of spending time with her son. But Pip remained glued to Victoria's side right up until the moment everyone went upstairs to get dressed for the party.

Not that Victoria minded. She liked Pip. She was witty and bright. A lot like Charles, really. She could even imagine them becoming friends, but there wouldn't likely be a chance for that.

"My parents really like you," Charles said, as they walked up the stairs together.

"I like them, too. I never expected your mum to be so attentive, though. At least, not toward me. Shouldn't she be showering her son with affection?"

"When I'm not here, she's desperate to keep in touch. And when I'm here, we have a few hours to catch up, then we run out of things to say to each other. The novelty wears off, I guess."

That sounded like someone else she knew. Always wanting what he couldn't have. And once he got it, he grew easily bored.

He hadn't gotten bored with her yet. But he would. It was inevitable.

Or was it?

Given his pathetically short attention span when it came to women, if he was going to grow tired of her, wouldn't it have happened by now?

She shook the thought from her mind, and not for the first time. That was dangerous ground to wander into. A place where she would undeniably get her heart smashed to pieces.

God knew it had happened enough times before.

"The party starts in three hours," he said, when they reached the top of the stairs, where they would part ways and go to their own rooms. "How much time do you need to get ready?"

She didn't have to ask why he wanted to know. It was clear in his sinfully sexy smile. And she had to admit, making love in his parents' home in the middle of the afternoon did hold a certain naughty appeal.

She took his hand, weaving their fingers together. "Your place or mine?"

Fourteen

Victoria sat on the edge of the bed, her stomach twisted into nervous knots as she waited for Charles to fetch her from her room. They were already half an hour late, no thanks to Charles, who had finessed his way into her bed, then wouldn't get back out. She'd had to practically dress him herself and shove him out the door.

Now that she was ready, with nothing to do but sit and think, she couldn't keep her mind off of those one hundred or so guests she was going to have to meet. And the fact that she barely knew a single one of them. And how out of place she could potentially feel. Even when she and her father still had a thriving business, this echelon of society had been far out of their reach.

She was so edgy that when Charles rapped on the door, she nearly jumped out of her skin.

Here we go.

She shot to her feet, adjusting her dress, making sure she looked her best. She took a deep cleansing breath, then blew it out and called, "Come in!"

The door opened and Charles appeared, looking unbelievably handsome in his tux. "We're late—we have to…" He trailed off the instant he laid eyes on her, and for one very long moment he just stood there and stared. She was wearing the dress he had picked and had complemented it with the diamond jewelry she had inherited from her mother. Simple, but elegant.

But why didn't he say something? She swallowed hard and picked nervously at the skirt of her dress. "Well?"

"You look…" He shook his head, as though searching for the right words. He opened his mouth to say something, then closed it again. Then he shrugged and admitted, "I'm speechless."

She bit her lip. "Speechless good or speechless bad?"

He stepped closer. "Victoria, there are no words for how amazing you look in that dress." He lifted a hand to touch her cheek, then he leaned forward and brushed his lips across hers. So sweet and tender. And something happened just then. Something between them shifted. She could see in his eyes that he felt it too. Their relationship had…*evolved,* somehow. Moved to the next level.

"Victoria," he said, and she knew deep down in her heart what he was about to say. He was going to tell her that he was falling in love with her. She could just *feel* it. Her heart skipped a beat or two, then picked up double time.

He came so close, then at the last minute, chickened out. "We should get downstairs now."

She nodded, and let him lead her downstairs. She couldn't blame him for being afraid to say the words, to admit his feelings. This was new ground for him. And maybe he was afraid of rejection. But if he had gone out on a limb and said the words, she would have told him that she was falling in love with him, too.

Victoria found herself thrust amidst the upper crust of Morgan Isle society. The beautiful people. The weird thing was, despite any preconceived notion she may have had, that was really all they were. Just people. Not a single one treated her as though she were below them. And if deep down any thought so, they were kind enough to keep it to themselves.

Pip made sure that Victoria was introduced to all the right people and whispered to her juicy bits of gossip about them that Victoria found disturbingly entertaining. One by one she was reintroduced to the members of the royal family, and each took the chance to not so subtly try to convince her to stay with the Royal Inn. All she would say was that she was considering her options. She had to admit it was tempting, especially now that it was obvious they'd hired her on merit and not because of her father. But at the same time, she felt she needed a fresh start. Maybe, though, if the other position fell through, or if Charles asked her not to leave...

Which she was beginning to think was more and more likely. It seemed as though he hadn't taken his eyes off of her for a single minute all evening. Every time she turned he was there, watching her with that hungry look in his eyes. And she knew exactly what he was thinking.

He liked her in the dress, but he couldn't wait to get her out of it.

And people were noticing. Especially the women who were volleying for his attention.

"He can't keep his eyes off you," Pip told her, wearing the hopeful and conspiratorial smile of a mother who was ready to marry off her son.

"I noticed" was all Victoria said.

"He keeps insisting that you two are just friends, but I've never seen him look at a woman that way."

Her words sent an excited shiver through Victoria. Maybe Charles really did love her.

He saw the two of them talking and walked up to them. "Victoria, would you dance with me?"

"Go ahead," Pip said, eagerly waving them away. Whatever had happened between Victoria and Charles upstairs, Pip seemed to be sensing it, too. And no doubt loving every second.

Charles offered his arm and led Victoria out on the dance floor. The band was playing a slow, sultry number. Charles pulled her close to him, gazing down into her eyes. She felt mesmerized.

"Having a good time?" he asked, and she nodded. "Don't tell my mother I said this, but you're the most beautiful woman here."

Whether it was true or not, he made her believe it was. He made her *feel* beautiful. He was the only man she'd ever been with who made her feel good about herself.

His eyes searched her face, settled on her lips. "You wouldn't believe how badly I want to kiss you right now."

She grinned up at him. "And you wouldn't believe how badly I'd like you to." But they had always had an unspoken agreement. No physical affection when they were out in public together. He was hiding the relationship from his family, and she was protecting herself from everyone else. She didn't want to be labeled another one of his flings. Only this didn't feel like a fling any longer. This was real.

"Maybe I should then," he said.

It seemed to happen in slow motion. He lowered his head, one excruciating inch at a time, while Victoria's heart leapt up into her throat. Then his lips brushed hers, right there on the dance floor in front of everyone, softly at first. Then he leaned in deeper, catching the back of her head in his hand.

It was like their first kiss all over again. Sexy and exciting, and oh so good. And people were looking. She could feel their curious stares.

Their secret affair was officially out, and she didn't even care. She just wanted this night to last forever. She wanted *them* to last forever.

They parted slowly, hesitantly, and she rested her cheek against his chest, realizing, as they swayed to the music, that she had never been so happy in all her life.

Maybe he was afraid to say the words, but she wasn't. For the first time in a long time, she wasn't afraid of anything.

"Charles," she whispered.

"Hmm?"

"I think I'm falling in love with you."

She waited for him to squeeze her tighter, to gaze down at her with love and acceptance.

Instead he went cold and stiff in her arms. It was like dancing with a store mannequin.

You just surprised him, she told herself. *Any second now he's going to realize how happy he was to hear those words.*

Say something, she begged silently. *Anything.* But he didn't. It would seem she'd managed to stun him speechless again.

This time in a bad way.

Her knees felt unsteady and dread filled her heart. It was more than clear by his reaction that he didn't feel the same way. And he wasn't too thrilled to know that she did.

She had done it again. Despite going into this affair with no expectations whatsoever, she still managed to fall for Charles and get her heart filleted in the process. How could she have been so foolish to believe he actually cared about her? That he'd changed? That she was any different from the many others who came before her?

A person would think she'd have learned by now.

Tears of humiliation burned her eyes, but she swallowed them back. She wouldn't give anyone there the satisfaction of learning she was just one of many whose hearts he'd crushed.

She looked up at him with what she was sure was a strained smile. Her face felt like cold, hard plastic. "Thanks for the dance. Now, if you'll excuse me."

She broke away from him and walked blindly from the room, wanting only to get the hell out of there. She didn't even care that people were interrupting their conversations to stop and watch her pass. And she did her best to smile cordially, and nod in greeting.

So no one would realize she was dying inside.

"What did you do?" his mother hissed from behind him, as Charles helplessly watched Victoria walk away.

He turned to her, and under his breath said, "Stay out of this, Mother."

"Whatever you said to her, the poor girl went white as a sheet."

"I didn't say a thing." And that was the problem.

He shook his head and cursed under his breath. This was not his fault. Why did she have to go and say something like that? They had such a good thing. Why ruin it? And how in the hell had she gone from refusing to accept even a temporary exclusivity to falling in love with him? It made no sense.

Maybe she had just gotten caught up in the moment. That was probably it, he realized, feeling relieved. He needed to talk to her, before this thing was blown way out of proportion.

He started to walk away and his mother grabbed hold of his sleeve. "Sweetheart, everything inside me says she's the woman for you. And deep down I think you know it, too. *Why* won't you let yourself feel it?"

He pulled his arm free. "Excuse me, Mother."

He took the stairs two at a time. Her bedroom door was closed, so he knocked and called, "Victoria, I need to speak with you."

He didn't really expect a response, but he heard her call back, "Come in."

She was standing beside the bed, her suitcases open in front of her. She had changed out of her dress and it was draped across the footboard.

"What are you doing?" he asked.

"I thought I would get a head start on my packing," she said, but she wouldn't look him in the eye. She gestured to the dress. "You may as well take that. I'll never have a need for it again. Maybe someone else can get some use out of it."

He knew in that instant that she meant what she said, she was falling in love with him.

"Victoria, I'm sorry."

She bit her lip and shook her head. "No, it's my fault. I never should have said that to you. I don't know what I was thinking. Temporary insanity."

"You didn't give me a chance to say anything."

"Your silence said it all, believe me."

"I'm sorry. I'm just not—"

"In love with me? Yeah, I got that."

"We agreed this was temporary."

"You're absolutely right."

"It's not that I don't care for you."

She finally turned to him. "Look, this was bound to

happen, right? It's a miracle we lasted this long. It was going to end eventually."

"It doesn't have to," he said. They could just go back to the way things have been.

"Yes," she told him, "it does."

They were doing the right thing, so why did it feel like a mistake? "I feel…really bad."

She nodded sympathetically, but her eyes said she felt anything but. "That must be awful for you."

"You know that isn't what I mean."

"Look, I appreciate you coming after me and all. But honestly, you didn't do anything wrong. You did what you always do. And I should have expected that."

Maybe this wasn't her fault. Maybe he…led her on somehow. Made her believe he felt more that was really there.

She walked past him to the door and held it open. "Please leave."

"You're kicking me out?"

She nodded. "I created this mess. Now it's time I fixed it."

The drive back to the city the next morning was excruciatingly silent. Charles tried to talk to Victoria, to reason with her, but she refused to acknowledge him. The worst part wasn't even that she wasn't acting angry or wounded. She was just…cold.

He didn't follow her up to her flat when the car dropped her off, convinced that if he gave her time to cool off, she would see reason. But by eleven a.m. Monday he hadn't heard a word from her and she hadn't shown up at work. He checked her office to see if she'd slipped quietly in without him hearing her, and he realized all of her things were gone.

What the hell?

She was pissed at him. He got that. But that didn't mean she could just quit her job, just...*abandon* him.

He grabbed his jacket from his office and stormed out past Penelope, tossing over his shoulder, "Cancel all of my appointments."

Her car was parked out in front of her building, and he took the stairs two at a time up to her floor. He rapped hard on her door and barked, "Victoria!"

She opened the door, but left the security chain on. "What do you want?"

She looked tired, and the anger that had driven him there fizzled away.

"You didn't come to work," he said. "I was concerned."

"Technically, my three weeks are up. I don't work there anymore."

"But we haven't found a replacement yet. Who will do the training?"

"I'm sure you'll manage."

But that hadn't been the deal. And he didn't like being exiled in the hall. The least she could do was invite him in. She owed him that much. "Are you going to let me in?"

She hesitated, then she unlatched the chain and stepped aside to let him pass. "Only for a minute. I have a lot of packing to do."

"Packing? Are you going on a trip?"

"I'm moving."

She had said something about having to get a cheaper place. If she would just accept the damned job at the Royal Inn, she could stay right here. Or hell, she could probably afford to buy a house. "Where are you moving to?"

"London."

"England?"

"I was offered a position at a five-star hotel there. I start next Monday."

"You're leaving the country?"

"This Friday." She paused and said, "You could congratulate me."

Congratulate her? Wait. This was all wrong. She wasn't supposed to find a new job. She was supposed to change her mind and agree to work at the Royal Inn. "Whatever they're paying you, the Royal Inn will top it."

"I told you weeks ago, I don't want to work at the Royal Inn."

"But they want you. They're counting on me to convince you to stay."

"You'll just have to tell them you failed."

"It doesn't work that way. You can't leave."

She seemed to find his predicament amusing. "Look, I know you're used to getting your way, getting everything your heart desires, but this time you're just going to have to suck it up like the rest of us."

"It's not about that."

"Then what *is* it about, Charles? Because to me it sounds like you're just being a sore loser."

What was he trying to say? What did he really want from her?

He stepped toward her as though he could bully her to comply.

She didn't even flinch.

"You can't leave."

"Why? What can you offer me if I stay? A real relationship?"

"What we have is real."

"A commitment?"

He cringed. "Why do we have to do that? Why do we have to put a label on it? Why can't we just keep doing what we're doing?"

"Because that isn't what I want."

"It was a week ago. And why not? It was the perfect relationship. Totally uncomplicated."

Her expression darkened. "For you, maybe it was. But I'm tired of always being on edge. Waiting around for the other shoe to fall, for you to get bored and dump me. I just can't do it anymore."

"So you're dumping me first, is that it?"

She shrugged. "Welcome to the world of the dumpee. It's not fun, but trust me when I say you'll get over it."

She was right. He was usually the one to do the leaving. The one to walk away. So this was how it felt.

He knew that if he let her go, he would probably never see her again. But what choice did he have? She was right. It was very likely that in time he would grow tired of their relationship and need something else. He would feel trapped and stifled and get that burning need to move on. Then he would hurt her all over again.

It would be cruel and selfish to try to persuade her to stay. So he didn't.

He turned and left, walked away from her for the last time, an odd ache, like a spear thrust through his chest, making it hard to breath.

It's just that your pride has been slightly bruised, he assured himself. In a day or two he'd be fine. And when Victoria left, he wouldn't say a single damned thing to stop her.

Fifteen

When Charles's doorbell chimed late Thursday afternoon, he was sure it was Victoria, there to tell him that she'd changed her mind. But instead he found Ethan standing on his front porch.

Ethan looked Charles up and down, took in his disheveled hair, wrinkled clothes, and four days' growth of facial hair. "Christ almighty, you look like hell."

Appropriately so, considering that was how he felt.

He stepped aside so Ethan could come in, then shut the door behind him. "I think I caught some kind of bug."

"I hope it's nothing catching," Ethan said warily. "Lizzy will kill me if I bring germs home. She's due any minute now, you know."

Only if wounded pride had become contagious. "I think you're safe."

"Could this have something to do with Victoria? Word is she took a job in England." At Charles's surprised look, Ethan said, "Did you think we wouldn't hear? I guess you didn't manage to convince her to stay, huh? And the way you were locking lips at the party, I'm guessing you ignored our request that you not sleep with her."

"Are you angry?"

He shrugged. "Let's just say I'm not surprised."

"If it counts for anything, I don't think it would have made a difference. Victoria Houghton is the most stubborn woman alive."

He walked to the kitchen, where he'd left his drink, and Ethan followed him. "What are you doing here, anyway?"

"You missed our squash game, genius. I called your office and your secretary said you've been out since last Friday."

"Yeah." Charles sipped his scotch and gestured to the bottle. "Want one?"

Ethan shook his head. "So, what happened?"

"I told you, I caught a bug."

"She dumped you, didn't she?"

Charles opened his mouth to deny it, but he just didn't have the energy.

Ethan flashed him a cocky grin and gave him a slap across the back. "The notorious Charles Mead was finally set loose by a woman. I never thought I would see the day. And she's moving all the hell the way over to England to get the away from you."

Charles glared at him. "I'm glad I could be a source of amusement."

"Welcome to the real world, my friend."

"Go to hell."

Ethan laughed. "What I find even more amusing, is that you're in love with her, and you probably didn't have the guts to tell her."

"I don't do love."

"Everyone does eventually."

"I'm not looking for a commitment," he insisted, but the familiar mantra was beginning to lose its luster. And the idea of being with anyone but Victoria left a hollow feeling in his gut.

That would pass.

"I know you see marriage as some kind of prison sentence, and I find that tragic. My life didn't truly begin until I married Lizzy."

Charles wanted to believe that it might be that way for him, too. It just seemed so far out of the realm of reality.

"You want to reschedule our game?" Ethan asked. "Or do you plan to mope in here for the rest of your life?"

"I'm not moping." Maybe he was a little depressed. Maybe it had been a slight shock to his system. But in a few days he would be back on his game. Besides, Victoria could still change her mind. She could realize that he was right and accept their relationship on his terms.

You just keep telling yourself that, pal.

Ethan's cell phone rang. He unclipped it from his belt and checked the display. "It's Lizzy." He flipped it open and said, "Hey, babe." He was silent for several seconds, then his eyes lit. "Are you sure?" Another pause, then, "Okay, I'll be there as soon as I can. Ten minutes, tops. Just hold on." He snapped his phone shut, grinning like an idiot. "Lizzy is in labor. Her water just broke." He laughed and slapped Charles on the back. "I'm going to be a father."

"Congratulations," Charles said, practically knocked backward by the intensity of Ethan's joy. What would it feel like to be that happy?

But he already knew the answer to that. He'd been that happy for a while. With Victoria. Right up until the instant when he'd screwed it all up.

Maybe he did love her. Maybe this so-called bug he'd contracted was really just lovesickness. Maybe his mum was right, and Victoria was the woman for him. Was it possible?

"You okay?" Ethan asked, wearing a concerned look. "You just got the weirdest expression on your face."

"Yeah," Charles said, unable to stifle the smile itching at the corners of his mouth. The same kind of goofy, lovesick smile Ethan had been wearing seconds ago. And he liked it. It felt…good. "I'm okay. In fact, I think I'm pretty great right now."

"If I didn't know any better, I would say you just came to your senses."

Maybe he did. Instead of feeling trapped or stifled, he felt free.

"What are you still doing here," he said, giving Ethan a shove in the direction of the foyer. "Are you forgetting your wife is waiting for you? You're going to be a father!"

Ethan grinned and looked at his watch. "How fast do you think I can get from here to the palace?"

"It's a twenty-minute drive, so probably about five. Now get out of here."

"I'm already gone," Ethan said, and Charles thought, with a chuckle, *Me too*.

As she was emptying the drawer of her bedside table into a box, Victoria saw the corner of a sheet of paper wedged between the headboard and mattress.

Probably just a magazine insert or an old message slip. She almost left it there, figuring it would fall loose when the movers took her bed apart. Then something compelled her to wedge her hand into the tight space and catch the corner of the paper with the tips of her fingers. When she pulled it free, and saw what it was, she wished she had just left it the hell alone.

It was an old shopping list, but what stopped her heart for an instant is what she found scribbled on the opposite side; the note that Charles had left her that first night they spent together

It must have slipped off the pillow and gotten caught. Reading it now, in Charles chicken-scratch scrawl, sent a sharp pain through her heart.

Victoria,
Have an early meeting but wanted to let you sleep. I had a great time last night. See you in the office.
XOXO
Charles
P.S. Dinner tonight?

She'd managed, up until just then, not to shed a single tear over him. But now she felt the beginnings of a precariously dammed flood welling up against the backs of her eyes.

Some silly part of her that still believed in fairy-tale endings actually thought he might come after her. That he might have a sudden epiphany, like a lightning bolt from the heavens, and realize that he was madly in love with her. That he couldn't live without her.

Well, that certainly hadn't happened. She hadn't seen or heard from him since Sunday when he walked out of her apartment without even saying goodbye.

"Victoria?"

She turned to see her dad standing in the bedroom doorway. "Yeah?"

His brow was wrinkled with concern. He'd been worried about her lately, claimed that she wasn't acting like herself. He even hinted that by taking this job she might be running away from her problems, rather than facing them. Sort of like he had done.

She was seriously wondering the same thing. But it was too late to back out now.

"Everything okay?" he asked.

She nodded, a little too enthusiastically, and stuffed the note in the pocket of her jeans. "Fine, Daddy."

"The movers called. They'll be here tomorrow at eight a.m."

"Great." But it wasn't great. She didn't want to move to England and leave the only home she'd ever known. But careerwise, there wasn't much left for her here. The Royal Inn was the biggest game on the island, and she definitely had no future there.

"Almost finished in here?" he asked, the worry still

set deeply in his face. She wished there was something she could do to ease his mind. This shouldn't have to be so hard on him. But she knew he felt responsible for sticking her in this position in the first place.

"I think I'll need one more box for the closet stuff," she said. "Other than that, it's pretty much packed."

The bell rang and her father gestured behind him. "You want me to get that?"

"Would you mind? And could you grab me a box while you're out there?"

"Sure thing, honey."

Her father had wanted to move to England with her right away, but she asked him to wait until she was settled and had her bearings. And she wanted time to find them a nice place. Preferably something close to the hotel. With her new salary, signing bonus and moving expense account, as long as she stayed out of Central London, money wasn't going to a problem. It was her chance to finally take care of him. And he deserved it.

She dumped the rest of the drawer contents into the box, then carried it over to the closet. She still had room for a few pairs of shoes.

She heard a noise in the bedroom doorway, and turned to her father, asking, "Did you get me a b—" Then she realized that it wasn't her father standing there.

It was Charles.

Her knees went instantly soft, and her heart surged up and lodged somewhere near her vocal chords.

He looked so good, so casually sexy it made her chest sting. And what was he doing here?

"I don't have a *buh*. But I do have a *box*," he said, holding it out to her. "Your father asked me to bring it in."

Her father actually let him into the apartment? Couldn't he have asked first? What if she didn't want to talk to him?

But you do, a little voice in her head taunted. *You're dying to know why he's here.*

He probably just came to say goodbye. To wish her the best of luck in her new life.

When she didn't step forward and take the box from him, he dropped it on the floor. "Your dad told me to tell you that he was heading home for the night, and he would be back tomorrow around seven."

Great, he left her to deal with this alone. Way to be supportive, Dad.

"I'm a little busy right now," she said.

He nodded, hands wedged in the pockets of his slacks, gazing casually around the naked room. "I can see that. It looks as though you're all ready to go."

"The movers will be here tomorrow morning at eight." Why had she told him that? So he could show up at the last minute and beg her not to go? Like *that* would ever happen.

"So, you're really going?" he said.

Did he think this was all for show? An elaborate hoax to throw him off her scent? "Yes, I'm *really* going."

The jerk had the gall to look relieved! Like her leaving was the best thing that had ever happened to him.

"I'm glad my eminent departure is such a source of happiness for you," she snapped, when on the inside her heart was breaking all over again. Why couldn't he just leave her alone?

"I am happy," he admitted. "But not for the reason you think."

Getting rid of her wasn't reason enough? "Let me guess, you have a new girlfriend. Or six?" *Way to go, Ace, make him think you're jealous.* She needed to keep her mouth shut.

"I'm happy," he said, walking toward her, "because for some reason I can't even begin to understand, knowing that you're really leaving makes me realize how damned much I love you, Victoria."

He said it so earnestly, that for a second she almost believed him. But this had nothing to do with love. Real or imagined. "You only want me because you can't have me. Give it time. You'll find someone to fill the void, then you'll forget all about me."

"Forget you?" he said with a wry laugh. "I can't even fathom the idea of being with another woman."

"For now, maybe."

He shook his head. "No, this is not a temporary state of mind. This is it. You're stuck with me, until death do us part."

Death do us part? Was he talking *marriage?* Charles? Who spent his life bucking the very thought of the institution?

She narrowed her eyes at him, unable to let herself believe it. Yet there was a tiny kernel of hope forming inside of her, that made her think, *Maybe, just maybe…*

She folded her arms across her chest, eyed him suspiciously. "Who are you, and what have you done with Charles?"

"This is your fault," he said. "If you weren't everything I could possibly want in a woman, we wouldn't even be having this conversation. I would still be living happily oblivious and totally unaware of how freaking fantastic it feels to realize you've met the person you want to spend the rest of your life with."

"I don't believe you," she said, although with a pathetic lack of conviction.

He just smiled. "Yes you do. Because you know I would never lie to you. And I would never say something like this if I didn't mean it."

She swallowed hard, those damned tears welling in her eyes again. But at least this time they were happy. "Does this mean I don't have to go to England?"

"I was really hoping you wouldn't."

"Thank God!" she said, throwing herself into his open arms. And she had that same feeling, the one she'd had the first time she kissed him.

He was the one.

She was exactly where she was supposed to be.

His whole body seemed to sigh with relief, and he rested his chin on the top of her head. "I love you, Victoria."

She squeezed him, thinking, you are not going to cry, you big dope. But a tear rolled down her cheek anyway. "I love you, too."

"I'm sorry it took me so long to come to my senses."

"You know what they say. The things we have to work hardest for, we end up appreciating more." It sure made her appreciate him.

"Since you're not going to London, how would you feel about that position at the Royal Inn."

She looked up at him and grinned. "When do I start?"

"I'll talk to Ethan tomorrow." He lowered his head, rubbed his nose against hers. "You realize this means you'll have to deal with my mother a lot more now. She's going to go into anaphylactic shock when she hears I'm finally settling down. Which reminds me…" He rifled around in his pocket. "You want to give me a little room, so I can do this right?"

She backed away from him, wondering what he was up to now, then she saw the small velvet box resting in his palm. Then he actually lowered himself down on *one knee*.

Oh, my God.

He flipped the box open and in a bed of royal blue velvet sat a diamond ring that made her gasp. Not only was the stone enormous, but it sparkled like a star in the northern sky.

"It's beautiful."

"It was my grandmother's," he said. "Given to me when she died, to give to the woman I chose to be my wife. And until I met you, I didn't think there was a finger in the world I would ever want to place it."

That was, by far, the sweetest thing anyone had ever said to her. And she was pathetically close to a complete emotional meltdown. Her head was spinning and her hands were trembling and she had a lump in her throat the size of small continent.

"Victoria, will you marry me?"

She knew if she dared utter a sound she would dissolve into tears, so she did the next best thing.

She dropped to her knees, threw her arms around Charles and hugged him.

He laughed and held her tight. "I'll take that as a yes."

* * * * *

ROYAL SEDUCER

BY
MICHELLE CELMER

To Nancy

One

Melissa Thornsby never got nervous.

She'd been raised in the pretentious and oftentimes eccentric New Orleans high society, where it wasn't all that uncommon to check one's back and occasionally find a knife or two sticking out. But that was par for the course.

After Katrina, she'd started a foundation to rebuild the city, and when she met presidents, past and present, actors, musicians and other celebrities eager to "do the right thing," it was just another day at the office.

Even when she'd learned she was the illegitimate princess of the country of Morgan Isle and made the decision to move there permanently to be with a family that was, to put it mildly, suspicious of her motives, she barely broke a sweat. She took her late mother's advice and viewed it as an adventure.

So, visiting Thomas Isle, the former rival of her native country, and meeting the royal family, really wasn't a big deal.

Until she saw *him.*

He stood on the tarmac of the small private airstrip in the bright afternoon sunshine, flanked by two very frightening-looking bodyguards and a polished black Bentley at the ready. And he was, for lack of a better word, *beautiful.* Tall, fit and well put together in a tailored, charcoal-gray pinstriped suit.

Prince Christian James Ernst Alexander, next in line to the throne of Thomas Isle. Confirmed bachelor and shameless playboy. His photos didn't do him justice.

She descended the steps of the Learjet and the prince approached, flashing her a million-watt stunner of a smile. Her heart leapt up into her throat and a curious tickle of nerves coiled in her belly. Was it too much to hope that he was to be her guide for the duration of her two-week stay? Although in her experience that task was typically left up to the princess since the crown prince was usually busy with slightly more significant tasks, such as preparing to run the entire country.

Flanked by her own equally threatening entourage— the security detail her half brother, King Phillip, insisted she have accompany her—she stepped forward to meet him halfway.

When they were face to face, he nodded his head in

greeting and said, in a voice as rich and as smooth as her favorite gourmet dark chocolate, "Welcome to Thomas Isle, Your Highness."

"Your Highness." She dipped into a curtsey, turning on the Southern-belle charm. "It's an honor to be here."

"The honor is all ours," he said with a lethal smile. Lethal because she could feel it, like a buzz of pure energy, from the roots of her hair to the balls of her feet.

He watched her intently with eyes a striking shade of green, and behind them she could see very clearly a hint of mischief and sly determination. She couldn't help wondering if he'd spent his previous life as a cat.

He noted her security detail and with one brow slightly raised, asked, "Expecting a revolution, Your Highness?"

Nodding to his own "muscle," she answered, "I was going to ask you the same thing."

If the question had been some sort of test, she could see that she'd passed. He grinned, playful and sexy, and the coil of nerves in her gut twisted into a hopeless knot. This really wasn't like her at all. Heaven knows, she was used to men flirting with her. Young and old, rich and poor, and all of them after the ludicrous trust her great-aunt and uncle had left her. But somehow, she didn't think the prince had money on his mind. He was one of the few men she'd met whose wealth exceeded her own. At least, she was assuming it did.

"The bodyguards were King Phillip's idea," she told him.

"Of course, you're welcome to keep them with you," he said, "but it's certainly not necessary."

Phillip had insisted she take the bodyguards with her, but he never said she had to *keep* them there. And call her optimistic, but entrusting her welfare to Prince Christian's staff seemed to her a valuable gesture of good faith. In the vast, stormy history of their two countries, the peace they had adopted was for all practical purposes still in its infancy. And her duty, the way she saw it, was to build on that.

"You'll see that they're flown back safely?" she asked.

He nodded. "Of course, Your Highness."

She cringed inwardly. She still hadn't grown used to the royal title. "Please, call me Melissa."

"Melissa," he said, with that sexy British accent. "I like that."

And she liked the way he said it.

"You can call me Chris. I imagine it best we drop the formalities, seeing as we will be spending a considerable amount of time together the next two weeks."

Would they? Another jolt of nerves sizzled inside her stomach. "Are you to be my guide?" she asked.

"If you're agreeable," he said.

As though she would say *no* to two weeks with a gorgeous and charming prince. She smiled and said, "I look forward to it."

He gestured to the waiting car. "Shall we go?"

She turned to her bodyguards, dismissing them with a simple, "Thank you, gentlemen."

They exchanged an uneasy glance, but remained silent. They knew as well as she did that Phillip would not be happy she'd sent them home.

Oh, well. If there was one thing her new family had learned, it was that she had a mind of her own. As deeply as she longed to be accepted as one of them, to have a real family for the first time since losing her parents, there was only so much of herself she was willing to sacrifice. At thirty-three, in many respects she was too set in her ways to change.

The prince touched her elbow to lead her to the car, and despite the layers of silk and linen of her suit jacket, her skin simmered with warmth. When was the last time she'd felt such a sizzling connection to a man? Or perhaps the better question was, when was the last time she'd let herself? This was as much vacation as business, and it wouldn't hurt to let her hair down and have some fun.

He helped her into the back, and she sank into the rich, butter-soft leather seat. He circled the car and climbed in the opposite side, filling the interior with a warm and delicious scent that left her feeling lightheaded. Were she home, she might have blamed it on the Southern heat, but the temperature here hadn't even topped eighty degrees and there was no humidity to speak of. Warm for mid-June on Thomas Isle, but mild by her standards.

As soon as the doors were closed they were off in the direction of the castle, which couldn't be more than a few minutes away, as they had flown past it just before landing. It appeared massive from the air—dare she say larger than the much more modern palace on Morgan Isle—and seemed to have acres of emerald-green lawns, ornately patterned gardens, and even a shrubbery maze.

A passionate lover of nature, she could hardly wait to explore it all. Her mother had been an avid gardener. Melissa's childhood home on Morgan Isle was renowned for its award-winning gardens, and she'd carried on the tradition at her own estate in New Orleans. Though it had been hard to leave that and move back to Morgan Isle, the U.S. had never really been her home. Since losing her parents, she had never felt as though she truly belonged anywhere.

"My parents, the king and queen, are anxious to meet you," Chris said.

"The feeling is mutual." She turned to him and realized he was studying her, a curious look on his face. "What?"

"Your accent," he said. "I can't quite place it."

"That's because it's a mishmash of different dialects. Little bits of every place I've lived pop out occasionally."

"How many different places have you lived?"

"Let's see…" she counted off on her fingers. "I lived on Morgan Isle until I was ten, then I relocated to New Orleans, then it was off to boarding school in France and summers in California, then college on the east coast, then back to New Orleans."

"Sounds exciting," he said.

One would think so, but really all she had ever wanted was to settle down, stay in one place. Of course, when she finally had, it just hadn't felt…right. She'd thought that moving back to Morgan Isle would give her the sense of home and family she had been longing for, but she'd been disappointed to find that despite it being her true home, she still felt like an outsider. It left her wondering if she would ever fit in anywhere.

"How about you?" she asked the prince.

"My diplomatic travels have taken me all over the world, but I've never lived anywhere but here, with my family."

She detected a vague note of exasperation in his tone. To her it sounded wonderful. After her parents died, she had been shuttled to the States to live with her great-aunt and uncle, who had little concept of family. Childless by choice, they saw their orphaned great-niece as more of an interloper than a part of the family. They wasted little time shipping her off to boarding school for her education and camp for the summers. Not that she blamed them. They'd done the best they could. Had they chosen not to take her in she would have become a ward of the state, and who knows where she would be today.

Melissa became aware that the car was climbing, and she knew that they were nearly there. Then the trees cleared and there sat the royal castle, like a scene from a child's picture book, high on a cliff overlooking the ocean and hovering like a sentinel above a charming village below. Far less modern than Morgan Isle, she thought with a tug of pride, but magnificent nonetheless.

She felt a little as though she had been thrown back into a past century.

From what she'd learned in her research, where Morgan Isle was modern and forward-thinking—a flourishing and expanding resort community—Thomas Isle was traditional and private. Most of their economy was based on export, primarily fishing and organic farming. Some considered it archaic, but she saw it as quaint and charming.

"It's magnificent," she told him, gazing up from the car window.

"Do you know the history between our two countries?"

"Only that they've been rivals for many years."

"It's a fascinating story. Were you aware that both islands used to be ruled by one family? A king and queen with two sons. Twins, born only minutes apart."

"Their names wouldn't have been Thomas and Morgan, would they?"

He smiled. "In fact, they were. When the king died, the princes became ensnared in a battle over who would be become the next ruler. They each felt they deserved the title. When an accord couldn't be reached, one challenged the other to a duel." He paused for dramatic effect. "To the death.

"The survivor would reign as king. But their mother couldn't bear the thought of losing either one of them, and begged them not to fight. She suggested a compromise. They could split the kingdom by each taking one of the islands. They agreed, but their discord was so bitter, they never spoke again."

"That's so sad."

"To spite the other, each chose his own name for his island. Their subjects, as a show of loyalty to their respective kings, were banned from visiting the island on which they didn't reside, or even communicating with its people. Many families were broken and businesses ruined."

"What about the queen? Which island did she choose?"

"She refused to choose between her sons and was banished from both islands."

She pressed a hand to her heart. "Oh, my goodness, how awful!" How could they banish their own mother?

"It took hundreds of years to put our history behind us," he said. "That's why it's so important that we maintain accord between our two countries. Joining our resources could benefit both our islands. Both of our societies. Both of our families."

"King Phillip feels the same way," she assured him. "That's why I'm here."

"I'm relieved to hear that. Matters such as these have the potential to be very…awkward."

"I'm a go-with-the-flow princess," she said, which was true, for the most part. "However, I take my new role very seriously. Anything for the good of the country."

He flashed her another one of those sizzling smiles. "Then I'm sure we'll get along quite well."

The car pulled up the drive to the gates, where a mob of press waited with microphones poised and cameras at the ready.

The gates swung open and guards in formal uniform

stepped forward to control the crowd. The car continued on past a stone wall that seemed to extend miles in
each direction, and what she saw on the other side took
her breath away. Everything looked green and vibrant,
and the castle itself was a towering edifice of stone and
mortar and ornate stained-glass windows, all meticulously maintained and preserved.

"Welcome to Sparrowfax Castle," Chris said.

It was clear, as they rounded the drive and she saw
the royal family and what appeared to be the entire staff
lined up awaiting their arrival, that they were pulling out
all of the royal stops. That annoying knot of nerves
coiled even tighter in her belly.

This sure seemed liked a lot of trouble to go to for a
simple diplomatic visit. Yet she couldn't let herself
forget how important this was to her family and country,
which would mean watching her behavior. Particularly
biting her sharp Southern tongue that sometimes had a
mind of its own.

As the car slowed to a halt, footmen in royal dress
approached to open the doors. Melissa took the prof-
fered hand thrust her way and rose from the back seat,
feeling underdressed in her basic linen suit. The family
was dressed and poised to receive royalty—which she
had to remind herself, *she was*—and for the first time
in her adult life she felt apprehensive about her suitability.

Chris's parents, the king and queen, stepped forward
to greet her. Though getting up in years, they appeared

healthy and vibrant. Their other children, Chris's brother and twin sisters, were as breathtakingly attractive as their sibling. What a privilege it would be, Melissa mused, to belong to such a beautiful family. It was a wonder that all of them had yet to marry.

Good looks, however, were only a fraction of a much larger picture. For all she knew they could be rude and unfriendly.

Chris appeared at her side, and though it was silly, his presence seemed to have a calming effect on her.

"All this for me?" she asked.

Her question seemed to perplex him. "Of course. You're an honored guest. Your visit marks a new era for both of our kingdoms."

Little ol' me? She hadn't realized her visit would be seen as quite that big of a deal. Her own family hadn't put up close to this much fuss when she'd come home to her native land. In fact, there hadn't been any fuss at all. Her return to Morgan Isle had been very hush-hush, to avoid a media frenzy.

But it wasn't as though she was going to complain. What woman didn't enjoy a little ego-stroking every now and then?

Chris offered his arm. "Are you ready to meet my family?"

She looped her arm through his, finding his solid warmth a decadent treat. And a comfort. He made her feel…safe.

She smiled up at him and nodded. Back in New

Orleans she sat at the very top of the social food chain. But none of that carried much weight here, where she was known only as the illegitimate daughter of the late King Frederick.

And she suspected that for the rest of her life no one would let her forget it.

Two

Within five minutes of meeting her, Chris suspected that he and Princess Melissa would get along quite well.

Though he typically preferred blondes, Melissa's dark hair and eyes and her warm complexion were unexpectedly exotic and appealing. She was not only attractive and seemingly pleasant, but as had been suggested by King Phillip, she had a resilient personality and a sharp wit. Traits some might find undesirable, but a necessity for the type of arrangement they were considering.

He walked her over to his family to start the introductions. It had already been determined how everyone was to behave. It was imperative they make her feel welcome.

"Melissa, I would like to introduce you to my parents, the king and queen of Thomas Isle."

Melissa curtsied and said, "It's an honor, Your Majesties."

His mother took her hand and said warmly, "The honor is ours, Melissa. We're so happy that you could visit us."

"I hope we find it mutually beneficial," his father said, his tone serious.

"I'm certain we will," Melissa answered with a warm smile.

The king cast Chris a sideways glance, one that conveyed the message *don't screw this up.* Despite his past resistance when it came to the idea of settling down, even Chris couldn't deny that an alliance with the royals of Morgan Isle would be a smart move. Politically and financially.

"Meet my brother and sisters," Chris said, introducing them each in turn. "Prince Aaron Felix Gastel, and princesses Anne Charlotte Amalia and Louisa Josephine Elisabeth."

"It's a pleasure to meet you all," Melissa said. She shook each of their hands, and just as planned, they all greeted her warmly. Aaron was simply relieved that it was Chris in this position and not himself, though at thirty-one he should have been ready for the responsibility.

Louisa, the younger fraternal twin by five minutes, greeted Melissa with her usual bubbly enthusiasm. From the time that she was a small child, Louisa loved everyone, often to her own detriment. Her siblings had spent a good deal of time sheltering her from harm.

Anne was the older and more cautious twin. Too many times her trust had been betrayed by people she had mistakenly considered her friends. But even she put her best foot forward and welcomed Melissa warmly. She, like everyone else, knew how important it was that this visit go smoothly.

The introductions complete, Chris gestured to the maid who would tend to Melissa for the duration of her trip.

"Elise, would you please show our guest to her quarters?" Then he asked Melissa, "How much time do you need to settle in?"

"Not long," she said, a light of excitement flashing in the dark depths of her eyes. "I'm anxious to see the gardens. They looked decadent from the air."

"Then that's where we'll begin," he told her. "Will an hour suffice?"

She nodded. "I'll expect you in an hour."

Elise stepped forward, curtsied, and said, "This way, Your Highness."

When they disappeared inside the castle and out of earshot, and the staff was dismissed to resume their duties, everyone seemed to let out a collective breath of relief.

"I think that went quite well," his mother said.

And from his father, "Have you discussed it with her?"

Chris refrained from rolling his eyes and struggled to keep the exasperation from his voice. "Of course not, Father. We've only just met."

His mother shot her husband a sharp look. "Give it time, James." Then she told Chris, "Take all the time you need, dear. A decision like this shouldn't be rushed. But I do have to say, I think she's lovely."

"Although illegitimate," the king reminded her.

"That's hardly her fault," she snapped back. "Besides, what family doesn't have its share of scandal? And *secrets*."

"Just some more than others," Aaron quipped, receiving a stern look from the his mother.

"Well, I like her," Louisa bubbled.

Anne shot her an exasperated look. "You like *everyone*."

"Not *everyone*. But I really like Melissa, and I'm an excellent judge of character."

Actually, Louisa was a rotten judge of character, but Chris hoped in this case she was right.

"We all have to remember to be on our best behavior," their mother said firmly. "Make her feel welcome." She took Chris's hands in hers and gave them a squeeze. "I think this might be the one, dear."

Though at first he had resisted, now Chris was inclined to agree.

He was quite sure already that Melissa would make a suitable wife.

"We need to talk," Aaron said quietly to Chris as the rest of the family dispersed.

Chris nodded and followed his brother away from the castle, where they could speak in private. "Is there a problem?"

"There might be," Aaron said, brow wrinkled with concern, which wasn't at all like him. It took a lot to put a frown on his face.

"Something about Melissa?"

Aaron shook his head. "No, no, nothing like that. I had an urgent message from the foreman of the east fields, saying he needed to see me as soon as possible. So I drove down there this morning."

The east fields, which made up close to a third of the royal family's vast acreage, was used primarily to grow soy and housed the largest of their research and greenhouse facilities. "What did he want?"

"There's some sort of disease causing a blight on the crops. A strain he doesn't recognize."

Due to the organic nature of their business, disease and insect infestations were at times a concern. "Is it treatable?"

"He's tried several methods, but so far it appears resistant. He called in a botanist from the university who he believes will be able to help. But at the rate it's spreading, we could lose half of the crop. Maybe more."

Which would be unfortunate, but not a devastating loss. Unless it spread. "You say it's confined to the east fields?"

"So far, yes."

"And there have been no problems reported from local farmers?"

"None that I've heard."

"Good. Lets try to keep it that way. The last thing we

need right now is an epidemic. Or the fear of one."
Which could be just as damaging. The timing couldn't
be worse. "And we shouldn't burden Father with this.
Not until it's absolutely necessary."

"I'll see that the situation is handled discreetly,"
Aaron assured him. "Although if it begins to spread we'll
have no choice but to post a countrywide bulletin."

"Let's hope it doesn't come to that." This alliance
with the royal family of Morgan Isle depended on a
stable economy and strong leadership. Their father's
health issues were a closely guarded secret known only
to the family and the king's personal physician. And
Chris intended to keep it that way. If he was to become
king, sooner rather than later as the case might be, he
needed a strong base on which to build.

"Try not to worry about it. Concentrate on your
princess." Aaron flashed Chris a sly grin. "Not that it
will be much of a hardship. She's very attractive."

"And just think, once I'm married off, you'll be next."

Aaron snorted out a rueful laugh. "I wouldn't hold
your breath. Only the crown prince is required to marry
and have an heir."

"That won't stop Mother from setting you up with
every eligible female on the island."

"She knows better."

Chris laughed and said, "You keep telling yourself
that. But mark my words, the instant I'm spoken for,
you'll be next."

Aaron glared at him. "Don't you have a princess to seduce?"

He did, and seduce her was exactly what he planned to do.

The interior of the castle was even more magnificent than the exterior.

As the maid led Melissa up to the room she would occupy for the duration of her visit, she took in with sheer wonder the high, ornately scribed ceilings and tall stained-glass windows, the authentic period furniture, magnificent tapestries and rich oriental rugs over gleaming polished wood and inlaid marble floors. On the walls hung amazing works of art, landscapes and portraits and even a few abstracts.

In New Orleans she'd seen many magnificent residences—her own estate had been highlighted in its share of newspaper and magazine articles—and the palace on Morgan Isle was the pinnacle of luxury and style. Yet none could compare to the grandeur of Sparrowfax Castle. Though she had anticipated a dark, dank atmosphere—it was after all built of stone and mortar—it was surprisingly bright and airy, her own room included.

While her things were unpacked, she took some time to change and freshen her makeup, then investigate her chamber. It wasn't a terribly large room, maybe only a third the size of her suite at the palace. But what it lacked in size, it made up for in luxury. The furnishings were rich and traditional, authentic to the period and meticulously preserved.

The bathroom was enormous and updated with all the modern amenities, including a whirlpool tub and three-headed shower. The stall, she noticed, was big enough for two. And she was sure that as good as Chris looked in his clothes, he probably looked better out of them.

Don't get ahead of yourself, Mel.

She unpacked her laptop, booted it up, and typed in her password, scanning for a wireless signal. Her family expected daily updates on her visit and trusted encrypted e-mails over a cellular line that could easily be intercepted. Not that Mel expected they would be doing espionage, but she supposed one could never be too careful.

She established a link and opened her e-mail program, addressing a note to Phillip. She wrote:

Arrived safely. Greeted warmly. Nothing to report yet.

A knock sounded at her door, so she hit Send and snapped her laptop shut. She crossed the room and opened the door.

Chris stood on the other side. He had changed out of his suit into dark slacks and a black silk dress shirt.

He looked delicious. Dark and sexy and a little mysterious.

"I hope I'm not interrupting," he said.

"Of course not." She flashed him a warm smile, and

noticed the way his eyes roamed slowly over her with no shame or hesitation, taking in the gauzy silk dress she had changed into. The deep, warm blue enhanced the gray of her eyes. She'd also let her hair down and brushed it out until it hung in rich, dark waves down her back.

She looked damned good, and it didn't go unnoticed.

"You look lovely," he said, heat flickering in the depths of his eyes like emerald flames. "How fortunate I am to have the privilege of spending the next two weeks with such a beautiful woman."

His words made her feel weak in the knees, and she was tempted to say *You're not so shabby yourself.* But she should at least play a little hard to get. Instead she batted her lashes and turned on the Southern charm. "You flatter me, Your Highness."

He grinned like a sly, hungry wolf anticipating his next meal. And, oh, how she hoped he would sink those pearly whites into her.

"Is the room satisfactory?" he asked.

"Quite," she said. "What I've seen of the castle is breathtaking."

"Are you ready to see the gardens?"

More than he could imagine. "I'd love to."

He offered his arm for her to take, and she slid hers through it. Again she felt that exciting little rush of awareness. That tingle of attraction. And she could tell by the heat in his gaze that he felt it, too.

He led her downstairs, gesturing to points of interest along the way. Family heirlooms that dated back hun-

dreds of years, gifted to the royal family from friends
and relatives and neighboring kingdoms. Melissa had so
little left of her own family. After her mother and the
man she'd known as her father had been killed, her aunt
and uncle had seen that all of their possessions had been
auctioned off and the proceeds put in a trust. But Mel
would have preferred their possessions, something to
remember them by, more than all the money in the
world.

She didn't even have the albums of photographs and
scrapbooks her mother had meticulously kept. They had
probably been tossed in the trash, deemed useless. The
only reminder Melissa had of her parents was a single
4x6 snapshot of the three of them taken only weeks
before their accident.

"It must be wonderful to be so connected to your
family," she said. "To be so close."

He shrugged. "It all depends on how you look at it,
I suppose."

"Well, it looks pretty good to me." She had hoped to
rediscover that closeness, that sense of continuity with
her half siblings, yet something was missing. Though
they made an effort to include her, she still felt like an
outsider. And maybe she always would.

She was the oldest, and illegitimate or not, technically, she had a rightful claim to the crown. But despite
signing documents swearing that she would never challenge Phillip's position as ruler, she didn't think they
were ready to trust her. Maybe someday.

Then again, maybe not.

Chris led her through an enormous great room and out a rear door onto a slate patio bordered by a meticulously tended perennial garden so alive with color its beauty made her gasp.

"It's amazing," she said. On the patio sat a variety of chairs, chaise longues and wrought-iron tables. She could just imagine herself out there in the morning, drinking coffee, or lounging in the afternoon, reading a book. She closed her eyes and breathed in the salty tang of ocean air, could hear the waves in the distance, lapping against the rocky bluff.

It felt like paradise.

"Do you spend much time out here?" she asked him.

He shook his head. "It's mostly used for entertaining. Although you might occasionally find Louisa out here practicing yoga."

If she lived in the castle, Melissa would be out here every day, weather permitting. Although that was easy to say. She hadn't spent nearly as much time as she would have liked in her gardens at her New Orleans estate. There always seemed to be more pressing business that needed tending.

"Can we walk to the bluff?" she asked.

"Of course." He offered his arm and they walked down a twisting sandstone path that wound its way through the gardens. His knowledge of the different varieties of flowers and shrubs impressed her, as did the steady strength of his arm, and his solid presence beside her.

She'd never been what one would consider a fading flower, she could hold her own in almost any given situation, but even she liked to be pampered every now and then.

"Can I ask you a personal question, Melissa?"

She didn't have to wait for the question to know what was on his mind. She could hear it in his tone, see the curiosity in his eyes.

She'd been getting that same look from many people lately.

"Let me guess. You're wondering if it was a shock to learn that I was an illegitimate royal?"

He grinned. "Something like that."

Her illegitimacy wasn't something Melissa tried to hide, or felt she should be ashamed of. After all, how could she be responsible for the actions of a mother she'd lost twenty-three years ago, and a father she had never even known? Nor was she shy about discussing it. Why attempt to hide something everyone already knew? It would only sit like the proverbial elephant in the room. She was who she was, and people either accepted her or they didn't. Loved her or hated her.

"I felt as though I'd been caught up in some surreal sequel to *The Princess Diaries*," she said.

His eyes crinkled with confusion. *"Princess Diaries?"*

"Suffice it to say, I was flabbergasted. I had no idea that I wasn't my father's daughter."

"Did it upset you that your parents never told you the truth?"

"On some level. But honestly, I have little room to

complain. If my father knew I wasn't his, he never let it show. I had an extremely happy childhood. And my real father…well, I honestly think he did me a favor by staying out of my life. Although after my parents died it would have been nice if he'd claimed me. But I understand why he didn't."

"Life after your parents passed away wasn't so happy?"

The directness of his question surprised her a bit. Most people tiptoed around the subject of her parents' deaths. It seemed almost as though he was testing her. Seeing how tough she was.

"To quote Nietzsche," she said "'That which does not kill me makes me stronger.'"

Chris smiled. "I believe he also said, 'No price is too high to pay for the privilege of owning yourself'."

And she did own herself. Despite everything that had happened, she was in control of her own life. Her own destiny. And she intended to keep it that way.

The path ended and the gardens opened up to a rocky bluff that seemed to stretch for miles in either direction. Over its edge was nothing but cloudless sky and calm blue ocean, and farther in the distance, the coast of Morgan Isle. Fishing boats dotted the expanse that lay between the two islands, and closer to the Morgan Isle shore she could just make out the luxury craft common to the tourist trade.

She toed closer to the edge and peeked over the side, to the jagged rocks below. It was a *long* way down. At least three or four stories, with no discernible beach that she could make out in either direction. She looked back at Chris. "Is there a path down?"

He shook his head. "Not for miles. It's a straight drop down to the water. Tactically speaking, it was the perfect place for my ancestors to build the castle. Invading forces would have been forced to dock their ships miles down the coast."

She leaned farther over, trying to see the sharp incline of the cliff wall.

"Be careful," he said, concern in his voice.

"I'm always careful." At least, *almost* always.

"Not afraid of heights, I guess."

She shrugged and backed away from the edge. "Not afraid of anything, really."

He regarded her curiously. "Everyone is afraid of *something*."

She though about it for a moment, then said, "Centipedes."

He grinned. "Centipedes?"

"All those legs." She shuddered. "They give me a serious case of the creeps."

"Well, then, you have nothing to fear here," he said, offering his arm and leading her back toward the castle. "We don't see many centipedes."

There was one other thing she feared. Feared it more than a stampede of creepy centipedes.

She was afraid she might fall for Prince Christian. Then get her heart broken as she had so many times before.

Three

Chris and Melissa strolled slowly back to the castle, she a soft and comfortable presence beside him. They chatted about the weather and the flowers and the different crops they grew on the island. She had an insatiable curiosity about practically everything, and always looked genuinely interested in his answers and explanations. But when he led her past the shrubbery maze, her eyes all but shimmered with excitement. She stopped him just outside the entrance. "It's taller than it looks from the air."

"Three meters, give or take," Chris said. "It takes an entire crew a full day to manicure."

"I'm sure it's worth it."

"This maze has been standing here, unchanged, for hundreds of years."

Her eyes filled with mischief. "Could we go inside?"

"You'd like me to lead you through?"

"Oh, no, I'll figure it out myself."

Chris looked at his watch. "Unfortunately, there's no time. We're to meet with my parents for drinks before supper."

"How long does it usually take?"

"Drinks or supper?"

She laughed. "No, the maze."

"If you know your way, not long. Ten minutes, maybe. For the novice, though, it's easy to get turned around. I've seen people wander through there for hours."

She shot him a cocky smile. "I'll bet I could figure it out in no time."

"It's more confusing than you might think."

"I have a very good sense of direction. And I like a challenge."

He didn't doubt that she did. She certainly had spunk. He liked that about her. In his opinion, it took a strong and independent woman to withstand a marriage of convenience. Melissa seemed to have what it would take. He hoped she felt the same way.

"Just in case, I think it should wait."

She looked disappointed, but she didn't push the issue. Duty was duty, and she seemed to embrace the concept. One more trait in her favor.

"Tomorrow, then?" she asked.

"Of course."

She gazed up at him through a curtain of thick, dark lashes, a wicked smile teasing the corners of her lips. "You promise?"

"I'm a man of my word," he said.

"I'm sure you've heard the saying 'Chivalry is dead.'"

"Not on Morgan Isle it isn't." He gazed down at her, into the smoky depths of her eyes, and swore he could see a shadow of apprehension. Maybe even sorrow. Then it was gone.

Either he'd imagined it, or she wasn't as tough as she wanted people to believe.

"Now," he said, "are you ready to have drinks with my parents?"

"I guess so." She took a long, deep breath, and blew it out. Then asked, "Anything I should know beforehand? It's important that I make a good impression."

"Just be yourself and I know they'll find you as enchanting and interesting as I do."

He could see from her smile that she appreciated his answer.

"I like you, Your Highness."

He returned the smile. "I would have to say, that's a very good thing."

"Why is that?"

"Because, Princess, I like you, too."

As Melissa had suspected, "drinks with the king and queen" was code for a thorough grilling by not only Chris's parents, but his brother and sisters as well. They

seemed to want to know all about her and her half
siblings, and the country of Morgan Isle. And they
weren't shy about asking. She tried to answer their questions as honestly as possible without giving away too
much, or in some cases, too little. She had been with her
new family such a short time that in some cases she
simply didn't know the answers.

Dinner was a five-course feast of seafood caught off
their own shores, organic vegetables from the royal
family's personal garden and bread baked fresh from
wheat grown in their own fields. They followed it up
with a dessert that was so mouthwateringly delicious
Melissa was tempted to ask for seconds.

Though she had never been one to choose organic or
natural products, it really did make a difference. She
would go so far as to say it was one of the tastiest,
freshest meals she'd ever eaten.

It was nine-thirty by the time dinner was over and she
thoroughly expected another round of drinks, and very
possibly more questions. Instead, Chris's parents excused themselves to their quarters. The king did look exhausted, but she supposed that was only natural when
she considered that he spent his days running an entire
country. And though he didn't exactly have one foot in
the grave, he was no kid, either. In his late sixties would
be her guess, but she wasn't rude enough to ask.

She also didn't miss the way his children seemed to
coddle him. The fleeting and furtive looks of concern
they would direct his way when they thought no one was

looking. She couldn't escape the feeling that there was something going on with his royal highness. Something they didn't want her to know.

Everyone said their good-nights, his brother and sisters included—although she doubted they all actually went to bed this early—and Chris walked her to her room.

"Everyone retires early here," she said when they stopped outside her door.

He leaned against the doorjamb. "Our primary business is farming. Early to bed, early to rise."

"In New Orleans, if I was in bed by one it was an early night. It's a totally different culture."

"To be honest," he said, "I've always been something of a night owl myself."

"Would you like to come in for a while?" she asked, gesturing inside her room. "We could have a drink and…talk."

He looked past her into the bedroom. A single lamp burned beside the bed and the maid had turned down the covers. There was no denying that it looked awfully inviting. "I'd like to, but I shouldn't."

"Tired of me already?" she teased.

"Quite the opposite." He took a step closer, his eyes simmering with desire. "If I allow myself to come into your room tonight, you know as well as I that we'll be doing much more than just talking. Is that what you want?"

Though a part of her wanted to say *yes*—the curious, reckless, and let's face it, *lonely* part—she knew it wouldn't be right. She'd met him only a few hours ago.

Shouldn't she at least get to know him a little before she let her hormones call the shots? Before she gave in to the inevitable? Because she knew without a doubt that sometime before she flew home to Morgan Isle, she would sleep with Chris.

But not tonight.

"No, I guess not." She took a step back from him, from the heady pull of attraction that would instead have her wrapping her arms around his neck and pulling him closer for a long, deep kiss.

He looked disappointed, but not at all surprised. "I thought we would take a tour of the island tomorrow. See the village and the fields we control."

She smiled. "I'd like that."

"Shall we have breakfast first? Say, eight o'clock. If that's not too early."

She doubted she'd be able to sleep late, if she slept at all. She smiled. "I'd like that."

"Good night, Melissa. Sleep well."

"Good night, Chris."

He took her hand in his and lifted it to his lips, brushing a soft kiss against it, and for an instant she thought he might take her in his arms and kiss her anyway, then he let go of her hand and backed away. He flashed her one last dark, sizzling smile, then disappeared down the hallway.

She closed the door and leaned against it.

Wow.

Her heart pounded and she felt drunk on the sensation of his lips against her skin. If she did sleep, she had no doubt whatsoever that she would dream of him.

She changed into her favorite silk nightgown—which also happened to be her sexiest, since one never knew—and because she wasn't the least bit sleepy, booted up her laptop to check her e-mail.

There was one from Phillip. It said simply:

Have you spoken with the king and queen?

No *How was your trip,* or *Are you having fun?* He didn't even ask why she'd sent the bodyguards home.

She couldn't help but feel he was relieved that she was gone. Which could very well be her imagination. Phillip was not what anyone could call warm and fuzzy. He was, she imagined, very much like their father. With the exception of his sleeping habits.

As in, Phillip was faithful to his wife, while their father, it seemed, hadn't been able to keep it in his pants.

She hit Reply and typed up a quick e-mail, giving Phillip a brief rundown on her visit so far. Leaving out the part about almost shacking up with Prince Christian. Phillip wanted her to become well acquainted with the royal family of Thomas Isle, particularly their future leader, but she didn't think he meant *that* well.

She'd never been one to sleep around, though that was not to say she was a prude in any respect, but maybe there was more of her father in her than she cared to admit.

She sent the e-mail and, with nothing better to do, opened her favorite card game, but after fifteen minutes or so was bored to tears. She tried curling up in bed and reading the book she'd brought along with her, but she couldn't concentrate.

She called down to the kitchen for a cup of herbal tea, but not even that would quiet her nerves. Back home in New Orleans, a stroll in the garden under the moon and the stars was usually the most effective cure for a sleepless night. She doubted anyone would mind if she took a quick walk. Besides, how would they even know? Unlike her, they were all soundly sleeping.

She slipped on her robe and opened her door, peering out into the hall. In the palace on Morgan Isle, it seemed there was always some sort of activity going on, day or night, whether it was midnight bottle feedings or diaper changes, or the guards' nightly rounds of the premises. In contrast, the castle was quiet and dark.

Melissa stepped into the hall and quietly made her way down the stairs and through the castle to the patio door. She slipped outside onto the patio, the slate smooth against her bare feet. The air was cool and damp, and the full moon cast a silver, ghostly glow across the land. In the distance she could hear the *whoosh* of the ocean against the bluff, but otherwise the night was eerily still.

To the east, just beyond the garden, stood the shrubbery maze, looking ominous in the dark. Yet it seemed to beckon her. If it was a challenge during the day, think of the thrill it would be to guess her way through with only the moon to light her way.

She glanced back at the castle, dark and still, and figured, *why the heck not?* This was supposed to be a

vacation. And what was the worst that could happen?
She would get lost and wander around in there all night.

She stepped off the patio onto the cool, damp grass
and cut across the lawn to the entrance of the maze, her
heart thumping a little faster with excitement.

Here goes nothin'.

She stepped forward and the maze swallowed her
into its depths like a hungry animal. Inside it was dark
and serene, and the towering greenery seemed to muffle
all sound beyond its walls.

She waited for her eyes to adjust, until she could see
the first turn ahead of her. She stepped forward, deeper
inside, the grass cool and slippery under her feet. She
turned the first corner to find herself at the end of a long,
ominous-looking passageway. Memorizing her steps in
case she needed to back her way out later, she walked
slowly forward. Halfway through she encountered
another passageway that hooked off to the right. Should
she maintain her present course, or turn down a path that
would take her deeper inside?

The adventurer in her said go deeper.

She turned and followed the passage, but after a few
yards she reached a T in the path. Should she go right,
or left? Logic dictated that turning right would put her
on course for a dead end, so she went left instead.

Behind her she swore she heard a rustling, but when
she turned to look, there was nothing there. Probably
just a bat, or some small animal. She shrugged and continued on through a few more twists and turns until she

reached another T. This time she chose right. She heard another noise, a distinct rustling of branches, but this time it seemed to be coming from in front of her. She strained to see in the dim light, and could swear she saw a dark figure cross the path somewhere in front of her.

Her imagination? A trick of the light?

Curious, she forged ahead, turning the same direction as the figure had, and found herself at a dead end. There wasn't anyone or anything there.

That was odd. She felt around, looking for some sort of secret passage. There was nothing but solid branches, far too thick and brittle to slip through. Then she heard the rustling again, this time from directly behind her.

She spun around, but there was no one there. Yet she had the distinct feeling she wasn't alone. "Hello?" she called. "Is someone there?"

There was another rustle, then the dark figure passed the T junction just ahead of her. It was too dark to tell who it was, or even if it was a man or a woman.

She darted after the ghostly figure, determined to catch up. But it seemed as though no matter how swiftly she moved, he or she was always rounding the next corner, out of sight before she could get very close. Whoever it was, they obviously knew the maze well. They had lured Melissa deep inside, and she'd been concentrating so hard on following him or her, she hadn't been memorizing her steps. Now she had no idea how to get out.

She suspected that had been the intention all along.

Whoever it was, he was taunting her. Trying to throw her off track, and it had worked. She was hopelessly turned around. And of course, her ghostly figure had chosen that moment to disappear without a trace.

"Swell," she mumbled to herself. She wandered around for another twenty minutes or so trying to get her bearings, hearing an occasional rustle in the leaves, sometimes in front of her, sometimes behind. If this was some sort of test, she was failing miserably. She strained to hear the ocean, to get a bearing on her direction, but it was useless, and since the idea of wandering around in there all night held little to no appeal, she threw in the towel.

"You win," she called. "I surrender."

"I told you it was confusing," a voice said softly into her ear.

She spun around and crashed into the wall of one very long, solid and—oh, Lord—blissfully bare chest.

Chris's chest.

Four

Melissa was so surprised she nearly toppled over backward. Chris grabbed her arms to steady her, the heat of his hands searing her through the thin silk of her robe. He wore a playful, slightly cocky grin that she felt all the way through to the center of her bones.

"What are you doing out here?" she asked.

"I was just about to ask you the same thing."

"I couldn't sleep. I decided to go for a walk."

"In the middle of the night?" His eyes raked over her and the gentle pressure on her arms increased. "In your night clothes?"

"I didn't expect to run into anyone." She didn't bother to point out that in baggy PJ bottoms and no shirt he wasn't exactly overdressed either. And it was taking all of her concentration not to stare at his smooth, muscular, *magnificent* chest. "I just assumed everyone had gone to sleep."

"I'm sure everyone else has."

"Except you."

"I was working. I saw you from my bedroom window. When you went into the maze, I worried you might get lost."

She doubted that. "Actually, I was doing just fine until someone got me all confused and turned around."

His teeth flashed white in the dark as he smiled. "Most people aren't brave enough to venture in here at night."

She shrugged. "What's the worst that could happen?"

"Giant, man-eating centipedes?" he suggested, then a sly smile curled his lips. "And there's always me."

"You?"

"You barely know me. I could be dangerous."

Only to her heart.

She smiled up at him. "Somehow I doubt that."

"You never know." His hands slid up to her shoulders, caressing her through the delicate, slippery silk. "I might try to take advantage of you. There's no one here to stop me."

"What if I didn't want you to stop?" She reached up and pressed her palms against the solid warmth of his chest, felt his heart thumping under warm skin and sinew. "Who knows? I might even take advantage of *you*."

Even in the dim light she could see flames of desire flicker in his eyes. His gaze settled on her mouth, making her lips feel swollen and warm. Her heart began to beat double time and her skin felt tingly and alive. She knew instinctively that he would be an accomplished lover. Probably because she'd known so many who weren't.

You're moving too fast, her subconscious warned her. She barely knew Chris, yet already she was sure that before she returned to Morgan Isle, she would be getting to know him a lot better. Maybe it was destiny. Or fate.

"Since the minute you stepped off that plane, I've thought of little else but kissing you, Melissa," he said, so close she could feel the whisper of his breath on her cheek. And, oh, how she loved that accent. When he spoke her name it gave her warm shivers.

A proper Southern belle would tease awhile, play hard to get. But she never had been one to play by the rules.

She smiled up at him and said, "So what's stopping you?"

He caressed the side of her face with one large, warm hand while the other slipped through her hair to delicately cradle the back of her head, as though she were a precious object he worried he might damage.

He lowered his head, leaned in and brushed his lips against hers. So sweet and gentle she went weak in the knees. But she wanted *more.* Every instinct she possessed was screaming that this was right. She wanted all of him, right that second.

She slid her arms around his neck, pulled him closer, deepening the kiss. Being in Chris's arms, feeling his warm hands on her skin, his lips, soft yet firm, on her own, felt like returning home after a long, arduous journey. For the first time since she was a child she felt as though she was exactly where she was supposed to be.

A rush of relief so intense that she felt like weeping washed over her. She'd never felt so vulnerable in her life, and frankly, it scared her to death.

She flattened her palms against his chest and gently pushed, severing their connection. And he knew why instinctively.

"We're going too fast," he said.

She nodded. So much for her brave claims that she might take advantage of him. That she wasn't afraid of anything. Right now she was terrified.

"Maybe I should walk you back up to your room," he said.

"You probably should," she agreed. Another time, another night, maybe she wouldn't tell him no.

"Give me your hand," he said.

She held it out, and he laced his fingers through hers. He led her through the maze and had them out in a few short minutes. They walked together in silence through the castle to her bedroom door.

She opened it, and turned to look at him. "I feel as though I should apologize for the way I acted out there. I'm usually not so forward."

He gave her hand a gentle squeeze. "I should be the one apologizing. I didn't mean to rush things. It's just that when I see something good, I go after it."

So did she. Maybe the problem was that Chris was too good. To perfect to be true.

But wouldn't it be nice if he was everything he seemed to be?

Despite the late night, Chris woke before dawn and for the life of him couldn't get back to sleep. Too much on his mind. Namely Melissa. Things were progressing more quickly than he'd imagined. Than he could have possibly hoped. And he was eager to take it to the next step.

He also had the crops to think about. He'd been doing Internet research last night when he saw Melissa outside. And now that he was awake, he might as well see what else he could find.

He booted up his computer, opened his browser and returned to the site he'd bookmarked—a study of botanical diseases in organic crops—immersing himself in the text.

A while later Aaron poked his head in. "You're up early," he said.

Chris looked at the clock. "It's half past seven."

"Which is early for someone who spent half the night traipsing through the gardens," Aaron said with a cocky grin.

Apparently Aaron hadn't been asleep either. Chris shot him a look. "I don't *traipse*."

"I take it things are moving right along with your princess."

"You might say that." He could see that his brother wanted details, but he wasn't going to get any. And he didn't push the issue.

"Oh, and by the way," Aaron said, "nice e-mail. You have a twisted sense of humor."

Chris didn't recall sending his brother anything lately, much less something that could be defined as twisted. "What e-mail?"

"The one you sent last night. I never knew you were such a poet."

Poet? "Seriously, Aaron, I haven't sent you an e-mail."

Aaron unclipped his cell phone from his belt. He punched a few buttons, then handed it to Chris. "This e-mail."

The address was definitely his. The subject was *Funny,* and the body of the e-mail read:

Eeny Meeny Miny Mo
String Prince Aaron by the toe
Light the fuse and watch him blow
Eeny Meeny Miny Mo

That was rather twisted, and it wasn't from him.

"That's my e-mail address," Chris said. "But I didn't send it."

Aaron frowned, looking perplexed. "Seriously?"

"I would tell you if I did. I've never seen it before."

"Do you think it could have been one of the girls?"

That wasn't Louisa's style, but he wouldn't put it past Anne. "Why don't you ask?"

The words were barely out of his mouth when Anne appeared at his bedroom door. She was still in her pajamas, her long hair pulled back in a ponytail and her face freshly scrubbed. In her hand she clutched a single sheet of paper. When she saw Aaron standing there, she speared daggers with her eyes.

"You're a jerk," she spat.

Aaron looked genuinely stunned. "What the hell did I do?"

She stormed over to him and shoved the paper at his chest.

He read it, his expression grim, then passed it over to Chris.

It was another e-mail with the subject *Funny,* and a similar, twisted version of a child's nursery rhyme:

Anne be nimble
Anne be quick
Anne jump over
The candlestick

Anne jumped high
But lost her foot
She burst to flames
And now she's soot

"I didn't send this," Aaron told Anne.

"Nice try," she snapped back, snatching the paper from Chris and pointing to the header. "It's your e-mail address, genius."

It had indeed come from Aaron's address.

Chris and Aaron exchanged a worried glance. It was disturbing to say the least. It was one thing to receive threatening e-mails, but from their own e-mail addresses?

"I didn't send that, and Chris didn't send this." He showed her the e-mail on his phone.

As she read it, the anger slipped from her face. "What the heck is going on?"

"I'm not sure, but odds are pretty good I got one, too." Chris opened his e-mail program. Sure enough, there was a message with the same subject, *Funny*, and it was sent from Louisa. But the contents were anything but humorous.

Star light, star bright
Crown Prince Christian will ignite
I wish I may, I wish I might
Watch him burst in flames tonight

"Somehow I doubt Louisa sent this," he said, gesturing to his monitor. Aaron and Anne crowded behind his desk to read it.

Aaron raked a hand through his hair. "Is it just me, or is there a theme here?"

"What the bloody hell is going on?" Anne said.

Chris shook his head. "I don't know. But we need to talk to Louisa and see if she got one, too."

"Is she up yet?" Aaron asked.

"If not," Anne said, already heading for the door, "we'll wake her."

Five

Louisa opened her bedroom door, sleepy-eyed and rumpled in pajamas better suited an adolescent than a grown woman, looking surprised to see all of her siblings standing there.

"Have you checked your e-mail this morning?" Anne asked her.

She yawned and rubbed her eyes. "I just woke up. Why?"

"You need to check it," Chris said.

Louisa frowned. "Right now?"

"*Yes,*" Anne shot back. "Right now."

"Fine, you don't have to get snippy." She opened the door so they could all pile into her room, which was still decorated in the pale pink and ruffles of her youth. Typical Louisa. Always a girly girl.

She walked over to her desk and booted up her computer. "Is there anything in particular I should be looking for?"

"An e-mail from one of us," Aaron told her.

"Which one?"

"Probably Anne," Chris said, figuring that everyone else had already been accounted for.

"You're not sure?"

Anne's patience seemed to be wearing thin. "Bloody hell, Louisa. Would you just look for the damned e-mail?"

"My, someone woke up cranky this morning," Louisa mumbled as she opened the program and scrolled through her e-mails. "Here's one from Anne."

"What's the subject?" Aaron asked.

"Funny."

Aaron turned to Chris. "That's it."

Louisa looked up at them. "Should I read it?"

"Please," Chris said. "Out loud, if you wouldn't mind."

Louisa shrugged and double clicked. "It says: I love you, a bushel and a peck. A bushel and a peck, and a noose around your neck." She paused and frowned before continuing. "With a noose around your neck, you will drop into a heap. You'll drop into a heap and forever you will sleep." She looked over at her twin. "Real nice, Anne."

"I didn't send it," Anne said, casting a worried look to Chris and Aaron. "Hanged or burned alive? These are our choices?"

Louisa looked back and forth between the three of them. "Does someone want to tell me what's going on?"

Anne handed her the printout of the e-mail she'd received, and told her about their brothers' similar rhymes.

Louisa shuddered and hugged herself. "That's creepy."

"Maybe it's just a prank," Anne offered.

"But they were sent from our own e-mail addresses," Aaron reminded her. "Personal addresses that few people outside of the family even know. That would be an awfully elaborate prank."

"Should we tell Father?" Louisa asked.

Chris shook his head. "No. At least, not yet. He doesn't need the extra stress."

"He looked tired at supper last night," Anne said. "And he hardly ate a thing. He looks as though he's losing weight."

Chris had noticed that, too. All the more reason not to say anything. He glanced at his watch and saw that it was almost eight. "I think we should take this to the head of security. Aaron, can I trust you to talk to him? I have a breakfast date with our guest. I don't want to give the impression anything is amiss."

Meaning she couldn't spend too much time with the king or she might notice his failing health, and he couldn't take her near the east fields or she might notice the diseased crops, and he certainly couldn't mention the e-mails.

At this rate, they would run out of things to do and say before the first week was up.

"God forbid she believe things are anything but

blissfully perfect," Anne said with a snicker. "Pretty ironic, don't you think, considering the mess that she came from?"

Aaron shot her a look, then turned to Chris. "I'll see that it's done immediately. And I'm sure the first thing he'll want is to see the e-mails themselves, so we should all forward them to him."

"I bet this will turn out to be nothing," Louisa assured them in her typical optimistic way. "Probably just some harmless computer hacker trying to impress his friends."

Deep down Chris hoped she was right, but in reality he sensed a disaster coming on.

Melissa stretched out on a lounge chair on the back patio, sipping her latte, the morning sun on her face. She closed her eyes and tipped her face up, breathing in the fresh ocean air, feeling as though she could nod off. She'd slept poorly last night. She had tossed and turned for hours, filled with longing and regret. And confusion. A part of her wished desperately that she'd invited Chris into her room, while another part of her was scared to death to get too close.

Hadn't she endured enough rejection in her life?

The trick was not *letting* him get close. After all, how could he hurt her if she didn't care? The problem with that was, it had only been a day and she already liked him far too much for her own good.

She'd never understood how it happened so easily for some people. Love just seemed to fall in their laps when they weren't even looking. But despite her desperate longing for a family, the right man constantly seemed to elude her. Around about her thirtieth birthday, she'd begun to worry that she might never find Mr. Right. And now, at thirty-three, she'd nearly given up on the concept of marriage and family and resigned herself to settling for Mr. Right Now.

Maybe the trick was not to look. To just sit back and let it happen naturally. Which was tough when, as every day passed, her biological clock ticked louder.

She heard the door open behind her and turned to see Chris step out onto the patio. He wore a pair of dark slacks and a white silk dress shirt with the sleeves rolled loosely to the elbows that contrasted his deeply tanned forearms.

"I thought I might find you out here," he said, flashing her one of those heart-stopping, deliciously sexy smiles. The man was far too attractive for his own good. Or hers. She could just imagine the gorgeous children he would have with the lucky woman who eventually nabbed him. Which was inevitable. For a crown prince, marriage and children weren't a luxury. They were a duty. Like her half brother, Phillip. But he'd been smart enough to marry a woman he loved.

Not that she considered herself unlovable. But the sad truth was, when Chris did choose a wife, she would be considerably younger, with plenty of fertile, child-bearing years ahead of her. A commodity Melissa no longer possessed.

But she wasn't going to let that fact ruin her vacation.

Love was nice, but there was also a lot to be said for smoking-hot, no-strings-attached sex.

She returned his smile and said, "Good morning, Your Highness."

He lowered himself into a chair across from her, his back to the sun, folding one leg casually atop the other. "Did you sleep well?"

"Very," she lied. "And you?"

"Quite." He gazed up at the cloudless blue sky, shading his eyes from the sun with one hand. "Beautiful morning."

"Yes, it is," she agreed. "The news this morning said it should be pleasantly warm this afternoon. Around seventy-nine degrees. And no humidity."

"Some might consider that a little too hot."

"That's because they haven't lived in the deep South of the United States. Seventy-nine is downright balmy."

He grinned, and for a moment he just looked at her, a spark of amusement in his eyes.

She narrowed her eyes at him. "Why are you looking at me like that?"

"When you talk about the U.S., your Southern accent thickens."

"Does it?"

He nodded. "I like it."

And she liked that he liked it. He certainly hadn't wasted any time with the flirting this morning. A full day of this and tonight she wouldn't even think of telling him no.

"Hungry?" he asked with a smoldering grin that said he had more than breakfast on his mind.

"Famished."

"Breakfast should be ready." He rose from his seat and held out a hand to help her from the chaise. She took it and his warm fingers curled around her own. He had strong, long-fingered, graceful-looking hands. The thought of what they would feel like on other parts of her body made her shiver.

She hoped she didn't have to wait too long to find out.

Despite all the natural beauty that Thomas Isle had to offer, Chris had found that most women grew bored with the tour of the family's vast acreage and green-house facilities within the first hour. In fact, with the situation in the east fields he might have welcomed it. He should have known Melissa would be different.

She spent the morning in rapt interest, taking in the sights and sounds and information, asking a million questions, soaking up the answers much the way a parched sponge absorbs moisture. Either she was gen-uinely interested, or she was one bloody good actress. The morning didn't lack for sexual teasing and in-nuendo, either.

The pale-orange sundress she wore barely reached mid-thigh and left all but a few narrow strips of her back exposed. She obviously spent a lot of time either in the sun or the tanning bed. Her skin looked bronzed and smooth and was suspiciously lacking any bathing suit lines, and her legs were a work of art. Long and slim and shapely. About as close to perfection as he'd ever seen.

She wore her long hair down, draped in shiny waves over one shoulder. The effect was exotic and sexy, as was her accent. He liked to test himself, guessing which dialect would emerge next. In serious instances, when she was asking questions about their business or meeting their employees, she sounded more east-coast U.S. When she was excited, she sounded decidedly more Southern. Only when she was teasing, or slaying with that sharp wit, did the deep drawl come through.

If he had to choose, he would say he preferred the drawl the most. And the sassy smile that partnered with it.

At one, when he suggested they head back to the castle for lunch, she seemed genuinely disappointed to be ending the tour.

"But we didn't see the east fields yet," she said.

"They're not going anywhere," he promised. "Besides, aren't you hungry?"

"Starved, actually."

He walked her to the car, hand pressed gently to the small of her back. They had done an awful lot of touching all morning. A caress here, a soft touch there. The accidental brush of their shoulders, or her elbow against his arm. Or maybe it wasn't accidental at all.

And frankly, he couldn't wait to get her alone.

"Couldn't we see the east fields, then have lunch?" she asked.

"I could call ahead and have the cook pack us a picnic

lunch," he suggested, knowing most women ate that romantic sort of thing up.

Her eyes lit and he knew he had her.

She smiled and said, "I suppose the east fields could wait."

Using his cell phone, he rang the kitchen, arranging for a variety of fruit, crackers and cheese, caviar and a bottle of their best champagne to be prepared. After he hung up, he helped Melissa into the car.

When they were comfortably seated, she turned to him and said, "I get the feeling, Your Highness, that you're trying to soften me up."

She didn't miss a thing. He liked that about her, and at the same time it could prove to be quite an inconvenience. Although there didn't seem much point in denying it.

He grinned instead and asked, "Is it working?"

She returned the smile, but added a touch of sass. "*Ridiculously* well."

Chris knew without a doubt that it would be a very interesting afternoon.

Six

Melissa couldn't help but wonder if something was up. While the tour of the fields he did show her was thorough, she had the distinct impression that the foremen she'd been introduced to were on edge about something. They seemed wary of her questions, especially when she brought up the subject of the downfalls of growing organic, things like pests and disease. And it hadn't escaped her attention that, although the east fields were the closest to the castle and had the largest of their greenhouse facilities, they were the only ones he'd chosen to skip.

That couldn't possibly be coincidence.

There was definitely something going on, something secret, and it could be any number of things. Possibly even something illegal.

Or maybe she was letting her imagination run wild. Just because the royal family of Morgan Isle was riddled with scandal, it didn't mean the Alexander family was as well. She would just be sure to keep her eyes open and her ears perked.

When they got back to the castle, a basket packed with everything Chris had requested was waiting for them, along with a thick, soft flannel throw to sit on.

"We could walk down to the bluff and eat by the water," he suggested.

That sounded like a wonderful idea to her, and she couldn't help but think that if he really was trying to soften her up, he was doing an excellent job. "I'd love to."

"Shall we?" he asked, offering his arm.

She took it and they walked to the bluff together, choosing a pleasant spot in the shade of a knotty old oak that looked as if it had stood on the property as long as the castle. It conveniently blocked the view from the castle windows. Which could be a good or a bad thing.

He spread out the blanket and they sat across from each other. Melissa kicked off her sandals and stretched out, breathing in the salty air, feeling the breeze ruffle her hair and hearing the rush of the ocean against the rocks below. They couldn't have asked for a more beautiful afternoon for a picnic.

Chris popped the champagne—which sold for several hundred dollars a bottle—and poured them each a glass while she investigated the contents of the basket.

She found a box of gourmet crackers, a can of caviar, a variety of cheeses already sliced and a plastic container with different kinds of fresh fruit. "Everything looks wonderful."

He handed her a glass of champagne and lifted his in a toast. "To new friends," he said. "And new beginnings."

Amen to that. She clinked her glass to his and sipped, the bubbles tickling her nose. She reached for the box of crackers and he gently pushed her hand away. "Why don't you let me?"

He opened the caviar, spread a dollop on a cracker, and handed it to her, then fixed one for himself. She took a bite and the caviar exploded like little bombs of salty flavor across her tongue. She closed her eyes and savored the decadent sensation. "Delicious."

"Try a strawberry. They were picked just this morning."

He held one out to her, already hulled and cut in half, and on impulse, rather than take it with her hand, she leaned forward and took it directly into her mouth, grazing the tip of his thumb with her tongue.

The fruit was plump and juicy and sweet. She moaned and closed her eyes as another explosion of flavor overwhelmed her taste buds.

Maybe it was the atmosphere, or the company, but it was probably the tastiest thing she had ever eaten. When she opened her eyes and looked at Chris, saw the way he was watching her from under lids heavy with desire, she knew that he enjoyed her enjoying it.

"Let's do that again," he said. This time he chose a

chunk of pineapple, and as he fed it to her, she caught his finger in her mouth to lick off the juice.

"It's so sweet," she said. "You should try it."

She fished a piece out of the bowl and held it out for him. His eyes locked on hers, he leaned forward and took it from her fingers, his tongue brushing the pad of her thumb, and she went limp all over. She watched him chew, mesmerized by his mouth and his jaw and the movement of his throat as he swallowed.

He licked his lips. "Hmm, delicious."

She wanted to try that again. This time she held out a cherry. He took it with his teeth and when the juice dripped down her finger, and he took the entire thing into his mouth, sucking it clean.

Oh. My. God.

He grinned, a lazy, sexy smile, and said, "Tasty."

His lips looked so full and inviting, tinted pink from the cherry juice, that she couldn't resist leaning in for a taste. And though the kiss was meant to be a brief one, he hooked a hand behind her head, tangling his fingers through the silky locks of her hair, and pulled her closer.

She wrapped her arms around his neck, leaning into the long, lean length of his body, and a low moan rumbled in his throat. He broke the kiss and gazed down at her, eyes glazed and half-closed. "Do you have any idea what you're doing to me?"

She knew exactly what she was doing. "You like it?"

He took her hand and placed it palm down on his

chest, so she could feel the heavy *thump-thump* of his heart. "What do you think?"

She slipped her hand inside the collar of his shirt and touched his bare skin. "Then maybe we should do it some more."

He reached for her, but she pushed him backward onto the blanket instead, moving the food containers aside so she could scoot closer.

He reached up with one hand to brush her hair back from her face and tuck it behind her ear. "I thought I was supposed to be seducing you."

She leaned down, brushed her lips against his, whispered against them, "That's not my style."

His arms went around her and he pulled her down for a deep, searching kiss. He tasted sweet and salty and even more delicious than the food. She fed off his mouth, feeling as though she could eat him up. His hands were on her face and in her hair, stroking her shoulders and her back. She may have been the one seducing him, but he was definitely in on the action. When he rolled her over onto the blanket she didn't try to stop him. She opened her eyes to find him propped up on one elbow, grinning down at her.

"I'm supposed to be seducing you," she reminded him. "That's harder to do from down here."

"Sorry, love. That's not my style, either."

Well, someone was going to have to relinquish control. "I think this could be a problem."

He shrugged. "So don't think."

She was poised for another snappy comeback, but before she could get the words out he was kissing her again, and she completely forget what she'd been about to say. In fact, she forgot everything but the feel of his mouth on hers, and his hands on her body. She wished they were in the castle, in her bedroom, where their clothes wouldn't have to be in the way.

He kissed her chin, down her throat and she let her head fall back against the blanket. He kissed lower still, across her collarbone, over the swell of her cleavage, whispering sweet words, telling her she was beautiful.

They may have only been words, but he wielded them skillfully and they cut through her defenses like the lethally sharp blade of a gilded sword.

Through a haze of desire, she gradually became aware of a presence beside them. She felt something warm and damp and foul-smelling against her cheek.

Dog breath, she realized.

She opened her eyes to find a small, canine face not an inch from her own. One of those cute little yappy dogs that people like Paris Hilton carted around with them, with bulging eyes and long, ginger-colored hair tied up with a blue ribbon.

"Well, hello there," she said, and he or she let out an excited yap, which had Chris looking up from Melissa's cleavage.

He cursed under his breath and said, "Get lost, Muffin."

Such an adorable name coming from a big tough prince like him made her laugh. "You named your dog Muffin?"

"It's not my dog." He sat up and shooed the furry invader away, which only made it jump around and yap excitedly. "He's Louisa's bag of fleas."

"He's so cute!" She sat up beside Chris and held out a hand for Muffin to sniff. He sniffed daintily, then lapped at her fingers with his tiny pink tongue. "Aren't you just a sweetheart?"

From a distance, behind the tree somewhere Melissa heard Louisa call out, "Muffin! Here, boy!"

Muffin's ears perked and he let out a short yap, as if to say *"Here I am!"*

"Shoo," Chris said. "Go get her."

Muffin didn't budge.

"Over here!" Melissa called to Louisa, and Chris cursed again, but at this point an interruption seemed inevitable. She just hoped her hair wasn't too much of a mess, or her makeup smeared. Though she was sure Chris has kissed away whatever had been left of her lip gloss.

Louisa rounded the tree, looking young and fresh in white capri pants and a pink blouse. Her hair looked soft and cute pulled back in a low bun. She was graceful and petite, almost to the point of looking fragile.

When she saw the three of them there—Chris, Melissa and Muffin—she smiled. Then she pointed a finger at her dog and said sternly, "Bad boy, Muffin. You know you're not supposed to run off like that."

"He's so cute," Melissa told her.

"I hope he's not bothering you."

Melissa said "no," and Chris said "yes" simultaneously. Melissa gave his shoulder a light shove and told Louisa, "He's not bothering us at all. Is he a shih tzu?"

"Purebred." Louisa said proudly, scooping him up and tucking him into the crook of her arm. "He probably smelled the food. He's a little eating machine. I swear, he's part pig."

"Would you like to join us?" Melissa asked, in part to be polite, but also because they had hardly eaten a thing and she hated to see all of that food go to waste.

Louisa opened her mouth to answer but Chris interrupted her. "Actually, we were just getting ready to pack up. Melissa was just saying how tired she is from her trip yesterday, and that she'd like to take a nap. I was going to walk her back to her room."

Oh, yes, that fifteen-minute plane ride from Morgan Isle was absolutely *exhausting* Although she was pretty sure that *napping* was the last thing he had on his mind.

"The nap can wait," she said.

"No," Chris insisted, spearing her with a sharp look. "I don't think it can. We wouldn't want you to get too tired."

"That's okay," Louisa said. "Muffin and I are going to take a walk." She smiled brightly and told Melissa, "Have a good rest."

Either she hadn't recognized the innuendo in the nap scenario, or she was just polite enough not to let on. Either way, she waved good-bye and walked off with Muffin trailing obediently while Melissa and Chris gathered the leftover food and packed it back into the basket.

"A nap, huh?" she said.

He grinned. "Yeah. You look *exhausted.*"

"She's very sweet, isn't she?" Melissa asked. "Louisa, I mean."

"Yes." His brow tucked into a frown. "Far too sweet for her own good."

"I get the impression she's a bit…naive."

"More than a bit." He closed the basket, then rose to his feet and shook out the blanket. "I fear someday someone will take advantage of that. And I think we've only perpetuated the problem by sheltering her."

"She may be tougher than you think."

"I hope so." He folded the blanket, grabbed the basket, then held out an arm for her to take, flashing one of those sizzling smiles. "Shall I walk you back for that nap?"

She wrapped her arm tightly through his and pressed herself against his side, smiling up at him. "The sooner the better."

She doubted it would be restful, but it would probably be the most pleasurable *nap* she'd ever taken.

Chris dropped the basket in the kitchen on the way in and led Melissa upstairs to her room. The halls were blissfully silent, and thankfully they didn't run into anyone on the way up. Not that it would have stopped Chris from going into her room. He'd have fabricated some reason they needed to be alone.

If Louisa hadn't interrupted them, he might have made love to Melissa right there on the blanket under the tree, the consequences be damned. Everything about her was so sweet and soft and sexy. He might not have been able to stop himself. He was pretty sure she wouldn't have put up much resistance, it was obvious she wanted him as much as he wanted her.

They were mere steps from her door, and Chris was already plotting just how he would get her out of her clothes, when a bodyguard named Flynn caught up with them.

"Sorry to interrupt, sire," he said, bowing his head to both Chris and Melissa. "Prince Aaron is looking for you."

Yeah, well, Prince Aaron was going to have to wait. "Tell him that I'll speak with him later."

"He said it's urgent," Flynn insisted. "Regarding the matter this morning, with the e-mail."

"Right!" Chris said, before the man said too much and piqued Melissa's curiosity. Aaron had obviously discovered something important. "Where is he?"

"The tech office, your highness."

"Fine, tell him I'll be right down." When he was gone, Chris turned to Melissa. "I'm sorry. I need to take care of this."

"Trouble getting your e-mail?" she teased.

If only it were that simple. "A security issue," he said, not wanting to give any more than that away.

"It's all right. I actually am a little tired. Maybe I'll lie down for a while." She grinned. "Reserve my strength for later."

"I'll try to make it quick."

She rose up on her toes and pressed a lingering kiss

to the corner of his lips, and it took everything in him not to say *to hell with it* and back her into her room. But he didn't want to feel rushed. When he made love to Melissa, he was going to take his time. With this security thing hanging over his head, he would be distracted.

"You know where to find me," she said, then she slipped into her room and closed the door.

Bloody hell. He lingered another second, tempted to follow her in, then he forced himself to turn and head down to the tech office, hoping Aaron had answers and they could wrap this up quickly. But the instant he stepped inside and saw the look of concern on Aaron's face, he knew this was going to take a while.

Seven

Chris stepped into the tech office and closed the door. "I'm guessing the news isn't good."

"Good guess," Aaron said.

The systems administrator, Dennis Attenborough—though everyone called him by his hacker name, Datt—gazed grimly at his computer screen. "This guy knows what he's doing."

"Guy?" Chris asked.

Datt shrugged. "Guy, girl, whatever."

"So we don't know who it is?"

"No, but statistically, most hackers are men."

"Whoever it is," Aaron said, "they managed to hack into the e-mail system undetected."

That wasn't good. "Were any other systems breached?"

Datt shook his head. "Nothing critical."

"Can you trace the ISP?"

"As I said, he knows what he's doing. He was in and out like a ghost. Completely untraceable."

"Could it be someone on the inside?"

"It's possible, but I doubt it."

"Could it happen again?"

"With any luck, yes."

At Chris's surprised look, Aaron told him, "Datt is setting a trap."

"How do you trap someone who sneaks in and out undetected?"

"You put out a net," Datt said.

"A net?"

"Think of it like a spiderweb," Datt told him. "If he gets back in, he'll get stuck. Although odds are he won't try it again."

"Why is that?"

"He's smart. He'll anticipate our next move."

"Meaning he'll just give up?"

"Or try to find another way in, through a different system."

Bloody fantastic. "Will he get in?"

Datt looked up at him. "No, sire, he won't."

"See that he doesn't. And if you learn anything, I want to be informed immediately."

"Of course."

With a jerk of his head, Chris gestured his brother

into the hallway. When they were alone, he said in a low voice, "We need to keep this to ourselves."

"The staff has been advised that the king should be left out of the loop. Although if he does find out, he'll be furious."

"Then we'll make sure that he doesn't. With any luck we've heard the last of this."

Somehow, Chris doubted they would get away that easy.

Melissa checked her e-mail, then fired off a quick message to Phillip, giving him a rundown on her day so far. Almost immediately a reply appeared in her inbox. It said simply:

Keep me posted.

Nice to hear from you, too, she thought. Though she wasn't the least bit surprised.

There was another e-mail, one from Chris that she had received early that morning. That was sweet, she thought. It read:

Meet me in the maze.
Midnight.

She smiled, and wondered exactly what he had in mind. If he would let her find her own way through this time, or send her on another wild-goose chase. Or it was possible he had other plans for her that didn't involve the maze at all?

She replied, I'll be there.

She hit Send, then shut down her computer.

She stretched out on the bed and closed her eyes. She would rest for just a few minutes, then maybe take a walk in the garden until Chris had finished with his business. When she opened her eyes again, he was sitting on the edge of the bed, smiling down at her.

She sat up, hazy and disoriented. The curtains were drawn and the room dark. She couldn't tell if it was morning or night. "What time is it?"

"Seven," he said. "It's time for dinner."

"How long have you been sitting here?" She hoped she hadn't done anything embarrassing, like snore or drool on the pillow.

"Only a few minutes."

She covered a yawn with the back of her hand. "I didn't mean to sleep so long. Did you just finish your meeting?"

"Hours ago. I came by to see you, but you were sound asleep."

"You could have woken me."

He shrugged. "I figured you could use the rest."

"For our date tonight?"

"Date?"

"I answered your e-mail," she said. "I guess you didn't get it yet."

There was a flicker of emotion in his eyes, something

that looked almost like apprehension, then it was gone. "You got an e-mail from me?"

He didn't remember? "Well, I assumed it was from you. Your name was on it."

"Refresh my memory. What did it say?"

"'Meet me at the maze. Midnight.'"

He nodded slowly. "Oh, yes, right."

How could he not remember? It was only this morning. "Is something wrong?"

"This is going to sound a little strange, but would you show me?"

"The e-mail?"

He nodded.

Something was definitely not right here. "Of course."

She walked over to the desk where her laptop sat. She opened it and booted it up. Chris averted his eyes while she typed in her password, then she opened her e-mail program and scrolled down to find the message from him. "Here it is."

He leaned over her shoulder to read it, brow furrowed with concern.

"Isn't that your e-mail address?" she asked.

"Yes," he said, sounding somewhat grim. "It is."

There was only one explanation for his behavior. "You didn't send that, did you?"

He hesitated, then said, "It's complicated."

That was a non-answer if she'd ever heard one. "Does it have to do with your e-mail security issues?"

"It's just a prank. I can't say more than that. Rest assured, there's no reason to be concerned."

If that was true, why did *he* look so concerned?

"Seems weird that whoever sent it would choose the maze as a meeting place," she said. "It's almost as though they saw us out there last night."

She could tell by his disturbed expression that he was thinking the same thing.

"You think it's someone on the inside?" she asked.

"I really can't say."

She wondered if that meant he couldn't tell her, or he didn't know.

"Would you mind if I forwarded this to our systems administrator?" he asked.

She stepped away from the computer and gestured him over. "Knock yourself out."

He hit Forward, typed in the e-mail address, then sent it off. He turned to look at her. "I'm not sure how to word this, so I'm just going to say it. I would appreciate your discretion on this."

"As in, don't go running to my family with this?"

"Yes, that, too…" He raked a hand through his hair, cursing under his breath.

"What?"

"Please don't say anything to my parents. Specifically, the king."

"He doesn't know?"

He shook his head. "As I said, it's complicated."

"Is it his health?"

Her question seemed to surprise him, and she could see she'd hit a nerve. "What do you mean?"

"I'm a fairly intelligent woman, Chris. I'd have to be daft or blind not to notice the way everyone pampers him. The logical explanation would be that he's in poor health."

He didn't seem to know how to answer that.

"You'll have to forgive me," she said. "I have a tendency to let my mouth run away from me."

He seemed to choose his next words very carefully. "It's just that it's a...*sensitive* issue."

Heaven knew, her family had its share of sensitive issues, too. "I haven't said anything to my family, and I won't. Your secret is safe with me."

"I appreciate that."

"If you ever need someone to talk to, to vent to—"

"It's congestive heart failure," Chris said, and his honesty surprised her. It seemed to surprise him, too. Maybe he did just need someone to talk to.

"And the prognosis?" she asked.

"Not good. At the present rate he's deteriorating, six months. Maybe a year."

Oh, how terrible. No wonder they wanted to keep it a secret. "What about a transplant?"

"He has a very rare blood type. The chances of finding a match are astronomical."

She could see that he loved his father very much, and the idea of losing him hurt Chris deeply.

She rested her hand on his forearm, gave it a gentle squeeze. "I'm so sorry."

"There is one treatment that he's considering. It's still experimental. He would be hooked to a portable bypass machine. The machine would take over all function, giving his heart a chance to heal."

She'd never heard of such a procedure. "That sounds promising."

"But it carries risks."

"What kind of risks?"

"The surgery itself is risky because his heart is so weak, and after the pump is in he would be prone to blood clots and strokes."

"How long would he be on the pump?"

He shrugged. "Six months. A year. The doctors don't know. They can't even say if the treatment will be effective. It depends on the patient, and the degree of damage."

"Your poor mother," Melissa said. "This must be awful for her."

"It's not something we talk about outside the family," he said. "I shouldn't have even said anything to you."

But the fact that he had made her feel even closer to him. "I won't say a word to anyone. I promise."

He laid his hand over hers. "Thank you, Melissa. For listening."

On impulse, she leaned forward and brushed her lips against his. His were soft and warm. His hand slipped behind her neck, drawing her in closer. His tongue teased the seam of her lips and they parted. The kiss was deep and searching and loaded with emotion.

Deep down she was a hopeless romantic, which had

earned her a good share of bumps and bruises in her life. Mostly to her heart, but more than a few to her pride as well. She had learned to be tough. But Chris seemed to be pushing all the right buttons, knocking down all of her carefully constructed defenses. Whether he meant to or not.

She wanted him. The way she had never wanted anyone in her life.

"This is going to sound a little crazy," she said. "But despite the fact that it's barely been a day, I feel as though I know you, Chris."

"Strange, isn't it?" His eyes searched her face. She couldn't help but wonder what he was looking for. If he saw something the others hadn't. Something special.

She reached up and touched his cheek, felt the hint of evening stubble under her fingertips. "What do you think it means?"

"I'm not sure," he said. "But I'd like to find out."

Chris sat beside Melissa during dinner, listening to her chat with his family. If they knew what he'd done, they would be furious with him. He and his siblings had made a pact, a promise to their parents and each other to keep the king's condition a closely guarded secret. Great pains had been taken with his doctors to keep his medical records restricted.

He wasn't one to confide in family or friends, but finally admitting the truth to someone outside the family seemed to take a bit of the pressure off. And as promised, she didn't say a thing about the king's health or the e-mail situation, nor did she give even a hint that she knew anything was amiss. He could only hope that she would keep it from her family as well, as it could jeopardize a potential alliance.

If she felt wary of the consequences, she hadn't let it show. Perhaps she wasn't familiar enough with the way the monarchy worked to recognize the potential complications the king's death could generate. Or maybe she just didn't care. It was possible that she believed the potential benefits would outweigh the disadvantages. And after all, when his father died, or was no longer physically capable of performing his duties, Chris would be crowned king, and if they were married, Melissa would be queen. That had to hold a certain appeal.

Whatever her motivation, she seemed willing to give this partnership consideration. He just needed a bit more time to make sure this was right before he made his move and formally asked for her hand. He needed to be sure that they were sexually compatible. If he was going to be forced to marry, then damn it, he was going to marry someone who could please him in the bedroom.

After dinner, the king retired to his quarters and Melissa and the queen went for a walk in the garden. Chris gestured his siblings into the study for an impromptu meeting regarding the latest developments with the e-mails. They fixed themselves drinks at the bar then took seats by the ceiling-high windows across the room. The last threads of evening sun shone in warm, golden-orange shafts across the oriental rug.

"Aaron showed you Datt's report?" he asked his sisters, and they both nodded. "Well, something else has happened, something involving our guest."

They listened grimly as he told them about the e-mail Melissa had received, and how the sender mentioned the maze.

Aaron and Anne wore identical frowns. Louisa looked downright scared. "Was someone watching you?" she asked.

"It could just be coincidence they chose the maze," Chris told her, but she didn't look reassured, and he didn't blame her. "I'd like to have security stake it out tonight, just in case. I forwarded the e-mail to Datt."

"She didn't find that at all suspicious?" Anne asked.

"She figured out that I hadn't sent it. And of course she was curious as to what was going on."

"What did you tell her?" Aaron asked.

"That it was a prank, and there was no reason to be concerned."

But it was clear that his siblings believed there was a damned good reason, and Chris agreed. He planned to talk to Randall Jenkins, the head of security, just as soon as he was finished here. He planned to have them keep a close eye on Melissa, just in case. They certainly couldn't risk something happening to her while she was in their care.

"Did she believe you?" Anne asked.

"She seemed to. I asked her not to mention it around our parents, or to her family. She promised not to."

"Can we trust her?"

Chris shrugged. "We don't really have a choice."

Louisa drew her knees up and hugged them. "I don't like this. Maybe we should tell Father."

"No," Chris said. "Not until we absolutely have to."

With any luck, Datt would get to the bottom of this and they could solve the problem without the king ever being the wiser.

Eight

Melissa walked arm in arm with the queen along the slate path through the gardens. She had been concerned, after the horror stories she'd been told about the queen of Morgan Isle, that Queen Maria might have the same cold and dreadful disposition. Instead she was warm and friendly and surprisingly down-to-earth. She was smaller than Melissa by several inches and very petite. Her hair was always perfectly in place, her makeup flawless and her clothes immaculate. If Melissa had to chose one word to describe her, it would probably be *classy.*

They slowly strolled along, chatting about their two countries, and what it had been like for Melissa growing up in the U.S. Did she miss it, or was she happy to be home on Morgan Isle? Melissa didn't see any point in sugarcoating the truth.

"It's been an adjustment," she admitted. "My family means well, but the last few months, I feel as though I've been in a sort of limbo."

"You feel out of place?"

She nodded. "I supposed I can't blame them for feeling wary of me."

"Well, we've very much enjoyed having you here as our guest," the queen told her, sounding as though she genuinely meant it. What reason did she have to lie?

"I really like being here," Melissa said.

"You feel welcome?"

She nodded. "Oh, yes, very."

"It seems that you and Chris are getting along rather well."

That was something of an understatement.

"He's an excellent host," she said. *And an above-average kisser.*

"You know, I've never seen Chris look at a woman the way he looks at you." She smiled, an undeniable hint of mischief in her eyes. "There's something there, I think."

Her words warmed Melissa from the inside out and she felt her cheeks flush. It was good to know that she approved.

She flashed Melissa a conspiratorial smile. "I can see that you think so, too."

"He's an intriguing man."

"He's a lot like his father," she said. "The strong,

silent type. And he does have something of a stubborn streak. All the Alexander men do."

"I think all *men* do," Melissa said.

"Chris is very loyal. His family means everything to him. He'll be a good husband and father some day. And a strong leader."

"I don't doubt that he would be." If the queen thought she had to sell Chris to Melissa, she couldn't be farther off the mark. She could already feel herself falling hard and fast.

The queen smiled and patted Melissa's hand. "I'm so glad you feel that way."

"How long have you and the king been married?"

"It will be thirty-seven years this Christmas," she said, but the smile she wore didn't quite reach her eyes. She was probably thinking of how little time they might have left with each other.

Melissa wished she could talk to her about the king's condition, tell her how terribly sorry she was, but she'd promised not to say anything. She just hoped that if he chose to try the heart pump, it would be effective.

"Life is fleeting," the queen told her, "you have to seize the moment. Live life to the fullest."

Amen to that. "That's always been my motto."

"And it's served you well?"

"So far."

"Oh, speak of the devil."

Melissa looked up and saw Chris walking down the path toward them. The pride in his mother's eyes was genuine and intense. It was clear that she truly adored all of her children.

"The king is requesting your presence," he told his mother, and though her smile didn't waver, there was worry in her eyes.

"I'll go right in." She took both of Melissa's hands and gave them a squeeze. "I'm so glad we could talk. Let's do this again."

Melissa smiled and nodded. "I'd like that."

She watched the queen hurry off, asking Chris, "Is anything wrong?"

"No more so than usual." He offered his hand and asked, "Can I walk you back to the castle, Your Highness?"

She smiled and took it, threading her fingers through his. His hand felt so big and warm and sturdy.

"What did you and my mother talk about?"

"Lots of things. You, mostly."

"I'm almost afraid to ask what she said."

"She told me how loyal you are, and what an exceptional leader you'll be. And that you'll be a good husband and father."

He winced. "Not very subtle, is she? I'm sorry if she embarrassed you, or put you on the spot."

"Actually, I thought it was kind of sweet."

"I almost forgot to mention, tomorrow I've arranged a tour of the village."

"And maybe afterward we can see the east fields?"

"I doubt there will be time. Another day." He looked up at the darkening sky and said, "We should get inside."

"Wouldn't you like to walk for a while? Maybe let me take another shot at the maze?"

"It's nearly dark."

"I think we already determined I'm not afraid of the dark."

"Maybe tomorrow," he said.

She wondered what the rush was. And maybe it was her imagination, but there seemed to be an unusually large number of security officers patrolling the grounds. She wondered if it might have something to do with the rogue e-mail. Maybe there was more to it than he'd led her to believe. An element of danger. Or maybe it was just a precaution.

She didn't question him as he led her inside the castle. It was barely nine-thirty and already it was quiet and dark.

"Are you ready to retire for the night?" he asked.

"Are you forgetting I took an afternoon nap? I'm wide awake."

"What would you like to do?"

"Something fun."

He flashed her a sizzling, suggestive grin. "What did you have in mind?"

"Do you play cards?"

She could see from his disappointed expression that he had something altogether different in mind. But he asked, "What sort of cards?"

"I was thinking along the lines of poker. I used to be quite the card shark back in college."

"Were you really?" he said, looking intrigued. "I'm

sure I could scrounge up cards and chips around here somewhere."

"Great. Although…"

"What?"

"Instead of chips, why don't we wager something a bit more…*interesting?*"

One brow rose a fraction higher than the other. It made him look young and mischievous. "Such as…?"

"I don't know. How about…our clothes?"

A wicked grin curled the corners of his lips. "Strip poker?"

"Have you ever played?"

"I can't say I have, but that does sound interesting."

"I have to warn you, I'm pretty good. But I'll go easy on you," she said, even though she had no intention of doing any such thing.

"I appreciate that."

"So, that's a yes?" she asked, not that she thought he would say no. Since they both knew exactly where it would lead.

He took her hand in his and asked, "Your room or mine?"

Chris found them a deck of cards, and they decided on his room to play. Unlike the full suites at the palace on Morgan Isle, Chris's room consisted of only a bedroom and full bath, but both were spacious and modern, decorated in a masculine theme of blues and grays, with a splash of red here and there, and dark cherrywood furnishings. The room was dim, lit only by a lamp beside the bed, and smelled of his aftershave. She couldn't help but think how well it suited his personality.

He shut the door and locked it, which sent a little shiver of excitement up her spine. He gestured to the king-size—or in his case, would that be prince-size?—bed. "Shall we sit?"

They sat across from each other, she by the headboard and he by the foot. His inexperience with the game showed. He kicked off his shoes before he sat. Knowing better, she left hers on, not that she thought he had a snowball's chance in hell of beating her. Hardly a night passed when she didn't play poker on her computer. It helped her relax after a long, stressful day.

It would be a nice change to play with a real person. She'd tried to get games going with her half siblings, but they were always too busy with their children or their spouses.

"How about five-card draw?" she asked. "Nothing wild."

"Sounds simple enough. Although you may need to give me a few hands to brush up on the rules."

Oh, this was going to be too easy.

She smiled sweetly and said, "Why, of course I will." She took the cards out of the pack, fished out the jokers, and shuffled. "Oh, one more thing. Rules are, we don't stop until someone loses."

"In other words, someone has to be naked."

She nodded.

He shrugged and said, "Okay."

Oh, yeah, *way* too easy.

They played a few practice hands so he could get the hang of it, and of course he lost miserably. "We could practice awhile longer," she offered, but he shook his head.

"I think I've got the gist of it," he said.

She didn't want this to go too quickly, so she suggested, "Best two out of three hands takes off one article of clothing. Fair?"

"Fine with me," he said. He obviously had no idea what he was getting himself into. Or maybe he just didn't care if he lost. Her philosophy was that if you were going to play, play to win. And she would.

She dealt the first hand, and though Chris still seemed a bit fuzzy on the rules, his defeat wasn't quite as bad this time. Three sixes to her straight. Unfortunately he lost the next hand, too. A pair of queens to her aces and tens.

"Let's have it," she said. "One item of clothing."

He sighed and peeled off one sock. He had nice-looking feet. Almost...elegant.

They started the second round. She took the first hand with a flush, but he came back strong with three kings to her measly pair of jacks. Despite that, she rounded out the match with a full house, which beat his two pair.

She gestured to his other foot. "Take it off."

"You are good," he said, peeling the other sock off.

Damn right she was. Three more rounds ought to do

it, unless he was wearing more than trousers, a shirt and underwear. She couldn't wait to see what he would take off next.

She dealt the next hand, sure that her natural straight would beat him, but he surprised her by laying down a flush.

"Flush beats a straight?" he asked.

"Barely," she said with a snort.

She shuffled and dealt again, and Chris won with three fives to her pair of eights.

"Your turn," he said with a smug grin.

"Beginner's luck," she mumbled, kicking off one sandal.

He lost the next two games in quick succession, and off came the shirt. She let her eyes wander across his chest, over his rock-hard abs. She couldn't wait to see more. Unfortunately for her, though, he creamed her the next two hands. Grumbling to herself, she toed the other sandal off and dropped it next to its mate.

"Not a gracious loser, are we?" he teased.

"The only one losing this game is you," she shot back, and he just smiled.

My turn, she thought, as she dealt the next hand. But he won that one, and the next. And she had the feeling that he wasn't quite so inexperienced as he'd led her to believe.

"I thought you said you never played poker."

"No. I said I never played *strip* poker."

"So what was that about the practice games?"

His lips turned up in a wicked smile. "They call it a bluff."

She should have known. But she hadn't lost yet.

"So, what's it going to be?" he said, eyes on her dress.

There was no way she was going to sit there in her underwear, so she unhooked her bra and wriggled out of it through the armholes of her dress.

"That's cheating," he said.

"We never said what order we had to take them off." And now they were tied up. Two articles of clothing left each.

He smiled and said, "Just deal the cards."

"Why don't you deal?" she said, handing the cards to him. Maybe it would change her luck.

He shuffled and dealt with the skill and finesse of a man who knew his way around a deck of cards. She had the distinct feeling she was in trouble. And sure enough, he won the next two hands.

He leaned back on his elbows to watch her. "Whenever you're ready."

She had only two choices. The dress or the panties. If she took off the dress, it would be pretty much over. Her skimpy thong barely covered the essentials. But if she took off the panties first, and then beat him the next two rounds, she would be the winner.

She got up on her knees, reached up her dress and slid the thong down her legs. Chris watched.

"I still say that's cheating," he said.

"Sue me."

He just looked amused. "My, don't we get lippy when we lose?"

"I'm not going to lose."

His confidence didn't waver, and there was a gleam of pure mischief in his eyes. "We'll see."

Melissa sat back down on the comforter, legs pressed primly together. Though she was still covered from mid-thigh to neck, she'd never felt so naked in her life.

The next round was hers, and he stripped down to a pair of plaid boxers. With no trace of shame or embarrassment, not that he had anything to be ashamed or embarrassed about. His body was…perfect.

They were even now. Winner take all.

Nine

"You ready to lose?" Chris asked.

"The only one losing here is you, Your Highness." There was no way she would let him have this one. He was going down.

He dealt the cards and she got a measly pair of aces, but she drew three and ended up with a full house. He only drew one card, and she held her breath as he set his hand down. Two pair.

She punched her fist in the air. "Yes!"

"That was luck," he said.

He dealt again, but this time he won. And looked quite pleased with himself, she couldn't help but notice.

"This is it," he said. He dealt the cards and when she picked hers up, her stomach plummeted. A pair of tens, which wasn't much, or four to a queen-high straight. All she needed was a nine and there was no way she would lose. But if she kept the tens, she could possibly draw another ten and end up with three of a kind, or even a full house. Or she could end up with a measly pair.

What the heck, she'd never been one to play it safe. Besides, she had a good feeling about the hand.

She smiled smugly and said, "I'll take one, please."

He handed her one card and she discarded one of the tens. When she looked at the card, and saw that it was a nine, she had to bite her lip to keep from whooping out loud.

"Dealer takes two," he said, meaning that at the most he had three of a kind, which wasn't going to beat her straight. He took his cards, but his expression gave nothing away. "What have you got?"

She set her cards down on the duvet. "Queen-high straight. Read 'em and weep."

He frowned and nodded. "That's good," he said, then a slow smile crept over his face. "But not good enough."

He was just trying to psyche her out, there was no way—

He laid his cards down. "Full house, fours over deuces."

Oh, damn. He won.

Chris grinned and gestured to her dress. "Hand it over, Your Highness."

Melissa squared her shoulders, accepting her defeat with dignity, but, oh, how she hated losing. "Fine."

She rose up on her knees, reached around and tugged

at the zipper, but it got caught in the fabric on the way down. If she wasn't careful, she might damage it.

"Problem?" he asked.

"It's stuck."

"Sure it is."

"I'm serious. I can't get it undone."

He slid the cards out of the way and knee-walked across the mattress to her. "Turn around."

She showed him her back and he tugged lightly on the zipper, the tips of his fingers brushing her skin. "It really is stuck."

"I told you."

"It's caught in the fabric. Hold still." He lifted her hair and draped it over one shoulder, then gently worked the zipper until it popped loose from the fabric. He tugged it slowly down and she felt a *whoosh* of cool air against her back. He leaned forward and she felt his warm breath against her neck.

"You smell so good," he said, then he brushed his lips softly against her skin, jut below her ear, making her shiver involuntarily. "Your skin is so soft."

He pulled her hair back over, running his fingers through it, then he eased the dress off one shoulder and pressed a kiss there.

One of his big hands curled around her rib cage, just under her breast, and as turned on as she was feeling, she tensed the slightest bit.

"Something wrong?" he asked, his face close to her

ear. She shook her head. "Are you sure? You seem a little nervous."

She wanted to deny it, but the truth was, she actually did feel a little nervous. She hadn't done this in quite some time. Her last serious boyfriend—serious enough to sleep with—had been more than two years ago.

It's like riding a bike, she assured herself. And what she did forget, she was sure would come back to her.

"I thought you wanted my dress off," she said.

She couldn't see his smile, but she could feel it. He drew his hand upward, over the swell of her breast to her other shoulder. He eased that side of her dress down, kissing his way across her skin. She no longer cared that she'd lost the game. In fact, she was glad she had, because what he was doing to her felt so impossibly wonderful, she couldn't imagine it happening any other way.

He eased the dress down slowly, exposing one breast, and the instant the cool air hit her, it pulled into a tight, aching point. He cupped her breast in his hand and lightly pinched her nipple. It was so sensitive the sensation was as painful as it was pleasurable. Moisture pooled between her thighs and she felt warm and tingly all over.

He had the dress pushed down to her waist, one hand flattened against her stomach, his muscular chest pressed against her back, his skin so hot it almost burned. She arched against him, could feel how turned on he was, how long and hard. Oh, how she wanted to feel him inside of her, that very second. And at the same time, she wanted it to last forever.

She took the hand resting on her belly and moved it downward, and Chris didn't have to be asked twice. He slipped it under the dress, between her thighs, touching her so intimately that she moaned and shuddered.

"You're so wet," he mumbled against her skin, kissing his way up the side of her neck. One hand toyed with her nipple while the other played between her legs. He found the sensitive little bundle of nerves and caught it between his thumb and forefinger, pinching lightly. The sensation was so erotic she cried out. Nothing in her life had *ever* felt this good. She wanted it to last, but she was so close already, just a heartbeat away from total oblivion.

Until there was a loud and insistent rap at the bedroom door.

Chris cursed under his breath and mumbled, "You have got to be kidding me."

Christ, talk about lousy bloody timing. He could feel how close Melissa was. He didn't want to stop.

"I could ignore it," he said. He nipped the skin where her shoulder met her neck and she groaned softly.

There was another loud knock.

"No," Melissa said, her voice soft and breathy. "It might be important. Maybe your father."

She was right.

"Don't move," he said, getting up from the bed. "And for God's sake, don't get dressed. We're not done." He grabbed his robe, shoving his arms in the sleeves and belting it at the waist.

There was another loud rap.

"Hold on!" he growled. He stomped to the door and pulled it open a crack, peering out. Aaron stood on the other side.

"This better be important," he barked.

Aaron looked taken aback by his sharp tone, then a slow, knowing grin curled his mouth. "Am I disturbing something?"

"You might be. Can we make this quick?"

"I'm afraid not." He lowered his voice so he wouldn't be overheard. "There's an issue."

Damn it.

"Security?" Chris asked softly.

Aaron nodded. "You're needed directly."

Chris cursed under his breath. "Give me a few minutes to get dressed and I'll meet you down there."

He shut the door and locked it, and turned to Melissa. She was sitting on the bed waiting for him, holding the dress up to cover her breasts. Her cheeks and chest were pink with arousal and her eyes looked glassy. He was so damned tempted to climb back into bed with her and finish what he'd started, but he didn't want to rush.

When they did this, they were going to do it right.

"I'm sorry," he said. "I have to go."

She nodded. "I figured as much. Is everything okay?"

"It's nothing you need to concern yourself with," he told her. "But I don't know how long this will take."

"I should probably wait in my room, then."

He wanted to tell her no, that she could wait here, but

since he had no idea when he would be back, it was probably best she sleep in her own bed. He needed to be marginally discreet, at least until they were engaged. And even then his mother would insist she sleep in her own quarters until the wedding. She was traditional that way.

Melissa tugged her dress up over her shoulders, reaching around to pull up the zipper.

"Let me," he said.

She stood and turned her back to him. He zipped her dress and pressed one last kiss to her shoulder. She turned to him and smiled. "I had fun tonight."

"So did I." He reached up and touched her cheek.

"Maybe next time we won't be interrupted."

"I'll see to it that we're not. And promise me that you won't sneak outside to the maze again tonight."

"I promise."

Not that she would have much luck getting past the guards at every door, but he suspected that if she was determined enough, she would figure out a way. Until they knew who they were dealing with, it was just too risky.

He walked her to the door and she rose up on her toes to kiss him. A sweet, lingering kiss. "Good night, Your Highness."

"Good night, Princess."

She opened the door and slipped out.

Damn, he hated to end it like that.

He dressed in jeans and a sweatshirt and headed down to the security office, where he found his brother, both his sisters and Randall Jenkins, the head of security, gathered around a desk. They were all grimly examining a sheet of paper sealed in a plastic bag.

"What did you find?" he asked.

"He was here," Louisa said, hugging herself, her eyes wide with concern. "He was right here on the property."

"What do you mean?" Chris asked.

Aaron handed him the paper. "They found this at the entrance of the maze."

It read, in neat block lettering:

RUN, RUN, AS FAST AS YOU CAN.
YOU CAN'T CATCH ME I'M THE GINGER-
BREAD MAN.

He certainly did like his rhymes.

"At least we know what to call him now," Anne said with a snicker. "What a freak."

She looked more angry that frightened. As though she was ready to go out there and kick some Gingerbread Man butt.

Chris handed it back to Aaron and asked Jenkins, "I thought you were going to post extra security outside?"

"We did, sire."

"And he got through?"

"Like a ghost. No one saw a thing."

There was that ghost reference again. But Chris doubted there was anything supernatural about him.

"Who found this? And when?"

"Avery, sir. Around ten. He was guarding the entrance

to the maze. He heard a noise from inside. He went in to investigate. When he came out the note was on the ground. He called it in immediately, and we searched the grounds, but there was no one."

"No one breached the perimeter?"

Jenkins shook his head firmly. "The gate and fence were secure."

"So it has to be someone on the inside," Louisa said with a shudder. "An employee. Someone we *trust*."

"Or someone skilled, or crazy enough, to scale the bluff in the dark," Chris said. Honestly, he couldn't decide which would be worse. A rogue employee would probably be a lot easier to expose. The idea that someone would be determined enough to risk plummeting to his death on the jagged rocks had everyone looking concerned. For that reason the bluff wasn't heavily guarded. But maybe they'd been lax. Maybe this Gingerbread Man was as crafty a rock climber as he was a computer hacker.

"We should interview the staff," Aaron said. "Just in case. Someone may have seen something."

"What if it gets back to Father?" Anne asked.

"We'll just make sure it doesn't," Chris said, then told Jenkins, "I'd like to see a detail of the current security posts. We're going to have to make some changes."

"Yes, sire."

"Do we have to do this now?" Anne asked.

"Why don't you and Louisa go back to bed?" Aaron said. "Chris and I will take care of this."

"I want to stay," Louisa said firmly.

"You'll just be in the way," Anne said, taking her arm. "They can update us in the morning."

Louisa grudgingly let her sister lead her out of the office. Chris glanced up at the clock. It was going on midnight. It looked as though it would be a very long night. And his date with Melissa would have to wait.

Ten

Hoping his meeting would end soon, Melissa stayed up until almost 1:00 a.m., waiting to hear a knock at her door. But it must have been a long one, and eventually she drifted off to sleep.

The following morning at breakfast Chris informed her that because of the beautiful weather, instead of a trip to the village, they would be spending the morning on the golf course with his parents and sisters, have lunch at the clubhouse, then spend the remainder of the day on the royal yacht.

"I hope you play golf," Chris said.

"About as well as I play poker. And I'm an above-average swimmer."

"So you'll save me if we capsize?" Chris teased,

wearing that sexy smile. And, oh, how she wished they were spending the day alone, just the two of them. Preferably in his bedroom. But with his family around all day, they couldn't so much as hold hands without raising eyebrows. They planned for private time following dinner, but after hearing from Chris what an accomplished poker player she was—he of course left out the stripping part—Aaron and Anne challenged Melissa and Chris to a game.

Chris left the decision to her, and since she couldn't exactly say *no thanks, I'd rather sleep with your brother,* she accepted their challenge. Louisa didn't play cards, but she and Muffin hung around, cheering them on. They played well past midnight, drinking beer brewed right on the island and nibbling on pretzels until Aaron—the true card shark of the group—cleaned everyone out of their chips and was declared the winner.

"I had *so much* fun tonight," Melissa told Chris as he walked her back to her room. More fun than she'd ever had with her own siblings. They didn't do things like play cards together. They were too wrapped up in their spouses and children.

They stopped outside her bedroom door. She looked up at him, and Chris smiled down at her, gently tucking her hair back from her face, his fingers caressing her cheek. "You look tired."

"I am." Between the sun and the water and the delicious food, not to mention the excellent company, she was beat.

"I should let you get some sleep," he said. "We have an early morning and a busy day ahead of us."

"The tour of the village?" she said, and he nodded. "And the east fields?"

"If there's time."

It probably would be best if she went to bed, otherwise she might sleepwalk through the day tomorrow. "Think we can fit in some private time tomorrow?" she asked.

That sexy grin was back, and it made her legs feel like limp noodles. "I'm sure we can work something out."

She could tell that he was just as anxious for that alone time, too.

"Good night, Chris."

"Sleep well, Melissa."

She rose up on her toes to brush a kiss across his lips, when what she really wanted to do was wrap her arms around him and drag him into her room. But before she could change her mind and do just that, she stepped into her room and closed the door.

She changed into her pajamas and brushed her teeth, then booted up her computer to check her e-mail. Other than the usual spam, and a few messages from old acquaintances in the U.S.—most looking for donations or an endorsement to one charitable cause or another— there was nothing of a personal nature. Nothing from Phillip or Ethan or even Sophie. It was as though the instant she left the palace they had forgotten she existed.

But could she blame them? They had their own lives, their own families. Sophie was newly married and traveling back and forth to the States with her husband, Alex. Ethan and his wife, Lizzy, had their infant son to keep them busy. Phillip and Hannah had Fredrick, and their second baby, a girl, due soon. Even their cousin Charles, whom she had felt an immediate kinship to, had settled down and married his personal assistant, Victoria, and recently announced that they were expecting their first child.

She considered sending Phillip a quick e-mail, a brief synopsis of her conversation with the queen, then thought *why bother?* If they wanted to know what she was doing, they would just have to contact her to find out.

You're being childish and immature, her aunt's voice chastised. The way it often had when they first took Melissa in. When she'd complained about being sent off to boarding school in a country whose language she barely spoke, with snobby girls who viewed her as an outsider. Or when they shipped her away to summer camp in an unfamiliar state where she didn't know a soul and was often the brunt of jokes and pranks. Because she talked with a strange accent, and she didn't have parents or siblings like the other girls. They got letters and care packages and visits on parents' day while she got nothing.

Eventually she'd learned that that all the begging and pleading and sob stories about being lonely had no effect on her cold, heartless guardians. She learned to go where they sent her without question or complaint. If nothing else it had made her tough. And the tougher she became, the less she cared, and the more the other girls seemed to respect her. But by then she was past needing their approval, or even their friendship. She was a force to be reckoned with all by herself. Besides, the fewer people she let close, the less likely she was to be hurt.

And yes, maybe shunning her siblings was a bit childish, but shouldn't this relationship be a two-way street? Was it too much to expect that they take the time to contact her every now and then? Why should it always be her making the effort? Why did she always feel like the third, or in her case, fourth wheel?

Maybe that was what she liked about Chris. He had no ulterior motives. His affection was genuine and he seemed to accept her for exactly who she was. She'd always known that if she found her one true love, her Mr. Right, she wouldn't need anyone else.

Feeling sorry for herself, and disgusted with herself for feeling that way, Melissa crawled beneath the covers and drifted off to sleep. She woke to the low rumbling of thunder and rain tapping against the bedroom window. She sat up and peered at the clock. It was already after eight.

She got out of bed, feeling cranky and out of sorts, and walked to the window, pushing the curtains aside to look out. The sky was an endless palette of dreary gray clouds that spit a steady drizzle of cold rain. It looked cold, anyhow. The sort of chilly damp that sank straight through the skin and into the bones. It had been on a day just like this that she'd lost her parents. She would never forget when her nanny had come into her room, her eyes red and swollen, cheeks streaked with tears, and told Melissa that her parents were never coming home.

She shivered and shook away the grim memories, letting the curtain drop to block out the inclement weather, but a dark shadow still loomed over her as she crossed the room to the bath.

Determined not to let the weather bring her down, Melissa showered and dressed, taking special care with her hair and makeup. Looking her best always made her feel better.

She was on her way out to find Chris when her maid, Elise, appeared to clean the room and change the linens. She had naturally red hair and freckled skin, and though she was small and very petite, there was a toughness about her. And a charm that Melissa found quite endearing. So different from her attendants at the palace. Friendlier. Not that the palace attendants had ever been rude or hostile toward her, but her routines and personality seemed to perplex them. And maybe even intimidate them.

Elise curtsied and said in a charming Irish brogue, "Did you sleep well, my lady?"

"I did Elise, thank you. Do you know where I might find Prince Christian?"

"In the parlor, I suspect. It's where he usually takes his morning coffee."

"Well then, that's where I'll look."

She headed downstairs and found Chris just where Elise had suggested. He sat in a comfortable-looking armchair by the window, a cup of coffee beside him and a newspaper draped across his lap.

"Good morning," she said.

He looked up and when he saw her standing in the doorway, he smiled. It was the sort of good-to-see-you grin that warmed the heart.

His eyes wandered over her, taking in the long, flowing dress that accentuated her slim figure, and the hair that tumbled in dark, silky waves across her shoulders. His grin said he liked what he was seeing. "Good morning."

The dark cloud that had hovered over her since she woke up dissipated and she actually felt…happy. Leave it to him to be the one person in the world who could drag her from the depths of a foul mood. And simply by smiling.

Chris folded the paper and rose to his feet. "You look lovely, Princess."

In dark linen slacks and a cream-colored tunic, he wasn't looking too shabby either. His hair was wet, which meant he had recently showered, and that had her recalling how he had looked sitting on his bed in his boxers last night, what it had felt like to have his hands on her body. How she couldn't wait to feel them again.

Even the dreary view from the window couldn't dampen her spirits.

She flashed him a sweet Southern smile. "Why, thank you, Your Highness."

"Shall I call for breakfast?" he asked.

"Just coffee for me."

He gestured to the chair opposite his, then called the butler to bring her a cup. When he was gone, Chris said, "You'll be happy to hear that I'm yours for the day."

"No interruptions?"

"No interruptions." He leaned forward slightly. "My parents had an appointment with a doctor in London." At her worried expression he added, "Just routine tests. My sisters went with them to shop, as if their closets aren't already overflowing."

"And Aaron?"

"Out in the fields and not expected back until late this evening."

This day was getting better and better. "So, what shall we do?"

"As you've probably assumed, due to the weather, our tour of the village will have to wait." There was a devilish gleam in his eye. "We'll just have to find something to do indoors."

She could think of a thing or two that would keep them busy for a very long time. "How about a rematch?"

"Poker?" He wore a wickedly sexy smile. "Are you sure you want to? After your humiliating loss the other night?"

She answered him in her sassiest Southern drawl. "What's wrong? Are you afraid you might be beaten by a girl?"

His grin was so hot she could swear she heard him sizzle. He gestured to the door and said, "Get ready to lose, Your Highness."

* * *

They never got around to that rematch.

Chris ushered her into his room, and the instant he closed and locked the door they were in each other's arms. No question, no hesitation, as though they couldn't stand to be apart another second. And when he kissed her it was so hot she worried they might both combust.

They didn't need cards to get naked this time. They tore at each other's clothes as he walked her backward in the direction of the bed. She didn't even care when she heard the delicate fabric of her dress rip as he tugged it down to her waist. She just wanted to feel his hands on her body. His lips on her mouth and her skin.

The curtains were open, but not even the sight of that depressing drizzle could drown her good mood. The gray, overcast sky couldn't smother her happiness. After this, she would never look at rain the same way again.

Melissa tugged Chris's shirt up over his head and tossed it aside. She placed her hands on his muscular chest. His skin was smooth and warm and she could feel the steady thud of her heart beating. She leaned forward and pressed a kiss against his throat, felt him shudder.

He took her hand and placed it on the clasp of his slacks. She unfastened it and shoved them down, taking his boxers along for the trip. He eased her dress and her thong down her hips, then they were both naked. For a moment they just looked at one another, and though she had been naked with men before, never in her life had she felt so exposed.

"I want to take this slow," he said, caressing her face. "But we've been building up to this for days and I'm getting impatient."

"To hell with slow," she said, wrapping her arms around his neck and kissing him. They tumbled onto the bed, a tangle of arms and legs. Skin against skin, making so much wonderful friction. One body fitting to the other like two pieces of a puzzle.

It all moved so fast, yet not nearly fast enough. She felt as though she had been anticipating this moment her entire life, and she couldn't bear to wait a second longer.

Chris wasted no time giving her exactly what she wanted, what she *needed*. He drove himself inside her, so swift and hard, so deep that she cried out with shock and ecstasy. He teased her, making her crazy with slow, steady thrusts. Speaking sweet words of encouragement. Until she was out of her mind, it felt so wonderful. So perfect.

Somewhere in her subconscious the question of protection penetrated the fog, but it was fleeting. By then she was too busy breaking the land-speed record for the world's fastest and most intense orgasm to worry about something so trivial as an unexpected pregnancy. And just as she started to come back to herself, regain her senses, every muscle in his body flexed and locked and she could swear she felt him swell inside her, and it was so damned erotic it drove her right over the edge again.

So this was what it was supposed to feel like, she mused afterward as they lay wrapped around each other, breath fast and raspy. This was how it felt to be with that one special person. The one she was destined to be with forever. Two halves coming together to make a perfect whole. It was terrifying and wonderful at the same time. And when he lifted his head from her shoulder, gazed into her eyes, she could tell that he felt it, too.

And all she could think to say was, *"Wow."*

He grinned and said, "I couldn't have said it better myself."

She should say something else, like, *by the way, did you use a condom?* But she couldn't imagine when he would have had time. Maybe, when she hadn't stopped him, he'd just assumed that she had it covered.

Which, unfortunately, she didn't.

Chris started kissing her again. Nibbling her lips and her throat, nipping her shoulder with his teeth. And she felt herself slipping, getting all mushy and turned on. Since the damage was already done, they could probably just talk about it later. Right? No point in bringing it up now and killing the mood.

No, that would be totally irresponsible. Not to mention underhanded. If the damage wasn't done yet, it could just as easily happen the second time. He needed to know right now what he might have just gotten himself into.

"We need to talk," she said.

He lifted his head to look at her. "About what?"

"Protection."

He raised one brow. "You feel your life is in danger?"

It was such a ridiculous thing to say, and she was so nervous, a bubble of laughter worked its way up. "Not *that* kind of protection. I meant *birth control.*"

"Oh. What about it?"

"You didn't use a condom."

"I guess I got a little carried away and forgot. Is that a problem?"

"It might be," she said, and Chris remained surprisingly composed. He probably wouldn't be for long. "You should know that I'm not on anything."

He nodded slowly. "And you're worried because…?"

He didn't know? Had he never had the birds-and-the-bees talk with his parents? "This may come as a shock, but unprotected sex can sometimes result in pregnancy."

He rose up on one elbow, looking more curious than concerned. "You think you could be pregnant?"

"Considering where I am in my cycle, I would say it's a possibility." In fact, she would go so far as to say that it was more of a *probability.*

His lips pulled into a frown, and she thought *here it comes, the inevitable talk of* what *if, and how we'll handle the "situation."*

Instead, he asked, "Is this your way of telling me that you don't want children?"

She was so stunned by his words it took her a second to find her voice. "No, of course not! I just…I thought…"

She didn't know what to say. This didn't make sense. Why wasn't he getting that cornered animal look? Shouldn't he be leaping out of bed, putting on his clothes, ranting about what a mistake they'd just made? Why was he still lying beside her, stroking her cheek with the backs of his fingers, gazing earnestly into her eyes?

"Are you worried what people will say?" he asked.

Apparently the fact that she very possibly could have conceived his child didn't bother him in the least.

"A—a little, I guess."

"Well then, there's only one thing we can do."

Here it comes, she thought. The big letdown. She had to force herself to ask, "What's that?"

"We'll just have to get married."

Eleven

"*Married?*" Melissa was so stunned the word came out high and squeaky, as though she had just sucked a balloon full of helium.

"Just in case," he said.

Aware that her jaw had gone slack, she snapped it shut, smacking her teeth together so hard that her skull rattled. "Just in case?"

He didn't even want to wait until they knew for sure?

He narrowed his eyes at her and said, his tone serious, "I'm moving too fast."

"No. It's not that. I'm just…" She was just what? Stunned into last Tuesday? She took a deep breath and blew it out. "You just surprised me a little."

He touched her face tenderly, his expression earnest.

"I know it's soon, and we still need time to get to know each other. But I think we both knew this was inevitable."

"Me getting pregnant?"

"Us ending up together."

Maybe she hadn't known, but she had certainly hoped. From the second she'd met Chris she'd felt there was something special there. The idea of marrying him, being a part of his wonderful family, feeling loved and accepted—it was everything she'd ever dreamed of.

"You're sure?"

"Unless you don't want to marry me."

"No. I mean, *yes, I do* want to marry you."

"Then I think if there is a possibility you're pregnant, we should do it sooner rather than later. Don't you agree?"

Though a small part of her was the slightest bit wary, the part that kept thinking this was too good to be true, the rest of her was practically screaming at her to throw caution to the wind and accept his proposal immediately. How often did an opportunity like this arise? And what if she was pregnant? They could be a family. Her and Chris and the baby. Her own little happy family. Wasn't that what she'd always hoped for?

She grinned up at him and asked, "When?"

"I imagine we'll need at least a few weeks to make all the arrangements. My mother will want something large and extravagant."

"Will a few weeks be enough time?"

"I'm sure they can pull it together. I'll have to call your brother. Formally ask for your hand."

She wondered what her siblings would think. Would they be surprised that it happened so quickly? Would they worry she was rushing into it? Or would they be relieved to be rid of her?

"I'll have to go back to Morgan Isle to pack and arrange to have my things moved. That shouldn't take more than a few days." Some of her things were still in boxes from her move to the palace. That arrangement had always felt somewhat temporary. But this, this new life, would be a keeper.

He grinned down at her. "This is a smart match."

She might have worded it differently, more affectionately, but she couldn't argue with his logic. Sentiments of love might have been nice, but she wasn't going to push it. Maybe Chris wasn't used to talking about his feelings.

That part of their relationship would come in time.

"We'll have to stay in separate rooms until our wedding night," he said. "My mother will insist."

"But she's not here right now," Melissa said, weaving her arms around his neck.

Chris grinned. "No, she isn't."

"I think we should try that again. Only a little slower this time."

"I think we should celebrate by spending the whole day in bed," he said.

It was the second-best offer she'd had all day.

As planned, Chris and Melissa spent the entire day in bed. He even arranged for their meals to be delivered to his room and they ate picnic-style on top of the covers. She kept waiting for some invisible shoe to drop, for something to happen that would ruin everything. But the day was absolutely perfect.

She even worried that their first fantastic time making love had been some sort of fluke, or beginner's luck, but over the course of the day, and then later that night, it only got better. They slept in each other's arms, then in the morning, after they showered and ate breakfast, he made it official. He locked himself in his office and called Phillip to ask for her hand.

She paced outside the door like an expectant father awaiting the birth of his first child. And when, after a god-awful twenty minutes, he finally emerged, she asked, "Well?"

"He released you. We have his permission to marry."

She took a deep breath and blew it out, surprised to find that she was relieved. Not that she thought he would demand she come home or that she would listen if he had. He was probably happy to be rid of her. Chris didn't say either way, and she didn't ask. It didn't matter anymore.

"Did you tell him why we're in such a rush?" she asked.

"Of course not. That's no one else's business." He glanced down to her belly, then up to her face, a grin unfolding across his lips. "When will we know for sure?"

"A few weeks, I guess. I'm really not sure how soon you can tell." Although deep down she knew already that she was. She could just...*feel* it. Feel the cells dividing and growing, building a tiny little person. And though things were moving along a little faster than she would have expected, she was excited at the prospect of starting a family.

The really amazing thing was how comfortable Chris seemed in their decision to marry now. He hadn't come right out and said it, but like her, he must have fallen hard and fast. To be fair, she hadn't said it either. She had the feelings, but wasn't quite ready to drop the love bomb. When the time was right, it would happen.

Chris's parents and sisters arrived home after noon, and he gathered the entire family together to announce their engagement. Melissa was so nervous her hands were trembling. They had been so nice to her during her visit, and his mother had gone so far as to hint that Chris had feelings for her, but what if they rejected the idea of their engagement?

"I think it's wonderful," the queen said, taking both of Melissa's hands and squeezing them. The king shook Chris's hand, then gave Melissa a hug and a kiss on the cheek. They made no mention about how quickly it had all happened, almost as though they'd been expecting it. Maybe, due to the king's health, they were anxious to see their son marry. And what would be more wonderful than giving him a grandchild.

Chris's siblings were a little less enthusiastic. They weren't negative or outwardly hostile, but as they expressed their congratulations, their embraces were a little stiff and their smiles didn't quite reach their eyes. She couldn't blame them for being wary. They hardly knew her. Put in their position, she would feel the same way.

She wasn't sure what to say to them to ease their concerns, so she said nothing at all. They would see in time that her feelings for Chris were genuine. She would have to be patient.

Sophie called later that evening to congratulate her, and Melissa was surprised to find that she sounded the slightest bit wary, too.

"You're sure you want to do this?" Sophie asked her. "Three weeks is so soon. You barely know him."

"I'm sure," Melissa insisted. If not one hundred percent, then a solid ninety-nine point nine.

"Well, the prince must really be something if you fell for him that fast."

He was everything she could have ever hoped for in a husband. "He is."

"I look forward to getting to know him. Maybe you two could spend a few days of your honeymoon here."

"I'll mention it to Chris. I'll be coming back to the palace for a few days to pack my things. After all of the wedding plans are made."

"I know these past months on Morgan Isle haven't been the easiest for you," she said. "I'm happy for you, Melissa. That you found someone."

More like happy that she was no longer their problem. Their burden to bear.

"We'll plan a celebratory dinner for when you're here," Sophie said. "Just the family."

"That would be nice." She didn't doubt they would all feel very much like celebrating her permanent departure.

When she hung up with Sophie, Melissa went looking for Chris and found him in his office. He rose to his feet as she entered the room. "How are you feeling?"

"Excited. And a little overwhelmed. There's so much to do, and so little time to do it."

"I mean, how are you *feeling?*" His gaze dropped to her stomach, and she realized what he meant.

"Oh, that." She laid a hand on her belly. "I think it's too soon to feel much of anything."

"You haven't changed your mind about marrying me?"

She grinned and shook her head.

He returned her smile. "Good, then, I have something for you." He took something from his top drawer, then stepped around his desk. When she saw that what he held was a small velvet ring box, her heart leapt up into her throat. It hadn't even occurred to her that he hadn't given her an engagement ring yet.

"My mother gave this to me after we told her the news. It was my grandmother's on my mother's side. She would be honored if you wore it." He flipped the box open and inside, on a bed of crimson satin, sat a ring so gorgeous it nearly brought her to tears. In the center, set in a wide gold band, was a flawless, princess-cut diamond surrounded by a ring of smaller, shimmering sapphires.

"Oh," she breathed. "It's beautiful."

"It's not very big. If you would prefer a larger stone…"

"I don't care how big it is. This is so special. It's a

part of your family history." Now *she* was a part of their family, too.

He took it from the box and she held out her hand. He gently slid the ring onto her finger.

It was a perfect fit.

Puzzled, she asked, "How did you know the size?"

"I didn't," he said, looking just as perplexed. "I haven't had it sized yet. Your finger must be the exact same size as my grandmother's."

Well, that had to mean something, didn't it? Maybe it was karma or fate.

She moved her hand in the sunlight shining through his office window and the stones shimmered. No one had ever given her such a special, meaningful gift.

Melissa threw her arms around his neck and hugged him. "I'll cherish it."

"When you become queen, you'll wear my mother's ring," he said.

If she never wore another ring in her life but this one, she would be eternally happy. The idea that she would someday be queen of the country was difficult to grasp. She'd barely gotten used to the idea of being a princess. But as long as she was with Chris, as long as they were a family, they could be beggars for all she cared.

This was the first day of the rest of her life, and she planned to live it to the fullest.

Exhausted from the excitement, Melissa went to bed early and Chris called a meeting with his siblings.

Though everyone should have been thrilled by the news—this was what they'd wanted, wasn't it?—the mood was gloomy at best. When he asked for their thoughts, Anne wasn't shy about speaking her mind.

"I think it's terrible," she said, arms folded stubbornly across her chest.

"This was the plan," Chris reminded her. "What's best for our country."

"But if you're going to marry someone," Louisa said, "it should be someone you love."

"I don't have that luxury," Chris told her. "I have to consider what's best for the country. And you can't argue that this is an ideal situation."

"It doesn't bother you that she's only in it for the benefits?" Anne asked. "That she's essentially waiting for our parents to pass on so that she can be queen?"

"You make her sound so cold and calculating," Aaron said.

Anne shrugged. "If the shoe fits."

"Don't forget," Chris told her, "that this arrangement will be mutually beneficial. We both know what we're doing. Neither of us is in it for love."

Louisa frowned. "It still seems wrong."

Chris wasn't exactly thrilled about it either. Given the choice, he might never marry. But that had never been an option for him. And if they were going to lose their father, he only hoped he could give him a grandchild first.

"If it makes you feel any better," Chris said, "I'm

quite fond of her. I think she'll make a fine wife and a good mother."

"I noticed that she slept in your room last night," Aaron said.

Did Aaron think Chris would agree to spend the rest of his life with a woman without first making sure they were sexually compatible? They should at least have that much in common. "And your point is?"

"If Mother finds out you're sleeping with her before the wedding, she'll blow a gasket."

"Yeah," Anne agreed. "She foolishly believes we're all still pure as the driven snow. Except for Louisa, who actually is."

Louisa pinned her with an irritated look.

"Who I sleep with is not our mother's business," Chris said. "But should the need arise, we'll be very discreet."

"How much do you plan to tell her about our current situations?" Aaron asked, meaning their new pal the Gingerbread Man, and the troubles with the crops.

"As little as possible. Especially before the wedding."

"And Father's health?" Louisa asked.

Chris figured he might as well tell them the truth. "She already knows."

Anne's jaw dropped. "You *told* her!"

"She figured it out by herself. She's an intelligent woman. She was bound to notice eventually. Besides, if he decides to try the heart pump, it's going to be impossible to keep it a secret."

"For all we know that worked in our favor," Aaron said. "The sooner he dies, the sooner she'll be queen."

"Enough!" Chris barked, startling not only his siblings, but himself as well. "She is a member of this family now and I expect everyone to treat her with respect. Understand?"

He received silent nods from everyone.

Even though much of what they said was probably true, he felt this irrational urge to defend Melissa. He refused to go through life having this constantly thrown back in his face. They were just going to have to accept the situation and learn to live with it.

So was he.

Twelve

Melissa had had no idea of everything that went into planning a wedding. The queen hired a world-renowned wedding planner, who brought with her hordes of assistants, not to mention list upon list upon list of all the things they needed to accomplish in only three weeks' time.

Only a few days into the planning, while they were deciding on the flowers, Melissa felt a twinge in her abdomen. Those telltale cramps that always warned her that her period would soon start. At first she hoped it was just a fluke, or maybe something she'd eaten. But the cramps became worse, and though she willed it with all her heart not to be true, she had no choice but to accept the inevitable. A sudden and overwhelming sob began to build in the back of her throat.

What was wrong with her? She hadn't cried since she was ten years old.

Mortified at the thought of embarrassing herself in front of the queen and the planner, she rose from her seat. "Will you ladies excuse me, please?"

Her distress must have shown on her face, because the queen's brow wrinkled with concern. "Is everything all right?"

She forced a smile and whispered, "Cramps."

They both nodded sympathetically.

"I'll just go take something," Melissa said.

"Why don't you lie down for a while?" the queen suggested, as though Melissa were some fragile flower. But right now she was relieved for the excuse.

"I think I will," she said. She excused herself and walked calmly up the stairs to her room, her stomach tied in knots. Though that pain didn't even come close to the ache in her heart. She had been so sure that she was pregnant. Had wanted it *so* badly. And what would Chris say? What if he wanted to postpone the wedding?

She considered not telling him until afterward. If he snuck into her room after everyone was asleep, as he had the past few nights, she could plead a headache, or tell him out of respect for his mother she wanted to wait until the honeymoon.

When she realized that she was actually considering lying to him, she felt disgusted with herself. Lies and deception were no way to start a marriage. She had to tell him the truth. If he was angry, or didn't understand, maybe he wasn't the man she thought he was.

She called his office from her room, but his assistant told her that he was in the east fields. He seemed to be spending a lot of time there lately.

"I could call down there," she told Melissa.

"Would you, please? Tell him I need to see him right away. It's urgent."

"I'll call right away, Your Highness."

Melissa hung up the phone, and all she could do was wait nervously. But she didn't have to wait long. After only ten minutes or so there was a knock on the door, then it opened and Chris was standing there.

When he saw her sitting on the bed, he frowned. "What's wrong? My assistant said it was urgent."

She opened her mouth to tell him that nothing was wrong, but her throat closed so tight she couldn't get any air to pass through. She could hardly breathe, much less speak, and her hands were trembling.

Chris's frown deepened. He walked over to the bed and sat beside her. "Melissa, tell me what's wrong."

She pushed down the knot of fear building in her chest and forced herself to say, in a clear, strong voice, "I'm not pregnant."

Not only did Chris not look angry or upset, he actually looked relieved. "Is that it?"

She wasn't sure how to take that. Deep down had he hoped she *wasn't* pregnant?

"I thought you wanted a baby."

"I do," he said. "But when my secretary told me it was urgent, I though something was wrong. Like maybe you'd changed your mind and decided not to marry me."

"And I thought you might be upset and decide you didn't want to marry me."

"I'm disappointed, but not upset." He took her in his arms and held her, and she hugged him fiercely. Maybe this was what happened when two people who barely knew each other jumped into a marriage. They just needed time to get to know one another a little better. They had all the time in the world.

He grinned down at her and said, "We'll just have to try again. Practice makes perfect, right?"

And, oh, she did enjoy the practicing they'd been doing. She did the math and grinned. "I should be ovulating while we're on our honeymoon."

"See," he said. "That will be perfect."

He was right, it would be. They could celebrate their marriage, their new life together, by creating a new life of their own. She hugged him close, pressing her cheek to of his chest. She heard the steady thump of his heart, felt his warmth seeping through the cotton of his shirt. She never should have worried that he would be anything but sympathetic and understanding. Once again she experienced that overwhelming sense of happiness. The feeling that this was right.

Melissa was so busy for the next two weeks planning every last detail of the wedding, she barely even saw

Chris. It seemed as though whenever she had free time, he was in a meeting, or out in one of the fields. Usually the east. One of these days they were going to have to finish that tour, and take the trip into the village. She was anxious to see the country she would now call home, and meet its people.

The idea of being queen someday was still a little overwhelming and frightening, but with any luck she wouldn't have to worry about that for a very long time. She learned from Chris that the king had made the decision to try the heart pump. His surgery had been scheduled for the beginning of August, barely more than a month away. Everyone was scared, of course, but hopeful that the procedure would be a success, and his heart would begin to heal.

Melissa made something of a monumental decision of her own.

"I'm going to sell my estate in New Orleans," she told Chris during their morning coffee, the brief time they were able to spend together most days.

"But that house has been in your family for generations," he said.

"In my great-aunt's family. I may have inherited it, but it never really was mine. I always sort of felt like a guest in my own home."

"You're sure you want to do this?" he asked, and if he looked concerned, she knew he was only considering her well-being.

"I am." In fact, she felt it was something that she

needed to do. Thomas Isle was her home now. New Orleans was just another place she'd lived, and she couldn't see herself ever going back. She smiled and said, "Besides, why do I need a house in the U.S., when my home, my *family,* is here?"

"Good point," he said, returning her smile. "What about all of your things?"

"All that's left belonged to my aunt and uncle." It would only serve as a reminder of unhappier times. She wanted to leave all of that behind. Start fresh. And she knew the perfect way. "I'd like to arrange for an auction, and with your blessing, donate the proceeds to cardiac research."

"Of course you have my blessing." He reached across the table and took her hand. "I would be honored."

There was sadness in his eyes. Though he didn't speak often of the king's health, she knew it troubled him.

She gave his hand a squeeze. "The heart pump will work. He'll probably outlive us all."

"I hope you're right." He looked down at their hands clasped together, grazing her palm with his thumb. "This is…comfortable."

"Yes," she agreed. "It is."

Four days before the wedding, Melissa flew back to Morgan Isle to pack her things. Her family greeted her warmly, and she was a little stunned when Sophie and Hannah threw her a surprise wedding shower. In attendance were her half sister and sister-in-law, Charles's wife Victoria, and a few family friends that Melissa had met only briefly at the last benefit hosted by the royal family. It was small and intimate, and to her surprise, a lot of fun.

"We planned to hire a male stripper," Sophie told her, "But Phillip found out and had a fit."

Melissa shrugged. "It's the thought that counts, right?"

"Yeah, but nothing beats a pair of tight buns wiggling an inch from your face," Sophie said.

Hannah shot her a curious look. "You know, I thought I heard music coming from your suite the other night. Alex must have some hidden talents."

Sophie grinned. "Oh, you have *no* idea."

"Must run in the family," Victoria said, and everyone laughed.

It was strange, but for the first time since Melissa had arrived on Morgan Isle she felt as though she belonged. She had finally gained access to the club, the secret handshake being her engagement, she supposed. She was finally one of them.

Melissa spent the next few days sorting her things, deciding what she would bring with her and what would go into storage. The night before the wedding, Phillip called her into his office.

"Close the door behind you," he said as she stepped inside.

"Is something wrong?"

"No." He gestured to the empty chair by his desk. "Sit down. Would you like a drink?"

She was half tempted to say *do I need one?* Instead she sat and said, "No, thank you. What's on your mind?"

"I just thought we should have a talk."

"About…?"

"I want you to know you're in no way obligated to do this."

She frowned. "Do what?"

"Marry Prince Christian."

Why would he think she'd feel obligated? Sure, the marriage would bring opportunities and benefits to both their countries, but there was so much more to it than that. She loved Chris. Even though she hadn't actually told him so. She'd decided to save that for their wedding night, to make it more special. And if all went as planned, she would come home from their honeymoon pregnant.

"I *want* to marry him," she told Phillip.

He looked relieved. "I'm glad to hear that."

Early the next morning the family boarded the royal plane and flew to Thomas Isle together, where they were whisked off to the castle in a motorcade of shiny black Bentleys decorated for the occasion. Outside the gates of the castle a crowd of villagers waited, cheering as they drove past.

It was a monumental day for their country, and for Morgan Isle as well. It was the first time in centuries that the two monarchies had come together under optimistic circumstances. And how much more optimistic could you get than two families uniting?

In the four days since she'd left, the castle grounds had been transformed to host the nuptials. Everywhere Melissa looked she saw curled ribbons and flowers. The ceremony would take place on the bluff overlooking the ocean, and the reception would follow directly after, held under a city of white tents on the castle grounds.

An outdoor wedding always held the risk of rain, but she couldn't have asked for a more beautiful day. Sunny, warm and dry, and not a cloud in the sky. Even the wind cooperated, and there wasn't more than a gentle breeze, even by the bluff.

There were so many people there—hundreds of guests, all focused on her—but as Phillip walked her down the aisle, the only one she saw was Chris. He stood waiting for her in his white, formal royal dress uniform. She wore the dress that her mother and grand-mother had both worn, a timeless creation of the finest silk and lace and priceless pearls.

If she'd had any doubts at all, they were erased when he took her hands and smiled down at her. After they exchanged vows and rings and were presented to the guests as husband and wife, everyone cheered.

The reception that followed was such a blur of new faces and conversation, Melissa felt dizzy. It seemed that everyone wanted to meet the future queen. She was so swamped she didn't even have time to eat, though everyone she spoke to told her the food was delicious. And through it all, Chris stayed close by her side.

Precisely at dusk, she and Chris had their first dance

as husband and wife, then Chris danced with his mother and Melissa with her father-in-law. The first man who would be any kind of father at all to her since she was ten years old.

He twirled her confidently across the dance floor, but underneath the smile he wore for the cameras and the guests, he looked exhausted.

"Maybe you should rest for a while," she told him. He'd been on his feet all day.

"They told you about my heart," he said.

She nodded, hoping he wouldn't be angry.

He just shrugged. "I suppose everyone will know soon enough. There will be no hiding it when I'm carting around a heart pump, will there?"

"Maybe we should sit down. Rest for a minute."

"I'm fine," he insisted. "It isn't every day a man's oldest son gets married."

"Yes, but you shouldn't push yourself."

"You'll be a good wife to my son." He winked and smiled. "You sound just like his mother."

She hoped she would be a good wife. It wasn't as though she had any experience. Good or bad. She was flying blind on this one.

"I want you to know how much this means to us," he said. "This marriage. What it will do for our countries."

Why did everyone seem to think that she was doing this for the country? Did no one believe that she was marrying Chris because she wanted to? Because he wanted to marry her?

She couldn't think of what to say, so she didn't say anything at all.

A short time later she and Chris said good-bye to their guests and family so they could change and catch a plane to Paris, where they would spend the first week of their honeymoon. It took three maids twenty minutes to get her unfastened and out of her dress. It would be the last time she used this room. While they were gone on their honeymoon, her things would be moved to Chris's room. No more sneaking around and worrying the queen might catch them being naughty. Although the thrill of it had been fun for a while. But it would be nice, even something of a relief, to finally settle into their life together.

She had just changed into the suit she would wear for the trip when Chris knocked on her door. Probably to warn her that they were running late.

She opened the door and the instant she saw his pale skin and shell-shocked look, her heart filled with dread. "What happened?"

"It's my father," he said grimly. "Something is wrong."

Thirteen

The doctor emerged from the king's room in the royal family's private wing at the hospital looking grim, and Chris steeled himself for the worst.

"It was a mild heart attack," he told them. "But there was damage."

The queen's face went ashen and Louisa began crying quietly. Melissa gave Chris's hand a gentle squeeze.

Chris couldn't help but feel that this was his fault. That the excitement the last few weeks was the catalyst for the attack. "Maybe if we'd postponed the wedding—"

"Don't even talk like that," Aaron said. "He wanted this wedding."

"He's right," Anne said. "It's been ages since I've seen him so happy."

"What do we do now?" his mother asked the doctor.

"The heart pump is going to have to go in as soon as possible."

"How soon?" Anne asked.

"As soon as the surgeon can fly in and prepare."

Chris frowned. "I though they would do the surgery in England."

"He's too weak to be moved. But don't worry, we have everything he needs right here."

"How is he now?" his mother asked.

"In surprisingly good spirits. But then, he's always been a resilient man."

"Can we see him?" Chris asked.

"Of course. Just remember that he does need his rest. I'll let you know the minute the surgery is scheduled."

After he was gone, Chris turned to his mother. "I'd like to go in alone for a minute."

She nodded. Melissa let go of his hand and flashed him an understanding, sympathetic smile. He couldn't help but wonder what she was really thinking. Was she upset that they'd had to cancel their honeymoon, or that they were spending their wedding night in a hospital waiting room? Or did she consider herself that much closer to the crown?

It was a terrible thing to wonder about the woman he'd just vowed to spend the rest of his life with. But what had he expected from a marriage of convenience?

He entered his father's room. He looked so small and pale lying in the bed, hooked to all those machines. Before his heart had begun to fail him, even in the first few years of his illness, he had always seemed larger than life to Chris. Indestructible. Though all of his life Chris had been told the crown would one day be his, and he'd spent every day preparing for it, he had never really fathomed the idea of his father dying. Now the end seemed to hover over them like a thick black cloud.

Chris wasn't ready.

His father's eyes were closed, but when he heard the door, he opened them, smiling when he saw Chris walking toward him.

"You sure do know how to liven up a party," Chris joked.

The king smiled. "You know me, always wanting to be the center of attention."

"They tell me it worked."

He sighed, the humor gone from his eyes. "Is it too much to expect that the five hundred guests I collapsed in front of will keep this to themselves?"

He took a seat on the edge of the bed. "It's a media frenzy outside the hospital."

He nodded. "I expected as much."

"To avoid rumors, we decided it would be best to just tell everyone the truth."

"A wise decision. I can see you'll do just fine without me."

"The pump is going to work," he said, though he didn't know whom he was trying to convince, his father or himself.

James shrugged. "Statistically speaking, it could go

either way. Maybe, now that you're married and ready to take the crown, my body knew it was time. It was ready to give out."

But Chris *wasn't* ready. "Don't even talk like that."

"Don't worry. My body may be ready to give up, but I'm not. But this will mean that you'll have to assume my duties until I'm well. Work with the prime ministers of both islands on the new trade agreements."

"I'm ready to do that."

"Just don't get *too* comfortable on the throne."

He grinned. "Of course not."

"Why don't you tell everyone else to come in?" he said, his way of telling Chris that everything that needed to be said had been said.

"Of course." He rose from the bed and walked to the door, but his father called back to him.

"I meant to ask you, is Datt making any progress with those threatening e-mails, and have you learned anything new about the situation in the east fields?"

Chris was so stunned he didn't know what to say. They had been so careful to keep it quiet. Obviously someone had snitched.

His father's voice was stern as he added, "I appreciate that you're trying to protect me, son, but I'm still the one running this country. From now on I expect to be kept in the loop."

It was nearly 3:00 a.m. when Melissa, Chris, Anne, Louisa and Aaron got back to the castle. The queen had insisted on staying at the hospital with her husband. She didn't say *in case he takes a turn for the worse,* but that was probably what everyone was thinking. He wouldn't be out of the woods until the pump was in, and even then it would be touch and go.

Melissa tried not to see it as a bad omen, her father-in-law's health taking a sharp decline on her wedding night. And she immediately felt guilty for even thinking that way.

Though no one had come right out and said it, she couldn't escape the feeling that Chris's siblings had resented her presence at the hospital. Maybe they blamed the excitement of the wedding for this setback.

Or it could just be her own insecurities skewing her judgment. They were worried and upset and didn't have time to think about how they were treating their new sister-in-law. This wasn't about her, or her marriage. And she was determined to do whatever was needed, whatever she could, to make this easier for Chris and his family. Although the idea of the king dying, and her becoming queen right away, terrified her.

She and Chris changed into their pajamas and crawled into bed—the bed they would share from now on. She assumed they would go right to sleep. God knew it had been an exhausting day. But Chris reached for her, pulling her against him. Then he kissed her, slow and sweet at first, then deeper. His hands began to roam, first on top of her nightclothes, then underneath them.

"We don't have to," she told him, so he wouldn't feel obligated just because it was their wedding night.

He pulled her nightgown up over her head and tossed it to the floor, his eyes raking over her, filled with lust and longing. "I want to."

"Me, too," she admitted.

"You said you would be ovulating. At least something good could come out of this night."

She tried not to let his words sting. She knew he hadn't meant that the way it sounded, that he saw nothing good in the fact that they had just been married. Or that the only reason he wanted to make love to his new wife was to impregnate her. He was upset, and exhausted and probably not thinking clearly. He needed her understanding, not her judgment. So instead of letting it bother her, she pulled him to her and kissed him.

Since the first time they had slept together, sex had been fantastic. Better than fantastic. Hot and urgent and almost frantic in its intensity. Tonight was different. His touch was so tender, his kisses so sweet it made her want to cry.

What better way to celebrate their wedding night, to possibly create a life?

Afterward she hugged herself close to his body. She closed her eyes and breathed in the scent of his skin. In her life she'd never felt so close to a man. To *anyone*. And she knew, without a doubt, that these intense feelings she had, this need to be with him, was love. She was finally ready to say it, to put her heart on the line.

"I love you, Chris," she said, rubbing her cheek against his warm chest, expecting him to immediately return the sentiment.

He didn't say a word.

He'd probably just fallen asleep, she told herself. It had been a long and exhausting day.

She looked up at him and saw that his eyes were open, fixed at some random spot on the ceiling above them. Maybe he hadn't heard her.

She rose up on her elbow and said it again, so this time he could hear. "I love you, Chris."

"I heard you the first time," he said, and his voice, his tone, were so cold a chill passed through her.

This is not as bad as it seems, she assured herself. It was just a misunderstanding. "And you have nothing to say to me?" she asked.

"I have to say, I'm a little disappointed."

He was disappointed?

"I didn't think you would feel the need to manipulate me," he said.

Manipulate him?

Melissa sat up, clutching the covers to her chest. "Maybe they do things differently here on Thomas Isle, but where I come from, it's customary for a wife to tell her husband she loves him."

Chris sat up beside her. "There's no point in pretending we don't know exactly what kind of marriage this is going to be."

She felt sick to her stomach. With fear and confusion and dread. "What kind of marriage is it?"

"This is a business arrangement. A pact between two countries. Love was never part of the deal."

Melissa felt a pain in her chest, as though someone had driven a dagger clear through her heart. In that instant everything became painfully clear, and the perfect life she'd imagined that she and Chris would have together disintegrated before her eyes.

It all made sense. The elaborate welcome and over-the-top hospitality. All the talk of their countries *uniting,* and what a good thing she was doing marrying the prince.

She'd been set up.

When they talked about their countries joining resources, she'd never guessed that the commodity they'd had in mind was her. She'd been invited here not for a diplomatic visit, but so that the prince could judge her suitability. They had paraded her around like a cow at auction, then essentially bought her from the family that had never wanted her around to begin with. They had to know. She wondered if Phillip and Chris had discussed it on the phone. Laughed together about the way she'd been so easily fooled.

And here she'd believed that for the first time in her life, a man really cared for her. *Wanted* her. But as usual, she was only good for her money and connections.

How could she have been so stupid? So blind to the truth? Was there something wrong with her, some defect in her personally that made people incapable of loving or caring about her?

Humiliation burned her like acid from the inside out. She wanted to run, but she had nowhere to go. No place to call home. Her home in New Orleans was on the auction block and they obviously didn't want her on Morgan Isle. And even if she did have somewhere to run to, leaving him now could strain the peace between their countries and lead to international disaster. What would that do to the king's heart?

Did she really want to be responsible for that? Her own foolishness and naïveté had gotten her into this mess. She'd been so desperate to be loved, she had seen something that wasn't there. She had done this to herself, and she was getting exactly what she deserved.

Chris switched on the lamp beside the bed, the light blinding her for a moment. It was about time she came out of the dark. When she saw the disbelief on his face, she wished he'd left it off.

"Are you trying to tell me that you had no idea?" Chris asked her.

She shrugged. "I guess the joke is on me."

The pity in his eyes nearly did her in.

"Melissa—"

She held up a hand to stop him. The last thing she wanted was him feeling sorry for her. "Please, don't say anything."

She was humiliated enough.

"It's been a long day. I think we both need to sleep,"

he said. "Things will be clearer tomorrow. We can talk about it then."

Oh, yes. Sleep was the answer. Everything would be better in the morning. Maybe she would grow a new heart, to replace the one he'd just torn to pieces.

And with any luck, this one would be made of stone.

Melissa and Chris didn't talk in the morning. Or the morning after that.

On the third morning the king had his surgery—and came through with flying colors—and the subject of their marriage, or lack of one, conveniently never came up again. Despite the fact that she felt like a phony and an outsider she stayed beside Chris at the hospital, enduring the indifference from his siblings. Apparently there was no more need for the warmth and courtesy they had shown her at first. If they even acknowledged her presence it was a good day. She wore a facade of indifference, refusing to let them see how deeply they were hurting her. She wouldn't give them the satisfaction.

Every night she and Chris crawled into bed and when he reached for her, and she was so desperate for affection, so lonely, she couldn't tell him no. And the way he made love to her, so tender and sweet, she couldn't believe it was possible that he had no feelings for her at all. She kept telling herself that in time he would learn to love her. Maybe when they had a child. She prayed every night those first few weeks that she had conceived. Then her period started, right on time, and she felt like even more of a failure. As though Mother Nature was playing a cruel trick on her.

Next month, she told herself. *It'll happen next month.* But it didn't, and not for lack of trying, either. The bedroom seemed to be the only place she saw Chris lately. With his father out of commission, he had taken over the majority of the king's duties. He was too busy to spend time with her. It was probably for the best, because even when he was there, he wasn't really *there.* She tried to talk with him, about anything, but it seemed as though he had completely shut her out.

She passed many hours with the king and queen. He only left the castle for doctor visits, so they spent most of their time taking slow walks in the garden or watching television. They were the only ones who treated her with any affection. But they had so many problems of their own, she never dared admit how unhappy Chris was making her, or the way the others had been treating her. She just kept a bright smile pasted on her face and pretended everything was okay. Besides, how long would their affection last? Would they eventually tire of her, too?

If she had a baby, at least there would be someone to love her. Someone who needed her.

After the second month and no luck, Chris suggested they talk to a fertility specialist.

"Just to be sure," he said.

To make him happy she agreed, and endured the humiliating tests, convinced all the while that there was nothing wrong. She wasn't ancient, but at thirty-three she probably wasn't quite as fertile as she'd been in her twenties. They just had to be patient and keep trying.

She was so sure that everything was fine she could hardly believe it when, on a cool and breezy fall morning, the doctor calmly informed them that Melissa had a bum ovary and the tube on her good side wasn't in the best shape, either.

"What does that mean?" Chris asked.

"Conceiving naturally could be a challenge."

Chris didn't look at her, but she knew exactly what he was thinking. Not only had he married a woman he didn't love, but she couldn't even manage to give him an heir. His family was going to have a field day with this.

"What do you suggest?" she asked the doctor, hoping there was some simple solution. Some quick surgery that would fix the problem.

"I think we should wait a few more months and see if we get lucky. If after that you're still not pregnant, we'll consider in vitro fertilization."

"How many months?" she asked.

"Let's give it six."

She didn't think she could endure the loneliness another six months. A baby was the only way she could see to make Chris love her. But what could she do? Beg the doctor to do the in vitro now? Insist?

"I'm sorry," she said, when she and Chris were alone in the car.

"It's not your fault," he told her, but she could tell he blamed her.

No matter how hard she tried to be a good wife, the woman he wanted her to be, she never seemed to measure up.

Fourteen

Melissa looked so devastated and sad that Chris wanted to take her in his arms and hold her. He knew it was what she needed, but he couldn't make himself do it. It wouldn't be fair to her. He would only be leading her on, making her believe he cared more than he actually did. That this marriage was more than a business deal.

Coming to her in bed every night, that wasn't leading her on? That was fair?

No, he kept telling himself. That was just sex. And sex, despite what a lot of people thought, had nothing to do with love. He couldn't help but wonder, if she was so unhappy, why not just leave? Why not go home to Morgan Isle?

The answer was clear.

Despite her claim to love him, she was only using him for his title, for the opportunity to be queen. She couldn't take the crown of her own country. So she would take his mother's instead. She was no different than all the other women who had used him over the years. She simply had the benefit of royal blood running through her veins.

To be fair, they were using each other.

And if that was true, why did he feel so damned guilty for making her unhappy? And why didn't she seem all that interested in his mother's title?

Despite what she believed, he didn't blame her for their fertility problems. Now that his father was stable that urgency to have a child had subsided. They wouldn't know for sure if his heart function had improved until they took him off the pump, but there had been a reduction in swelling already. The doctors were hopeful it would work.

Chris had to give Melissa credit. She'd stayed by him through it all. All those long, boring hours in the hospital, she'd never left his side. She'd endured the indifference from his siblings, who for the most part chose to pretend she wasn't even there, and the occasional scathing remark when they decided to acknowledge her.

And why did she bother? She had no one to impress. No one to win over. She was already in, a shoo-in for the throne. Unless that wasn't really her motivation.

Lately, he just wasn't sure anymore. And those doubts had been gnawing at him.

His brother and sisters certainly weren't making it easy for her. Chris assumed that eventually they would learn to accept her, but it wasn't working out that way, and he was losing patience with them. Finally he broached the subject at one of their mandatory weekly meetings.

They had just finished discussing how the added security measures seemed to have taken care of their Gingerbread Man. Everyone started to rise from their chairs, and Chris told them, "There's one more thing I'd like to discuss. The issue with Melissa."

Everyone settled back into their seats and Anne asked, "What issue is that?"

"We've been married nearly three months now, and it's time you all began showing her a little respect."

"Respect?" Anne scoffed. "You've seen the way she sits there all high and mighty, not saying a word to anyone, thinking she's better than us."

"How do you know what she's thinking?" Chris asked.

"You can see it in her eyes."

What they never saw, what Melissa didn't allow them to see, was the hurt in her eyes when they rejected her. They didn't see the sadness she only let show when she thought no one was around. They didn't hear her crying softly in the middle of the night when she thought he was asleep.

Louisa, who never had a bad thing to say about anyone, added, "She is a little…cold."

"And when was the last time either of you said

anything to her?" Chris asked, then qualified that with, "Something that wasn't rude or sarcastic."

"It's a two-way street," Aaron said. "She doesn't talk to us either."

"And who could blame her, when she knows that all she'll receive in return is a snide remark or cold glare? Has it never occurred to any of you that she's terrified of being rejected? That her cold nature is a defense mechanism?"

Had it never occurred to him either?

"What does she have to be afraid of?" Anne said. "She has us exactly where she wants us."

"And where is that?" Chris asked.

Anne looked at him like he was dense. "She's going to be queen."

"Are you sure that's what she wants?"

"Why else would she be here?" Aaron asked.

A good question. One he'd been asking himself.

"Something happened on the night of Father's surgery," he told them. "Something I've been thinking a lot about lately. Melissa and I were sitting alone, waiting for news, and just in case he didn't make it, I was telling her what to expect. You know, the series of events that would lead to the coronation. What her duties would be as queen. I'm not sure how I expected her to react."

"How did she react?" Aaron asked.

"She looked absolutely *terrified.* She went so pale I was afraid she might faint or be sick. When Father came through the surgery I could swear she was more relieved than we were. Every time I mention her becoming queen she changes the subject, or tells me that Father will be fine. That he'll probably outlive us all."

His siblings all looked at one another, then Aaron asked, "What are you trying to say?"

Something he'd been denying for a long time now. Something even he wasn't ready to accept. "I don't think she has any interest in being queen."

"Then why did she marry you?" Anne asked.

"I think," Chris said. "that she...*loves* me."

Everyone looked at him in stunned silence.

She had never told him again after that first time, not that he blamed her when he considered the way he'd rejected her, but she'd shown it in a million little ways. She'd done everything she could to be a good wife, and he'd given her nothing in return. He honestly didn't know if he was capable of giving her what she really needed.

"You're serious?" Anne asked. "You're not just trying to guilt us into being nice to her?"

"She told me she loved me on our wedding night," he said.

"What did you do?" Aaron asked.

"I accused her of trying to manipulate me."

Anne winced. "That was brutal."

He shot her a look. "Thanks. I hadn't already figured that out."

"I feel so awful," Louisa said, tears welling in his eyes. "We were so mean to her."

"If our genius brother hadn't waited until just now

to tell us this," Anne told her, "we never would have been mean in the first place."

"You want to feel even worse?" Chris asked them. "She claimed not to know why she was invited here."

"So, what, she thought you married her because you were madly in love?" Aaron asked.

Chris shrugged. "I guess so."

Louisa slapped a hand over her mouth, looking as though she might be sick.

"Why didn't you tell us?" Anne asked.

"Because I didn't believe her. I didn't want to believe."

"Typical man," Anne scoffed.

"I screwed up," Chris said. "And now things are going to have to change."

"Of course," Aaron said, and the girls nodded in agreement.

It was a bit of a relief to finally admit the truth. Not only to his family, but to himself.

"We're flying to Morgan Isle for some hotel's grand opening tomorrow. We'll be back the following afternoon. Maybe you could all do something nice for her."

"Maybe a welcome-home party," Louisa suggested.

"We'll figure something out," Anne told him. "And maybe you should do something nice for her, too. I'd probably start with an apology."

He would have to do something.

As everyone got up and left, Chris realized, there was one obvious question no one had asked.

Did he love Melissa?

And he was glad no one had, because he didn't have a clue what he would have told them.

It was good to be back on Morgan Isle. It surprised Melissa how much she had missed it, missed being in the palace, and around people who actually acknowledged her presence. Everyone seemed genuinely happy to see her and told her how much they had missed her. At the party they treated her like family. For the first time in months she felt...*happy*. It was such a relief, she felt like clinging to them all at once and weeping. And she used to be so strong. What had happened to her? What had she let happen?

People talked to her and men asked her to dance, and for the first time in a while, it didn't sting so much that her own husband didn't love her. Perhaps the problem wasn't that she was unlovable, but that Chris was just incapable of love. Maybe he was the defective one, not her. Which she found to be both a relief and inexplicably sad. For once, instead of craving his attention, longing to be noticed, she actually felt sorry for him.

The idea of going back to Thomas Isle, back to that life, left her feeling hollow and lonely. It was at the party that she made a decision, a decision she should have made months ago. She doubted her family would be happy, and she was very sorry about that. If it caused an international disaster, so be it. She couldn't live like this another day. Another minute. She deserved better. And though she might never find it, she had to at least try.

Just making the decision made her feel a million times better. Lighter, and free, as if a heavy burden had been lifted from her shoulders.

She felt like her old self again.

As the party began to wind down, Melissa pulled Sophie aside and asked, "Can we talk? Privately?"

Sophie frowned. "Is something wrong?"

"Maybe. Sort of."

Her brow crinkling with worry, Sophie looked around the ballroom, but there was really no place for a private conversation. She took Melissa by the arm and led her to the door. "Come with me."

They walked out to the lobby, then down a corridor to the business offices. When they were inside one of the offices she closed the door, turned to Melissa and asked, "Is he hurting you?"

The question, and the ferocity with which she asked it, stunned Melissa for a second. "Hurting me?"

"I could tell from the second you arrived that something was wrong. Is he physically abusing you? Because if he is, royalty or not, I'll have to hurt him back."

"Of course not! Chris would never do that. He's a good man." *Just not so hot a husband.*

"Then what's wrong?"

She'd had no idea she was so transparent. That it was so obvious she was unhappy. Or maybe Sophie was just exceptionally perceptive.

In that case, she might as well be totally honest. "I asked to speak to you because frankly, I'm afraid of what Phillip's reaction will be. The blow might be gentler coming from you."

"What blow?"

"I'm leaving Chris."

Sophie stunned Melissa again by pulling her into her arms and hugging her. "I am so sorry. I was afraid this might happen when you rushed into this the way you did."

Melissa pulled back from her embrace. "That was the whole point, wasn't it?"

"What do you mean?"

"Look, I know it was a setup. That it was never meant to be more than a business deal. I thought I could handle it, for the good of the country and all that, but the truth is, I'm miserable."

Sophie frowned. "Back up a minute. What do you mean, about it being a setup?"

"The invitation to Thomas Isle. All the attention they showered on me to make me feel welcome. That was a nice touch, by the way."

Sophie looked hopelessly confused. "Melissa, what are you talking about?"

"Prince Christian needed a wife and I was the convenient choice. A pawn in your political game."

Sophie gaped at her. "My God, Melissa, you don't honestly think we would do that to you?"

She had, until just then. Now she had to wonder if she'd been wrong. "I figured you never really wanted me around anyway."

Sophie took her by the shoulders. "I assure you, if

there was any sort of setup, we knew *nothing* about it. As far as we knew it was just a diplomatic visit. We were *stunned* when you decided to stay and marry the prince. And why in heaven's name would you think we didn't want you around?"

"I was an outsider…a complication. You can't say it hasn't been easier with me gone."

Sophie sighed, looking inexplicably sad. "Melissa, our father left a legacy of scandal, and all we could do is pick up the pieces and move on. Was it complicated? You bet. Has it been easy? Not always. But that certainly wasn't your fault. Despite the circumstances, you're *family.* One of us. You were *always* welcome at the palace. And you always will be."

She hoped that was true. "You don't think Phillip will be angry?"

"Of course not. He'll be happy to have you home. We all will."

Melissa felt limp with relief, as though the nightmare was truly over. "It may not be a sound move diplomatically."

"Screw diplomacy. You're coming home."

Home. The idea sounded so wonderful she felt like weeping. She loved Chris, and she so desperately wanted him to love her back, but that was never going to happen. And they were both miserable.

"I'll talk to Phillip and make the arrangements," Sophie said. "We'll have your things sent here so you don't even have to go back there."

The thought of never seeing the king and queen again made her heart sting. They had been good to her, and she hated the idea of disappointing them. They were the closest thing to parents that she'd had since she lost her own mother and father. She would always appreciate that. She didn't expect them to understand what she was going to do, but she hoped some day they would forgive her.

It was well after 1:00 a.m. when they got back to the palace. As usual, when she and Chris climbed into bed, he reached for her, and for the first time she refused him.

"I'm tired," she said, turning away from him. She wondered if he would insist, or try to convince her, but after a moment of silence, he turned over and went to sleep.

If only he'd told her he loved her. That's all it would have taken. But she couldn't expect him to say something he didn't mean. That wouldn't mean anything to her.

Though it saddened her to the depths of her soul, she knew their marriage was over.

Phillip called Melissa to his office the next morning. "I talked to Sophie. She says that you want to come home."

There was that word again. *Home.* But what if, unlike Sophie, he really didn't want her there?

"Are you angry?" she asked.

"Angry?" He looked surprised by the question. "Why would I be angry?"

"I just want you to know that I don't have to stay at

the palace. I'm sure I could find a nice place in town, or even build something new."

He gestured to the sofa. "Please, have a seat."

She sat down, and he sat beside her. "Melissa, I know that my disposition is not always the warmest. A trait I inherited from our father, unfortunately. Hannah is constantly telling me that I need to lighten up. But I want you to know, and I mean this sincerely, from the bottom of my heart, that you were always, and always will be welcome to stay at the palace. It doesn't matter how or why, you're our family, and your place is with *us*."

His words, said so sincerely, touched her somewhere deep down. If only she had known that months ago, when she first came to Morgan Isle. She might not have been so vulnerable. She would have seen Chris's so-called affection for what it really was.

Not that she was blaming Phillip. This was no one's fault but her own.

"That's good to know," she said.

"I know Sophie already told you this, but I just wanted to clarify that there was never any 'arrangement.' Not of the marital kind. Although in retrospect, I see that whatever was said was misconstrued by them or us, or maybe both. And I take full responsibility."

"To be honest, I think it was all a big, stupid misunderstanding. As much my fault as theirs. It would be best if we all just let it drop."

"Have you talked to him yet?"

"Chris?" she asked and he nodded. She shook her head.

He looked at his watch. "Your plane is due to leave in less than an hour. If you're not going home with him, you should probably let him know."

"You're right."

This wasn't something she was looking forward to, but it had to be done.

Melissa found Chris in the guest suite, packing the last of his things.

"Our flight leaves in forty minutes," he said without looking at her. Maybe he was upset that she'd turned him down last night. Maybe his feelings had been hurt. It could mean that he did care.

Don't do that to yourself, Melissa. Just get this over with.

"I know it does," she said. "I won't be on it."

"You want to stay here longer?"

A lot longer. Like, forever. "Something like that."

He finally turned to her. He looked tired, as though he'd barely slept. "You're mad at me. I get it."

"Why would you think I'm mad?"

"You pretty much ignored me all last night at the party. Dancing with just about every man in the room but me."

She was surprised he noticed. "Not *every* man."

He glared at her. "You want to get on with it? Just say what you have to say, and let's go home."

He really was upset. Their first real fight as husband and wife. Their first and their last.

"I can't do this anymore, Chris."

"Do what?"

"Be with you. Stay on Thomas Isle. I'm lonely and miserable."

"I've talked to my brother and sisters," he said. "Things will be different when we get back. They'll be nice to you now."

And that was supposed to fix everything? "The only person whose actions I give a damn about are yours. The way you treat me, I feel so...*used*."

"It isn't like that," he insisted.

"That's sure how it feels to me."

"So you're just going to give up?"

"At least I *tried*. What have you contributed to this marriage?"

He didn't seem to know how to answer that, so he didn't. "So you're saying it's over?"

"It is for me. The truth is, it has been for a while."

"You're leaving me?"

"Don't worry, I'm sure there are countless women out there who would be happy to marry themselves into a royal title. Younger ones, who will have no trouble bearing lots of children for you."

His expression darkened. "Our fertility issues have nothing to do with my feelings for you."

"You mean *my* fertility issues."

"I never once blamed you."

"But you didn't *not* blame me. And I didn't feel any less like a failure." She stepped closer, feeling almost sorry for him. He probably wasn't used to being rejected. When it came right down to it, she was the stronger one. She had the courage to let go.

"Look, we gave it a shot," she said. "We should quit while we're ahead. Call it even. But this won't affect the trade agreements. I'll see to that."

He shook his head, as though searching for the right thing to say. Something that would make her change her mind, although for the life of her, she didn't know why he cared.

Finally he said, "I can't change who I am, Melissa."

He'd hit the nail right on the head.

"I know," she told him, "and that's exactly why I have to go."

Fifteen

Chris had looked forward to getting back home, getting on with his life, but as the car pulled up to the castle and he saw Aaron, Anne and Louisa waiting— probably for that warm welcome home they'd talked about—he wished he was anywhere else.

The car rolled to a stop, and when he climbed out alone, all three looked confused.

"Melissa isn't with you?" Louisa asked.

"Do you see her anywhere?" Chris snapped.

Startled, she shrank away, looking wounded.

Anne wasn't affected by his sharp tone. "Where is she, then?"

He stomped past them to the door, tossing back over his shoulder, "Morgan Isle."

"When is she coming back?" Aaron called.

He stopped abruptly and turned. He wanted to shout at them, say that if they'd only been nicer to her, this never would have happened. But the only one to blame for this mess was him. "Never," he told them. "She's never coming back."

He left them in stunned silence and went straight to his room. He didn't feel up to explaining this to his parents. He didn't even know where to begin.

The second he stepped in his room and closed the door, he knew it was a mistake. Everything here reminded him of Melissa. The trinkets and keepsakes on the dresser, and the photo of her and her parents. He could even smell her. A mix of her shampoo and soap and the citrus body spray she used. She'd left an indelible mark on everything.

He walked over to the dresser and picked up the photo. She and her parents looked so happy. She didn't talk about it much, but he knew how devastating it had been for her to lose them, then to feel so unwanted by her guardians. She'd moved to Morgan Isle, where she had admittedly never felt as though she fit in. Then they'd invited her here, where she was welcomed with open arms and affection, and the instant she became family, was treated like a trespasser. And all she'd ever wanted was someone to love her.

Talk about playing a cruel trick. And all because of a few crossed wires. Because he thought they were on the same page in regard to their arranged marriage.

It's a wonder she hadn't left him that first week. They might all have been better off.

He wanted to believe that this was for the best, but he wasn't sure what to believe. He would be lying if he said he hadn't grown fond of her. He actually liked having her around. And not just for the sex, although that was beyond satisfying. The idea of not waking up to feel her curled against him, not seeing her beautiful smile again, caused a strange aching sensation in his chest.

Maybe it he wasn't ready to let go. To give up. Maybe things could be different.

He set the photo back down. She'd asked him to have her things shipped home to her. But *this* was her home. She belonged here, with him. She had to know that. Maybe it was like poker and she was bluffing in attempt to get him to call his hand. Trying to *make* him love her.

If she really loved him, she would be back, he told himself, feeling better already. He gave her a couple of days, a week, tops, before she came crawling back to him. But all he got at the end of that week was a fat envelope from her attorney filled with divorce papers. There was also a very firmly worded letter demanding he return her things to her immediately.

Not exactly the actions of a woman planning to come back.

He tossed it all directly in the trash.

In that week, the curious ache in his chest had turned into a searing pain, as though someone had driven a hot iron through him and then proceeded to yank it back and forth until he felt like his insides were leaking to the outside. Soon he would be just a shell of a man. Skin and bone with no substance.

No soul.

Melissa had taken it with her.

When a group of her henchmen flew to the island to physically fetch her things themselves, he refused to let them past the main gate.

"You obviously love her," Aaron said. "Why don't you just go get her?"

"She'll be back," he said.

He looked at Chris like he was hopeless. Everyone had been looking at him that way lately. Except his mother, who wasn't looking at or speaking to him at all. And hadn't been since he'd told her the truth about everything that had happened. He hadn't really had a choice. She'd demanded to know the truth, and when she wanted something, the word *no* wasn't part of his vocabulary.

She'd had pretty much the same reaction as his siblings. "She didn't know it was an arrangement?"

He told her the entire story, and when he was finished explaining, she looked as though she wanted to strike him. "That poor girl. I raised you better than this."

He tried to make excuses, and all he got from her was, "I want my daughter-in-law back."

He'd never seen her look so disappointed in him, which stung more than any form of corporal punishment ever could.

By the end of the second week, when he hadn't gone after Melissa and still refused to turn over her things, holding them like some warped form of ransom, his brother and sisters stopped talking to him, too.

"What the bloody hell is the matter with you?" was the last thing Anne said to him. Louisa just stood there shaking her head sadly, then said, "I'm so disappointed in you." Which coming from her was pretty harsh.

The next morning as he was in his closet dressing for work, he heard the bedroom door open. He got up and walked out, and when he realized who it was standing in his bedroom, her back to him, for an instant he was sure he was hallucinating. "Melissa?"

She spun around, clutching the photo of herself and her parents, looking as surprised to see him as he was to see her. "What are you doing here?"

Was that some sort of trick question? "Uh...I live here?"

"You're not supposed to be here," she snapped with that sharp Southern twang. Over the last few months she'd lost that, and only now did he realize how much he'd missed it. Missed *her.* It was good to hear her sounding like her old self. The one that was fun and spunky, and wasn't afraid to talk back to him, tell him what was on her mind. It pained him to know that he'd made her so miserable he'd broken her spirit.

It was a bit ironic that now he was the one feeling isolated, lonely and like a complete failure. And finally, when he thought it would never be clear, never make sense, something in his head, or maybe in his heart, finally snapped, or shifted into place. He wasn't sure exactly what happened. All he knew was that one minute he was confused as hell, unsure of what to do next, how to fix the mess he'd made, and the next he knew without a shadow of doubt that he was in love with Melissa. It seemed so damned simple he didn't know why he hadn't figured it out before.

This may have started out as a business arrangement, but something had happened to him. Slowly, gradually, being with Melissa had changed him. He used to believe that marriage was nothing more than a duty. He could take it or leave it. And maybe with any other woman as his wife, that would still be true.

Now he couldn't imagine his life without Melissa by his side. He could only hope she would give him a chance to make it up to her.

He had to tell her, convince her to come home. And the only way that was going to happen was if he swallowed his outrageously over-inflated pride, stuck his tail between his legs where it belonged, and went crawling back to her.

Though he could see she was angry as hell, he couldn't help smiling. He could hardly wait for the opportunity to gather her into his arms and just hold her. Although he feared that if he were to try now, she was likely to deck him.

"Where am I supposed to be?" he asked her.

"Away on business."

"I am?"

"Your mother called and said you would be gone, and that I should come and get my things."

His mother had said she wanted Melissa back. She must have figured that if Chris wouldn't come to his senses, she would do it for him. And damned if she hadn't been right.

"Well, as you can see, I'm here. Not away on business." He took a step toward her, and she took one back, colliding with the dresser.

She looked genuinely alarmed. "I'm just here for my things. I don't want any trouble."

"What kind of trouble were you expecting?"

Her chin rose a notch. "That kind that would necessitate the two very large bodyguards I brought with me."

He looked around the room. "I don't see any bodyguards."

She drew her lower lip between her teeth, glancing nervously past him to the door. "They're downstairs, watching the doors in case you come in and try to stop me. All I have to do is yell and they'll come running."

Even if they heard her they would never make it in time. He was between her and the door. Not to mention they were outnumbered two to a couple dozen in the castle alone.

"You would really sic your bodyguards on me?"

"If necessary."

He walked slowly backward toward the door, and her

eyes widened a little. "What is it you think I'm going to do to you?"

"If you're trying to intimidate me, it isn't going to work."

He backed the door shut, and when he snapped the lock, she flinched. "Maybe it's just me, but you sure look intimidated."

She swallowed. "I could scream."

He started walking slowly toward her. "Why would you do that?"

"I know karate," she warned him.

He knew for a fact that she didn't. "Again, I ask, what is it you think I'm going to do to you?"

"I don't know!" she said, looking exasperated. "That's the problem. Your behavior these last few weeks has been...odd."

"Odd?"

She narrowed her eyes at him. "You don't think it's just a little creepy that you refuse to give me back my things?"

He shrugged. "Maybe a little. But I had a good reason."

"What reason?"

"I wanted them here for you when you came home."

"See, that makes you sound like a stalker."

"Having my wife home makes me sound like a stalker? In what penal system?"

"This isn't my home. And as soon as you sign the divorce papers, I won't be your wife anymore."

"I tossed them in the trash."

"Why?"

"Because you love me."

She frowned and shook her head, rubbing her temples as if the whole conversation was giving her a headache. "I'm not doing this again. Please just let me get my things and go."

She started to move toward the door but he stepped in her way. "Just hear me out. Five minutes, that's all I'm asking."

Since it was obvious she had little choice in the matter, she said, "Okay, five minutes."

"The way I figure it, you don't want the man you married."

She nodded slowly, looking totally confused. "Hence the divorce papers."

"What I mean is, you want the man I was before we were married. The man I was before our wedding night. That's the man you love. Right?"

She looked suddenly and inexplicably sad. "But you aren't that man."

"Yes, I am. He's always been in there. And that man loves you."

She cupped her hands over her ears and scrunched up her face as though she was in pain. "Please don't say things like that."

"You want to know the truth?"

She shook her head.

"On our wedding night, when you told me you loved me, you scared the living hell out of me. Since the day

I was born, my life has been meticulously planned out for me. And never, in all that preparation, was love ever mentioned. It was not part of that plan."

Her face was still scrunched, but she wasn't holding her hands very tightly over her ears. He walked closer until he was standing right in front of her.

"I really cared about you, Melissa. The day we were married, maybe it wasn't love yet, but I had very strong feelings for you. I trusted you. Then you said you loved me. Since that had never been part of the plan, I was sure you were only saying it to manipulate me. It wouldn't be the first time. And I honestly had believed you were different. I felt...*betrayed*."

Her hands dropped to her sides. "I would never say it if I didn't mean it."

"I know that now."

"You made me miserable."

"I know that, too. And I'm sorry. All I can do is promise that I'll never do it again. If you give me another chance."

"Why should I believe you?"

"Because I wouldn't say it if I didn't mean it."

"I knew this would happen," she said, looking up at him. "This is why I didn't want to come here."

"Why?"

"Because I knew you would start saying all of these wonderful things and then I would start to melt." The hint of a grin curled one corner of her mouth. "Then, even if I knew it was bad for me, I'd end up falling in love with you all over again. Which I have. Thanks a lot."

"Does that mean you're coming home?"

She hesitated, then bit her lip and nodded.

He smiled and held out his arms, and she stepped into them. She wrapped her arms around him, and he wrapped his around her, and they just held each other.

"I love you, Chris."

This time when she said it he didn't feel confused or betrayed. He felt like he was probably the happiest man on earth. "I love you too."

"Both?"

"The first Chris and the second Chris."

"And for the record, I loved you both."

"You did?"

"Yeah, but the first you was my friend, too, and I really missed him."

But he was here now. Exactly where he was supposed to be. And so was Melissa.

In his arms, right where she belonged.

* * * * *

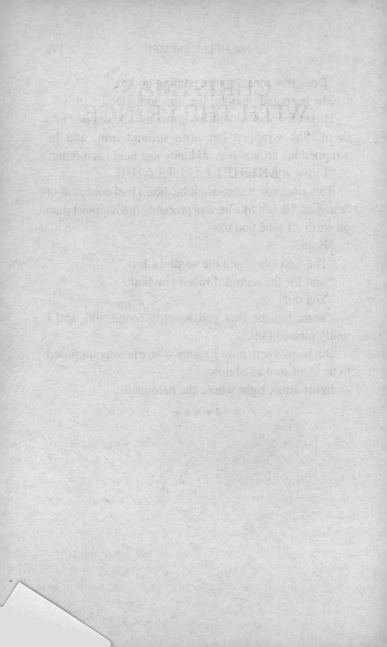

CHRISTMAS WITH THE PRINCE

BY
MICHELLE CELMER

To my mom,
who has been not only my teacher, my confidante,
and my most dedicated fan, but one of my best friends.
Love you!

One

Olivia Montgomery was attractive for a scientist.

Attractive in a brainy, geeky sort of way. From a distance, at least. And not at all what Prince Aaron had expected.

He watched her gaze up at the castle from his office window, a look of awe on her heart-shaped face, her bow mouth formed into a perfect *O* beneath eyes as large as dinner plates.

He supposed it wasn't every day that a woman was asked to uproot her entire life, stay at a royal castle for an indeterminable period and use her vast knowledge to save an entire country from potential absolute financial devastation.

Of course, from what he'd read of their new guest, her life to date had been anything but typical. Most kids didn't graduate from high school at fifteen, receive their Ph.D. at twenty-two and earn a reputation as a pioneer in the field of botanical genetics at twenty-four. He would swear she didn't look a day over eighteen, due in part to the long, blondish-brown hair she wore pulled back in a ponytail and the backpack she carried slung over one shoulder.

He watched as Derek, his personal assistant, led her into the castle, then he took a seat at his desk to wait for them, feeling uncharacteristically anxious. He had been assured that in the field of genetic botany, she was the best. Meaning she could very well be their last hope.

Specialist after specialist had been unable to diagnose or effectively treat the blight plaguing their crops. A disease that had begun in the east fields, and spread to affect not only a good portion of the royal family's land, but had recently been reported in surrounding farms, as well. Unchecked, the effects could be financially devastating to their agriculturally based economy.

His family—hell, the entire country—was counting on him to find a way to fix it.

Talk about pressure. He used to believe that his older brother, Christian, the crown prince, had it rough, carrying the burden of one day taking over as ruler, and the responsibility of marrying and producing a royal heir. But to Aaron's surprise, after a slightly rocky start, Chris seemed to be embracing his new title as husband.

For Aaron, the thought of tying himself down to one woman for the rest of his life gave him cold chills. Not that he didn't love women. He just loved lots of different women. And when the novelty of one wore thin, he liked having the option of moving on to something new. Although, now that Chris was blissfully married off, their mother, the queen, had taken an active and unsettling interest in Aaron's love life. He never knew there were so many eligible young women with royal blood, and his mother seemed hell-bent on setting him up with every single one of them.

She would figure out eventually that all the meddling in the world wouldn't bring him any closer to the altar. At least, he hoped she would. She could instead focus on marrying off his twin sisters, Anne and Louisa.

Several minutes passed before there was a rap at Aaron's office door. Undoubtedly Derek had been explaining policy for meeting members of the royal family to their guest. What she should and shouldn't do or say. It could be a bit overwhelming. Especially for someone who had never been in the presence of royalty before.

"Come in," he called.

The door opened and Derek appeared, followed

closely by Miss Montgomery. Aaron rose from his chair to greet her, noticing right away her height. He was just over six feet tall, and in flat-heeled, conservative loafers she stood nearly eye level. It was difficult to see her figure under the loose khaki pants and baggy, cable-knit sweater, although she gave the impression of being quite slim. *Too* slim, even. All sharp and angular.

Missing was the lab coat, pocket protector and cola-bottle glasses one might expect from a scientist. She wore no makeup or jewelry, and was for all accounts quite plain, yet she was undeniably female. Attractive in a simple way. Cute and girlish. Although at twenty-five, she was definitely a woman.

"Your Highness," Derek said, "May I introduce Miss Olivia Montgomery, of the United States." He turned to Miss Montgomery. "Miss Montgomery, may I present Prince Aaron Felix Gastel Alexander of Thomas Isle."

Miss Montgomery stuck her hand out to shake his, then, realizing her error, snatched it back and dipped into an awkward, slightly wobbly curtsy instead, her cheeks coloring an enchanting shade of pink. "It's an honor to be here, sir—I mean, Your Highness."

Her voice was softer than he'd expected. Low and breathy, and dare he say a little sexy. He'd always found an American accent undeniably appealing.

"The honor is mine," he said, reaching out for a shake. She hesitated a second, then accepted his hand. Her hands were slender and fine-boned, with long fingers that wrapped around his with a surprisingly firm grip. Her skin was warm and soft, her nails short but neatly filed.

She gazed at him with eyes an intriguing shade—not quite brown, and not quite green—and so large and inquisitive they seemed to take up half her face. Everything about her was a little overexaggerated and…unexpected.

But she couldn't be any less his type. He preferred his women small and soft in all the right places, and the more beautiful the better. Not particularly smart, either, because frankly, he wasn't in it for the conversation. The fewer brains, the less likely he was to become attached. As long as she could navigate a golf course or squash court, or rock a pair of cross-country skis. Sailing experience was a plus, as well, and if she could climb a rock wall, he would be in sheer heaven.

Somehow he didn't see Miss Montgomery as the athletic type.

"I'll be in my office if you need me, sir," Derek told him, then slipped out of the room, closing the door behind him. As it snapped shut, he could swear he saw Miss Montgomery flinch.

He gestured to the chair opposite his desk. "Miss Montgomery, make yourself comfortable."

She set her backpack on the floor beside her and sat awkwardly on the very edge of the cushion. She folded her hands in her lap, then unfolded them. Then she tucked them around the sides of her thighs and under her legs. She looked very *un*comfortable.

"I apologize for being so late," she said.

He perched on the corner of his desk. "I hear you hit some bad weather on the way over."

She nodded. "It was a bumpy flight. And I'm not real crazy about flying to begin with. In fact, I might look into taking a ship home."

"Can I offer you a drink, Miss Montgomery?"

"No, thank you. And please, call me Liv. Everyone does."

"All right, Liv. And because we'll be spending quite some time together, you should call me Aaron."

She hesitated, then asked, "Is that...allowed?"

He grinned. "I assure you, it's perfectly acceptable."

She nodded, her head a little wobbly on the end of a very long and slender neck. She had the kind of throat made for stroking and nibbling. But somehow he didn't see her as the nibbling type. She had shy and repressed written all over her. No doubt, he could teach her a thing or two. Not that he intended to. Or even possessed the desire.

Well, maybe just a little, but purely out of curiosity.

"My family apologizes that they couldn't be here to greet you," he told her. "They're in England to see my father's cardiologist. They'll be back Friday."

"I look forward to meeting them," she said, although she sounded more wary than enthusiastic.

She had no reason to be apprehensive. In the history of his father's reign as king, her visit might very well be the most anticipated and appreciated. Not that she was offering her services for free. They had agreed to make a handsome donation to fund her research. Personally she hadn't asked for anything more than room and board. No special amenities, or even a personal maid to tend to her care.

"I'm told that you looked at the disease samples we sent you," he said.

She nodded, not so wobbly this time. "I did. As well as the data from the other specialists."

"And what conclusion have you drawn?"

"You have yourself a very unusual, very resistant strain of disease that I've never seen before. And trust me when I say I've pretty much seen them all."

"Your references are quite impressive. I've been assured that if anyone can diagnose the problem, it's you."

"There is no *if*." She looked him directly in the eye and said firmly, "It's simply a matter of *when*."

Her confidence, and the forceful tone with which she spoke, nearly knocked him backward.

Well, he hadn't seen that coming. It was almost as though someone flipped a switch inside of her and a completely different woman emerged. She sat a little straighter and her voice sounded stronger. Just like that, he gained an entirely new level of respect for her.

"Have you thought about my suggestion to stop all agricultural exports?" she asked.

That was *all* he'd been thinking about. "Even the unaffected crops?"

"I'm afraid so."

"Is that really necessary?"

"For all we know, it could be lying dormant in the soil of areas that *appear* unaffected. And until we know what this thing is, we don't want it to get off the island."

He knew she was right, but the financial repercussions would sting. "That means we have only until the next season, less than five months, to identify the disease and find an environmentally friendly cure."

Environmentally friendly so that they could maintain their reputation as a totally organic, green island. Millions had been spent to radically alter the way every farmer grew his crops. It was what set them apart from other distributors and made them a valuable commodity.

"Can it be done in that time frame?" he asked.

"The truth is, I don't know. These things can take time."

It wasn't what he wanted to hear, but he appreciated her honesty. He'd wanted her to fly in, have the problem solved in a week or two, then be on her way, making him look like a hero in not only his family, but also his country's eyes.

So much for that delusion of grandeur.

"Once I get set up in the lab and have a few days to study the rest of the data, I may be able to give you some sort of time frame," she said.

"We have a student from the university on standby, should you need an assistant."

"I'll need someone to take samples, but in the lab I prefer to work alone. You have all the equipment I need?"

"Everything on your list." He rose to his feet. "I can show you to your room and give you time to settle in."

She stood, as well, smoothing the front of her slacks with her palms. He couldn't help wondering what she was hiding behind that bulky sweater. Were those breasts he saw? And hips? Maybe she wasn't as sharp and angular as he'd first thought.

"If you don't mind," she said, "I'd rather get right to work."

He gestured to the door. "Of course. I'll take you right to the lab."

She certainly didn't waste any time, did she? And he was relieved to know that she seemed determined to help.

The sooner they cured this blight, the sooner they could all breathe easy again.

Two

Liv followed her host through the castle, heart thumping like mad, praying she didn't do something stupid like trip over her own feet and fall flat on her face.

Prince Aaron was, by far, the most beautiful man she had ever laid eyes on. His hair so dark and soft-looking, his eyes a striking, mesmerizing shade of green, his full lips always turned up in a sexy smile.

He had the deep and smoky voice of a radio DJ and a body to die for. A muscular backside under dark tailored slacks. Wide shoulders and bulging pecs encased in midnight-blue cashmere. As she followed him through the castle she felt hypnotized by the fluid grace with which he moved.

He was…perfect. An eleven on a scale of one to

ten. And the antithesis of the scientists and geeks she was used to keeping company with. Like William, her fiancé—or at least he would be her fiancé if she decided to accept the proposal of marriage he had stunned her with just last night in the lab.

Fifteen years her senior and her mentor since college, Will wasn't especially handsome, and he was more studious than sexy, but he was kind and sweet and generous. The truth was, his proposal had come so far out of left field that it had nearly given her whiplash. They had never so much as kissed, other than a friendly peck on the cheek on holidays or special occasions. But she respected him immensely and loved him as a friend. So she had promised to give his proposal serious thought while she was away. Even though, when he'd kissed her goodbye at the airport—a real kiss with lips and tongue—she hadn't exactly seen fireworks. But sexual attraction was overrated and fleeting at best. They had respect and a deep sense of friendship.

Although she couldn't help wondering if she would be settling.

Yeah, right. Like she had a mob of other men pounding down her door. She couldn't even recall the last time she'd been on a date. And sex, well, it had been so long she wasn't sure she even remembered how. Not that it had been smoking hot anyhow. The one man she'd slept with in college had been a budding nuclear physicist, and more concerned with mathematical equations than figuring out sexual complexities. She bet Prince Aaron knew his way around a woman's body.

Right, Liv, and I suppose the prince is going to show you.

The thought was so ridiculous she nearly laughed out loud. What would a gorgeous, sexy prince see in a nerdy, totally *unsexy* woman like her?

"So, what do you think of our island?" Aaron asked as they descended the stairs together.

"What I've seen of it is beautiful. And the castle isn't at all what I expected."

"What did you expect?"

"Honestly, I thought it would be kind of dark and dank." In reality, it was light and airy and beautifully decorated. And so enormous! A person could get hopelessly lost wandering the long, carpeted halls. She could hardly believe she would be spending weeks, maybe even months, there. "I expected stone walls and suits of armor in the halls."

The prince chuckled, a deep, throaty sound. "We're a bit more modern than that. You'll find the guest rooms have all the amenities and distinction you would expect from a five-star hotel."

Not that she would know the difference, seeing as how she'd never been in anything more luxurious than a Days Inn.

"Although..." He paused and looked over at her. "The only feasible place for the lab, short of building a new facility on the grounds, was the basement."

She shrugged. It wouldn't be the first time she'd worked in a basement lab. "That's fine with me."

"It used to be a dungeon."

Her interest piqued. "Seriously?"

He nodded. "Very dark and dank at one time, complete with chains on the wall and torture devices."

She gazed at him skeptically. "You're joking, right?"

"Completely serious. It's been updated since then of course. We use it for food and dry storage, and the wine cellar. The laundry facilities are down there, as well. I think you'll be impressed with the lab. Not dark or dank at all."

Because the majority of her time would be spent staring in a microscope or at a computer screen, what the lab looked like didn't matter all that much to her. As long as it was functional.

He led her through an enormous kitchen bustling with activity and rich with the scents of fresh baked bread and scintillating spices. Her stomach rumbled and she tried to recall the last time she'd eaten. She'd been way too nervous to eat the meal offered on the plane.

There would be time for food later.

Aaron stopped in front of a large wood door that she assumed led to the basement. "There's a separate employee entrance that the laundry staff use. It leads outside, to the back of the castle. But as a guest, you'll use the family entrance."

"Okay."

He reached for the handle but didn't open the door. "There is one thing I should probably warn you about."

Warn her? That didn't sound good. "Yes?"

"As I said, the basement has been updated."

"But…?"

"It did used to be a dungeon."

She wasn't getting his point. "Okay."

"A lot of people died down there."

Was she going to trip over bodies on her way to the lab or something? "Recently?"

He laughed. "No, of course not."

Then she wasn't seeing the problem. "So…?"

"That bothers some people. And the staff is convinced it's haunted."

Liv looked at him as though he'd gone completely off his rocker.

"I take it you don't believe in ghosts," Aaron said.

"The existence of spirits, or an afterlife, have never been proven scientifically."

He should have expected as much from a scientist. "Well, then, I guess you have nothing to fear."

"Do you?" she asked.

"Believe in ghosts?" Truthfully, he'd never felt so much as a cold draft down there, but people had sworn to hearing disembodied voices and seeing ghostly emanations. There were some members of the staff who refused to even set foot on the stairs. Also there was an unusually high turnover rate among the laundry workers. But he was convinced that it was more likely overactive imaginations than anything otherworldly. "I guess you could say I try to keep an open mind."

He opened the door and gestured her down. The stairwell was narrow and steep, the wood steps creaky under their feet as they descended.

"It is a little spooky," she admitted.

At the bottom was a series of passageways that led to several different wings. The walls down here were still fashioned out of stone and mortar, although well lit, ventilated and clean.

"Storage and the wine cellar are that way," he said, pointing to the passages on the left. "Laundry is straight ahead down the center passage, and the lab is this way."

He led her to the right, around a corner to a shiny metal door with a thick glass window that to him looked completely out of place with its surroundings. He punched in his security code to unlock it, pulled it open and hit the light switch. The instant the lights flickered on he heard a soft gasp behind him, and turned to see Liv looking in wide-eyed awe at all the equipment they'd gotten on loan from various facilities on the island and mainland. The way one might view priceless art. Or a natural disaster.

She brushed past him into the room. "This is perfect," she said in that soft, breathy voice, running her hands along pieces of equipment whose purpose he couldn't begin to imagine. Slow and tender, as if she were stroking a lover's flesh.

Damn. He could get turned on watching her do that, imagining those hands roaming over him.

If she were his type at all, which she wasn't. Besides, he wasn't lacking for female companionship.

"It's small," he said.

"No, it's perfect." She turned to him and smiled, a dreamy look on her face. "I wish my lab back home were this complete."

He was surprised that it wasn't. "I was under the impression that you were doing some groundbreaking research."

"Yes, but funding is an issue no matter what kind of work you're doing. Especially when you're an independent, like me."

"There must be someone willing to fund your research."

"Many, but there's *way* too much bureaucracy in the private sector. I prefer to do things my way."

"Then our donation should go far."

She nodded eagerly. "The truth is, a few more weeks and I might have been homeless. You called in the nick of time."

She crossed the room to the metal shipping containers that had preceded her arrival by several days. "I see my things made it safely."

"Do you need help unpacking?"

She vigorously shook her head. "There are sensitive materials and equipment in here. I'd rather do it myself."

That seemed like an awful lot of work for one person. "The offer for the assistant is still good. I can have someone here Friday morning."

She looked at her watch, her face scrunching with confusion. "And what's today? The time change from the U.S. has me totally screwed up."

"It's Tuesday. Five o'clock."

"P.M.?"

"Yes. In fact, dinner is at seven."

She nodded, but still looked slightly confused.

"Out of curiosity, when was the last time you slept?"

She scrunched her face again, studied her watch for a second, then shrugged and said, "I'm not sure. Twenty hours at least. Probably more."

"You must be exhausted."

"I'm used to it. I keep long hours in the lab."

Twenty hours was an awfully long time, even for a workaholic, and he'd traveled often enough to know what jet lag could do to a person. Especially someone unaccustomed to long plane trips. "Maybe before you tackle unpacking the lab you should at least take a nap."

"I'm fine, really. Although, I guess I wouldn't mind a quick change of clothes."

"Why don't I show you to your room."

She looked longingly at all of the shiny new equipment, then nodded and said, "All right."

He switched off the lights and shut the door, hearing it lock automatically behind him.

"Will I get my own code?" she asked.

"Of course. You'll have full access to whatever and wherever you need."

He led Liv back through the kitchen and up the stairs to the third floor, to the guest rooms. She looked a bit lost when they finally reached her door.

"The castle is so big and confusing," she said.

"It's not so bad once you learn your way around."

"I don't exactly have a great sense of direction. Don't be surprised if you find me aimlessly wandering the halls."

"I'll have Derek print you up a map." He opened her door and gestured her in.

"It's beautiful," she said in that soft, breathy voice. "So pretty."

Far too feminine and fluffy for his taste, with its flowered walls and frilly drapes, but their female guests seemed to appreciate it. Although he never would have pegged Liv as the girly-girl type. She was just too…analytical. Too practical. On the surface anyhow.

"The bathroom and closet are that way," he said, gesturing to the door across the room. But Liv's attention was on the bed.

"It looks so comfortable." She crossed the room to it and ran one hand over the flowered duvet. "So soft."

She was a tactile sort of woman. Always stroking

and touching things. And he couldn't help but wonder how those hands would feel touching him.

"Why don't you take it for a spin," he said. "The lab can wait."

"Oh, I shouldn't," she protested, but she was already kicking off her shoes and crawling on top of the covers. She settled back against the pillows and sighed blissfully. Her eyes slipped closed. "Oh, this is heavenly."

He hadn't actually meant right that second. The average guest would have waited until he'd left the room, not flop down into bed right in front of him. But he could see that there was nothing average about Olivia Montgomery.

At least she hadn't undressed first. Not that he wasn't curious to see what she was hiding under those clothes. He was beginning to think there was much more to Liv than she let show.

"You'll find your bags in the closet. Are you sure you wouldn't like a maid to unpack for you?"

"I can do it," she said, her voice soft and sleepy.

"If you change your mind, let me know. Other than that, you should have everything you need. There are fresh towels and linens in the bathroom. As well as toiletries. If you need anything else, day or night, just pick up the phone. The kitchen is always open. You're also welcome to use the exercise room or game room, day or night. We want you to feel completely comfortable here."

He walked to the window and pushed the curtain aside, letting in a shaft of late-afternoon sunshine. "You have quite a lovely view of the ocean and the gardens from here. Although there isn't much to see in the gardens this time of year. We could take a walk out there tomorrow."

Or not, he thought, when she didn't answer him. Then he heard a soft rumbling sound from the vicinity of the bed.

She had turned on her side and lay all curled up in a ball, hugging the pillow. He walked over to the bed and realized that she was sound asleep.

"Liv," he called softly, but she didn't budge. Apparently she was more tired than she'd realized.

He found a spare blanket in the closet, noticing her luggage while he was in there, and the conspicuously small amount of it. Just two average-size bags that had seen better days. The typical female guest, especially one there for an extended stay, brought a whole slew of bags.

He reminded himself once again that Liv was not the typical royal guest. And, he was a little surprised to realize, he liked that about her. It might very well be a refreshing change.

He walked back to the bed and covered her with the blanket, then, for reasons he couldn't begin to understand, felt compelled to just look at her for a moment. The angles of her face softened when she slept, making her appear young and vulnerable.

She's not your type, he reminded himself.

If he was going to be honest with himself, his "type" had plenty to offer physically, but intellectually, he was usually left feeling bored and unfulfilled. Maybe it was time for a change of pace.

Seducing a woman like Liv might be just what he needed to spice things up.

Three

It was official. Liv was lost.

She stood in an unfamiliar hallway on what she was pretty sure was the second floor, looking for the staircase that would lead her down to the kitchen. She'd been up and down two separate sets of stairs already this morning, and had wandered through a dozen different hallways. Either there were two identical paintings of the same stodgy-looking old man in a military uniform, or she'd been in this particular hallway more than once.

She looked up one end to the other, hopelessly turned around, wondering which direction she should take. She felt limp with hunger, and the backpack full of books and papers hung like a dead weight off one shoulder. If she didn't eat soon, her blood sugar was going to dip into the critical zone.

She did a very scientific, eenie-meenie-minie-moe, then went left around the corner and plowed face-first into a petite, red-haired maid carrying a pile of clean linens. The force of the collision knocked her off balance and the linens fell to the carpet.

"Oh my gosh! I'm so sorry!" Liv crouched down to pick them up. "I wasn't watching where I was going."

"It's no problem, miss," the maid said in a charming Irish brogue, kneeling down to help. "You must be our scientist from the States. Miss Montgomery?"

Liv piled the last slightly disheveled sheet in her arms and they both stood. "Yes, I am."

The maid looked her up and down. "Well, you don't much look like a scientist."

"Yeah, I hear that a lot." And she was always tempted to ask what she did look like, but she was a little afraid of the answer she might get.

"I'm Elise," the maid said. "If you need anything at all, I'm the one to be asking."

"Could you tell me where to find the kitchen? I'm starving."

"Of course, miss. Follow this hallway down and make a left. The stairs will be on your right, about halfway down the hall. Take them down one flight, then turn right. The kitchen is just down the way."

"A left and two rights. Got it."

Elise smiled. "Enjoy your stay, miss."

She disappeared in the direction Liv had just come from. Liv followed her directions and actually found the kitchen, running into—although not literally this time—Prince Aaron's assistant just outside the door.

"Off to work already?" he asked.

"Looking for food actually. I missed dinner last night."

"Why don't you join the prince in the family dining room."

"Okay." She could spend another twenty minutes or so looking for the dining room, and possibly collapse from hunger, or ask for directions. "Could you show me where it is?"

He smiled and gestured in the opposite direction from the kitchen. "Right this way."

It was just around the corner. A surprisingly small but luxurious space with French doors overlooking the grounds. A thick blanket of leaves in brilliant red, orange and yellow carpeted the expansive lawn and the sky was a striking shade of pink as the sun rose above the horizon.

At one end of a long, rectangular cherry table, leaning casually in a chair with a newspaper propped beside him, sat Prince Aaron. He looked up when they entered the room, then rose to his feet.

"Well, good morning," he said with a smile, and her stomach suddenly bound up into a nervous knot.

"Shall I take your bag?" Derek asked her.

Liv shook her head. That backpack had all of her research. She never trusted it to anyone else. "I've got it, thanks."

"Well, then, enjoy your breakfast," Derek said, leaving her alone with the prince. Just the two of them.

Only then did it occur to her that she might have been better off eating alone. What would they say to each other? What could they possibly have in common? A prince and an orphan?

The prince, on the other hand, looked completely at ease. In jeans and a flannel shirt he was dressed much more casually than the day before. He looked so…*normal*. Almost out of place in the elegant room.

He pulled out the chair beside his own. "Have a seat."

As she sat, she found herself enveloped in the subtle, spicy scent of his aftershave. She tried to recall if William, her possibly-soon-to-be fiancé, wore aftershave or cologne. If he had, she'd never noticed.

The prince's fingers brushed the backs of her shoulders as he eased her chair in and she nearly jolted against the sudden and intense zing of awareness.

He was *touching* her.

Get a grip, Liv. It wasn't like he was coming on to her. He was being *polite* and she was acting like a schoolgirl with a crush. Even when she *was* a schoolgirl she had never acted this way. She'd been above the temptation that had gotten so many other girls from high school in trouble. Or as her last foster mom, Marsha, used to put it, *in the family way.*

Then the prince placed both hands on her shoulders and her breath caught in her lungs.

His hands felt big and solid and warm. You are not going to blush, she told herself, but already she could feel a rush of color searing her cheeks, which only multiplied her embarrassment.

It was nothing more than a friendly gesture, and here she was having a hot flash. Could this be any more humiliating?

"Do you prefer coffee or tea?" he asked.

"Coffee, please," she said, but it came out high and squeaky.

He leaned past her to reach for the carafe on the table, and as he did, the back of her head bumped the wall of his chest. She was sure it was just her imagination, but she swore she felt his body heat, heard the steady thump of his heart beating. Her own heart was hammering so hard that it felt as though it would beat its way out of her chest.

Shouldn't a servant be doing that? she wondered as he poured her a cup and slid it in front of her. Then he *finally* backed away and returned to his chair, resuming the same casual, relaxed stance—and she took her first full breath since she'd sat down.

"Would you care for breakfast?" he asked.

"Please," she said, though her throat was so tight,

she could barely get air to pass through, much less food. But if she didn't eat something soon, she would go into hypoglycemic shock. She just hoped she didn't humiliate herself further. She was so used to eating at her desk in the lab, or in a rush over the kitchen sink, she was a little rusty when it came to the rules of etiquette. What if she used the wrong fork, or chewed with her mouth open?

He rang a bell, and within seconds a man dressed in characteristic butler apparel seemed to material-ize from thin air.

"Breakfast for our guest, Geoffrey," he said.

Geoffrey nodded and slipped away as stealthily as he'd emerged.

Liv folded her hands in her lap and, because most of her time was spent huddled over her laptop or a microscope, reminded herself to sit up straight.

"I trust you slept well," the prince said.

She nodded. "I woke at seven thinking it was last night, then I looked outside and noticed that the sun was on the wrong side of the horizon."

"I guess you were more tired than you thought."

"I guess so. But I'm anxious to get down to the lab. You said I'll get a password for the door?"

"Yes, in fact…" He pulled a slip of paper from his shirt pocket and handed it to her. As she took it, she felt lingering traces of heat from his body and her cheeks flushed deeper red.

She unfolded the paper and looked at the code—

a simple seven-digit number—then handed it back to him.

"Don't you want to memorize it?" he asked.

"I just did."

His eyes widened with surprise, and he folded the paper and put it back in his pocket. "Your ID badge will be ready this morning. You'll want to wear it all the time, so you're not stopped by security. It will grant you full access to the castle, with the exception of the royal family's quarters of course, and any of our agricultural facilities or fields."

"You mentioned something about a map of the castle," she said, too embarrassed to admit that she'd actually gotten lost on her way to breakfast.

"Of course. I'll have Derek print one up for you."

"Thank you."

"So," Prince Aaron said, lounging back in his chair and folding his hands in his lap. "Tell me about yourself. About your family."

"Oh, I don't have any family."

Confusion wrinkled his brow. "Everyone has family."

"I'm an orphan. I was raised in the New York foster care system."

His expression sobered. "I'm sorry, I didn't know."

She shrugged. "No reason to be sorry. It's not your fault."

"Do you mind my asking what happened to your parents?"

It's not like her past was some big secret. She had always embraced who she was, and where she came from. "No, I don't mind. My mom died a long time ago. She was a drug addict. Social services took me away from her when I was three."

"What about your father?"

"I don't have one."

At the subtle lift of his brow, she realized how odd that sounded, like she was the product of a virgin birth or something. When the more likely scenario was that her mother had been turning tricks for drug money, and whoever the man was, he probably had no idea he'd fathered a child. And probably wouldn't care if he did know.

She told the prince, "Of course *someone* was my father. He just wasn't listed on my birth certificate."

"No grandparents? Aunts or uncles?"

She shrugged again. "Maybe. Somewhere. No one ever came forward to claim me."

"Have you ever tried to find them?"

"I figure if they didn't want me back then, they wouldn't want me now, either."

He frowned, as though he found the idea disturbing.

"It's really not a big deal," she assured him. "I mean, it's just the way it's always been. I learned to fend for myself."

"But you did have a foster family."

"Families," she corrected. "I had twelve of them."

His eyes widened. "Twelve? Why so many?"

"I was…difficult."

A grin ticked at the corner of his mouth. *"Diffi-cult?"*

"I was very independent." And maybe a little arrogant. None of her foster parents seemed to appreciate a child who was smarter than them and not afraid to say so, and one who had little interest in following their *rules.* "I was emancipated when I was fifteen."

"You were on your own at *fifteen?"*

She nodded. "Right after I graduated from high school."

He frowned and shook his head, as if it was a difficult concept for him to grasp. "Forgive me for asking, but how does an orphan become a botanical geneticist?"

"A *lot* of hard work. I had some awesome teachers who really encouraged me in high school. Then I got college scholarships and grants. And I had a mentor." One she might actually be marrying, but she left that part out. And that was a big *might.* William had never given her this breathless, squishy-kneed feeling when he touched her. She never felt much of anything beyond comfortable companionship.

But wasn't that more important than sexual attraction? Although if she really wanted to marry William, would she be spending so much time talking herself into it?

The butler reappeared with a plate that was all but

overflowing with food. Plump sausages and eggs over easy, waffles topped with cream and fresh fruit and flaky croissants with a dish of fresh jam. The scents had her stomach rumbling and her mouth watering. "It looks delicious. Thank you."

He nodded and left. Not a very talkative fellow.

"Aren't you eating?" she asked Prince Aaron.

"I already ate, but please, go ahead. You must be famished."

Starving. And oddly enough, the prince had managed to put her totally at ease, just as he'd done the night before. He was just so laid-back and casual. So...*nice.* Unlike most men, he didn't seem to be put off or intimidated by her intelligence. And when he asked a question, he wasn't just asking to be polite. He really listened, his eyes never straying from hers while she spoke. She wasn't used to talking about herself, but he seemed genuinely interested in learning more about her. Unlike the scientists and scholars who were usually too wrapped up in their research to show any interest in learning about who she was as a person.

It was a nice change of pace.

The prince's cell phone rang and he unclipped it from his belt to look at the display. Concern flashed across his face. "I'm sorry. I have to take this," he said, rising to his feet. "Please excuse me."

She watched him walk briskly from the room and realized she was actually sorry to see him go. She couldn't recall the last time she'd had a conversation with a man who hadn't revolved in some way around her research, or funding. Not even William engaged in social dialogue very often. It was nice to just talk to someone for a change. Someone who really listened.

Or maybe spending time with the prince was a bad idea. She'd been here less than a day and already she was nursing a pretty serious crush.

Four

"Any news?" Aaron asked when he answered his brother's call.

"We have results back from Father's heart function test," Christian told him.

Aaron's own heart seemed to seize in his chest. Their father, the king, had been hooked to a portable heart pump four months ago after the last of a series of damaging attacks. The procedure was still in the experimental stages and carried risks, but the doctors were hopeful that it would give his heart a chance to heal from years of heart disease damage.

It was their last hope.

Aaron had wanted to accompany his family to

England, but his father had insisted he stay behind to greet Miss Montgomery. *For the good of the country,* he'd said. Knowing he'd been right, Aaron hadn't argued.

Duty first, that was their motto.

"Has there been any improvement?" Aaron asked his brother, not sure if he was ready to hear the answer.

"He's gone from twenty percent heart capacity to thirty-five percent."

"So it's working?"

"Even better than they expected. The doctors are cautiously optimistic."

"That's fantastic!" Aaron felt as though every muscle in his body simultaneously sighed with relief. As a child he had been labeled the easygoing one. Nothing ever bothered Aaron, his parents liked to brag. He was like Teflon. Trouble hit the surface, then slid off without sticking. But he wasn't nearly as impervious to stress as everyone liked to believe. He internalized everything, let it eat away at him. Especially lately, with not only their father's health, but also the diseased crops, and the mysterious, threatening e-mails that had been sporadically showing up in his and his siblings' in-boxes from a fellow who referred to himself, of all things, as the Gingerbread Man. He had not only harassed them through e-mail, but also managed to breach security and trespass on the castle grounds, slipping in and out like a ghost despite added security.

There had been times lately when Aaron felt he was days away from a mandatory trip to the rubber room.

But his father's health was now one concern he could safely, if only temporarily, put aside.

"How much longer do they think he'll be on the pump?" he asked his brother.

"At least another four months. Although probably longer. They'll retest him in the spring."

Aaron had been hoping sooner. On the pump he was susceptible to blood clots and strokes and in rare cases, life-threatening infections. "How is he doing?"

"They had to remove the pump to test his heart and there were minor complications when they reinserted it. Something about scar tissue. He's fine now, but he's still in recovery. They want to keep him here an extra few days. Probably middle of next week. Just to be safe."

As much as Aaron wanted to see his father home, the hospital was the best place for him now. "Is Mother staying with him?"

"Of course. She hasn't left his side. Melissa, the girls and I will be returning Friday as planned."

The girls being Louisa and Anne, their twin sisters, and Melissa, Chris's wife of only four months. In fact, it was on their wedding night that the king had the attack that necessitated the immediate intervention of the heart pump. Though it was in no way Chris and Melissa's fault, they still felt responsible for his sudden downturn.

"Now that Father is improving, maybe it's time you and Melissa rescheduled your honeymoon," Aaron told him.

"Not until he's off the pump altogether," Chris insisted, which didn't surprise Aaron. Chris had always been the responsible sibling. Of course, as crown prince, slacking off had never been an option. But while some people may have resented having their entire life dictated for them, Chris embraced his position. If he felt restricted by his duties, he never said so.

Aaron wished he could say the same.

"Did Miss Montgomery arrive safely?" Chris asked.

"She did. Although her flight was delayed by weather."

"What was your first impression of her?"

He almost told his brother that she was very cute. And despite what she'd told him, he couldn't imagine her as ever being difficult. She was so quiet and unassuming. But he didn't think that was the sort of *impression* Chris was asking for. "She seems very capable."

"Her references all checked out? Her background investigation was clean?"

Did he honestly think Aaron would have hired her otherwise? But he bit back the snarky comment on the tip of his tongue. Until their father was well, Chris was in charge, and that position deserved the same respect Aaron would have shown the king.

"Squeaky-clean," Aaron assured his brother. "And after meeting her, I feel confident she'll find a cure."

"Everyone will be relieved to hear that. I think we should—" There was commotion in the background, then Aaron heard his sister-in-law's voice, followed by a short, muted conversation, as though his brother had put a hand over the phone.

"Is everything okay, Chris?"

"Yes, sorry," Chris said, coming back on the line. "I have to go. They're wheeling Father back to his room. I'll call you later."

"Send everyone my love," Aaron told him, then disconnected, wishing he could be there with his family. But someone needed to stay behind and hold the fort.

He hooked his phone on his belt and walked back to the dining room. Liv was still there eating her breakfast. She had wiped out everything but half of a croissant, which she was slathering with jam. He didn't think he'd ever seen a woman polish off such a hearty meal. Especially a woman so slim and fit.

For a minute he just stood there watching her. She had dressed in jeans and a sweater and wore her hair pulled back into a ponytail again. He couldn't help grinning when he recalled the way she seized up as he put his hands on her shoulders, and the deep blush in her cheeks. He knew he wasn't exactly playing fair, and it was wrong to toy with her, but he'd never met a woman who wore her emotions so blatantly on her sleeve. There was little doubt that she was attracted to him.

She looked up, saw him standing there and smiled. A sweet, genuine smile that encompassed her entire face. She wasn't what he would consider beautiful or stunning, but she had a wholesome, natural prettiness about her that he found undeniably appealing.

"Sorry about that," he told her, walking to the table.

"S'okay," she said with a shrug, polishing off the last of her croissant and chasing it down with a swallow of coffee. "I think that was the most delicious breakfast I've ever eaten."

"I'll pass your compliments on to the chef." Instead of sitting down, he rested his arms on the back of his chair. "I'm sorry to say you won't be meeting my parents until next week."

Her smile vanished. "Oh. Is everything all right?"

"My father's doctors want to keep him a few days longer. Just in case."

"It's his heart?" she asked, and at his questioning look, added, "When I was offered the position, I looked up your family on the Internet. A ton of stuff came back about your father's health."

He should have figured as much. The king's health had been big news after he collapsed at Chris's wedding reception. But other than to say he had a heart "problem," no specific information had been disclosed about his condition.

"He has advanced heart disease," Aaron told her.

Concern creased her brow. "If you don't mind my asking, what's the prognosis?"

"Actually, he's in an experimental program and we're hopeful that he'll make a full recovery."

"He's getting a transplant?"

"He has a rare blood type. The odds of finding a donor are astronomical." He explained the portable heart pump and how it would take over all heart function so the tissue would have time to heal. "He's very fortunate. Less than a dozen people worldwide are part of the study."

"Heart disease is genetic. I'll bet you and your siblings are very health-conscious."

"Probably not as much as we should be, but the queen sees to it that we eat a proper diet. You know how mothers are." Only after the words were out did he realize that no, she probably didn't know, because she'd never had a real mother. He felt a slash of guilt for the thoughtless comment. But if it bothered her, she didn't let it show.

She dabbed her lips with her napkin, then set it on the table beside her plate. Glancing at the watch on her slender wrist, she said, "I should get down to the lab. I have a lot of unpacking to do."

He stepped behind her to pull her chair out, and could swear he saw her tense the slightest bit when his fingers brushed her shoulders. She rose to her feet and edged swiftly out of his reach.

He suppressed a smile. "You're sure you don't need help unpacking?"

She shook her head. "No, thank you."

"Well, then, lunch is at one."

"Oh, I don't eat lunch. I'm usually too busy."

"All right, then, dinner is at seven sharp. You do eat dinner?"

She smiled. "On occasion, yes."

He returned the smile. "Then I'll see you at seven."

She walked to the door, then stopped for a second, looking one way, then the other, as though she wasn't sure which direction to take.

"Left," he reminded her.

She turned to him and smiled. "Thanks."

"I'll remind Derek to get you that map."

"Thank you." She stood there another second, and he thought she might say something else, then she shook her head and disappeared from view.

The woman was a puzzle. Thoughtful and confident one minute, then shy and awkward the next. And he realized, not for the first time, that she was one puzzle he'd like to solve.

After a long morning in the fields and an afternoon in the largest of their greenhouse facilities, Aaron looked forward to a quiet dinner and an evening spent with their guest. Even though normally he would arrange some sort of physical, recreational activity like squash or tennis or even just a walk in the gardens, he was more interested in just talking to Liv. Learning more about her life, her past. She was the first woman in a long time whom he'd found both attractive and intellectually stimulating. And after a few drinks to loosen her up a bit, who knew where the conversation might lead.

He changed from his work clothes and stopped by her room on his way downstairs to escort her to the dining room, but she wasn't there. Expecting her to already be at the table waiting for him, he headed down, but found all of the chairs empty.

Geoffrey stepped in from the pantry.

"Have you seen Miss Montgomery?" Aaron asked.

"As far as I know she's still in the lab, Your Highness."

Aaron looked at his watch. It was already two minutes past seven. Maybe she'd lost track of the time. "Will you wait to serve the first course?"

Geoffrey gave him a stiff nod. "Of course, Your Highness."

A servant of the royal family as long as Aaron could remember, Geoffrey prided himself on keeping them on a strict and efficient schedule. Tardiness was not appreciated or tolerated.

"I'll go get her," Aaron said. He headed through the kitchen, savoring the tantalizing scent of spicy grilled chicken and peppers, and down the stairs to the lab. Through the door window he could see Liv, sitting in front of a laptop computer, typing furiously, papers scattered around her.

He punched in his code and the door swung open,

but as he stepped into the room, Liv didn't so much as glance his way.

Her sweater was draped over the back of her chair and she wore a simple, white, long-sleeved T-shirt with the sleeves pushed up to her elbows. Her ponytail had drooped over the course of the day and hung slightly askew down her back.

"It's past seven," he said softly, so as not to startle her, but got no response. "Liv?" he said, a little louder his time, and still she didn't acknowledge that he was there.

"Olivia," he said, louder this time, and she jolted in her chair, head whipping around. For a second she looked completely lost, as though she had no clue where she was, or who *he* was.

She blinked several times, then awareness slid slowly across her face. "Sorry, did you say something?"

"It's past seven."

She stared at him blankly.

"Dinner," he reminded her.

"Oh…right." She looked down at her watch, then up to her computer screen. "I guess I lost track of time."

"Are you ready?"

She glanced up at him distractedly. "Ready?"

"For *dinner.*"

"Oh, right. Sorry."

He gestured to the door. "After you."

"Oh…I think I'll pass."

"Pass?"

"Yeah. I'm right in the middle of something."

"Aren't you hungry?"

She shrugged. "I'll pop into the kitchen later and grab something."

"I can have a plate sent down for you," he said, even though he knew Geoffrey wouldn't be happy about it.

"That would be great, thanks," she said. "By the way, were you down here earlier?"

He shook his head. "I've been in the field all day."

"Does anyone else know the code for the door?"

"No, why?"

"A while ago I looked over and the door was ajar."

"Maybe you didn't close it all the way."

"I'm pretty sure I did."

"I'll have maintenance take a look at it."

"Thanks," she said, her eyes already straying back to the computer screen, fingers poised over the keys.

Geoffrey wouldn't consider it proper etiquette for a guest of the royal family to refuse a dinner invitation and then dine alone at a desk, but even he couldn't argue that Liv was not the typical royal guest.

She could eat in the bathtub for all Aaron cared, as long as she found a cure for the diseased crops.

"I'll have Geoffrey bring something right down."

She nodded vaguely, her attention back on her computer. He opened his mouth to say something else, but realized it would be a waste of breath. Liv was a million miles away, completely engrossed in whatever she was doing.

Doing her job, he reminded himself. They hadn't flown her in and paid good money so that she could spend her time amusing him.

He wondered if this was a foreshadow of what her time here would amount to. And if it was, it was going to be a challenge to seduce a woman who was never around.

Five

Liv studied the data that had been compiled so far regarding the diseased crops and compared the characteristics with other documented cases from all over the world. There were similarities, but no definitive matches yet. She wouldn't know for sure until she compared live samples from other parts of the world, which she would have to order and have shipped with expedited delivery.

She yawned and stretched, thinking maybe it was time for a short break, and heard the door click open.

She dropped her arms and turned to see Prince Aaron walking toward her. At least this time there was actually someone there. Despite a thorough check from a maintenance man, she'd found the door open several times, and once she could swear she'd seen someone peering at her through the window.

"Dinner not to your liking?" he asked.

Dinner? She vaguely remembered Geoffery coming by a while ago.

She followed the direction of his gaze to the table beside her desk and realized a plate had been left for her. Come to think of it, she was a little hungry. "Oh, I'm sure it's delicious. I was just wrapped up in what I was working on."

"I guess you were. You haven't slept, have you?"

"Slept?" She looked at her watch. "It's only ten."

"Ten *a.m.*," he said. "You've been down here all night."

"Have I?" It wouldn't be the first time she'd been so engrossed in her work that she forgot to sleep. Being in a lab with no windows probably didn't help. Unless she looked at her computer clock, which she rarely did, it was difficult to keep track of the time, to know if it was day or night. She'd been known to work for days on end, taking catnaps on her desk, and emerge from the lab with no idea what day it was, or the last time she'd eaten.

And now that she'd stopped working long enough to think about it, she realized that her neck ached and her eyes burned with exhaustion. A good sign that it was time for a break.

"When we hired you, we didn't expect you to

work 24/7," he said, but the playful smile said he was just teasing her.

"It's just the way I work." She reached back to knead the ache that was now spreading from her neck into the slope of her shoulders.

"Neck ache?" he asked, and she nodded. "I'm not surprised. Although gripping the muscles like that is only going to make it hurt more."

"It's stiff," she said.

He expelled an exasperated sigh and shook his head. "Why don't you let me do that."

Him?

She didn't think he was serious…until he stepped behind her chair. He was actually going to do it. He was going to rub her neck. He pushed her hands out of the way, then draped her ponytail over her left shoulder.

"Really," she said. "You don't have to—"

The words died in her throat as his hands settled on her shoulders.

The warmth of his skin began to seep through the cotton of her shirt and her cheeks exploded with heat. And as if that wasn't mortifyingly embarrassing and awkward enough, he slipped his fingers underneath the collar of her shirt. She sucked in a surprised breath as his hands touched her bare skin.

"The trick to relax the muscle," he told her, "is not to pinch the tension out, but to instead apply even pressure."

Yeah, right. Like there was any way she was going

to be able to relax now, with his hands touching her. His skin against her skin.

He pressed his thumbs into the muscle at the base of her neck and, against her will, a sigh of pleasure slipped from her lips. He slid his thumbs slowly upward, applying steady pressure. When he reached the base of her skull, he repeated the motion, until she felt the muscles going limp and soft.

"Feel good?" he asked.

"Mmm." Good didn't even begin to describe the way he was making her feel. Her head lolled forward and her eyes drifted shut.

"It would be better with oil," he said. "Unfortunately I don't have any handy."

The sudden image of Prince Aaron rubbing massage oil onto her naked body flashed through her brain.

Oh, no. Don't even go there, Liv. This was not a sexual come-on. He was just being polite. Although at that moment she would give anything to know what it would feel like. His oily hands sliding across her bare skin…

As if that would ever happen.

He sank his thumbs into the crevice beside her shoulder blades and a gust of breath hissed through her teeth.

"You have a knot here," he said, gently working it loose with his thumbs.

"You're really good at this," she said. "Did you take a class or something?"

"Human anatomy."

"Why would a prince in an agriculturally based field need a human anatomy class?"

"It might surprise you to learn that there was a time when I was seriously considering medical school."

Actually that didn't surprise her at all. She had the feeling there was a lot more to Prince Aaron than he let people see. "What changed your mind?" she asked.

"My family changed it for me. They needed me in the family business, so I majored in agriculture instead. End of story."

Somehow she doubted it was that simple. There was a tense quality to his voice that belied his true feelings.

"I guess that's the benefit of not having parents," she said. "No one to tell you what to do."

"I guess" was all he said, and she had the distinct impression she'd broached a subject he preferred not to explore. He gave her shoulders one last squeeze, then backed away and asked, "Feel better?"

"Much," she said, turning toward him. "Thank you."

"Sure," he said, but the usual, cheery smile was absent from his face. In fact, he looked almost...sad. Then she realized the inference in what she'd just said. His father was *dying,* his only hope a risky experimental procedure, and here she was suggesting that not having parents was a good thing.

Here he was being nice to her, and she was probably making him feel terrible.

Way to go, Liv. Open mouth, insert foot.

"Aaron, what I said just then, about not having parents—"

"Forget it," he said with a shrug.

In other words, *drop it*.

The lack of sleep, especially after that relaxing massage, was obviously taking its toll on her. She was saying stupid and inappropriate things to a man she knew practically nothing about. A virtual stranger.

A stranger who had the authority to fire her on a whim if it suited him.

"You should get some rest," he said.

He was right. She was long overdue for a power nap. "Now, if I can just find my way back to my room," she joked.

"Didn't Derek bring you a map?"

She looked down at her desk, papers strewn everywhere. "It's here. Somewhere."

He smiled and gestured to the door. "Come on, I'll walk you up."

"Thank you." She slipped her laptop in her backpack and slung it over her shoulder, grabbing the plate of uneaten food on her way out.

Even though he was silent, the tension between them seemed to ease as she followed the prince out of the lab and up the stairs. She left the plate in the kitchen and received a distinct look of disapproval from the butler.

"Sorry," she said lamely, and he answered with a stiff nod. That on top of what she'd said to the prince filled her with a nagging sense of guilt as they walked up to her room. She was obviously way out of her league here. This was going to take a lot of getting used to.

When they reached her door, she turned to him and said, "Thanks for walking me up."

He smiled. "My pleasure. Get some rest."

He started to turn away.

"Aaron, wait!"

He stopped and turned back to her.

"Before you go, I wanted to apologize."

His brow furrowed. "For what?"

"What I said in the lab."

"It's okay."

"No, it isn't. It was really…thoughtless. And I'm sorry if I made you feel bad."

"Liv, don't worry about it."

"I mean, I basically suggested you would be better off without parents, which, considering your father's health, was totally insensitive of me. My verbal filter must be on the fritz."

He leaned casually against the doorjamb, a look of amused curiosity on his face. "Verbal filter?"

"Yeah. People's thoughts go through, and the really dumb and inappropriate stuff gets tossed out before they can become words. Lack of sleep must have mine working at minimum capacity. I know it's a pretty lame excuse. But I'm really, *really* sorry. I'm just an employee. I have no right asking you personal questions or talking about your family, anyway."

For several long, excruciating seconds he just looked at her, and she began to worry that maybe he really was thinking about firing her. Then he asked, "Will you have dinner with me tonight?"

Huh?

She insulted him, and he invited her to share dinner with him? She might have thought he was extending a formal invitation just to be polite, but he looked sincere. Like he really *wanted* to have dinner with her.

"Um, sure," she said, more than a touch puzzled.

"Seven sharp."

"Okay."

"I'll warn you that Geoffrey loathes tardiness."

"I'll be on time," she assured him.

He flashed her one last smile, then walked away.

She stepped into her room and shut the door, still not exactly sure what just happened, but way too tired to try to sort it out. She would think about it later, after she'd had some sleep.

As inviting as the bed looked, the draw of a steaming shower was too appealing to resist. The sensation of the hot water jetting against her skin was almost as enjoyable as Aaron's neck massage had been. After her shower she curled up under the covers, planning to sleep an hour or two before heading back down to the lab.

She let her tired, burning eyes drift shut, and when she opened them again to check the clock on the bedside table, it was six forty-five.

* * *

Liv had been so wracked with guilt when Aaron walked her to her room this morning, she hadn't been paying attention to how they got there. And of course her handy map was in the lab, buried under her research. Which was why, four minutes before she was supposed to be in the dinning room, she was frantically wandering the halls, looking for a familiar landmark. The castle was just so big and quiet. If only she would run into someone who could help. She was going to be late, and she had the feeling she was already in hot water with Geoffrey the butler.

She rounded a corner and ran—literally—into someone.

Plowed into was more like it. But this time it wasn't a petite maid. This time it was a hulk of man, built like a tank, who stood at least a foot taller than her own five-foot-ten-inch frame. If he hadn't caught her by the arms, the force of the collision probably would have knocked her on her butt.

He righted and swiftly released her.

"Sorry," she apologized, wondering how many more royal employees she would collide with while she was here. "It was my fault. I wasn't looking where I was going."

"Miss Montgomery, I presume?" he said in a slightly annoyed tone, looking, of all places, at her chest. Then she looked down and realized she'd forgotten to pin on her ID badge. She pulled it from the outer pocket of her backpack and handed it to him. "Yeah, sorry."

His badge identified him as Flynn, and she couldn't help thinking that he looked more like a *Bruno* or a *Bruiser.*

He looked at the photo on her badge, then back at her, one brow raised slightly higher than the other. He didn't say, *You don't look like a scientist,* but she could tell he was thinking it.

He handed it back to her. "You should wear this at all times."

"I know. I forgot." She hooked it on her sweater, managing not to skewer her skin as she had yesterday. "Maybe you can help me. I'm trying to get to the dining room," she told him. "I've lost my way."

"Would you like me to show you the way?"

She sighed with relief. "That would be wonderful. I'm about three minutes from being late for dinner, and I'm already in the doghouse with Geoffrey."

"We can't have that," he said, gesturing in the direction she'd just come from. "This way, miss."

This time she paid attention as he led her downstairs to the dining room and she was pretty sure that she would be able to find her way back to her room. But she would keep the map with her at all times, just in case.

Prince Aaron was sitting in the dining room waiting for her, nursing a drink, when they walked in.

"I found her, Your Highness," Flynn told him.

"Thank you, Flynn," the prince said.

He nodded and left, and Liv realized it was no accident that she'd encountered him in the hallway.

"How did you know I would get lost?" she asked him.

He grinned. "Call it a hunch."

He rose from his chair and pulled out the adjacent chair for her, and as she sat, his fingers brushed the backs of her shoulders. Was he doing it on purpose? And if so, why did he feel the need to touch her all the time? Did he get some morbid kick out of making her nervous?

The only other time she'd had an experience with a touchy-feely person was back in graduate school. Professor Green had had a serious case of inappropriately wandering hands that, on a scale of one to ten, had an ick factor of fifteen. All of his female students fell victim to his occasional groping.

But unlike her professor, when Aaron touched her, she *liked* the way it felt. The shiver of awareness and swift zing of sexual attraction. She just wished she knew what it meant.

He eased her chair in and sat back down, lounging casually, drink in hand. "Would you like a drink? A glass of wine?"

"No, thank you. I have to stay sharp."

"What for?"

"Work."

He frowned. "You're working tonight?"

"Of course."

"But by the time we finish dinner, it will be after eight o'clock."

She shrugged. "So?"

"So, I have an idea. Why don't you take a night off?"

"Take a night off?"

"Instead of locking yourself in the lab, why don't you spend the evening with me?"

Six

The confused look on Liv's face was as amusing as it was endearing. She was as far from his type as a woman could be, yet Aaron wanted inside her head, wanted to know what made her tick.

Geoffrey appeared with the first course of their dinner, a mouthwatering lobster bisque. He knew this because he'd managed to sneak a taste before the chef had chased him out of the kitchen.

"How about that drink?" he asked Liv.

"Just water, please. Bottled, if you have it."

Geoffrey nodded and left to fetch it.

"You never answered my question," he said.

She fidgeted with her napkin. "I'm here to work, Your Highness."

"Aaron," he reminded her. "And you just worked a twenty-four-hour shift. Everyone needs a break every now and then."

"I had a break. I slept all day."

He could see he was getting nowhere, so he tried a different angle: the guilt card. He frowned and said, "Is the idea of spending time with me really so repulsive?"

Her eyes widened and she vigorously shook her head. "No! Of course not! I didn't mean to imply…" She frowned and bit her lip.

He could see that she was this close to giving in, so he made the decision for her. "It's settled, then. You'll spend the evening with me."

She looked hesitant, but seemed to realize that she had little choice in the matter. "I guess one night off wouldn't kill me."

"Excellent. What do you do for fun?"

She stared blankly.

"You do have fun occasionally, right?"

"When I'm not working I read a lot to catch up on the latest scientific discoveries and theories."

He shot her a skeptical look.

"That's fun."

"I'm talking social interaction. Being with other human beings."

He got a blank look from Liv.

"What about sports?" he asked.

She shrugged. "I'm not exactly athletic."

A person would never know it by her figure. She

looked very fit. He knew women who spent hours in the gym to look like Liv, and would kill to have a figure like that naturally.

"Do you go to movies?" he asked. "Watch television?"

"I don't get to the movies very often, and I don't own a television."

This time his eyes widened. "How can you not own a television?"

"What's the point? I'm never home to watch it."

"Music? Theater?"

She shook her head.

"There must be *something* you like to do besides work and read about work."

She thought about it for a moment, chewing her lip in concentration, then she finally said, "There is *one* thing I've always wanted to try."

"What's that?"

"Billiards."

Her answer surprised him. "Seriously?"

She nodded. "It's actually very scientific."

He grinned. "Well, then, you're in luck. We have a billiards table in the game room, and I happen to be an excellent teacher."

Ten minutes into her first billiards lesson, Liv began to suspect that choosing this particular game had been a bad idea. Right about the time that Aaron handed her a cue and then proceeded to stand behind her, leaning her over the edge of the table, his body pressed to hers, and demonstrating the appropriate way to hold it.

Hard as she tried to concentrate on his instructions, as he took her through several practice shots, she kept getting distracted by the feel of his wide, muscular chest against her back. His big, bulky arms guiding her. His body heat penetrating her clothes and warming her skin. And oh, did he smell good. Whatever aftershave or cologne he'd used that morning had long since faded and his natural, unique scent enveloped her.

It's just chemical, she reminded herself. And wholly one-sided. He wasn't holding her like this for pleasure, or as some sort of come-on. He was giving her a billiards lesson. Granted, she'd never had one before, but it stood to reason this was the way one would do it. Although the feel of him guiding the cue, sliding it back and forth between her thumb and forefinger, was ridiculously erotic.

If he did have some other sort of lesson on his mind, one that had nothing to do with billiards, she was so far out of her league that she couldn't even see her own league from here. Although, she had to admit, the view here was awfully nice.

"Have you got that?" Aaron asked.

She realized all this time he'd been explaining the game to her and she had completely zoned out. Which was absolutely unlike her. She turned her head toward him and he was so close her cheek collided with his chin. She could feel his breath shifting the wisps of hair that had escaped her ponytail.

She jerked her head back to look at the table, swallowing back a nervous giggle. Then she did something that she hardly ever did, at least, not since she was a rebellious teen. She *lied* and said, "I think I've got it."

He stepped back, racked up the balls, then said, "Okay, give it a try."

She lined the cue up to the white ball, just the way he'd shown her, but she was so nervous that when she took the shot she hit the green instead, leaving a chalky line on the surface. She cringed and said, "Sorry."

"It's okay," he assured her. "Try it again, but this time get a little closer to the ball. Like this." He demonstrated the motion with his own cue, then backed away.

She leaned back over, following his actions, and this time she managed to hit the ball, but the force only moved it about six inches to the left, completely missing the other balls, before it rolled to a stop. "Ugh."

"No, that was good," he assured her. "You just need to work on your aim and put a little weight behind it. Don't be afraid to give it a good whack."

"I'll try."

He set the cue ball back in place and she leaned over, lining it up, and this time she really whacked it. A little too hard, because the ball went airborne, banking to the left, right off the table. She cringed as it landed with a sharp crack on the tile floor. "Sorry!"

"It's okay," he said with a good-natured chuckle, rounding the table to fetch the ball. "Maybe not quite so hard next time."

She frowned. "I'm terrible at this."

"You just started. It takes practice."

That was part of the problem. She didn't have *time* to practice. Which was exactly why she was hesitant to try new things. Her motto had always been, If you can't be the best at something, why bother?

"Watch me," he said.

She stepped aside to give him room. He bent over and lined up the shot, but instead of keeping her eyes on his cue, where they were supposed to be, she found herself drawn to the perfect curve of his backside. His slacks hugged him just right.

She heard a loud crack, and lifted her gaze to see the balls scattering all over the table.

"Just like that," he said, and she nodded, despite the fact that, like before, she hadn't been paying attention. He backed up and gestured to the table. "Why don't you knock a few around. Work on your aim."

Despite her awkwardness, somehow Aaron always managed to make her feel less…inept. And after some practice and a couple of false starts, she was actually getting the hang of it. She even managed to keep all the balls on the table where they belonged and sink a few in the pockets. When they played a few actual games, she didn't do too badly, although she had the sneaking suspicion he was deliberately going easy on her.

After a while, despite having slept most of the day, she started yawning.

"Maybe we should call it a night," he said.

"What time is it?"

"Half past twelve."

"Already!" She had no idea they'd been playing that long.

"Past your bedtime?" he teased.

"Hardly." As if on cue, she yawned again, so deeply moisture filled her eyes. "I don't know why I'm so sleepy."

"Probably jet lag. It'll just take a few days for your system to adjust. Why don't you go to bed and get a good night's sleep, then start fresh in the morning."

As eager as she was to get back down to the lab, he was probably right. Besides, she really needed samples and her assistant wouldn't be here until the next morning. Maybe she could take some time to catch up on a bit of reading.

"I think maybe I will," she told him.

He took her cue and hung it, and his own, on a wall rack. "Maybe we can try this again, tomorrow night."

"Maybe," she said, and the weird thing was that she really wanted to. She was having fun. Maybe *too* much fun. She had a job to do here. That disease wasn't going to cure itself. It had been hours since she'd even thought about her research, and that wasn't at all like her.

"I'll walk you to your room," Aaron said.

"I think I can find my way." They were somewhere on the third floor, and if she took the nearest steps down one floor she was pretty sure she would be near the hallway her room was on.

"A gentleman always walks his date to the door," he said with a grin. "And if nothing else, I am *always* a gentleman."

Date? Surely he was using that word in the loosest of terms, because she and Aaron were definitely not *dating*. Not in the literal sense. He meant it casually, like when people said they had a *lunch date* with a friend. Or a *dinner date* with a work associate.

She picked up her backpack from where she'd left it by the door, slung it over her shoulder and followed him out into the hall and down the stairs. She wanted to remember how to get there, should she ever decide to come back and practice alone every now and then.

"By the way, do you play poker?" he asked as they walked side by side down the hall toward her room.

"Not in a long time."

"My brother, sister and I play every Friday night. You should join us."

"I don't know…"

"Come on, it'll be fun. I promise, it's much easier than billiards."

She wondered if that would be considered proper. The hired help playing cards with the family. Of course, since she'd arrived, he'd treated her more like a guest than an employee.

"If you claim you have to work," he said sternly, "I'll change the door code and lock you out of the lab."

She couldn't tell if he was just teasing her, or if he would really do it. And who knows, it might be fun. "They won't mind?"

"My brother and sister? Of course not. We always invite palace guests to join in."

"But I'm not technically a guest," she said as they stopped in front of her door. "I work for you."

He was silent for a moment as he seemed to digest her words, looking puzzled. Finally he said, "You don't have the slightest clue how valuable you are, do you?"

His words stunned her. Her? Valuable?

"What you've been through. What you've *overcome*..." He shook his head. "It makes me feel very insignificant."

"I make you feel that way?" she asked, flattening a hand to her chest. *"Me?"*

"Why is that so hard to believe?"

"You're royalty. Compared to you, I'm nobody."

"Why would you think you're nobody?"

"Because...I am. What have I ever done?"

"You've done a hell of a lot more than I ever have. And think of all that you still have the chance to do."

She could hardly believe that Aaron, a *prince,* could possibly hold someone like her in such high esteem. What was he seeing that no one else did?

"I'm sure you've done things, too," she said.

He shook his head. "All of my life I've had things

handed to me. I've never had to work for *anything*. And look at the adversity you've overcome to get where you are."

She shrugged. "I just did what I had to do."

"And that's my point exactly. Most people would have given up. Your determination, your *ambition,* is astounding. And the thing I like most is that you don't put on airs. You don't try to be something that you're not." He took a step closer and his expression was so earnest, so honest, her breath caught. "I've never met a woman so confident. So comfortable in her own skin."

Confident? Was he serious? She was constantly second-guessing herself, questioning her own significance. Her worth.

"You're intelligent and interesting and kind," he said. "And fun. And I'm betting that you don't have a clue how beautiful you are."

Did the guy need glasses? She was so...plain. So unremarkable. "You think I'm beautiful?"

"I don't think you are. I *know* you are. And you wouldn't believe how much I've wanted to..." He sighed and shook his head. "Never mind."

She was dying to know what he was thinking, and at the same time scared to death of what it might be. But her insatiable curiosity got the best of her.

Before she could stop herself she asked, "You wanted to do what?"

For a long, excruciating moment he just looked at

her and her heart hammered relentlessly in anticipation. Finally he grinned that sexy simmering smile and told her, "I wanted do this." Then he wrapped a hand around the back of her neck, pulled her to him and kissed her.

This was not the wishy-washy version of a kiss that Liv had gotten from William the day she left. Not even close. This kiss had heart. And soul. It had soft lips and caressing hands and breathless whimpers— mostly from her.

It was the kind of kiss that a girl remembered her entire life, the one she looked back on as her first *real* kiss. And she was kissing him back just as enthusiastically. Her arms went around Aaron's neck, fingers tunneled through his hair. She was practically *attacking* him, but he didn't seem to mind. She felt as though she needed this, needed to feed off his energy, like a plant absorbing the sunlight.

She kept waiting for him to break the kiss, to laugh at her and say, *Just kidding* or *I can't believe you fell for that!* As if it was some sort of joke. What other reason would he have for kissing someone like her? But he didn't pull away. He pulled *her* closer. Her breasts crushed against the solid wall of his chest, tingling almost painfully, and just like that, she was hotter and more turned on than she'd ever been in her life.

But what about William?
William who?

Aaron's hands were caressing her face, tangling through her hair, pulling the band free so it spilled out around her shoulders. He pulled her closer and she nearly gasped when she felt the length of his erection, long and stiff against her belly. Suddenly the reality of what she was doing, where this was leading and the eventual conclusion, penetrated the lusty haze that was clouding her otherwise-rational brain. In the back of her mind a guilty little voice asked, *Is this how you treat the man who asked you to marry him?*

She didn't want to think about that. She wanted to shut him out of her mind, pretend William didn't exist. But he *did* exist, and he was back in the States patiently awaiting an answer from her. Trusting that she was giving his proposal serious thought.

She broke the kiss and burrowed her head against Aaron's shoulder, feeling the deep rise and fall of his chest as he breathed, the rapid beat of his heart. Her own breath was coming in shallow bursts and her heart rate had climbed to what must have been a dangerously high level. Had anyone under the age of seventy ever actually died of heart failure brought on by extreme sexual arousal?

"What's wrong?" he asked, genuine concern in his voice.

She struggled to catch her breath, to slow her pounding heart. "We're moving too fast."

He chuckled. "Um, technically, we haven't actually done anything yet."

"And we shouldn't. We *can't*."

He was quiet for several seconds, then he asked, "Are you saying you don't want to? Because, love, that kiss was hot as hell."

He called her *love*. No one had ever used a term of endearment like that with her. Certainly not her foster parents. Not even William. It made her feel special. Which made what she had to do next that much harder.

"I want to," she said. "A lot."

He rubbed his hands softly up and down her back. "Are you…afraid?"

She shook her head against his shoulder. She was anything but frightened, although maybe she should have been, because nothing about this made any sense. It wasn't logical, and her entire life revolved around logic and science.

Maybe that was what made it so appealing.

"There's something I haven't told you," she said.

"What is it?"

She swallowed the lump in her throat and looked up at him. "I'm kind of…engaged."

Seven

"You're *engaged?*" Aaron backed away from Liv, wondering why this was the first time he'd heard this. Especially when he considered all of the blatant flirting that had been going both ways between them the past couple of days. Well, some of it went both ways, but in all fairness he was always the one to initiate it.

"Um…sort of," she said, looking uneasy.

Sort of? "Wait, how can a person be *sort of* engaged? And if you are engaged, why aren't you wearing a ring?"

"We kinda didn't get to that part yet."

He narrowed his eyes at her. "What part did you get to exactly?"

"He asked me, and I told him I would think about it."

There was this feeling, low in his gut. A surge of sensation that he didn't recognize. The he realized he was jealous. He envied a complete stranger. "Who is *he?*"

"His name is William. We work together."

"Another scientist?"

She nodded. "He's my mentor."

"Are you in love with him?" he asked.

She hesitated a moment, then said, "He's a good friend. I have an immense amount of respect for him."

Was that relief he'd just felt? "That isn't what I asked you."

She chewed her lip, as though she was giving it deep consideration, then she said, "Love is highly overrated."

Normally he would have agreed, but this was different. *She* was different. He couldn't imagine Liv being happy with a man she only *respected*. She deserved better. She'd fought all of her life to get exactly what she wanted. Why quit now?

And how did he know *what* she wanted when he barely knew her?

Somehow, he just did. And she was special. He couldn't even vocalize exactly why. It was just something he knew deep down.

"He must be a damned good shag, then," Aaron said, aware of how peevish he sounded.

He expected a snappy response, a firm, *Butt out, buster,* or *Mind your own business.* Instead Liv bit her lip and lowered her eyes. It didn't take him long to figure out what that meant.

He folded his arms across his chest and said, "You haven't slept with him, have you?"

"I didn't say that."

But she didn't deny it, either. "Out of curiosity, how long have you been dating this William fellow?"

Her gaze dropped to her feet again and in went the lip between her teeth. She didn't say a word. But her silence said it all.

"Are you telling me that you two have never even dated? Let me guess, you've never kissed him, either?"

She leveled her eyes on him. "I have so!"

He took a step toward her. "I'll bet he doesn't make you half as hot as I do."

He could tell by her expression, from the sudden rush of color to her cheeks, that he was right.

"I wasn't *that* hot," she said, but he knew it was a lie.

"You won't be happy," he said. "You're too passionate."

She looked at him like he was nuts. "I've been accused of a lot of things, but being passionate is not one of them."

He sighed. "There you go, selling yourself short again."

She shook her head in frustration. "I can't believe we're having this conversation. I hardly even know you."

"I know. And that's the bizarre part, because for some reason I feel as though I've known you forever." He could see by her expression that she didn't know how to respond to that, and she wasn't sure what to make of him. And oddly enough, neither did he. This wasn't at all like him.

She grabbed the knob and opened her door. "I should get to sleep."

He nodded. "Promise me you'll think about what I said."

"Good night, Aaron." She slipped inside her room and closed the door behind her.

He turned and walked in the direction of his own room. What he'd told her wasn't a lie. He'd never met anyone quite like her. She sincerely had no idea how unique, how gifted she was.

At first he'd planned only to seduce Liv and show her a good time while she was here, but something had happened since then. Something he hadn't expected. He really *liked* her. And the idea of her marrying this William person—a man she obviously didn't love— disturbed him far more than it should have.

Liv closed the door and leaned against it, expelling a long, deep breath.

What the heck had just happened out there? What did he want from her? Was he just trying to seduce her? To soften her up with his sweet words? Or did he really mean what he said? Did he really think she was interesting and fun? And *beautiful.* And if she really was, why had no one told her until now?

Just because no man had said the words, it didn't mean it wasn't true. And although she would never admit it to his face, he was right about one thing, no man had ever made her even close to as hot as he just had. With barely more than a kiss. Had it gone any further, she may have become the first scientifically genuine victim of spontaneous human combustion.

And oh how she had wanted it to go further. But to what end? A brief, torrid affair? Yeah, so what if it was? What was so wrong with that? They were consenting adults.

Yeah, but what about William?

So what if William wasn't an above-average kisser, and who cared that he didn't get her all hot and bothered the way Aaron did. William was stable and secure, and he respected her, and she was sure that he thought she was beautiful, too. He just wasn't the type of man to express his feelings. She was sure that once they were married he would open up.

But what if he didn't? Was that enough for her?

She heard a muffled jingle coming from her backpack and realized her phone was ringing. She pulled it out and saw that it was, *speak of the devil,* William. She hadn't spoken to him since she left the States. No doubt he was anxious for an answer.

She let it go to voice mail. She would call him

back tomorrow once she'd had a night to think things through. When she'd had time to forget how Aaron's lips felt against hers, and the taste of his mouth, and what it had been like to have his arms around her, his fingers tangling in her hair.

What if she never forgot? Could she go through life always wondering *what if?* Would it really be so awful, for once in her life, to do something just because she wanted to. Because it felt good. It wasn't as if he would want a relationship, and frankly, neither would she. Just one quick roll in the hay. Or maybe two. Then she could go home to William, who would never be the wiser…and live the rest of her life in guilt for betraying him.

Ugh.

But if they weren't technically engaged yet, could it really be counted as cheating?

As she was changing into her pajamas, her cell phone rang again. It was William. She considered letting it go to voice mail again, then decided she at least owed him a few words.

When she answered, his voice was filled with relief.

"I thought maybe you were avoiding me." He sounded so apprehensive and vulnerable. So unlike the confident, steadfast man she was used to, and the truth was, hearing him that way was just the slightest bit…off-putting. It knocked the pedestal she'd always kept him up on down a notch or two.

"Of course not," she said. "I've just been very busy."

"Is this a bad time? I could call back later."

"No, this is fine. I was just getting ready for bed. How have you been?"

"Swamped." He gave her a rundown on everything that had been going on in the lab since she left.

When he'd finished his dissertation, she asked him again. "How are *you*, William?"

"Me?" He sounded confused, probably because they never really talked about their personal lives.

"Yes, *you*."

Finally he said, "Good. I'm good."

She waited for him to elaborate, but he didn't. Instead he asked, "How are *you?*"

Exhausted, but excited, and having more fun than I've ever had in my life, not to mention nursing a pretty serious crush, and considering an affair with, of all people, a prince.

But she couldn't tell him that. "I'm…good."

"The reason for my call," he said, getting right to the point—because William *always* had a point. "I was just wondering if you'd given any thought to my proposal."

He said it so drily, as though he were referring to a work proposal and not a lifetime commitment.

"I have," she said. "It's just…well, I've been so busy. I'd like a little more time to think it over. It's a huge decision."

"Of course. I don't mean to rush you. I realize that it probably came as something of a surprise."

"A little, yes. I never realized you had those kinds of feelings for me."

"You know that I deeply respect you. Both personally and professionally. We make a good team."

Yes, but a good professional relationship and a good marriage were two entirely different animals. Again she had to wonder, did she want to marry a man who respected her, or one who loved her? A man whom she worked well with, or one who found her so sexually appealing he couldn't keep his eyes, or hands, off her? One who made her feel all warm and breathless and squishy inside, the way Aaron did.

Don't even go there, she warned herself. Aaron had no place in this particular equation. Besides, for all she knew William would be fantastic in bed. She'd always considered good sex more of a perk than a necessity.

If that was true, why wasn't she jumping at his offer?

"Can I ask you a question, William?"

"Of course."

"Why now? What's changed from, say, two months ago?"

"Well, I've been doing a lot of thinking lately. I've always imagined that one day I would get married and have a family. And as you know, I'm not getting any younger. It seemed like a good time."

It sounded so logical, but that hadn't exactly been what she was hoping for.

"I guess what I want to know is, why me?"

"Why you?" he said, sounding puzzled. "Why not you?"

"What I mean is, was there a particular reason you asked *me?*"

"Who else would I ask?"

She was seriously fishing here, and he just didn't seem to get it. She wasn't desperate enough to beg for a kind word or two. Like, *You're beautiful* or *I love you.* That would come with time.

Then why, deep down, was a little voice telling her that this was all wrong?

"Things are just so crazy right now," she told him. "Can you give me a few weeks to think about it?"

"Of course," he said, his tone so patient and reasonable that it filled her with shame. "Take your time."

They made random and slightly awkward small talk for several minutes, and William seemed almost relieved when she said she had to go.

She hung up wondering what kind of marriage would they have if the only thing they ever talked about was work? And even worse, he didn't seem all that interested in getting to know her on a personal level. Would that just take time? Or should the years she had already known him have been time enough?

She thought of Aaron, who asked her questions and seemed genuinely interested in getting to know her Why couldn't William be more like that?

Thoughts like that wouldn't get her anywhere.

William would never be like Aaron—a rich, charming prince. Which was a good thing, because as she'd reminded herself so many times now, Aaron, and men like him, were out of her league. Granted, she had never actually had a relationship with a man like Aaron, but she wasn't so naive that she didn't know the way these things worked. Even if Aaron did find her interesting at first, see her as a novelty, it wouldn't take him long to grow bored with her, for him to realize that she wasn't as special as he thought. Then he would be back to pursuing a proper mate. A woman with the right family and the proper breeding.

Yet she couldn't help but think of all the fun they could have in the meantime.

Eight

Liv was on her way to breakfast the following morning when she was greeted—more like accosted—by one of Aaron's sisters at the foot of the stairs on the main floor. Was it Friday already?

She was nowhere near as tall as her brother and had a slim, frail-looking build, and while they didn't exactly look alike, there was a strong family resemblance. She was dressed in a pale pink argyle sweater and cream-colored slacks and wore her hair pulled back in a low bun. In the crook of one arm she cradled a quivering ball of fur with bulging eyes. A dog, Liv realized. Probably a shih tzu.

The first impression that popped into Liv's head

was sweet and demure. Until the princess opened her mouth.

She squealed excitedly when she saw Liv and said, "You must be Olivia! I'm Aaron's sister Louisa."

Liv was so stunned by her enthusiasm—weren't princesses supposed to be poised and reserved?—she nearly neglected protocol and offered a hand to shake.

"It's nice to meet you, Your Highness," she said, dipping into a slightly wobbly curtsy instead. She had barely recovered when Louisa grabbed her hand and pumped it enthusiastically.

"Call me Louisa." She scratched the canine behind its silky ears. "And this is Muffin. Say hello, Muffin."

Muffin just stared, his little pink tongue lolling out of his mouth.

"I can't tell you how excited we are to have you here," she said, smiling brightly. "Aaron has told us *wonderful* things about you."

Liv couldn't help but wonder exactly what he'd told them. She would be mortified if he'd said something about their kiss last night. Having had the entire night to think it over, she decided that it would definitely never happen again. At least, not until she'd decided what to do about William. Although, probably not then, either. What she needed to concentrate on was the job she had come here to do.

"Has my brother been a good host?" Louisa asked.

Good didn't even begin to describe the sort of

host he'd been. "He has," Liv assured her. "He's made me feel very welcome."

"I'm so glad. I can't *wait* for you to meet the rest of the family! Everyone is so excited that you're here."

"I'm anxious to meet them, too."

"Well, then, let's go. Everyone should be having breakfast."

Everyone? As in, the *entire* family? Louisa expected her to meet them all at once?

Her heart slammed the wall of her chest. She never had been much good in groups of people. She preferred one-on-one interaction. She opened her mouth to object, but Louisa had already looped an arm through hers and was all but dragging her in the direction of the dining room. Liv felt like a giant beside her. Too tall, awkward and totally unrefined.

This was a nightmare.

"Look who I found!" Louisa announced as they entered the dining room. She probably didn't mean to, but she gave the impression that Liv had been aimlessly wandering the halls when this was the first morning she *hadn't* gotten lost.

She did a quick survey of the room and realized that other than Geoffrey, who was serving breakfast, there were no familiar faces. Where was Aaron?

Aaron's brother and his wife sat at one side of the table, while his other sister sat across from them.

"Everyone, this is Olivia Montgomery," Louisa

gushed. "The scientist who has come to save our country!"

Wow, no pressure there. She stood frozen beside Louisa, unsure of what to say or do. Then she felt it. The gentle and soothing pressure of a warm hand on her back. Aaron was standing there to rescue her.

She turned to him, never so happy in her life to see a familiar, friendly face. He was dressed to work in the field, in jeans and a soft-looking flannel shirt over a mock turtleneck.

He must have sensed how tense she was because he said under his breath, so even Louisa wouldn't hear, "Relax, they won't bite."

Miraculously, his deep, patient tone did just that. Her tension and fear seemed to melt away. Most of it at least. As long as Aaron was there, she was confident the introductions would go well. He would never feed her to the wolves.

His hand still on her back, he led her to the table where his brother sat.

"Liv," Aaron said, "meet my brother, Prince Christian, and his wife, Princess Melissa."

"Your Highnesses," she said, dipping into a near-perfect curtsy.

Prince Christian rose to his feet and reached out to shake her hand. She shifted her backpack to the opposite shoulder and accepted it.

His grip was firm and confident, his smile genuine. "I know I speak for everyone when I say it's an honor and a relief to have you here with us."

She pasted on her face what she hoped was a confident and capable smile. "I'm honored to be here."

"If there's anything you need, anything at all, you need only ask."

How about a valium, she was tempted to say, but had the feeling he might not appreciate her brand of humor. Instead she said, "I will, thank you."

"My parents send their regards and apologies that they weren't here to welcome you. They'll return in several days."

Liv wasn't sure if she was supposed to know the facts surrounding their father's situation, so she only nodded.

"You've already met Princess Louisa," Aaron said. "And this is my other sister, Princess Anne."

Louisa and Anne may have been twins, but they didn't look a thing alike. Anne was darker. In color, and considering her guarded expression, in personality, as well.

"Your Highness," Liv said, curtsying in her direction. She was getting pretty good at this.

"I understand you think you can find a cure for the diseased crops," Anne said, sounding slightly antagonistic, as though she questioned Liv's credentials. Was Anne trying to intimidate her? Put her in her place?

It was one thing to question Liv personally, but as a scientist, they wouldn't find anyone more capable.

She lifted her chin a notch. "I don't *think* I can, Your Highness. I *will* find a cure. As I told Prince Aaron, it's simply a matter of time."

A vague smile pulled at the corners of Anne's mouth. If it had been some sort of test, it appeared Liv had passed.

"Shall we sit?" Aaron said, gesturing to the table.

She turned to him. "Actually, I was planning to get right to work."

He frowned. "You're not hungry?"

Not anymore. The idea of sitting and eating breakfast surrounded by his entire family was only slightly less intimidating than facing a firing squad. "If I could get a carafe of coffee sent down to the lab that would be great."

"Of course." He addressed the butler. "Geoffrey, would you take care of that, please?"

Geoffrey nodded, and although Liv couldn't say for sure, he might have looked a bit peeved.

"It was nice to meet everyone," Liv said.

"You'll join us for dinner?" Princess Melissa asked, although it came across as more of a statement than a question.

Before she could form a valid excuse to decline, Aaron answered for her, "Of course she will."

She wanted to turn to him and say, *I will?*, but she held her tongue. Besides, much as she'd like to, she couldn't avoid them forever.

She would feel so much more comfortable if they

treated her like the hired help rather than a guest and left her to her own devices.

"I'll walk you down to the lab," Aaron said, and though her first instinct was to refuse his offer, she didn't want everyone to think there was a reason she shouldn't be alone with him. Like the fact that she was scared to death he would kiss her again. And even more terrified that if he did, she wouldn't be able to make herself stop him this time.

He led her from the room, and when they were in the hall and out of earshot he said, "I know they can be intimidating, especially Anne, but you can't avoid them forever. They're curious about you."

"I just want to get an early start," she lied, "before my assistant arrives."

He shot her a we-both-know-that's-bull look.

"You don't have to walk me to the lab."

"I know I don't." His slightly mischievous grin said he was going to regardless, and the warmth of it began melting her from the inside out. When he rested a hand on her back to lead her there, her skin tingled under his touch.

If this was the way things would be from now on, she was in *big* trouble.

"I think we need to talk," Aaron told Liv as they walked through the kitchen to the basement door.

"About what?" she asked and he shot her a what-do-you-think look. She frowned and said, "Oh, *that*."

"In the lab," he said, "where we can have some privacy." She nodded and followed him silently through the kitchen and down the stairs. She wasn't wound nearly so tight as she'd been facing his family. She'd been so tense when he stepped into the dining room that he was hesitant to touch her for fear that she might shatter.

She trailed him down the stairs and waited while he punched in the door code. When they were in the lab with the door closed, she turned to him and said, "I've decided that what happened last night can't ever happen again."

So, she thought she would use the direct approach. That shouldn't have surprised him. And he was sure she had what she considered a very logical reason for her decision.

He folded his arms across his chest. "Is that so?"

"I'm serious, Aaron." She did look serious. "I talked to William last night."

An unexpected slam of disappointment and envy pegged him right in the gut.

"You've made your decision, then?" he asked, knowing that if she'd said yes to the engagement, he would do everything in his power to talk her out of it. Not for himself of course, but for her sake.

All right, maybe a *little* for himself.

"I haven't made a decision yet, but I told William that I'm still considering it. And until I accept or refuse his proposal, I don't feel it's right to…*see* anyone else."

He grinned. "See."

"You know what I mean."

"Why?"

His question seemed to confuse her. "Why?"

"You're not engaged. Admittedly you're not even *dating* him. So, logically, *seeing* me or anyone else wouldn't technically be considered infidelity."

She frowned. "You're splitting hairs."

"Not to mention that, if you really *wanted* to marry him, why would you need time to think about it? Wouldn't you have said *yes* as soon as he asked?"

She looked troubled, as though she realized he was right, but didn't want to admit it. "It's…complicated."

"And you think it will be less complicated after you're married? You think he'll miraculously change?"

"That's not what I meant."

"It doesn't work that way, Liv. Problems don't go away with the vows. The way I hear it, they usually get worse."

She expelled a frustrated breath. "Why do you even care? Or is this just your way of trying to get me in bed?"

He grinned. "Love, if I wanted in your knickers, I'd have been there last night."

Her cheeks blushed bright pink.

He took a few steps toward her. "I'm not going to insult your highly superior intelligence and say I don't want to get you into bed. But more than that, I like you, Liv, and I don't want to see you make a mistake."

"Ugh! Would you please stop saying that I'm making a mistake?"

"Are you afraid you're going to start believing me?"

"You think that my sleeping with you *wouldn't* be a mistake?"

He knew now that she'd at least been thinking about it. Probably as much as he had. "No, I don't. In fact, I think it would be beneficial to us both."

"Well, you're not exactly biased, are you?" She collapsed in her chair and dropped her head in her hands. "I want to do the right thing, and you're confusing me."

"How could anything *I* say confuse you? Either you want to marry him, or you don't."

"I don't know if I want to marry *anyone* right now!" she nearly shouted, looking shocked at her own words.

Then why fret over it? "If you're not ready to get married, tell him no."

She looked hopelessly confused and completely adorable. He could see that she wasn't used to not having all the answers. For some reason it made him like her that much more.

She gazed up at him, eyes clouded by confusion. "What if I don't get another chance?"

"To marry William?"

"To marry *anyone!* I do want to get married someday and have a family."

"What's stopping you?"

"What if no one else ever asks?"

That was the most ridiculous thing he'd ever heard. She was an attractive, desirable woman that any man would be lucky to have. If she spent some time outside of her lab and living her life, she might already know that. Men would probably be fighting each other to win her hand.

He knelt down in front of her chair, resting his hands on her knees. "Liv, trust me, someone will ask. Someone you want to marry. Someone you *love*."

She gazed into his eyes, looking so young and vulnerable and confused. What was it about her that made him want take her in his arms and just hold her? Soothe her fears and assure her that everything would be okay. But even if he'd wanted to, she didn't give him the chance. Instead, she leaned forward, wrapped her arms around his neck and kissed him.

Nine

That guilty little voice inside Liv was shouting, *Don't do it, Liv!* But by then it was already too late. Her arms were around Aaron's neck and her lips were on his. She was kissing him again, and he was kissing her back. The feel of his mouth, the taste of him, was already as familiar as it was exciting and new. Maybe because she'd spent most of the night before reliving the first kiss and fantasizing what it would feel like to do it again. Now she knew. And it was even better than she remembered. Better than she could ever have imagined.

Aaron cupped her face in his hands, stroking her cheeks, her throat, threading his fingers through her hair. She hooked her legs around his back, drawing him closer, clinging to him. She might have been embarrassed by her brazen behavior, but she felt too hot and needy with desire to care. She needed to feel him. She just plain *needed* him. Nothing in her life had ever felt this good, this…right. She hadn't even known it was possible to feel this way. And she wanted more—wanted it all. Even though she wasn't completely sure what *it* was yet. Was this just physical, or was there more to it?

Of course not. What did she think, they were going to have some sort of relationship? She didn't want that any more than he did. Her work was too important to her.

That didn't mean they couldn't have a little fun.

She tugged the tail of his flannel from the waist of his jeans, but he grabbed her hands and broke the kiss, saying in a husky voice, "We can't."

Shame burned her cheeks. Of course they couldn't. Hadn't she just told him that very same thing? What the hell had she been thinking? Why, the instant she was near him, did she seem to lose all concept of right and wrong?

She jerked her hands free and rolled the chair backward, away from him. "You're right. I'm sorry. I don't know what I was thinking. This isn't like me at all."

He looked puzzled for a moment, then he grinned and said, "I don't mean *ever*. I just meant that we can't *here*. Any minute now Geoffrey is going to walk through that door with your coffee, not to mention the lab assistant who's due here this morning."

"Oh, right," she said, feeling, of all things, relieved. When what she should have felt was ashamed of herself, and regretful for once again betraying William. Although, as Aaron had pointed out, she and William weren't technically a couple.

You're rationalizing, Liv. When there was absolutely nothing rational about this scenario. This was not the way the world was supposed to work. Brainy, orphaned scientists did not have flings with rich, handsome princes. No matter what the storybooks said.

Nothing that felt this wonderful could possibly be good for her.

"We can't do this again," she told him. "Ever."

Aaron sighed. "We're back to that again?"

"It's wrong."

Aaron rose from his knees and tucked his shirt back in. "It felt pretty good to me."

"I'm serious, Aaron."

"Oh, I know you are."

So why didn't he look as though he was taking her seriously? Why did she get the feeling he was just humoring her?

"I have to get to work," he said. "I'll see you at dinner?"

Was that a statement or a request? She could say no, but she suspected he wouldn't take no for an answer, and that if she tried to skip it, he would come down to the lab and fetch her. At least with his family around he wouldn't try anything physical with her. At least, she hoped he wouldn't. She seriously doubted his family would approve of Aaron messing around with the hired help. Especially one who ranked so abysmally low in the social ladder.

"Seven sharp," she said.

He leaned over and before she could stop him, he gave her a quick kiss—just a soft brush of his lips against hers, but it left her aching for more—then he walked to the door. As he opened it, he turned back to her and said, "Don't forget about the poker game tonight." Then he left, the door closing with a metallic click behind him.

Ugh. She had forgotten all about that. But she already said she would play, so she doubted he would let her back out now.

As much as she didn't want to spend the evening with his family, she dreaded even more spending it alone with him.

She turned to her desk, reaching for the pen she'd left beside her keyboard, but it wasn't there. She searched all over the desk, under every paper and text. She even checked the floor, in case it had somehow rolled off the desk, but it wasn't there. It was as if it had vanished into thin air.

She got a new one from her backpack, and as she was leaning over she heard a noise behind her, from the vicinity of the door. She thought maybe it was Geoffrey with her coffee, or her lab assistant, but when she turned, there was no one there.

And the damn door was open again.

After breakfast Aaron pulled Chris aside and asked, "So, what did you think of Liv?"

"Liv?"

"Miss Montgomery."

Chris raised one brow. "We're on a first-name basis, are we?"

Aaron scowled a him. "I'm being serious."

Chris chuckled. "I'll admit she's not at all what I expected. She doesn't look like a scientist and she's much younger than I imagined. She does seem quite confident, though, if not a bit…*unusual*."

"Unusual?"

"Not the typical royal guest."

Despite having thought that very same thing, Aaron felt protective of Liv. "What does that matter, so long as she gets the job done?"

Chris grinned. "No need to get testy. I'm just making an observation."

"An observation of someone you know nothing about." Knowing his siblings had the tendency to be more judgmental, Aaron wouldn't tell them about Liv's past. Not that he believed she had anything to be ashamed of—quite the contrary in fact—but the things she'd told him had been in confidence. If they wanted to know more about her, they would have to ask themselves—which he didn't doubt they would.

"If I didn't know better, I might think you fancy her," Chris said. "But we all know that you prefer your women with IQs in the double digits."

Even though he couldn't exactly deny the accusation, Aaron glared at him. "By the way, I invited her to our poker game tonight."

Chris looked intrigued. "Really? She doesn't strike me as the card-playing type."

Aaron wanted to ask, *What type does she strike you as?*, but he was afraid he might not like the answer he got. "Are you saying you don't want her to play?"

Chris shrugged. "It's fine with me. The more the merrier." He looked at his watch. "Is there anything else? I have a conference call in fifteen minutes."

"No, nothing else."

Chris started to turn away, then stopped and said, "I almost forgot to ask, have there been any new developments since I left?"

Aaron didn't have to ask Chris what he meant. It had been in the back of everyone's minds for months now. The person who referred to himself as the Gingerbread Man. "No e-mails, no security breaches. Nothing. It's as if he disappeared into thin air."

Chris looked relieved. "I hope that means it was a harmless prank, and we've heard the last of him."

"Or it could mean that he's building up to something big."

His relief instantly turned to irritation. "Always the optimist."

Aaron grinned. "I like to think that I'm realistic. Whoever he was, he went through an awful lot of trouble breaching our security systems. All I'm saying is that we should keep on our toes."

"I'll keep security on high alert, but at some point we'll have to assume he's given up."

"Call it a hunch," Aaron said, "but I seriously doubt we've seen or heard the last of him."

In her life Liv had never met such an inquisitive group of people. It must run in the family because during dinner she was overwhelmed by endless questions from every side of the table. And like their brother, they seemed genuinely interested in her answers. They asked about her work and education mostly, and they were nothing if not thorough. By the end of the evening she felt picked over and prodded, much like one of the soil samples she'd studied that afternoon. It could have been worse. They could have completely ignored her and made her feel like an outsider.

"See?" Aaron whispered as they walked to the game room to play cards. "That wasn't so bad."

"Not too bad," she admitted.

As they took seats around the table, Geoffrey took

drink orders while Prince Christian—Chris, as he'd asked her to address him—divvied out the chips.

"We start with one hundred each," Aaron told her. "I can front you the money."

She hadn't realized they would play for real money. In college and grad school the stakes had been nickels and dimes, but one hundred euros wasn't exactly out of her budget range. She'd checked the exchange rate before leaving the U.S. and one hundred euros would be equivalent to roughly one hundred thirty-one dollars, give or take.

"I can cover it," she told him.

He regarded her curiously. "You're sure?"

Did he think she was that destitute? "Of course I'm sure."

He shrugged and said, "Okay."

She was rusty the first few hands, but then it all started to come back to her and she won the next few rounds. A bit unfairly, she would admit, even though it wasn't exactly her fault. Besides, she was actually having fun.

Louisa apparently didn't play cards. She sat at the table with her dog, to her siblings' obvious irritation, chatting.

"Where are you from originally?" she asked Liv. She was definitely the friendlier of the twins. A glass-is-half-full kind of girl. And Liv used the term *girl* because Louisa had so sweet a disposition.

"I'm from New York," Liv told her.

"Your family still lives there?" she asked.

"Five card draw, nothing wild," Chris announced, shooting Louisa a look as he shuffled the cards.

"I don't have family," Liv said.

"Everyone has some family," Melissa said with the subtle twang of a Southern accent. Aaron had mentioned that she was born on Morgan Isle, the sister country of Thomas Isle, but had been raised in the U.S. in Louisiana.

"None that I know of," Liv told her. "I was abandoned as a small child and raised in foster homes."

"Abandoned?" Melissa repeated, her lower lip beginning to quiver and tears pooling in her eyes. "That's *so* sad."

"Easy, emotio-girl," Chris said, rubbing his wife's shoulder. When the tears spilled over onto her cheeks, he put down the cards he'd been dealing, reached into his pants pocket and pulled out a handkerchief. Neither he nor anyone else at the table appeared to find her sudden emotional meltdown unusual.

Melissa sniffed and dabbed at her eyes.

"You all right?" he asked, giving her shoulder a reassuring squeeze.

She gave him a wobbly nod and a halfhearted smile.

"You'll have to excuse my wife," Chris told Liv. "She's a little emotional these days."

"Just a little," Melissa said with a wry smile. "It's these damn fertility drugs. I feel like I'm on an emotional roller coaster."

"They're trying to get pregnant," Aaron told Liv.

"She's a scientist, genius," Anne said. "I'm sure she knows what fertility drugs are for."

Aaron ignored her.

"I don't know much about it myself, although I have a colleague who specializes in fertility on a genetic level," Liv said. "I never realized how common it is for couples to have some fertility issues."

"We're trying in vitro," Melissa said, tucking the handkerchief in her lap while Chris finished dealing. "Our doctor wanted us to wait and try it naturally for six months, but I'm already in my midthirties and we want at least three children, so we opted for the intervention now."

"We do run the risk of multiples," Chris said. "Even more so because obviously twins run in the family. But it's a chance we're willing to take."

It surprised Liv that they spoke so openly to a stranger about their personal medical issues, although she had found that, because she was a scientist, people assumed she possessed medical knowledge, which couldn't be further from the truth. Unless the patient happened to be a plant.

"I'll open for ten," Aaron said, tossing a chip in the pot, and everyone but Anne followed suit.

She threw down her cards and said, "I fold."

"I can hardly wait to have a little niece or nephew to spoil. Or both!" Louisa gushed. "Do you want children, Olivia?"

"Someday," Liv said. After she'd had more time to develop her career, and of course she would prefer to be married first. Would William be that man? Would she settle out of fear that she would never get another chance? Or would she take a chance and maybe meet a man she loved, and who loved her back? One who looked at her with love and affection and pride, the way Chris looked at Melissa. Didn't she deserve that, too?

If she never married and had kids, would it be that big of a tragedy? She always had her work.

"I love kids," Louisa said. "I'd like at least six, maybe eight."

"Which is why when you meet men, they run screaming in the opposite direction," Anne quipped, but her jab didn't seem to bother her sister.

"The right man is out there," Louisa said, with a tranquil smile and a confidence that suggested she had no doubt. She was probably right. What man wouldn't want to marry a sweet, beautiful princess? Even if it meant having an entire brood of children.

"We all know that Aaron doesn't want kids," Anne said, shooting Liv a meaningful look.

Did she suspect that something was going on between Liv and her brother? And if so, did she honestly believe that Liv would consider him as a potential father to her children? Nothing could be further from the truth. If they did have a fling, which was a moot point because she had already decided they wouldn't, she would never expect more than a brief affair.

Unsure of how to react, Liv decided it was best to give her no reaction at all and instead studied her cards.

"I'm just not cut out to be a family man," Aaron said to no one in particular. If he caught the meaning of his sister's statement, he didn't let on. Or maybe he was saying it for Liv's benefit, just in case she was having any delusions of grandeur and thought they had some sort of future together.

"You would have to drop out of the girl-of-the-month club," Anne said with a rueful smile and a subtle glance in Liv's direction.

"And miss out on that fantastic yearly rate they give me?" Aaron said with a grin. "I think not."

"Are we going to talk or play?" Chris complained, which, to Liv's profound relief, abruptly ended the conversation.

Louisa tried occasionally to engage them in conversation, earning a stern look from her oldest brother each time. She finally gave up and said good-night around ten. Half an hour later Melissa followed. At eleven-thirty, when Liv was up by almost two hundred euros, they packed it in for the night.

"Good game," Chris said, shaking her hand, and added with a grin, "I hope you'll give us a chance to win our money back next week."

"Of course," she said, although she would have to throw the game to make it happen.

"I'll walk you to your room," Aaron said, gesturing to the door, and he had a curious, almost sly look on his face. Something was definitely up.

"Why are you looking at me like that?" she asked.

"Because we finally get some time alone."

Ten

The idea of being alone with Aaron again both terrified and thrilled Liv, then he went and added another level of tension by saying, "You do realize that counting cards is considered cheating."

Oh damn.

She really hadn't thought anyone was paying that close attention. They were playing for only a couple hundred euros, so what was the harm?

She plastered on a look of pure innocence that said, *Me? Cheat?* But she could see he wasn't buying it.

She sighed and said, "It's not my fault."

He raised one disbelieving brow at her.

"I don't even do it consciously. The numbers just kind of stick in my head."

"You have a photographic memory?"

She nodded.

"I wondered how you managed to memorize the code for the lab door so quickly. Although for the life of me I don't understand how you kept getting lost in the castle."

"It only works with numbers."

For a second she though he might be angry, but he shot her a wry smile instead. "At least you made a bit of money for your research."

He apparently had no idea of the going rate for genetic research. "A couple hundred euros won't get me very far."

"You mean thousand," he said.

"Excuse me?"

"A couple hundred thousand."

She nearly tripped on her feet and went tumbling down the stairs. "That's not even funny."

He shrugged. "I'm not trying to be funny."

"You're serious?"

"*Totally* serious."

"You said we were starting with one hundred."

"We did. One hundred thousand."

She suddenly felt weak in the knees. All this time she thought she'd been betting a dollar or ten, it had actually been thousands? What if she'd lost? How would she have ever paid her debt?

"I'll give the money back," she said.

"That would look suspicious. Besides," he reminded her, "you already told Chris you would play again next Friday."

Damn it, she had, hadn't she? If the rest of the family figured it out, they might think her some sort of con artist. Next week she would just have to lose on purpose, claim that her first time must have been beginner's luck, then pretend to be discouraged and vow never to play again. Only she and Aaron would know the truth.

When they reached her room she opened the door and stepped inside. A single lamp burned beside the bed and the covers had been turned down. Standing in the doorway, she turned to him and said, "I had fun tonight."

He leaned against the doorjamb, wearing that devilish, adorable grin. "Aren't you going to invite me in?"

"No."

"Why not?"

"I told you earlier, we can't be…intimate." Just saying the word made her cheeks flush.

"You said it, but we both know you didn't mean it." He leaned in closer. "You want me, Liv."

She did. So much that she ached. He smelled so good and looked so damn sexy wearing that wicked, playful smile, and he was emitting enough phero-mones to make any woman bend to his will.

"That doesn't make it right," she told him, but

with a pathetic degree of conviction. She didn't even believe herself.

Which was probably why, instead of saying good-night and closing the door in his face, Liv grabbed the front of his shirt, pulled him into her room and kissed him.

He reacted with a surprised, "Oomf," which she had to admit gave her a decadent feeling of power. But it took him only seconds to recover, then he was kissing her back, pulling her into his arms. He shut the door and walked her backward to the bed, tugging the hem of her shirt free from the waist of her pants. She did the same to him, their arms getting tangled. They broke the kiss so that they could pull the shirts over their heads, and the sight of his bare chest took her breath away. He didn't even seem put off by her very plain and utilitarian cotton bra. His eyes raked over her, heavy with lust, and when his hands settled on her bare skin, she shuddered. He was so beautiful, so perfect, she could hardly believe it was real. That he wanted someone like her.

It's just sex, she reminded herself, although deep down, it felt like more.

He tugged the band from her hair and it spilled down around her bare shoulders.

"You're beautiful," he said, looking as though he sincerely meant it. She wished she could see what he saw, see herself through his eyes for one night.

He lowered his head, brushing his lips against the

crest of one breast, just above the cup of her bra. She shuddered again and curled her fingers through his hair.

"You smell fantastic," he said, then he ran his tongue where his lips had just been, up one side and down the other, and a moan slipped from between her lips. "Taste good, too," he added with a devilish grin.

"What are we doing?" she asked.

He regarded her curiously. "As a scientist, I'd have thought someone would have explained it to you by now."

She couldn't help but smile. "I know *what* we're doing. I just don't understand *why*."

"I don't know what you mean."

"Why me?"

She expected him to tease her, to tell her that she was underestimating herself again; instead his expression was serious.

"Honestly, I'm not sure." He caressed her cheek with the backs of his fingers. "All I know is, I've never wanted a woman the way I want you."

She might have suspected it was a line, but his eyes told her that he was telling the truth. That he was just as stunned and confused by this unlikely connection as she was.

Then he kissed her and started touching her, and she didn't care why they were doing it, her only thought was how wonderful his hands felt on her skin, how warm and delicious his mouth felt as he tasted and nipped her. With a quick flick of his fingers he unhooked her bra, and as he bared her breasts, he didn't seem to notice or care how voluptuous she wasn't, and as he drew one nipple into his mouth, flicking lightly with his tongue, she didn't care, either. He made her feel beautiful and desirable.

There was this burning need inside her like she'd never felt before, a sweet ache between her thighs that made her want to beg him to touch her, but he was still concentrating all of his efforts above her waist—and it was driving her mad.

Thinking it might move things along, she ran her hand down his chest to his slacks, sliding her fingers along his waistline, just below the fabric, then she moved her hand over his zipper, sucking in a surprised breath when she realized how long and thick he felt. She should have expected that he would be perfect everywhere.

She gave his erection a gentle squeeze and he groaned against her cleavage.

He reached behind him and she wasn't sure what he was doing, until he tossed his wallet down on the mattress. Intelligent as she was, it took her several seconds to understand why, and when she did—when she realized that he kept his condoms in there—the reality of what they were doing and exactly where this was leading hit her full force.

The fading flower who in college wouldn't even let a man kiss her until the third date was about to have sex with a man she'd known only four days. A playboy prince who without a doubt was far more experienced than she could ever hope to be.

So why wasn't she afraid, or at least a little wary? Why did it just make her want him that much more?

"Take them off," he told her, his voice husky.

She gazed up at him, confused. Only when she saw the look on his face did she realize how aroused he was, and that she was rhythmically stroking him without even realizing it. Reacting solely on instinct.

"My pants," he said. "Take them off now."

With trembling fingers she fumbled with the clasp, then pulled down the zipper. She tugged the slacks down, leaving his boxers in place.

"All of it," he demanded, so she pulled the boxers down, too. "Now, do that again."

She knew what he wanted. He wanted her to touch him again. She took him in her hand and the skin was so hot, she nearly jerked her arm back. Instead she squeezed.

The point of touching him, or at least, part of the point, had been so that he would touch her, too, but so far he was the one getting all of the action. With that thought came a sudden jab of concern that he was one of *those* men. The kind who took pleasure and gave nothing in return. She'd never been with a man who had taken the time to even try to please her, so what made her think Aaron would be any different?

Before she could even complete the thought, Aaron clasped her wrist to stop her. "That feels too good."

Wasn't that the point?

But she didn't argue because he *finally* reached down to unfasten her chinos—much more deftly than she'd managed with his. He eased her pants and panties down together and she kicked them away.

"Lie down," he said, nodding toward the bed. She did as he asked, trembling with anticipation. But instead of lying down beside her, he knelt between her thighs. If she had been more experienced with men, or more to the point, with men like *him,* she probably would have known what was coming next. Instead it was a total surprise when he eased her thighs open, leaned forward and kissed her there. She was so surprised, she wasn't sure what to do, how to react. Then he pressed her legs even farther apart and flicked her with his tongue. The sensation was so shockingly intimate and intense she cried out and arched off the bed. He teased her with his tongue, licking just hard enough to drive her mad, to make her squirm and moan. When she didn't think she could stand much more he took her into his mouth and every muscle from head to toe locked and shuddered in ecstasy, sending her higher and higher, and when it became too much, too intense, she pushed his head away.

She lay there with her eyes closed, too limp to do more than breathe. She felt the bed shift, and the warmth of Aaron's body beside hers. She pried her eyes open to find him grinning down at her. "Everything all right?"

It took all of her energy to nod. "Oh, yeah."

"Are you always that fast?"

"I have no idea."

"What do you mean."

"No man has actually ever done that."

He frowned. "Which part?"

"Either. Both. The few men I've been with weren't exactly...adventurous. And they were more interested in their own pleasure than mine."

"Are you saying no man has ever given you an orgasm?"

"Nope."

"That's just...*wrong*. There's nothing more satisfying for me than giving a woman pleasure."

"Really?" She didn't think it worked that way. Or maybe he was in a class all by himself.

"And you know the best part?" he said.

"Huh?"

He grinned that wolfish smile. "I get to spend the rest of the night proving it to you."

In his life Aaron had never been with a woman so responsive or easy to satisfy as Liv. She climaxed so quickly, and so often, just using his hands and mouth, that it sort of took the challenge out of it. But the way he looked at it, he was helping her make up for lost time. Those other men she'd been with must have been totally inept, completely self-absorbed or just plain stupid. That gave all men a bad rap. He'd never seen anything as fantastic as Liv shuddering in ecstasy, eyes blind with satisfaction.

"I want you inside me," she finally pleaded, gazing up at him with lust-filled eyes, and he couldn't resist giving her exactly what she wanted. He grabbed a condom and tore the package open with his teeth. He looked down at Liv and realized she was staring at his hard-on with a look on her face that hovered somewhere between curiosity and fascination.

"Can I do it?" she asked, holding out her hand.

He shrugged and gave her the condom. "Knock yourself out."

He expected her to roll it on; instead she leaned forward and took him in her mouth. Deep in her mouth. He groaned and wound his hands through her hair, on the verge of an explosion.

She took him from her mouth, looked up at him and grinned.

"I figured it would go on better this way. Besides, I've always wanted to try that."

She could experiment on him anytime. And he truly hoped she would.

He gritted his teeth as she carefully rolled the condom down the length of him.

"Like that?" she asked.

"Perfect," he said, and before he could make another move she lay back, pulling him down on top of her, between her thighs, arching to accept him.

She was so hot and wet and *tight* that he nearly lost

it on the first thrust. And though he was determined to make it last, she wasn't making it easy. Her hands were all over him, threading through his hair, her nails clawing at his back and shoulders, and she wrapped those gloriously long legs around his waist, whimpering in his ear. Then she tensed and moaned and her body clamped down around him like a fist, and it was all over. They rode it out together, then lay gasping for breath, a tangle of arms and legs.

"I had no idea it could be like this," she said.

Neither did he. "You say that as if we're done."

She rose up on one elbow and looked down at him, her expression serious. "I can't marry William."

"That's what I keep telling you," he said. He just hoped she hadn't decided to set her sights on him instead. They had fantastic sexual chemistry, but that didn't change the fact that he had every intention of remaining a free man. William wasn't the right man for her, but neither was he.

"If I wanted to marry him, I would feel guilty right now, wouldn't I?"

"I would think so."

"I don't. Not at all. In fact I almost feel…*relieved*. Like this huge weight has been lifted from my shoulders."

"That's good, right?"

She nodded. "I'm not ready to get married. And even if I was, I can't marry a man I don't love, that I'm not even sexually attracted to. I want more than that."

"You deserve more."

"I do," she agreed, looking as though, for the first time in her life, she finally believed it. "We have to keep this quiet."

"About William?"

"No. About us. Unless…" She frowned.

"Unless what?"

"Well, maybe we shouldn't do this again."

"Don't you think that's a bit unrealistic? Since you got here we haven't been able to keep our hands off each other."

"Then we'll have to be very discreet. Anne already suspects something."

He shrugged. "So what?"

"I'm going to go out on a limb here and assume that your family wouldn't approve of you slumming it with the hired help."

"You're a *guest*," he reminded her. "Besides, I don't give a damn what my family thinks."

"But I do. I spent most of my life trying not to be one of *those* girls. Having sex for the sake of sex."

"This is different."

"Is it really?"

He wanted to say yes, but they were by definition having an affair. And although he hated to admit it, if he were sleeping with a woman of his own social level, his siblings wouldn't bat an eyelash. Liv's humble beginnings and lack of pedigree put her in an entirely different category.

Even though *he* didn't think of her any differently than a duchess or debutante, she was probably right in believing other people would.

It wasn't fair, but it was just the way the world worked. No point in making this any more complicated than necessary.

"They won't hear a word about it from me," he told her.

"Thank you."

"Now," he said with a grin, "where were we?" He pulled her down for a kiss, but just as their lips met, his cell phone began to ring. "Ignore it."

"What if it's something about your father?"

She was right of course. He mumbled a curse and leaned over the edge of the bed to grab it from the floor. He looked at the display and saw that it was Chris. He answered with an irritated, "What?"

"Sorry to wake you, but we need you in the security office."

He didn't tell him that he hadn't been sleeping. And that he had no intention of sleeping for quite some time. He and Liv weren't even close to being finished. "It can't wait until morning?"

"Unfortunately, no. Besides, you wouldn't want to pass up the opportunity to say I told you so."

Eleven

The Gingerbread Man, as he liked to call himself, was back in business.

Posing as hospital housekeeping staff, he'd made it as far as the royal family's private waiting room. Hours after he was gone, security found the chilling calling card he'd left behind. An envelope full of photographs of Aaron and his siblings that the Gingerbread Man had taken in various places. The girls shopping in Paris, and one of Chris taken through the office window of a building where he'd recently had a meeting with local merchants. Every shot of Aaron showed him with a different woman.

It wasn't a direct threat, but the implication was

clear. He was watching them, and despite all of their security, they were vulnerable. And either he'd gotten bolder or he'd made a critical error, because he'd let himself be caught on the hospital surveillance. Aaron stood in the security office with Chris watching the grainy image from the surveillance tape.

"How in the hell did he get so close to the king?" Aaron asked.

"His ID checked out," Randal Jenkins, their head of security, told him. "He must have either stolen a badge from another employee or fabricated one. He never actually looks up at the camera, so he may be difficult to identify."

"We need to tighten down security at the hospital," Chris told him.

"Already done, sir."

"The king knows?" Aaron asked.

"He and the queen were informed immediately as a precaution," Jenkins said. "The London police are involved, as well. They're talking with the hospital staff to see if anyone remembers him, and they're suggesting we take the news public, run the security tape on television in hope that someone will recognize him."

"What do you think?" Aaron asked his brother. "Personally, I'd like to see this lunatic behind bars, but it's your call."

"Take it to the public," Chris told Jenkins. "And until we catch him, no one will leave the castle without a full security detail, and we'll limit any unnecessary travel or personal appearances."

"That will be difficult with the holidays approaching," Aaron said. "Christmas is barely a month away."

"I'm confident that by then he'll be in custody," Chris said.

Aaron wished he shared that confidence, but he had the feeling that it wouldn't be that easy.

Though Aaron assured her that the king was fine and it was nothing more than a security issue that needed his attention, Liv tossed and turned, sleeping fitfully. She roused at 5:00 a.m. so completely awake that she figured she might as well get to work.

The castle was still dark and quiet, but the kitchen was bustling with activity.

"Getting an early start, miss?" Geoffrey asked, sounding almost...friendly.

"I couldn't sleep," she told him.

"Shall I bring you coffee?"

Was he actually being *nice* to her? "Yes, please. If it's no trouble."

He nodded. "I'll be down shortly."

Liv headed down the stairs, grinning like an idiot. Though it shouldn't have mattered what Geoffrey thought of her, she couldn't help but feel accepted somehow, as if she'd gained access to the secret club.

As she rounded the corner to the lab door, she stopped abruptly and the smile slipped from her face.

She distinctly remembered turning out the lights last night before going up for dinner. Now they were blazing. The assistant, a mousy young girl from the university, didn't have a code for the door. As far as Liv knew, no one but herself, Aaron, Geoffrey and the security office had access, and she couldn't imagine what business they might have down there.

She approached the door cautiously, peering through the window. As far as she could see, there was no one there. So why did she have the eerie sensation she was being watched?

"Problem, miss?"

Liv screeched with surprise and spun around, her backpack flying off her shoulder and landing with a thud on the ground. Geoffrey stood behind her carrying a tray with her coffee.

She slapped a hand over her frantically beating heart. "You scared me half to death!"

"Something wrong with the door?" he inquired, looking mildly amused, the first real emotion she had ever seen him show.

"Do you know if anyone was down here last night?" she asked.

"Not that I'm aware of." He stepped past her and punched in his code. The door clicked open and he stepped inside. Liv grabbed her backpack and cautiously followed him.

"I know I turned out the lights when I left last night, but they were on when I came down."

"Maybe you forgot." He set the coffee down on the table beside her desk.

When she saw the surface of her desk, she gasped.

He turned, regarding her curiously. "Something wrong, miss?"

"My desk," she said. The papers and files that had been strewn everywhere were now all stacked in neat piles. "Someone straightened it."

"They're just trying to get your attention," he said, pouring her a cup of coffee.

"Who?" Had someone been snooping down there?

"The spirits."

Spirits?

She had to resist rolling her eyes. It surprised her that a man as seemingly logical as the butler would buy in to that otherwordly garbage. "I don't believe in ghosts."

"All the more reason for them to ruffle your feathers. But you needn't worry, they're perfectly harmless."

It would explain how the door kept opening on its own, when security claimed the log had shown no record of the keypad being used, and maintenance had found nothing amiss with the controls. Yet she still believed it was far more likely that someone was messing with her head or trying to frighten her. Maybe even Geoffrey?

But why?

"Shall I call you for breakfast?" Geoffrey asked.

"I think I'll skip it," she said.

Geoffrey nodded politely, then let himself out of the lab.

Liv wasn't exactly looking forward to facing Aaron's family again. What if someone else had figured out how she'd done so well at poker? Or even worse, what if they knew Aaron had been in her room last night?

If it were possible, she would stay holed up in her lab until the day she was able to go home to the States.

She took her computer out of her backpack and booted it up. As she did every morning, she checked her e-mail first and among the usual spam the filter always missed, she was surprised to find a message from William. There was no subject, and the body of the e-mail said simply, *Just checking your progress.* That was it. Nothing personal like, *How are you?* Or, *Have you made a decision yet?*

She was going to have to tell him that she couldn't marry him. Let him down easy. She would be honest and explain that she just wasn't ready to marry anyone yet, and hope that it wouldn't affect their friendship or their working relationship.

But she couldn't do it through e-mail; that would be far too impersonal, and she hadn't yet worked up the nerve to call him. Maybe it would be better if she waited until she flew home and did it face-to-face.

But was it really fair to string him along? If he knew what she'd been up to last night…

A pleasant little shiver tingled through her body

when she recalled the way Aaron had touched her last night. The way he'd driven her mad with his hands and his mouth. Just thinking about it made her feel warm all over. Even though deep down something was telling her that she would end up regretting it, that she was way out of her league and headed for imminent disaster, she could hardly wait to be alone with him again.

Maybe last night was a total fluke and the next time they had sex it would only be so-so, even though she doubted it. If she kept thinking about it, about *him,* she wouldn't get a thing done today.

She answered William's mail with an equally impersonal rundown of her progress so far, and asked him to please go over the data she planned to send him later that afternoon—a fresh eye never hurt—then she got back to work analyzing the samples her assistant had taken yesterday.

Although she usually became engrossed in her work, she couldn't shake the feeling that she was being watched, and kept looking over to the door. The window wasn't more than ten-by-ten inches square, but a few times she could swear she saw the shadow of a figure just outside. Was it possible that Aaron or one of his siblings had someone keeping an eye on her? What did they think she might be doing down there, other than saving their country from agricultural devastation?

Or maybe it was just her mind playing tricks.

Some time later she heard the sound of the door clicking open, and thought, Here we go again. She was relieved when she heard footsteps moving in her direction. Assuming it was probably Geoffrey fetching the empty coffee carafe, she paid no attention, until she felt a rush of cool air brush past her and the unmistakable weight of a hand on her shoulder. She realized it had to be Aaron, there to say good morning. She pried herself away from her computer and spun in her chair to smile up at him, but there was no one there. She looked over at the door and saw that it was still firmly closed.

She shot to her feet and an eerie shiver coursed through her. It had to be her imagination. Could she have dozed off for a second? Maybe dreamed it?

If she had been sleeping, she wouldn't feel completely awake and alert. She glanced back up at the door and saw distinct movement outside the window, then it clicked and swung open. She sat there frozen, expecting some ghoulish apparition to float through, relieved when it was Aaron who stepped into the lab.

Her apprehension must have shown because when he saw her standing there, he stopped in his tracks and frowned. "You look as though you've just seen a ghost."

"Do you have someone spying on me?"

Taken aback by Liv's question, Aaron said, "Good morning to you, too."

"I'm serious, Aaron. Please tell me the truth."

Not only did she look serious, but deeply disturbed by the possibility. How could she even ask him that? "Of course not."

"You mean it?"

"Liv, if I felt you needed constant supervision, I never would have invited you here."

"Could your brother or one of your sisters have someone watching me?"

"I can't imagine why they would."

She shuddered and hugged herself. "This is too weird."

He walked over to her desk. "What's wrong?"

"I keep getting this feeling like someone is watching me, and when I look up at the window in the door, I see a shadow, like someone is standing just outside."

"Maybe someone on the laundry staff has a crush on you," he joked, but she didn't look amused. "I don't know who it could be."

"You know that the door kept popping open yesterday, and the technician said there wasn't anything wrong with it. Then this morning when I came down here, the lights were on and I know I turned them off last night."

He shrugged. "Maybe you thought you did, but didn't hit the switch all the way or something."

"Then explain how the papers that were strewn all over my desk were stacked neatly this morning."

He frowned. "Okay, that is kind of weird."

"There's something else."

"What?"

She looked hesitant to tell him, but finally said, "This is going to sound completely crazy, but a few minutes before you came in I heard the door open and footsteps in the room, then someone touched my shoulder, but when I turned around no one was there and the door was closed."

He might have thought it was crazy, but he'd heard similar stories from the staff. "Lots of people have reported having strange experiences down here."

"I don't believe in ghosts," she said, but without a whole lot of conviction. "Scientific labs aren't typically hot spots for paranormal activity."

"But how many labs have you been in that used to be dungeons?"

"None," she admitted.

"If it eases your mind, no one has ever been physically harmed down here. Just frightened."

"I don't feel as though I'm in physical danger. It's just creepy to think that someone is watching me. And—" she shuddered again "—*touching* me."

"Do you want to leave?"

"You mean, permanently?"

He nodded. God knows he didn't want her to; they needed her expertise and would be hard-pressed to find someone equally qualified, but he would understand if she had to.

"Of course not," she said, and he felt a little too relieved for comfort.

He tried to tell himself that he was only concerned

for his country's welfare, but he knew that was nonsense. He wanted more time with Liv. At least a few weeks to get her out of his system.

He grinned and told her, "I guess that means I'll just have to protect you."

He wrapped a hand around her hip and tugged her to him. She resisted for about half a second, then gave in and melted into his arms, resting her head on his shoulder. She felt so warm and soft and she smelled delicious. If they weren't in the lab, he would already be divesting her of her clothing.

"I had fun last night," he said and he could swear he felt her blush.

She wrapped her arms around him and hugged herself to his chest. "Me, too. Did you resolve your security problem?"

"In a manner of speaking." Because it wasn't a secret, and she would eventually be informed of the security lockdown, he figured he might as well tell her about the Gingerbread Man.

"That's really creepy," she said, gazing up at him. "Why would someone want to hurt your family?"

Aaron shrugged. "There are a lot of crazy people out there."

"I guess."

He kissed the tip of her nose. "I didn't think I'd find you in the lab. I figured, because it's the weekend, you might not be working today. I thought you might be up to a game of billiards."

"I work every day."

"Even Sunday?"

She gazed up at him and nodded. "Even Sunday."

"That reminds me. Chris wanted to know how long you'll need for the holidays."

She looked confused. "Need for what?"

"To go home."

"Oh, I won't be going home. I don't celebrate Christmas."

"Why not?" he asked, thinking that maybe it was some sort of religious issue.

She shrugged. "No one to celebrate with, I guess."

He frowned. "You must have friends."

"Yes, but they all have families and I would feel out of place. It really is not a big deal."

But it was. It was a very big deal. The thought of her spending the holidays alone disturbed him in a way he hadn't expected. It made him…*angry*. If her so-called friends really cared about her, they would insist she spend the holidays with them.

"If you're worried about me getting in the way, I'll keep to myself," she assured him. "You won't even know I'm here."

What kind of person did she think him to be? "That is the most ridiculous thing I've ever heard," he said, and she looked startled by his sharp tone. "I won't let you spend Christmas alone. You'll celebrate with us."

"Aaron, I don't think—"

"This is *not* negotiable. I'm *telling* you. You're spending the holidays with my family."

She opened her mouth to argue, so he did the only thing he could to shut her up. He leaned forward, covered her lips with his and kissed her.

Twelve

Aaron was making it really difficult for her to tell him no. Literally. Every time they came up for air, and she would open her mouth to speak, he would just start kissing her again. She was beginning to feel all soft and mushy-brained and turned on. Yet she couldn't shake the feeling they were being watched.

She opened one eye and peered at the door, nearly swallowing her own tongue when she saw a face staring back at her through the window. A woman she didn't recognize, with long, curly blond hair wearing some sort of lacy bonnet. Liv's first thought was that someone had discovered their secret, and they were both in big trouble. Then before her eyes the face went misty and translucent and seemed to dissipate and disappear into thin air.

She let out a muffled shriek against Aaron's lip, then ripped herself free so fast that she stumbled backward, tripped over her chair and landed on her rear end on the hard linoleum floor.

"Bloody hell, what's wrong?" Aaron asked, stunned by her sudden outburst.

She pointed to the door, even though whoever, or *whatever,* she'd seen in the window was no longer there. "A f-face."

He spun around to look. "There's no one there."

"It disappeared."

"Whoever it was probably saw you looking and ran off."

"No. I mean, it actually disappeared. One minute it was there, and the next minute it vanished. I don't even know how to explain it. It was as if it...dissolved."

"Dissolved?"

"Like mist." It was scary as hell, but the scientist in her couldn't help feeling intrigued. She had always clung to the belief that there was no such thing as heaven or an afterlife. When you were dead, you were dead. Could this mean there was some sort of life after death?

He looked at the window again, then back to her, still sprawled on the floor. "Are you saying that you saw a ghost?"

"A few days ago I never would have believed it,

but I can't think of any other logical explanation." And for some reason, seeing it with her own eyes, knowing it was real, made her more curious than frightened. She wanted to see it again.

He held out a hand to help her up, and when she was on her feet he tugged her back into his arms. "If someone was watching us, alive or otherwise, they nearly got one hell of a view, because I was about two seconds from ravishing you."

So much for being discreet. "Suppose someone on this plane of existence did happen to come down and look in the window?"

"So we'll cover it," he said, nibbling on her neck. "A sheet of paper and some tape should do the trick."

What he was doing felt deliciously wonderful, but now wasn't the time for fooling around. Although she had the feeling that when it came to women, he was used to getting his way. If he was going to be with her, he was going to have to learn to compromise.

"Aaron, I have to work," she said firmly, planting her hands on his chest.

"No, you don't," he mumbled against her skin.

She gave a gentle but firm shove. "Yes. *I do.*"

He hesitated a moment, then grudgingly let her go. "Do I get to see you at all today?"

Though she could easily work late into the evening, if he had to compromise, then so should she. "How about a game of billiards tonight after dinner?"

He grinned. "And after billiards?"

She just smiled.

"I'm holding you to it," he said, backing toward the door.

"Oh, and about Christmas," she said.

"It's not up for discussion."

"But your family—"

"Won't mind at all. Besides, if Melissa were to get wind of you spending the holidays alone, she would probably have an emotional meltdown."

He was probably right. If Aaron didn't insist she join them, Melissa probably would. Or maybe she was rationalizing.

Compromise, Liv. Compromise.

"Okay," she said, and that seemed to make him very happy.

"See you at dinner," he said as he walked out.

She'd never had what anyone would consider a conventional Christmas holiday. Her foster families never had money for gifts and extravagant meals. If she got candy in her stocking—hell, if she even *had* a stocking—it was a pretty good year. It used to make her sad when the kids at school returned after the holiday break sporting new clothes and handheld video games and portable CD players, but she'd learned to harden her heart.

Even now Christmas was just another day to her. But she would be lying if she said it didn't get a *little* lonely, knowing everyone else was with their families.

But there were definite benefits, too. She didn't

have to fight the holiday crowds shopping for gifts, or have outrageous credit card bills come January. The simpler she kept her life, the better. Although it might be a nice change to spend Christmas somewhere other than alone in the lab. With a real family.

Or maybe, she thought as she sat down in front of her computer, it would make her realize all that she'd been missing.

Liv fidgeted beside Aaron as they neared the king's suite. His parents had returned from England yesterday, several days later than expected due to mild complications caused by the reinsertion of the pump. But he was feeling well, in good spirits and happy to be home with his family.

"Maybe we shouldn't bother them," Liv said, her brow furrowed. "I'm sure the king needs rest."

"He *wants* to meet you," he assured her. She'd grown much more comfortable in the castle this past week. She seemed to enjoy spending time with his siblings, and the feeling was remarkably mutual. Even Anne had lowered her defenses within the past few days and seemed to be making a genuine effort to get to know Liv, and of course Louisa loved everyone.

He took Liv's hand and gave it a reassuring squeeze, and even though no one was around, she pulled from his grasp. He was breaking her rule of no public displays of affection. Although he was quite sure that if his siblings hadn't already begun to suspect their affair, it was only a matter of time. Nearly every moment Liv wasn't in the lab, Aaron was with her and he'd spent every night for the past seven days in her room.

If they did suspect, no one had said a word to him.

"I'm so nervous. I'm afraid that when I curtsy I'm going to fall on my face."

"If you fall, I'll catch you," he assured her. He knocked on the suite door then pushed it open, feeling Liv go tense beside him.

His father had dressed for the occasion, though he was reclined on the sofa. His mother rose to greet them as they entered the room.

"Liv, meet my parents, the King and Queen of Thomas Isle. Mother, Father, this is Olivia Montgomery."

Liv curtsied, and even though it wasn't the smoothest he'd ever seen, she was nowhere close to falling over.

"It's an honor to meet you both," she said, a slight quiver in her voice.

"The honor is all ours, Miss Montgomery," his father said, shaking her hand, which she did gingerly, Aaron noticed, as though she worried she might break him. "Words cannot express how deeply we appreciate your visit."

His mother didn't even offer to shake Liv's hand. Maybe the king's health and all that time in the hospital was taking its toll on her. Although she'd seemed fine yesterday. Just a bit tired.

"My children speak quite highly of you," the king said, and added with a grin, "in fact, I hear you're something of a card shark."

Liv smiled nervously. "I'm sure it was beginner's luck, Your Highness."

"I'm assuming you've had time to work since you arrived," his mother said and her curt tone took him aback.

Liv looked a little stunned as well, so Aaron answered, "Of course she has. I practically have to drag her out of the lab just to eat dinner. She would work around the clock if I didn't insist she take a break every now and then."

She ignored him and asked Liv in an almost-demanding tone, "Have you made any progress?"

As was the case when she talked about her work or someone questioned her professionally, she suddenly became the confident and assertive scientist. The transformation never ceased to amaze him.

"I'm very close to discovering the strain of disease affecting the crops," she told his mother. Usually she explained things to him in layman's terms, so he had at least a little hope of understanding what she was talking about. She must have been trying to make a point because when she explained her latest developments to his mother, she used all scientific terms and jargon. Though the queen had spent the better part of her life farming, botanical genetics was *way* out of her league.

By the time Liv finished with her explanation, his mother looked at least a little humbled.

"Would you mind excusing us, Miss Montgomery," the queen said. "I need to have a word with my son."

"Of course," Liv said. "I need to get back down to the lab anyway. It was a pleasure to meet you both."

"I'll walk you out," Aaron said, leading her from the room.

When they were in the hallway with the door closed, Liv turned to him and said, "I'm so sorry."

Her apology confused him. He should be the one apologizing for his mother's behavior. "For what? I thought you were fantastic."

She frowned, looking troubled. "I was showing off. It was rude of me."

"Love, you've earned the right to show off every now and then."

"Your mother hates me."

"Why would she hate you?"

"Because she knows."

He frowned. "Knows what?"

She lowered her voice, even though they were alone. "That something is going on between us."

"How could she?"

"I don't know, but that was a mother lion protecting her cub. Her message clearly said back off."

"You're being paranoid. I think between my

father's health, the security breach at the hospital and the diseased crops, she's just stressed out."

Liv didn't look as though she believed him, but she didn't push the issue.

"I'll come see you in the lab later." He brushed a quick kiss across her lips, ignoring her look of protest, then let himself back into his parents' suite. He crossed the room to where they still sat, determined to get to the bottom of this.

"What the bloody hell was that about?" he asked his mother.

"Watch your tone," his father warned.

"*My* tone? Could she have been any more rude to Liv?"

"Don't think I don't know what's going on between you two," his mother said.

So Liv had been right. She did suspect something. He folded his arms over his chest. "And what *is* going on, Mother?"

"Nothing that your father and I approve of."

"You haven't even been here, so how could you possibly know what's been going on? Do you have the staff watching me?"

"There's someone I want you to meet," she said. "She's a duchess from a *good* family."

Unlike Liv who had *no* family, was that what she meant? That was hardly Liv's fault. "If you're concerned that I'm going to run off and marry Liv, you can stop worrying."

"It isn't proper. She's not of noble blood."

If his mother had the slightest clue about the behavior of those so-called *proper* women she set him up with, she would have kittens. The spoiled brats whose daddies gave them everything their hearts desired, while they dabbled in drugs and alcohol, and were more often than not sexually promiscuous. Liv was a saint in comparison.

"Maybe you should take the time to know her before you pass judgment."

"I know all I need to. She's not good enough for you," his mother said.

"Not *good* enough? I can safely say she's more intelligent than all three of us combined. She's sweet, and kind, and down-to-earth. And she could very well be saving our *asses* from total financial devastation," he said, earning a stern look from his father. "Can you say that of your princesses or duchesses?"

"The decision has already been made," his mother said. "You'll meet the duchess next Friday."

Since Chris married Melissa, their mother had been determined to find Aaron a wife, and even though he'd told her a million times he didn't want to settle down, the message seemed to go in one ear and out the other. But he'd gone along with the blind dates and the setups because it was always easier than arguing. Easier than standing up for himself.

He thought of Liv, who had fought like hell for everything she'd ever gotten, how strong she was, and wondered what had he ever done but settle? From the day he was born his family told him who he was supposed to be. Well, he was tired of compromising himself, tired of playing by their rules. It ended today.

"No," he said.

She frowned. "No, what?"

"I won't meet her."

"Of course you will."

"No, I won't. No more blind dates, no more setups. I'm finished."

She huffed out a frustrated breath. "How will you ever find a wife if you don't—"

"I don't *want* a wife. I don't want to settle down."

She rolled her eyes. "Every man says that. But when the right one comes along you'll change your mind."

"If that's true, I'll find her without your help."

She gave him her token you-would-be-lost-without-me-to-run-your-life look. "Aaron, sweetheart—"

"I mean it, Mother. I don't want to hear another word about it."

She looked stunned by his demand; his father, on the other hand, looked amused. "He's made his decision, dear," he said. And before she could argue, he sighed and said, "This conversation has worn me out."

"Why didn't you say something?" She patted his shoulder protectively and summoned the nurse, shooting Aaron a look that suggested his father's sudden fatigue was his fault. "Let's get you to bed. We'll talk about this later."

No, they wouldn't, he wanted to say, but for his father's sake he let it drop. She would come to realize that he wasn't playing by her rules any longer.

While the nurse helped his father into bed, his mother turned to him and said, "Please let Geoffrey know that your father and I will be taking dinner in our suite tonight."

"Of course."

She smiled and patted his cheek fondly. "That's a good boy."

A good boy? Ugh. What was he, twelve? He turned and left before he said something he regretted. She seemed to believe she'd won, but nothing could be further from the truth. Knowing Liv had made him take a good hard look at his own life and he didn't like what he was seeing. It was time he made a few changes.

Thirteen

The following Monday was December first and overnight the castle was transformed to a holiday wonderland. Fresh evergreen swags dotted with red berries and accented with big red bows hung from the stair railings, making everything smell piney and festive, and mistletoe hung in every door and archway. Life-size nutcrackers stood guard in the halls and every room on the main floor had a Christmas tree decorated in a different color and theme. From one hung various styles and flavors of candy canes and other sugar confections, while another was festooned with antique miniature toy ornaments. Some were draped in all shades of purple, and others in creamy whites. But the most amazing tree was in the ballroom. It stood at least twenty feet high, decorated in shimmering silver and gold balls.

The outside of the castle was the most incredible of all. What looked to be about a million tiny multicolored lights edged the windows and turrets and lit the shrubs.

Liv had never seen anything like it, and she couldn't help but get drawn into the holiday spirit. For the first time in her life Christmas wasn't something she dreaded or ignored. This time she let herself feel it, get caught up in the atmosphere. And she almost felt as if she had a family. Aaron's siblings made her feel so welcome, and Liv was particularly fond of the king. He was warm and friendly and had a surprisingly thorough understanding of genetic science and an insatiable curiosity. They had many evening conversations about her research, sitting by the fire in the study sipping hot cider.

"Science is a hobby of mine," he once told her. "As a child I used to dream of being a scientist. I even planned to go to university and study it. That was before I was crown prince."

Much the way Aaron had dreamed of being a doctor, she thought. "You weren't always crown prince?"

"I had an older brother, Edward. He would have been king, but he contracted meningitis when he was fifteen. It left him blind and physically impaired, so the crown was passed on to me. It's a bit ironic, really. We would spend hours in this very room, sitting by the fire. I would read to him, or play his favorite music. And now here I am, the incapacitated one."

"But only temporarily," she reminded him.

He just smiled and said, "Let's hope so."

The queen didn't share her husband's affection for Liv. She wasn't cruel or even rude. She was just…indifferent. Liv had overcome enough adversity in her life to understand that she couldn't let herself be bothered by the opinions of one person, but she would be lying if she said it didn't hurt her feelings just a little. Particularly because she was being judged not on the merits of her accomplishments, or even her morals, but on her lack of pedigree.

The Sunday before Christmas a blizzard dropped nearly a foot of snow and Liv let Aaron talk her into trying cross-country skiing. He wanted to take her to their ski lodge on the other side of the island, but with the Gingerbread Man still on the loose, the king insisted they stay on the castle property.

As Liv anticipated, she spent the better part of the first hour sitting in the snow.

"It just takes practice," Aaron told her as he hauled her back up on her feet again, and she actually managed to make it two or three yards before she fell on her face. But he assured her, "You're doing great!"

As inept as she felt, and embarrassed by her lack of coordination, Aaron's enthusiasm was contagious and she found that she was having fun. Since she arrived on Thomas Isle, he had intro-

duced her to so many things that she otherwise
would have never tried. If not for him, she would
still be in her lab 24/7, working her life away
instead of living it.

As much fun as they had been having, Liv knew
it wouldn't last. She was in the process of testing
compounds in hope of finding one that would kill
the disease, and when she found the right combination, there would be no reason for her to stay.
Leaving would be hard because she'd grown
attached to Aaron. In fact, she felt she may even be
in love with him, but that didn't change who they
were. Besides, he had made it quite clear that he
didn't want to be tied down. It was destined to end,
and all she could do was enjoy the time they had
left together.

An hour before sundown, exhausted to the center
of her bones and aching in places she didn't even
know she could ache, Liv tossed down her poles and
said enough.

"You have to admit that was fun," he said as they
stripped out of their gear.

"Oh, yeah," she said, hissing in pain as she bent
over to unclip the ski boots. "Spending an entire day
sitting in the snow has always been my idea of fun."

He shot her a skeptical look.

"Okay," she admitted with a shrug that sent spirals
of pain down her back. "Maybe it was a *little* fun."

"You were getting pretty good near the end there."

It was her turn to look skeptical.

"I'm serious," he said. "By the end of winter I'll have you skiing like a pro."

The *end* of winter? How long did he expect her to stay? Did he *want* her to stay? And even more important, did *she* want to?

Of course he didn't. It was just an off-the-cuff remark that he probably hadn't thought through.

They walked up the stairs—well, he walked and she limped—to her room.

"I'm going to dress for dinner," he said. "Shall I pick you up on my way back down?"

"I don't think so."

"Are you sure?"

"Not only am I not hungry, but I'm exhausted and everything hurts. I'd like to lie down for a while."

"I'll come by and check on you later." He brushed a quick kiss across her lips, then headed to his room. She still wasn't comfortable with him showing her physical affection where someone might see. Although she didn't doubt that his family knew what was going on. They had just been kind enough not to say anything. She was sure they saw it for what it was. A fling. But she still didn't feel comfortable advertising it.

She went into her room and limped to the bathroom, downing three ibuprofen tablets before she stepped into the shower. She blasted the water as hot as she could stand, then she toweled off and crawled into bed naked. She must have fallen asleep the instant her head hit the pillow because the next thing she remembered was Aaron sitting on the edge of the mattress.

"What time is it?" she asked, her voice gravelly with sleep.

"Nine." He switched on the lamp beside the bed and she squinted against the sudden flood of light. "How do you feel?"

She tried to move and her muscles screamed in protest. "Awful," she groaned. "Even my eyelids hurt."

"Then you're going to like what I found," he said, holding up a small bottle.

"What is it?"

He flashed her one of his sexy, sizzling smiles. "Massage oil."

He eased back the covers, and when he saw that she was naked, he growled deep in his throat. "I swear, you get more beautiful every day."

He'd told her that so many times, so often that she was beginning to believe him, to see herself through his eyes. And in that instant in time everything was perfect.

He caressed her cheek with the backs of his fingers. "I love…"

Her heart jolted in her chest and she thought for sure that he was going to say he loved her. In that millisecond, she knew without a doubt that her honest reply would be, *I love you, too.*

"…just looking at you," he said instead.

The disappointment she felt was like a crushing weight on her chest, making it difficult to breathe. Tell him you love him, you idiot! But she couldn't do that. Love wasn't part of this arrangement. Instead she didn't say a word, she just wrapped her arms around him and pulled him down for a kiss. And when he made love to her, he was so sweet and gentle that it nearly brought her to tears.

She loved him so fiercely it made her chest ache, and she desperately wanted him to love her, too.

She wasn't sure how much longer she could take this.

It took some convincing on his part, but Aaron talked Liv into another afternoon of skiing on Christmas Eve. And despite her reservations she did exceptionally well. So well that he looked forward to introducing her to other recreational activities, like biking and kayaking and even low-level rock climbing. The problem was, she probably wouldn't be around long enough. He was sorry for that, but in a way relieved. He'd grown closer and more attached to Liv than he had any other woman in his life. Dangerously close. And even though he knew he was walking a very fine and precarious line, he wasn't ready to let go yet.

Christmas morning he woke Liv at 5:45 a.m., despite the fact that they had been up half the night making love.

"It's too early," she groaned, shoving a pillow over her head.

He pulled it back off. "Come on, wake up. We're gathering with everyone in the study at six."

She squinted up at him. "*Six?* What for?"

"To open presents. Then afterward we have a huge breakfast. It's been a tradition as long as I can remember."

She groaned again and closed her eyes. "I'd rather sleep."

"It's *Christmas*. And you promised you would spend it with me and my family, remember?"

"I was thinking that you meant Christmas dinner."

"I meant the entire day." He tugged on her arm. "Now come on, get up."

She grumbled about it, but let him pull her to an upright position. She yawned and rubbed her eyes and asked, "What should I wear?"

"Pajamas." At her questioning look, he added, "It's what everyone else will be wearing."

She made him wait while she brushed her hair and teeth, and when they got to the study his siblings and sister-in-law were already gathered around the tree, waiting to open the piles of gifts stacked there. Their father sat in his favorite armchair and their mother beside him at the hearth. Geoffrey stood at the bar pouring hot cider. Christmas music played softly and a fire blazed in the fireplace.

"Hurry up, you two!" Louisa said excitedly.

"I shouldn't be here," Liv mumbled under her breath, standing stiffly beside him, looking as though she were about to go to the guillotine.

"Of course you should." When she refused to move, he took her hand and pulled her over to the tree and sat her by Louisa. The second she was off her feet she pulled her hand from his.

"Merry Christmas!" Louisa gushed, giving Liv a warm hug, and after a slight hesitation, Liv hugged her back. If anyone could make Liv feel like part of the family, it was Louisa. Although right now she just looked overwhelmed. She looked downright stunned when Anne, who wore the santa hat and passed out the gifts, announced, "And here's one for Olivia from the king and queen."

Liv's jaw actually dropped. "F-for me?"

Anne handed it to her. "That's what the tag says."

She took it and just held it, as if she wasn't sure what to do.

"Aren't you going to open it?" Aaron asked.

"But I didn't get anything for anyone."

His mother surprised him by saying, "Your being here is the only gift we need."

Liv bit her lip, picking gingerly at the taped edge of the paper, while everyone else tore into theirs enthusiastically. It was almost as though she had never opened a gift before or had forgotten how. What disturbed him most was that it might be true. When was the last time anyone had given her anything?

She finally got it open and pulled from the layers of gold tissue paper a deep blue cashmere cardigan.

"Oh," she breathed. "It's beautiful."

"You keep the lab so dreadfully cold," his mother said. "I thought it might come in handy."

"Thank you so much."

Anne passed out another round of gifts and this time there was one for Liv from Chris and Melissa, a pair of thick wool socks.

"For skiing," Melissa told her.

Louisa got Liv a silver bracelet decorated with science-themed charms, and Anne gave her a matching cashmere mitten, scarf and hat set. Aaron had gotten her something, too, but she would have to wait until later to get it.

The last present under the tree was for the king and queen from Chris and Melissa. Their mother opened it and inside was what looked like an ultrasound photo. Did that mean…?

"What is this?" their mother asked, looking confused.

"Those are your grandchildren," Chris said with a grin. "All three of them."

"Three grandchildren!" his mother shrieked, while his father beamed proudly and said, "Congratulations!"

"They implanted five embryos," Melissa said. "Three took. It's still very early, but we couldn't wait to tell you. My doctor said everything looks great."

Aaron had never seen his mother look so proud or

excited. She knelt down to hug them both, then *everyone* was hugging Chris and Melissa and congratulating them.

"Isn't it great? I'm going to be an uncle," Aaron said, turning to Liv, but she wasn't smiling or laughing like the rest of them. In fact, she looked as though she might be sick. "Hey, are you okay?"

She shook her head and said, "Excuse me," then she bolted from the room, seven startled pairs of eyes following her.

"What happened?" his mother asked, and Louisa said, "Did we do something wrong?"

"I don't know," Aaron said, but he was going to find out.

Fourteen

Liv reached her room, heart beating frantically and hands shaking, and went straight to the closet for her suitcase. She dropped it on the bed and opened it just as Aaron appeared in the doorway.

"What happened down there?" he asked, looking concerned. "Are you okay?"

"I'm sorry. Please tell everyone that I'm *so* sorry. I just couldn't take it another minute."

He saw her suitcase and asked, "What are you doing?"

"Packing. I have to leave."

He looked stunned. "Was being with my family really that awful?"

"No, it was absolutely wonderful. I had no idea it could be like that. I just… I can't do this anymore."

"What do you mean? I thought we were having fun."

"I was. I *am*. The time we've spent together has been the best in my life."

She started toward the closet to get her clothes, but he stepped in her way, looking so hopelessly confused she wanted to hug him. "So what's the problem?"

Did he honestly have no idea what was going on? "I know it's illogical and totally irrational, but I've fallen in love with you, Aaron."

She gave him a few seconds to return the sentiment, but he only frowned, looking troubled, and it made her inexplicably sad. She hadn't really believed he would share her feelings, but she had hoped. But as she had reminded herself over and over, the world just didn't work that way. Not the world she lived in.

"We don't have any further to go with this," she said. "And I'm just not the kind of person who can tread water. I think it would be better for us both if I leave now. The work I have left to do, I can finish in my lab in the States."

"You can't leave," he said, looking genuinely upset.

"I have to."

"I *do* care about you."

"I know you do." Just not enough. Not enough for her, anyway. She wanted more. She wanted to be part of a family, to feel as if she belonged somewhere. And not just temporarily. She wanted forever.

She wanted it so badly that she ached, but she would never have that with him.

His brow furrowed. "I just… I can't…"

"I know," she assured him. "This is not your fault. This is *all* me. I never meant to fall in love with you."

"I…I don't know what to say."

Just tell me you love me, she wanted to tell him, but Aaron didn't do love. He didn't get serious and settle down. And even if he did, it wouldn't be with someone like her. She didn't fit in. She wasn't good enough for someone like him.

"I'll pack up the lab today," she told him. "Can you arrange for a flight off the island tomorrow?"

"Won't you at least have dinner with us? It's Christmas."

She shrugged. "It's just another day for me."

That was a lie. It used to be, but after this morning it would forever be a reminder of how wonderful it could be and everything she'd been missing out on, and so *desperately* wanted. In a way she wished she'd never met Aaron, that he'd never called for her help. She would still be living in blissful ignorance.

"You should get back to your family," she told him.

"You're sure I can't convince you to spend the day with us?"

"I'm sure."

He looked disappointed, but he didn't push the issue, and she was relieved because she was this close to caving, to throwing herself into his arms and saying she would stay as long as he wanted. Even if he couldn't love her.

"I'll have Geoffrey bring your gifts up and inform you of your travel arrangements," he said.

"Thank you."

"You're *sure* I can't change your mind?"

There was an almost pleading look in his eyes, and she wanted so badly to give in, but her heart just couldn't take it. "I can't."

"I'll leave you alone to pack."

He stepped out of the room, closing the door behind him, and though it felt so final, she knew she was doing the right thing.

She packed all of her clothes, leaving out one clean outfit for the following day, then she went down to the lab to start packing there, feeling utterly empty inside.

She never had seen the ghost again, but she'd made her presence known by occasionally stacking Liv's papers, hiding her pen or opening the lab door. Maybe she should have felt uncomfortable knowing she wasn't alone, but instead the presence was a comfort. She'd even caught herself talking to her, even though the conversation was always one-sided. She realized now that when she was gone she might even miss her elusive and unconventional companion.

She was going to miss everything about Thomas Isle.

Geoffrey came down around dinnertime with a

plate of food. She wasn't hungry, but she thanked him anyway. "I bet you're happy not to have to deal with me anymore," she joked, expecting him to emphatically agree.

Instead his expression was serious when he said, "Quite the contrary, miss."

She was too stunned to say a word as he turned and left. And here she thought he viewed her as a nuisance. The fact that he hadn't only made her feel worse.

She packed the last of her equipment by midnight, and when she went up to her room, waiting for her as promised were the gifts the family had given her and the itinerary for her trip. She sat down at the desk by the window writing them each a note of thanks, not only for the presents, but for accepting her into their home and treating her like family. She left them on the desk where Elise would find them when she cleaned the room.

She climbed under the covers around one-thirty, but tossed and turned and slept only an hour or two before her alarm buzzed at seven. She got out of bed feeling a grogginess that even a shower couldn't wash away. At seven-forty-five someone came to fetch her luggage, then a few minutes later Flynn from security came to fetch her.

"It's time to go to the airstrip, miss," he said.

"Let's do it," she said, feeling both relieved and heartsick. She wanted so badly to change her mind, to stay just a little bit longer and hope that he would see he loved her. But it was too late to turn back now. Even if it wasn't, she knew in her heart that it would be a bad idea.

She followed Flynn down the stairs to the foyer, and when she saw that the entire family lined up to say goodbye, the muscles in her throat contracted so tight that she could barely breathe. This was the last thing she'd expected. She had assumed her departure would be as uneventful as her arrival.

The king was first in line. If she had expected some cold and formal goodbye, a handshake and a "have a nice life," she couldn't have been more wrong. He hugged her warmly and said, "I've enjoyed our talks."

"Me, too," she said, realizing he was the closest thing she had ever had to a father figure. She hoped with all her being that the heart pump was successful and he lived a long, productive life. Long enough to see his daughters marry and his grandchildren grow. She wasn't a crier, but she could feel the burn of tears in her throat and behind her eyes. All she could manage to squeak out was, "Thanks for everything."

The queen was next. She took Liv's hands and air kissed her cheek. "It's been a pleasure having you with us," she said, and actually looked as though she meant it.

"Thank you for having me in your home," Liv said.

Chris and Melissa stood beside the queen. Chris kissed Liv's cheek and Melissa, with tears running in a steady river down her face—no doubt pregnancy hormones at work—hugged her hard. "Watch the mail for a baby shower invitation. I want you there."

If only. It was a lovely thought, yet totally unrealistic. She was sure by then they would have forgotten all about her.

Louisa scooped her up into a bone-crushing embrace. "We'll miss you," she said. "Keep in touch."

Anne hugged her, too, though not as enthusiastically. But she leaned close and Liv thought she was going to kiss her cheek, but instead she whispered, "My brother is a dolt."

Of all the things anyone could have said to her, that was probably the sweetest, and the tears were hovering so close to the surface now that she couldn't even reply.

Aaron was last, and the one she was least looking forward to saying goodbye to. He stood aside from his family by the door, hands in his pants pockets, eyes to the floor. As she approached he looked up at her.

The tears welled closer to the surface and she swallowed them back down. Please let this be quick and painless.

"You'll contact me when you have results," he said, all business.

She nodded. "Of course. And I'll send you updates on my progress. At the rate it's going, you should have it in plenty of time for the next growing season."

"Excellent." He was quiet for a second, then he said in a low voice, "I'm sorry. I just can't—"

"It's okay," she said, even though it wasn't. Even though it felt as though he was ripping her heart from her chest.

He nodded, looking remorseful. She had started to turn toward the door when he cursed under his breath, hooked a hand behind her neck, pulled her to him and kissed her—*really* kissed her—in front of his entire family. He finally pulled away, leaving her feeling breathless and dizzy, said, "Goodbye Liv," then turned and walked away, taking her heart with him.

The flights to the U.S. couldn't have been smoother or more uneventful, but when Liv got back to her apartment and let herself inside it almost didn't feel like home. She'd barely been gone a month, but it felt as if everything had changed, and there was this nagging ache in the center of her chest that refused to go away.

"You just need sleep," she rationalized.

She climbed into bed and, other than a few trips to the bathroom, didn't get back out for three days. That was when she reminded herself that she'd never been one to wallow in self-pity. She was stronger than that. Besides, she needed to see William. She hadn't spoken to or even e-mailed him in weeks. Maybe they could have a late lunch and talk about his proposal and she could let him down easy.

She tried calling him at the lab, but he wasn't there and he wasn't answering his house or cell phone. Concerned that something might be wrong, she drove to his house instead.

She knocked, then a minute later knocked harder. She was about to give up and leave when the door finally opened.

Being that it was the middle of the afternoon, she was surprised to find him in a T-shirt and pajama bottoms, looking as though he'd just rolled out of bed.

"Oh, you're back," he said, and maybe it was her imagination, but he didn't seem happy to see her. Maybe he was hurt that she hadn't readily accepted his proposal. Maybe he was angry that she'd taken so long and hadn't been in contact.

"I'm back," she said with a smile that she hoped didn't look as forced as it felt. She thought that maybe seeing him again after such a long time apart would stir up feelings that had been buried or repressed, but she didn't feel a thing. "I thought we could talk."

"Um, well…" He glanced back over his shoulder, into the front room. "Now's not the best time."

She frowned. "Are you sick?"

"No, no, nothing like that."

Liv heard a voice behind him say, "Billy, who is it?"

A *female* voice. Then the door opened wider and a young girl whom Liv didn't recognize stood there dressed in, of all things, one of William's T-shirts.

"Hi!" she said brightly. "Are you a friend of Billy's?" *Billy?*

"We work in the lab together," William said, shooting Liv a look that said, *Go along with it*. He obviously didn't want this girl to know that she and William had had anything but a professional relationship. Which, if you wanted to get technical, they never really had.

"I'm Liv," Liv said, because William didn't introduce them. She had the feeling he wished she would just disappear. "And you are?"

The girl smiled brightly. "I'm Angela, Billy's fiancée."

Fiancée? William was *engaged*?

She waved in front of Liv's face a hand sporting an enormous diamond ring. "We're getting married in two weeks," she squealed.

"Congratulations," Liv said, waiting to feel the tiniest bit of remorse, but what she felt instead was relief. She was off the hook. She didn't have to feel bad for turning him down.

"Could you give us a second, Angie?" he said. "It's work."

"Sure," she said, smiling brightly. "Nice to meet you, Liv."

William stepped out onto the porch, closing the door behind him. "I'm so sorry. I wasn't expecting you."

If he'd answered his phone, he would have been, but she was pretty sure they had been otherwise occupied. "It's okay," she said. "I only came here to tell you that I can't marry you."

"Yes, well, when you stopped calling, I just assumed…"

"It just wasn't something I wanted to do over the phone. I guess it doesn't matter now."

"I'm sorry I didn't have a chance to prepare you. I mean, it was very sudden. Obviously."

"I'm very happy for you." And jealous as hell that even he had found someone. Not that he didn't deserve to be happy. It just didn't seem fair that it was so easy for some people. Of course, falling in love with Aaron had been incredibly easy. The hard part was getting him to love her back.

He smiled shyly, something she had never seen him do before, and said, "It was love at first sight."

She left William's house feeling more alone than she had in her entire life. She'd gone from having seven people who accepted her as part of the family—even if the queen had done it grudgingly—to having no one.

Fifteen

Aaron sat in his office, staring out the window at the grey sky through a flurry of snow, unable to concentrate on a single damn thing. He should be down in the greenhouse, meeting with the foreman about the spring crops, but he just couldn't work up the enthusiasm to get his butt out of the chair. The idea of another long season of constantly worrying about growth rates and rainfall and late frosts, not to mention pests and disease, gave him a headache. He was tired of being forced into doing something that deep down he really didn't want to do. He was tired of duty and compromise and putting everyone else's wishes ahead of his own. And even though it had taken a few days for him to admit it to himself, he was tired of shallow, meaningless relationships. He was sick of being alone.

He missed Liv.

Unfortunately she didn't seem to share the sentiment. It had been two weeks since she left and he hadn't heard a word from her. Not even an update on her progress. Yet he couldn't bring himself to pick up the phone and call her. Maybe she'd run back to William.

"Are you going to mope in here all day?"

Aaron looked up to see Anne standing in his office doorway. "I'm working," he lied.

"Of course you are."

He scowled. "Do you need something?"

"I just came by to let you know that I talked to Liv."

He bolted upright in his chair. "What? When?"

"About five minutes ago. She wanted to update us on her progress. And inquire about father's health."

"Why did she call you?"

Anne folded her arms across her chest. "Gosh, I don't know. Maybe because you *broke her heart.*"

"Did she say that?"

"Of course not."

"Well," he said, turning toward the window, "she always has William to console her."

"William?"

"He's another scientist. He asked her to marry him before she came here." Not that Aaron believed for a minute she would actually marry William. Not when she admitted she loved Aaron.

"Oh, so *that* was what she meant."

He swiveled back to her. "What?"

"She mentioned that, with the wedding coming up, it might be several weeks before we get another update. I just didn't realize it was *her* wedding."

She was actually going to do it? She was going to compromise and marry a man she didn't love? How could she marry William when she was in love with Aaron?

The thought of her marrying William, or anyone else for that matter, made him feel like punching a hole in the wall. And why? Because he was jealous? Because he didn't like to lose?

The truth hit him with a clarity that was almost painful in its intensity. He loved her. She couldn't marry William because the only man she should be marrying was him.

He rose from his chair and told Anne, "If you'll excuse me, I need to have a word with Mother and Father."

"Something wrong?" Anne said with a grin.

"Quite the opposite." After weeks, maybe even *years* of uncertainty, he finally knew what he had to do.

Aaron found his parents in their suite watching the midday news. "I need to have a word with you."

"Of course," his father said, gesturing him inside.

He picked up the remote and muted the television. "Is there a problem?"

"No. No problem."

"What is it?" his mother asked.

"I just wanted to let you both know that I'm flying to the States today."

"With the Gingerbread Man still on the loose, do you think that's wise?" his father asked.

"I have to see Liv."

"Why?" his mother demanded.

"So I can ask her to marry me."

Her face transformed into an amusing combination of shock and horror. "*Marry* you?"

"That's what I said."

"*Absolutely not.* I won't have it, Aaron."

"It's not up to you, Mother. This is my decision."

"Your father and I know what's best for this family. That girl is—"

"Enough!" his father thundered, causing both Aaron and his mother to jolt with surprise. It had been a long time since he'd been well enough to raise his voice to such a threatening level. "Choose your words carefully, my dear, lest you say something you'll later regret."

She turned to him, eyes wide with surprise. "You're all right with this?"

"Is there a reason I shouldn't be?"

"I know you're fond of her, but a *marriage?* She isn't of noble blood."

"Do you love her, Aaron?" his father asked.

"I do," he said, never feeling so certain of anything in his life.

He turned and asked Aaron's mother, "Do you love our son?"

"What kind of question is that? Of course I do."

"Do you want him to be happy?"

"You know I do. I just—"

"Since Liv has come into his life, have you ever seen him so happy?"

She frowned, as though she didn't like the answer she had to give. "No…but…"

He took her hand. "She's not of noble blood. Who cares? She's a good person. Thoughtful and sweet and kind. If you'd taken any time to get to know her, you would realize that. Royal or not, our son loves her, so she deserves our respect. And our *acceptance.* Life is too short. Shouldn't he spend it with someone who makes him happy? Someone he loves?"

She was silent for a moment as she considered his words, and finally she said, "I want to state for the record that I'm not happy about this."

Aaron nodded. "So noted."

"However, if you love her and she loves you, I suppose I'll just have to learn to accept it."

"You have our blessing," his father told him.

"There's one more thing. I'm going back to school."

His mother frowned. "What for?"

"Because I still need a few science credits before I can apply to med school."

"*Med* school? At your age? What in heaven's name for?"

"Because I've always wanted to."

His father mirrored her look of concern. "But who will oversee the fields?"

"I'm sure we can find someone capable to fill my position. You'll manage just fine without me."

The king didn't look convinced. "Why don't we discuss this when you get back? Maybe we can reach some sort of compromise."

He wanted to tell his father that he was through compromising, but this was a lot to spring on them in one day. It would be best if he gave it some time to sink in.

"All right," he agreed. "We'll talk about it when I get home."

"I want you to take a full security detail with you," his father said. "I know we haven't had any more threats, but I don't want to take any chances."

"Of course," he agreed, and as he left his parents' suite to make the arrangements, he felt an enormous weight had been lifted from his shoulders. That for the first time instead of just watching his life pass by before him, he was finally an active participant. And he knew with a certainty he felt deep in his bones that until he had Liv by his side, life would never be complete.

And he would do anything to get her back.

* * *

It was late in the evening when his limo pulled up in front of Liv's apartment. The building was very plain and unassuming, which didn't surprise him in the least. Hadn't she claimed to spend most of her time in the lab? He hoped she wasn't there now, or, God forbid, at William's place. Not that he wouldn't hunt her down and find her wherever she happened to be. And if William tried to interfere, Aaron might have to hurt him.

Flynn opened the door for him.

"I'm going in alone," Aaron told him.

"Sir—"

"I don't imagine there's an assassin staked out on the off chance that I drop by. You can wait outside."

He nodded grudgingly. "Yes, sir."

Aaron went inside and took the stairs up to the third floor. Her apartment was the first on the right. There was no bell, so he rapped on the door. Only a few seconds passed before it opened, and there stood Liv wearing flannel pajama bottoms and a faded sweatshirt, looking as sweet and sexy and as irresistible as the first time he'd met her.

She blinked several times, as if she thought she might be imagining him there. "Aaron?"

He grinned. "The one and only."

She didn't return his smile. She just looked…confused. In every scenario he had imagined, she had immediately thrown herself into his arms and thanked him for saving her from a life of marital disaster. Maybe this wouldn't be quite as easy as he'd anticipated.

"What are you doing here?" she asked.

"Can I come in?"

She glanced back inside the apartment, then to him, looking uneasy. Had it not occurred to him that William could be there, in her apartment?

"Is someone...*with* you?" he asked.

She shook her head. "No, it's just that my apartment is kind of a mess. I'm getting ready to do some redecorating."

"I won't hold it against you," he said.

She stepped back and gestured him inside. Her apartment was small and sparsely furnished. And what furniture she did have was covered in plastic drop cloths.

"I was getting ready to paint," she explained. She didn't offer to take his coat, or clear a seat for him. "What do you want?"

"I'm here to prevent you from making the worst mistake of your life."

She frowned and looked around the room. "Painting my apartment?"

She looked so hopelessly confused that he had to smile. "No. I'm here to stop you from marrying a man you don't love."

"Why would you think I'm getting married?"

It was his turn to look confused. "Anne said..."

Before he could finish the sentence, reality slapped him in the face. Hard. He'd been set up. Anne was trying to get him off his behind, so he would go after Liv. And he'd given her just the ammunition she needed when he told her about William.

The next time he saw his sister, he was going to give her a big hug.

"I take it you never said anything to my sister about a wedding?"

She shook her head.

"So, you're definitely not marrying William," he confirmed, just to be sure.

"I should hope not, considering he's engaged to someone else."

That was by far the best news Aaron had had all day.

"What difference does it make?" she asked. "Why do you care who I marry?"

"I care," he said, taking a step toward her, "because the only man you should be marrying is me."

Her eyes went wide with disbelief. "I beg your pardon?"

"You heard me." He got down on one knee and pulled the ring box from his coat pocket. He opened it, offering her the five-carat-diamond family ring that sat nestled in a bed of royal-blue velvet. "Will you, Liv?"

For several excruciating seconds that felt like hours, she just stared at him openmouthed, and he began to wonder if she'd changed her mind about him, if, now that they'd been apart for a while, her affection for him had faded. For an instant he genuincly worried that she would actually tell him no.

But when she finally spoke, she said, "You don't want to get married. You're not cut out to be a family man. Remember?"

"Liv, you told me that you love me. Is that still true?"

She bit her lip and nodded.

"And I love you. It took me a while to admit it to myself, but I do. And I couldn't imagine spending the rest of my life with anyone else."

A smile twitched at the corner of her mouth. "What about that excellent rate you get from the girl-of-the-month club?"

He grinned. "I already cancelled my subscription. The only girl I want in my life is you. Now, are you going to make me kneel here all night?"

"But what about your parents? They'll never let you marry a nonroyal."

"They've already given their blessing."

Her eyes went wide. "Your *mother* gave her blessing? Did you have to hold a gun to her head?"

"I'll admit she did it grudgingly, but don't worry, she'll come around. If we give her a grandchild or two, she'll be ecstatic."

"You want that?" she asked. "You really want children?"

"Only if I can have them with you, Liv."

That hint of a smile grew to encompass her entire face. "Ask me again."

He grinned. "Olivia, will you marry me?"

"Yes." She laughed as he slid the ring on her finger, then he pulled her into his arms. "Yes, Your Highness, I definitely will!"

* * * * *

MILLS & BOON®

Why not subscribe?
Never miss a title and save money too!

Here's what's available to you if you join the
exclusive **Mills & Boon Book Club** today:

- ✦ *Titles up to a month ahead of the shops*
- ✦ *Amazing discounts*
- ✦ *Free P&P*
- ✦ *Earn Bonus Book points that can be redeemed*
  against other titles and gifts
- ✦ *Choose from monthly or pre-paid plans*

Still want more?
Well, if you join today we'll even give you
50% OFF your first parcel!

So visit **www.millsandboon.co.uk/subs**
or call **Customer Relations on 020 8288 2888**
to be a part of this exclusive Book Club!